THERE WAS A CROOKED MAN

Also by Katrina Morgan

Echoes in the Walls (2011)

These Animals Are Killing Me (2016, 2019)

There Was A Crooked Man

Katrina Morgan

ISBN:
SOFTCOVER 978-1709093302
HARDCOVER 978-1087861128
E-book: AISN

Library of Congress Control Number: 2020903445

Printed in the United States of America

Author's Note:
This is a work of fiction. Names, characters, places, and incidents either are the product of the author's imagination or are used fictitiously, and any resemblance to actual person living or dead, events, or locales is entirely coincidental.

"Hope is being able to see that there is light despite the darkness."
~Desmond Tutu

Dedication:

This book came about after a group that I was a part of sponsored a local Battered Women's Shelter. To listen to the women's desperate stories, and understand they left their previous life with nothing and still had hope, left an indelible mark on my mind, heart, and soul.

Many, within our group (including me), could not comprehend how the women found themselves in such circumstances and did not understand why they stayed so long. In listening and paying more attention, I realized many people, not just women, are imprisoned in relationships and situations they cannot easily escape.

This book, this story, although fictional, hopes to give them a voice.

Chapter 1

The little girl with dishwater blond hair slid her chair back, careful not to catch it on the torn linoleum. She eased her way out of the kitchen, tiptoeing and barely breathing. It was important to get away without being seen or heard.

Mom and Dad were arguing about money, and that never ended well. She mentally counted the number of drinks they'd had, too. Three. Each. That wasn't good either.

Pushing a chair against her bedroom door, she huddled in the dark, while the argument raged louder. She crawled to the closet and pulled the string for the overhead light bulb. Even with her hands over her ears, she heard the bottle smash against the living room wall.

She opened a book of nursery rhymes Aunt Susan had let her borrow from the library. Choosing one randomly, she started reading aloud, "There was a crooked man, and he walked
a crooked mile. He found a crooked sixpence against
a crooked stile. He bought a crooked cat which caught a crooked mouse, and they all lived together in a little, crooked house."

Katie read it over and over until she could no longer hear her parents.

The rhyme served her well over the years, becoming her go-to whenever she felt threatened or insecure.

Chapter 2

An alto saxophone wept soft jazz while a drummer kept a steady four-four beat—mixing with the hum of conversation from the three-hundred people gathered. Katie took in the elegant ballroom, shimmering with crystal, china, and ego and wondered briefly what it would be like to be a guest. Rolling her eyes at the notion, she kept moving.

The state auditor had invited members from Georgia's county zoning boards to celebrate their highly profitable fiscal year. Listening to snippets of conversation, Katie concluded the guests didn't give a damn about Georgia's bottom-line. The auditor had political aspirations, and most in attendance were interested in riding his coattails.

The blond man working the room held Katie's attention, though. He inserted himself seamlessly into conversations, giving specific compliments and asking thoughtful questions. Katie considered him more closely. The man caught Katie's stare and gave a slow, welcoming smile. She turned away, feeling heat rush up her neck.

The congested area by the bar had Katie sliding past clumps of people feasting and drinking to their heart's content. She adjusted the hated bow tie as she offered delicacies and champagne from her tray.

Hands slid across her body, and Katie spun toward the source. Two men standing nearby—the blond one she'd been admiring and an older, balding man in a tweed jacket. They spoke at the same time.

"Sorry."

"It's crowded in here."

Unsure who to blame, Katie smiled tightly, familiar with the game. The blond man followed her and waited nearby as she served hors d'oevres. She changed direction. *Stupid.* Katie chastised herself. *I shouldn't have made eye contact.*

She was relieved when her tray was empty. It gave her a chance to escape. She bumped her hip on the swinging kitchen door and entered the steamy room. It was crowded with dishes--clean on the right, dirty to the left. Prep stations were bustling, and dishwashers ran non-stop. The soft music from the grand ballroom would never be heard in here. Katie leaned against the counter, rubbing her lower back.

Donette, another server from the restaurant, shoved her way into the kitchen. "Assholes," she muttered and caught Katie's eye. "They're all assholes, right?"

Katie gave a meaningful look at Donette's breasts spilling out of her white tuxedo shirt. "The accidental rub against the chest move?"

Renae, slammed through the doors, harried and pissy. She caught the last bit of the conversation. "Oh yeah. Or how about the hand on the ass routine? They're all such assholes."

"Been there done that," Katie admitted.

"At least we get paid more for catering than we would at the restaurant," Donette added.

Renae threw her tray on the pile of dirty dishes and joined the two women for a quick break. "Still get mauled--just by richer asshats."

Katie snorted. She did love that expression "asshats."

"Laugh if you want, Princess. But we saw Boy Wonder watching you." Renae bumped her shoulder against Donette's. "Didn't we?"

"Mr. Tall, blond, and sexy? Perfect hair. Perfect clothes. Yeah, I saw him, for all the good it did me. He's got eyes for our Katie here."

Renae pretended to pout as she toyed with the end of her dark braid. "I guess we'll have to settle for the asshats, huh Donette?"

Katie waved their comments aside. "Trust me, he's not interested in anything serious."

Donette glanced at the clock. "It's only eight-thirty?" She rolled her shoulder to release the tension. "God. I hope this goes by fast."

The women shoved away from the counter and picked up newly prepared trays laden with bacon-wrapped scallops, and chocolate-dipped strawberries.

As they re-entered the ballroom, Katie stopped in her tracks. The blond man from earlier was leaning against a wall just outside the kitchen. Donette and Renae saw him too and elbowed Katie.

"See?"

"He's been waiting."

Renae pivoted right, and Donette spun left, forcing Katie to face him alone. Katie narrowed her eyes. "Can I help you?"

He pushed away from the wall, blocking her forward progress.

"I wanted to explain that *thing* earlier. It was an accident." He gave Katie a sheepish smile. "Maybe I can call you later?"

Katie's tone frosted, "Call me? You don't even know me."

"That's not true," he rushed forward until he was just inches away, "You have a contagious laugh, and you're sweet even when men," he pointed at his chest, "are total jerks.

Katie looked at her watch and tapped her foot.

'You're smart too," he hurried to explain, "I heard the conversation you had about tonight's theme. All I need now is a name."

Had he complimented her face or her figure, she'd have flat out refused. His remarks about her as a person had her considering. Survival instincts had her shaking her head and stepping around him.

He pursued her the rest of the evening, making eye contact, and mouthing, "Just your name."

Charmed, she finally whispered, "Katie."

"Well, Katie, I'm pleased to meet you. I'm Jack. Jack Werner."

He continued to flirt throughout the evening, winking and sending secret smiles. As the night wound down, Jack found her one more time.

"I rode here with my friends from work, so I have to go. Can I have your number?"

Katie rattled it off as he typed it into his phone. As she watched him leave, she couldn't stop grinning. Donette and Renae teased her mercilessly as they hauled supplies to the catering van.

"I'm Jack," Donette said in an over-modulated deep voice, "I'm the next best thing to God."

"Can I have your number, sweetie?" Renae batted her eyelashes.

Leaving the event well past one in the morning, Katie parked her ancient Honda as near to a streetlight as she could. She scanned the area, ensuring herself the streets were empty and jogged toward building C.

Oblivious to the cold March air, she took the stairs to her apartment two at a time, hopeful for the first time in, well, ever.

Chapter 3

Katie's cell phone vibrated across the nightstand, and she squinted at the clock: eight-o-nine. Not recognizing the number, she answered cautiously, "Hello?"

"Katie?"

"Who is this?"

"It's Jack. I couldn't wait to talk to you."

Katie curled into the blankets, stunned he'd called.

The phone calls came daily, growing in length as Jack and Katie got to know one another better. It's how Jack learned she was virtually alone. "Your mom and dad are both gone? No sisters or brothers?"

"Nope, just my Aunt Susan. "What about *your* family?" Katie asked, eager to change the subject. No way was she going to have a conversation about her mom and dad this early in the game. He'd never call again.

The long chats with Jack lifted her spirits, and Katie often bounced into work at the *City Palette*—an established restaurant in the old part of town. Renae and Donette tormented her by singing lyrics from any song they could think of that had Jack in the title: "Jack and Diane" from John Mellencamp, "Jumpin' Jack Flash" by the Rolling Stones and "Hit the Road Jack." The last one was a favorite, and Donette and Renae would belt out Ray Charles' well-known chorus.

Katie shook her head playfully. "You two are just jealous!"

"Damn straight," Donette answered. "I need a Jack."

Me too!" Renae added as she slid past with a tray of drinks. "Get me out of this hellhole."

Katie and Jack's budding relationship had one barrier: She lived in Atlanta, and Jack in Savannah. Two weeks of daily phone calls hadn't dulled the attraction, and Jack offered to make the drive to Atlanta. "I want to spend time with you, go on a date, see where this leads. How 'bout Saturday?"

When Katie hesitated, Jack pressed for an answer, "What? You don't think it's a good idea?

"No, I mean, yes. It's just a little scary, you know? Talking the next step."

"We don't have to *do* anything," Jack laughed, "but it is a four- hour trip each way, Katie. I'd rather not have to drive half the night."

Katie agreed, "I work until two on Saturday. Let me give you the building code in case I run late." She rattled off a four-digit number. "I'll leave a key under the mat."

Jack purposely arrived at her apartment early. He used the extra time to explore her rooms, rifling through the mail haphazardly stacked on the counter and sifting through her medicine cabinet in the bathroom. He looked for evidence of men's clothing in her closet and investigated her bedside drawer. Seeing a 'Thinking of You' card, his fingers curled into fists until he saw the signature, 'Love, Aunt Susan.' Checking his watch, Jack replaced each item exactly where it had been and hurried to the kitchen.

A few minutes later, Katie sailed in the door and angled straight into Jack for a hug. "Hello, handsome!" She took off her work apron and frowned at the papers on the counter. They were stacked perfectly, not messy the way she remembered leaving them that morning. "Have you been here long?"

"No, I got here a few minutes before you."

Katie dismissed the papers, thinking maybe she'd straightened them after all. She stuck her nose down into the bouquet of flowers Jack had brought. "These are beautiful."

"Not as beautiful as you." Jack pulled her close, stroking her brown-blond hair.

"Stop. I look awful—my hairs a mess, makeup's gone. And I definitely need a shower."

"You look perfect to me." Jack bent her backward, kissing her thoroughly.

"Whew! Aren't you romantic?" Katie laughed up into his face.

Later, after a perfect night out involving dinner, a slow walk home, and a fair amount of kissing and caressing, Katie pushed away. "Ummm. Ok. Whew." She ran a hand through her hair. She stood, unsure of what to do with her hands.

"This is actually only the second time I've seen you." She hurried to a tiny closet and pulled out blankets and a pillow and walked them back toward the couch where Jack sat. Setting them down carefully on the arm of the sofa, she stammered, "I'm…I'm sorry. I know this seems weird."

"It's okay, Katie. I know you're not ready."

Appreciating his patience, Katie promised to drive to Savannah the next weekend. "Who knows? Maybe you'll get lucky?" She gave Jack a wink.

On Monday, Katie made her announcement to Donette and Renae, "So, I'm heading to Savannah on Saturday."

Renae swiveled her head, "Whoa. This is getting serious."

Donette latched onto the other part of the sentence, "Saturday? That's our busiest night."

"I know," Katie said. "I'll make it up to you guys. I promise."

Renae wiggled her eyebrows, "You gonna do the deed, girl?"

Donette leaned in to hear the answer.

Seeing Katie give a timid shrug, Donette high-fived Renae and started talking lingerie. "You've got to get something silky and tiny."

"Lingerie? Shit. I didn't think about that." Katie mentally sifted through the few items she had at home.

"Something black and lacy," Renae insisted.

"It's been a while," Katie admitted, and let out a sigh. "I'll probably screw the whole thing up."

"Girl, when a man sees a woman half-naked, she's already in control." Renae flipped her braid over her shoulder. "Relax," she did a slow hip roll, "experiment, and never underestimate foreplay."

"And then come back here and tell us all the details!" Donette added with a laugh.

Renae agreed, "We deserve it after covering your sorry ass on a Saturday night."

Chapter 4

Katie did buy lingerie—pink, not black. She then drove to a pharmacy blocks from home, snatched the first box of condoms she saw, and paid without making eye contact with the cashier.

Her geriatric Honda, unused to long excursions, coughed a couple of times along the trip. Katie turned up the radio to cover the noise. Her phone beeped three times in succession, and Katie glanced at the screen. Texts from Renae, Donette, and Jack were waiting.

At the next gas station, Katie filled the gas tank and tried not to worry about the money. Opening her phone, she read her messages.

"Where r u on the drive?" Jack.

"OMG! Jack sent flowers!" Donette's text screamed.

Renae sent a picture of the bouquet and Jack's card: "Thanks for covering for Katie!"

Katie responded to each, proud to be with a man who would send flowers to her friends. When she pulled into Jack's apartment building, he was waiting outside, holding a poster, "Welcome, Katie!"

Katie popped out of the car. "I made it! But I don't think my car is happy about the drive." On cue, her Honda let out a small belch from its rusty tailpipe.

Jack took her hand. "I'll show you around before dinner."

Katie nervously toured his apartment, admiring the kitchen, and running her hand along the expanse of the counter. "It's all so new." She stood in an overly neutral living room, wondering why there was nothing on the walls, before following Jack upstairs. The small second bedroom was a homey office: a landscape on the wall, bookcases, and a newer computer. "This is better." Katie nodded to herself.

"What do you mean?"

Katie shrugged. "It's just obvious you spend more time here."

Jack looked at the room through Katie's eyes. "That's true, I guess. I don't cook much or watch much TV. I do, however," he wiggled his eyebrows and steered her by the elbow, "also spend time in here." He led her to his bedroom.

She poked her head into the room, noting it was tidy and decorated in shades of browns. The queen bed centered between the two windows screamed for attention. Katie backed out and ran into Jack's chest.

"Can I freshen up before dinner?" she asked, trying to mask her anxiety.

He grinned. "I take it you don't want to use my bathroom?"

She shook her head and jogged down the stairs. Squeezing into the tiny powder room, she took a big breath. *Get a grip, Katie! He's your boyfriend, for God's sake.* She dug through her purse, pulling out lipstick, and mascara.

Jack opened the door. "You okay in here?"

Surprised he hadn't knocked, Katie stood with the mascara wand suspended in midair.

He watched her in the mirror.

"What are you doing?"

"I wanted to see you."

Katie kissed him quickly and tried to shut the door, but his foot was in the way. The room grew claustrophobic with his tall frame half inside the doorway. She eased past him, eager for space.

Jack drove to a nearby Chinese restaurant and introduced Katie to a pot of potent saké.

"Mmmm. This is so good." Katie downed her second cup and held it out toward Jack.

"You want more?"

"Yep. Saké to me!" She giggled. "Get it? Saké to me?"

"Yeah, I get it." Jack glanced around the crowded restaurant. "Maybe you'd better take it easy."

His warning embarrassed her, and she mentally searched for a dignified subject. "Your parents? They live nearby, right?"

"They do. But, as I've said, we aren't exactly close."

"But you've never explained why." Katie leaned forward, eager to hear the story

Jack sampled his General Tso's chicken, choosing his words. "They were never around much—always headed to some fundraiser or committee meeting. When they were home, they spent their time telling me I wasn't good enough." His eyes grew stormy, and his speech quickened as he listed a litany of issues: grades, friends, girls, sports, extra-curricular. "Nothing was good enough, and I was punished for everything," he said for the third time.

None of the transgressions seemed overly serious to Katie, but she stayed silent.

"After I got my job, my parents and I went to dinner to celebrate. They spent the whole night berating me." Jack rolled his eyes. "They didn't approve of me reporting my predecessor's mistakes, but I sure as hell wasn't getting blamed for something he'd done." Jack flung his right hand in the air. "Whatever."

Katie's brow creased. "Go on," she encouraged.

"There's nothing else to say. I walked out." Jack scrubbed his neck below his right ear. "Let's talk about what's under that pretty pink shirt instead." He strained to look down her blouse, making her laugh and effectively ending the conversation.

Katie wasn't quite steady on her feet as they left the restaurant and clung to Jack's arm. "Whew. You better take me to bed, Jack, before I change my mind."

Once back at his place, he led her straight to his room, lighting candles and turning on soft music. Easing her back on the bed, Jack drew her in for a long kiss, licking her lips, nibbling her neck.

"God. You're beautiful. I've been dreaming of you here with me. Let me love you, Katie."

Smiling slowly, she murmured, "Yes."

Remembering her earlier purchase, Katie pushed herself up, looking for her purse.

"What are you doing?"

Her cheeks colored, "I brought some protection."

Stunned, Jack laughed, "Trust me. I've got that under control."

Once he returned to the bed, she let him take the lead, sinking deeper into the mattress, and growing accustomed to his weight. He unbuttoned her blouse. "Look at you." He kissed the top of one breast.

She stiffened and balled her hands into fists.

"You don't like that."

"I do. I'm just nervous. If I'm honest, it's been a while."

Jack grinned. "Good to hear there's no competition."

"You've seen where I live. Not a lot of fabulous boyfriend choices there."

He ran a feather-light caress across her stomach. "So, I'm your Prince Charming?"

Her hands wound around his neck, fingering his hair. "You are."

He undid the front clasp of the bra, and her nipples puckered. Katie sighed, enjoying the feel of his hands on her skin. He caressed down to her belly, moving further and sliding her skirt down. "Ahhh, look at you. Matching lingerie." He traced the lacy pattern, running his finger under the waistband, making her shiver. He eased the lingerie bottoms off and slid them down the long expanse of her leg so slowly, the entire process was a long caress.

He slid up her body, and she closed her eyes when he eased inside her. Katie squeezed her thigh muscles in reaction, and it nearly undid Jack. He slid deeper inside her. "Look at me, baby."

She met his gaze, and the age-old dance commenced. Jack's pace increased, and Katie matched his movements, arcing with each thrust. With nerve endings over-sensitized, she climbed higher, riding the wave and close to shattering. When Jack collapsed on top of her, Katie's senses were still jangling. She felt as though she'd eaten a fabulous meal but still had room for dessert.

When Jack lifted himself, she raised herself slightly on her elbows, anticipating a kiss that never came.

"Katie?" Jack watched her closely.

She stretched lazily. "Hmm."

"I'll be your only."

Overwhelmed, Katie heard only promises.

Chapter 5

Susan Garrison adjusted her thick glasses and squinted at the phone. She didn't recognize the number and answered sharply, "Hello?" Her voice still rasped despite ten years without her beloved cigarettes.

"Aunt Susan, it's Katie."

"Oh, hello, babycakes. Are you calling me from work?"

"No. Jack bought me a new cell phone. Can you believe it? My old one was crap and only worked half the time. He calls three or four times a day and got nervous when he couldn't reach me."

The older woman frowned. "Three or four times a day? That sounds over the top, don't you think?"

Katie giggled. "He just worries."

"That's more than worrying."

"No offense, Aunt Susan, but you're not exactly out there dating. This is how we do it nowadays. We call, we text, we send emojis."

"What the hell's an emoji?"

Katie laughed, dismissing her Aunt's concerns. "Jack's talking about getting married! He's even looking at houses to buy!"

Aunt Susan rolled her eyes. Since meeting Jack, Katie ended every sentence with an exclamation mark. "You know that tingly feeling you get when you meet someone you're really attracted to?"

Katie answered with a breathy sigh, "I do."

"Well, that's common sense leaving your body," Susan snorted.

"Aunt Susan!"

"Well, he sounds too good to be true. Maybe I should meet this young man."

"We should have dinner together! I'll cook your favorites and pick you up next Saturday. I work the early shift, so it shouldn't be any trouble. Six o'clock work for you?"

"Fine, fine. I can't wait to see you." Aunt Susan mentally shoved down the growing trepidation in her gut.

Jack was even less enthused. "I hardly ever see you, and now we have to give up our Saturday night?"

"She wants to meet you. She's my angel, the one who saved me." Katie waited through a long silence. "Hello?"

"I thought *I* was the one who saved you."

Hearing his clipped tone, Katie rushed to clarify, "She's my angel, but you're my Prince Charming. You two are the most important people in my life. I want you to meet each other."

Sighing, Jack agreed to dinner but inserted new parameters, "I'm sure it'll be great, sweetheart." his voice oozed through the line. "But let's do it earlier. Say four or four-thirty? We can have dinner, drive her back to the retirement joint by eight, and still have time for us."

"Retirement joint? What's that supposed to mean?" Katie held the phone away from her face and glared at the screen.

Jack backtracked again, "Is it wrong to want you all to myself?"

"Well, when you put it like that…" Katie pulled her shoulders up toward her chin, giving herself a hug.

On Saturday, Katie scrubbed her tiny apartment. Despite her parents having been gone four years, the rooms still held a whiff of hopelessness and gin. Katie drove the shadows away by cooking until her hair was damp and the kitchen steamy. She sang along with the radio and slid across the newly mopped floor in her socks.

Bubbling with enthusiasm, Katie was early picking up Aunt Susan. The older woman touched her newly permed hair. "Do I look all right?"

"You're beautiful." Katie kissed her leathery cheek and sped back toward the city. She steadied her aunt as they climbed the stairs. "Sorry. The elevator's out again." The ladies laughed at their staccato gait--up one stair, stop, regain balance, repeat.

"I can't let aging get me down."

"I know. I'm sorry."

"No, it's not that."

"What?"

"It's that I can't get back up!" Aunt Susan snickered at Katie's pretend swat.

The women were chatting when there was a knock on the door. Katie bounded from the couch. "Oh, there he is!"

Jack waltzed in before Katie could answer the door, and Susan scowled at his presumptuous manner.

Jack pulled a bouquet out from behind his back and walked toward the older woman. "You must be Aunt Susan. Katie talks about you all the time," Jack held out the flowers.

"For me?"

Susan forgave Jack for not knocking and rushed to find a vase. Catching Katie's eye, Susan winked and nodded once in approval.

Aunt Susan returned to the living room, eager to know Jack better. Within five minutes, her initial impression faded. Jack said all the right things and sounded interested, but the words never touched his eyes. Aunt Susan straightened her spine.

Dinner wasn't as fun as Katie had hoped. Aunt Susan zeroed in on details. She'd been to Savannah dozens of times, and still had friends there.

Fork in the air as if she'd just remembered something, Susan grilled Jack, "You grew up near Garden City? I thought you said you went to Johnson High School."

"I did."

"Johnson High School, the one I'm thinking of, is in Midtown. Hmm. I must be thinking of something else." She smiled ever so slyly. Midtown wasn't as posh as Garden City, and Susan smelled a healthy dose of bullshit.

She neatly turned the conversation toward college. "Katie didn't go to college, but you've got a degree, don't you, Jack?"

"Yes, ma'am. I went to Strayer University and, four years later, landed myself a job with the zoning commission. That may have been luck since the previous guy died." Jack laughed, relieved to be a safe topic. "They were still doing their accounting on spreadsheets. I introduced new software, and productivity went up." He smiled, showing overly white teeth, "I should be getting another promotion soon,"

Aunt Susan fiddled with the last of her scalloped potatoes. "Isn't Strayer a two-year college?"

Katie nudged her aunt's knee under the table.

When Aunt Susan looked up, Katie raised her eyebrows. "Please, stop," Katie mouthed.

Susan pretended she didn't understand and turned her attention back to Jack.

Jack narrowed his eyes, spinning out a lie. "They do specialize in associate degrees, but I stayed for four."

Aunt Susan nodded, and Jack pursed his lips.

Aunt Susan got up to help clear dishes, noticing Jack did not. From the kitchen sink, she looked over her shoulder and asked more questions. "Your parents still living, Jack?"

"Yes, ma'am, they are." He offered no other information.

"You've met them, Katie? I bet they love you to pieces, don't they?" Aunt Susan knew damn well Katie hadn't met his parents or anyone in his life for that matter. Susan smiled, innocent, and supposedly well-meaning.

Katie glanced at Jack and shrugged her shoulders. "Not yet. Jack says they don't get along well. I'm sure I will--meet them, I mean." Katie wiped her hands on her jeans. "What's with all the questions? It feels like an interrogation."

Jack nodded.

Aunt Susan's eyes grew large. "I'm sorry, Jack. I don't mean to pry. You know how it is, right? No one's ever going to be good enough for my Katie." Susan fluttered her hands, making her ever-present bracelets clatter together, transforming herself into a doddering aunt. "I get a little protective, but Katie's got nothing but praise for you."

After dessert, they drove back to Great Oak Estates. Jack accompanied the women to Aunt Susan's front door. "It was a pleasure meeting you, Aunt Susan."

Manners had Susan inviting Jack inside.

"No," Jack forced himself to smile. "I'll let you two ladies have a few minutes together."

He walked toward the car with his forehead deeply furrowed.

Katie followed Aunt Susan inside the villa, flicking on lights as she went. "So, isn't he great?" Katie asked while turning up the thermostat and closing curtains.

"He seems to be a nice man, Katie, but slow down. I don't think he's going anywhere."

Katie hugged Aunt Susan and called out, "I love you!" before racing back to the car.

As summer waned, Katie worked less to spend time with Jack. Donette and Renae began to echo Aunt Susan.

"Slow down, girl!"

"Play hard to get, for God's sake!"

"Seriously? Would either of you slow down? I've got a man who pays attention, comes to see me, brings me flowers. And, here's a miracle, he has a *job* and his own place. I could get out of here!" Katie's arms swept the restaurant, but her tone encompassed the neighborhood. Renae and Donette nodded and grew quiet.

Aunt Susan, for the first time, had to initiate calls to Katie. "Katie? Are you all right? You said you'd call yesterday."

"I'm sorry. I was running errands before heading to Savannah." Katie balanced the laundry hamper against her hip, still trying to do two things at once.

"Wait," Aunt Susan injected with force, "Savannah? Are you going again? You can't keep missing work, honey."

Katie's boss, Ricky, had said the same thing that morning.

Consumed by Jack and his promises, Katie ignored them all.

Chapter 6

Even if Katie had wanted to slow down, Jack had other ideas. Without including her in the decision, Jack bought a house. His county job gave him early access to foreclosed homes and properties in financial trouble. When the listing for a house, near Forsyth Park, came across the back-tax report, Jack drove by the address after work. Seeing the prestigious neighborhood, he called a realtor, toured the house, and placed a contract on it the same night.

Jack called Katie to share the exciting news.

"You bought a house? Where? When?" Katie asked.

"Consider it an early birthday present."

"But I've never even seen it," Katie protested.

"I had to act fast. Do you have any idea what houses in that neighborhood typically sell for? Seven, maybe eight hundred thousand! Even the foreclosed ones are half a million. Three-seventy-five is cheap."

"It doesn't sound cheap to me. Can we afford it?"

"Are you saying I don't make enough money?"

Katie heard the change in tone and panicked. Old habits rushed to the forefront, and she worked to defuse the situation. "I didn't say anything close to that. I have no idea what your salary is, or if you've got money saved."

"Trust me. I've got it under control." He would, of course, never admit he'd exhausted his savings, demanded five-thousand-dollars from his parents, and taken out a first-time home buyer's loan, which teetered on the brink of financial disaster.

Katie tried one more time, "But I've never seen it. What if I don't like it?"

"I'll show it to you this weekend. You'll love it." With that pronouncement, Jack dismissed Katie's concerns.

Katie hardly noticed. *What do I know about buying houses?*

As soon as Katie arrived at Jack's apartment early Friday evening, Jack scooted her into his car. He drove the cobblestone streets of historic Forsyth Park, and past the famous fountain, enjoying Katie's awe. After making a few more turns, he pulled up in front of a skinny, yellow house. The tiny circle of light afforded by the gas lamps edging the tree line was more ambiance than practical, and Katie peered through the windshield.

Jack sat in the driver's seat, beaming.

"This is it?" Katie craned her head further. The house was two and a half stories, with a neglected widow's walk sitting cautiously on the slate roof. A few upstairs windows were broken, and vines wound through the porch rails, sending reconnaissance tendrils up the side of the house. The home had once been a showcase, and Katie could see it in her mind, freshly painted, with flowers blooming.

"Wow," she said softly, and Jack was pleased.

"It needs a lot of work, doesn't it?" His smile slipped.

"You didn't mention it was so big! She was halfway out of the car. "Can we get inside?"

"Well, not technically." Jack shot her a wicked grin. "However," he tapped his head twice. "I memorized the code when the real estate lady was here last time."

"Can we get in trouble?"

"Not if we don't get caught. I'll move the car, so we don't attract attention."

He left her to wander the outside, and she trailed her hand along the overgrown bushes. A downspout, missing its last two feet, oozed slimy green algae. Katie bent her neck back, scanning the roofline, and wondering if there was water damage inside.

Jack jogged toward the porch. "Stay to the left. There's a big hole."

Katie laughed at the one-foot gap and skirted around the waiting disaster.

"Hold my phone by the lock." The meager cell phone light illuminated the three-digit lockbox, which Jack worked quickly. The key dropped into his hand, and he was through the door, pulling Katie inside.

Standing in the dim foyer, Katie let her eyes adjust. Dust and spider webs clung to all surfaces and congregated in corners. "I guess it's been vacant a while?" She headed towards the curved staircase, head swiveling back and forth to take in the details.

"Almost three years."

Katie gestured toward a carved rosette at the top of a door frame. "They don't build 'em like this anymore, do they? Aunt Susan used to take me on old house tours—her way of teaching me culture. I'm guessing this house was built around the first of the century. Am I right?"

"Close. 1914."

"Can you imagine? World War I had just started. The Panama Canal opened. People were buying cars as fast as they could make them." Katie's voice trailed off, soft and dreamy. Her eyes were on the tall ceilings, following the cracks zigzagging across the living room.

Jack fisted his hands on his hips. "How do you know that stuff? The Canal? The war?"

"Well, everyone remembers when World War I started. The rest?" She shrugged. "I loved history and took every class offered in school." She pulled at a pocket door, but it stuck halfway. She pushed her face through the opening. "Oh, look! It's a den." Delighted, she squeezed herself through the door.

Jack glared at her back.

Turning, Katie saw the look. "What?"

"Nothing." Jack pulled her back toward the dining room. Looking out the window, Katie ducked under the frame.

Jack eyed Katie, half crouched on the floor. "What are you doing?"

"Hiding! A car just went by."

Jack rolled his eyes. "Act like you're supposed to be here. No one will question a thing."

Not convinced, Katie stayed low. From her vantage point, she scrutinized a hole in the ceiling where a chandelier must have hung. "What happened to the people who lived here?"

"They couldn't pay the taxes, and after three years, it reverts to the county. Some old couple who'd bought it forty years ago. The area's grown, gotten more popular, so taxes rose. They couldn't keep up."

"That's sad." Katie rose and followed Jack, who was still talking.

"Sad? It's not sad. It's life. Their loss is our gain."

"Well, I think it's sad—living here all that time, maybe raising a family, watching things fall apart, losing your home."

They'd made their way to the kitchen, a throwback to the 1950s. "Whew. Not as sad as this kitchen, though," Katie snickered. "What color are those cabinets? Turquoise? And look at the black and white floors. Good Lord!" Katie shook her head.

"Did I say it was perfect?" Jack snapped. "Do you like it or not?"

"I'm kidding. You didn't do this." Katie gestured broadly at the room.

"You've complained ever since we got inside."

"I'm sorry. I love the house."

He continued to pout.

Katie took his hand and winked. "Show me upstairs, sir?"

The flirting and apology softened Jack's mood. "There are three bedrooms upstairs." He wiggled his eyebrows and cupped her butt as she climbed the stairs. Giggling, she smacked at his hands.

He opened and shut the doors to the two smaller bedrooms quickly before she noticed the broken windows. He ushered her into the master bedroom, which was at least passable.

She wandered the space. "Wow. This is ours?"

He circled her from behind, running eager hands across her nicely shaped breasts. Katie started to laugh, but his breathing quickened, and she realized he was serious.

"Jack, we can't do anything here." She pushed him back, light-heartedly, but he pulled her closer, drowning her in a kiss that had her close to gagging.

He pushed her shirt aside, eager to get past the bra and what lay beneath.

Katie broke free. "What are you doing? We have to get out of here." She pulled her shirt down, but he grabbed her hands, pulled them up over her head and backed her against a wall. Holding her in place with his knees and one arm, she heard his belt hit the floor.

Shock kept her silent. He held her arms over her head with his left hand, while his right hand fisted in her hair, pulling it upward to expose her neck. He bit and chewed while she rose involuntarily on her tiptoes to relieve the pressure. He bent his head and nipped her left breast.

"Jack. Stop. You're hurting me!"

Jack dropped her arms to yank at her pants.

"Jack. Stop. Seriously." She held onto the waistband with one hand and rubbed the other across her bruised breast.

Oblivious to her protests, Jack wrestled her pants down. A button clattered loose across the floor, breaking Jack's focus. Katie held her shirttail and pants tightly clenched at her waist. Trembling, she reverted to her little girl self—the one who hid in her closet, praying the monsters would go away. "There was a crooked man, who walked a crooked mile." Her voice barely registered above a whisper, making Jack lean in to hear her.

"What are you doing? Who's a crooked man? Me?"

"He bought a crooked cat…"

"What the hell are you doing?" Jack jiggled her slightly.

Katie brushed his hands away, needing to finish the rhyme. "And they all lived together in a little, crooked house." She shook her head to clear the tune. "It's just a silly nursery song I say when I'm scared."

"Scared? Why would you be scared?"

"*You* scared me. You've never acted like that."

He kissed the bruised breast, and she jerked away.

He laughed. "You've got a lot to learn. Couples get wound up--a little physical sometimes. I think you being here in the house, our future so close, I went a little crazy."

She considered his words and blinked twice. "I want to go home."

"I said I didn't mean it."

"I still want to go home."

"Marry me, Katie."

"What?" She swiveled her head toward him, blindsided for the second time that night.

"I said, marry me, Katherine Follings."

"You're asking me to marry you after what just happened?"

Jack pulled a box out of his pocket and opened it. A silver ring winked in the light as Jack dropped to one knee. "It was my grandmother's ring, and I'd be honored if you'd wear it."

As Katie stared at the ring, overwhelmed, and a bit unsure, Jack's mind drifted briefly back to his encounter with his parents just a few days prior.

Fred and Sylvia's pleasure at Jack's unexpected appearance had evaporated quickly when he bypassed the pleasantries and launched into his requests: money towards a downpayment on the house and the ring for Katie.

Fred Werner shook his head at Jack. "Son, you're going to need to learn to stand on your own two feet. You can't be asking your parents for money all the time."

"Actually, Dad, this is the first and last time I will ever ask you for money."

Fred shrugged, "Still…" and he took his time writing out the check.

The statement made Jack angry, but he needed the money more than an argument.

His mom had been no better. Sylvia had gone upstairs to retrieve the heirloom ring, but it remained clenched in her hand. "Are you sure this girl is the one, Jack? What do you really know about her? It seems awfully sudden."

Jack hadn't answered. Instead, he reached forward to take the box and exited as quickly as he could.

Unaware of Jack's thoughts, Katie watched his face. He was mentally a million miles away. "Jack? Is everything alright?"

Jack shook his head and re-focused on Katie. Holding the ring box higher, he asked, "So? What do you think? Will you marry me?"

Wanting love, a home, anything other than what she'd grown up with, Katie dismissed the earlier scene with Jack. *He's probably right. I just over-reacted.* "Yes! Yes, I'll marry you!"

Jack put the ring on her finger, and then lifted her off her feet, spinning her in a circle. "Let's get married tomorrow!"

"Tomorrow? We can't get married tomorrow!"

"Sure, we can. We'll go to Vegas! Why should we wait?"

Katie threw out the first excuse that crossed her mind. "I've got to work on Sunday."

"Call in sick. Better yet, quit--move in with me. In less than a month, we can live here, happily ever after."

"But my friends? Your parents? Aunt Susan will be crushed."

"Crushed? Crushed her niece is getting married and heading off to a better life?"

"I imagined a white dress, flowers, a church--" Katie trailed off.

"A church is just a building, Katie. No big deal," Jack stated.

It was a big deal to her, but she wasn't sure how to explain. She chewed her lip instead.

"We'll throw a huge party when we get back. It's the promises that matter, not the place they're made." Jack leaned in and kissed Katie. "Make me the happiest man on earth."

Chapter 7

Katie grabbed the possibility of a new life with both hands. When Jack confessed he'd put his entire savings into the down payment for the house, Katie offered up the money in her checking account. Before she could blink twice, he purchased two last-minute airline tickets and booked the cheapest room he could find at Circus Circus.

They landed late Saturday afternoon. "Oh, my God! Look at all the lights and the people!" Katie, who'd never been anywhere, wanted to take in the entire scene, but Jack dragged her to The Little White Chapel to register for marriage.

"We have an opening at 4:40 or 6:10 p.m. Take your pick." The grumpy clerk never looked up from the computer screen.

Three days before her twenty-third birthday, Katie became Mrs. Jack Werner. It should have been monumental. Unfortunately, her wedding left a lot to be desired. She wore a rented dress, carried a used bouquet, and a stranger stood as witness. The clerk took pictures on Katie's phone and then directed them to another room to sign the license. "That's it?" Katie asked, bewildered. The clerk nodded and called out the next number. Jack was eager to consummate the marriage, and she saw very little of the city.

Jack did manage to gamble, though. Watching Jack blow her last fifty-dollar bill at the craps table, made her uneasy. Katie decided not to tell him about the savings account she'd opened after her parents died. She remembered her own mother secreting money away so Katie's dad wouldn't spend it on lousy business ventures or booze.

Exhausted from the city, the wedding, and the pace, they flew back to Savannah on Sunday. Katie made the long drive back to Atlanta with her mind still in a whirl.

Aunt Susan answered her door Monday morning to find Katie shaking a bag of bagels and juggling a tray with two big to-go cups of coffee. "It's not even decaf!" Katie laughed and pushed her way inside. Sharing the news, Katie spun out a tale of romance and spontaneity, "We couldn't wait any longer!"

"Oh, my." Aunt Susan fanned her face and sat down. "I hope you're right. It's so fast, Katie. Not even a year."

Katie's face fell.

Susan pulled Katie into a hug. "I bet you were a beautiful bride. I want to hear every detail."

Katie showed her all four pictures on her phone and gushed about Vegas. "As for the wedding? Well, it was over so fast, I hardly remember the details."

Katie's nerves unwound after seeing Aunt Susan. She drove back to her apartment, making mental lists of what needed to happen in the upcoming week. Entering her apartment, Katie leaned against the door and concentrated on her breathing. "I still can't believe it." She stared at her wedding ring and opened the photo gallery on her phone to see the pictures again. The phone vibrated. Jack was calling.

"Hey there, handsome!"

"Hey there, beautiful. Whatcha been up to?"

"I went to see Aunt Susan today. Talk about surprised." Katie filled him in and then asked his opinion about the best way to let her landlord know she was moving.

"Do everything through email, so it's date-stamped. And Katie?"

"Ummm?" She'd been doodling across the top of her to-do list.

"I can't wait for you to get here. This is going to be a long week waiting for my *wife*."

They passed sweet comments back and forth. After they hung up, Katie bounced toward the tiny second bedroom where she kept her outdated computer. She spent the next hour sending a termination of her lease, canceling utilities, and drafting a resignation for work.

Her growling stomach took her to the kitchen. Eating salami right out of the deli bag, she took a good look around the apartment, evaluating what she would take to Savannah. Eyeing the second-hand furniture and drab surroundings, she blew out a breath. "Most of this isn't worth packing."

She decided to take an antique table from her grandmother, a woman she'd never met. That the delicate piece had outlived years of her parent's drunken arguments was a good sign.

Because Jack had none, the pictures and decorative items would all go to their new house. Katie picked up one of her favorite pieces, a tall, amber-colored candlestick. Turning it over in her hands and feeling the weight, she was surprised it had survived all the fights as well. "This thing could be a weapon." She set it back down in a corner and continued her inventory.

The only other things she chose to keep were her bedroom set and a sofa table she'd bought months before. She designed a flyer listing all the items she wanted to sell.

With that done, she sorted clothes and accessories into three piles: Trash, things to keep, and Goodwill. The music was blaring when Jack called again. "Hello?"

"It's me," he announced unnecessarily, "just checking on you, making sure you haven't changed your mind."

"For God's sake, we talked, what--" she angled her head to see the clock, "two hours ago? I haven't changed my mind. In fact, I'm packing."

"Keep it light. We don't close on the house for three weeks, and there's nowhere to store anything. Besides, I don't think the stuff from your place will go well with the house anyway." Katie didn't think his ultra-modern chrome and black furnishings were going to be a good fit either, but she didn't say it aloud.

She handed in her resignation on Tuesday morning, and it went over as expected. Ricky scanned it and yelled, "Immediately? I don't even get two weeks to find a replacement?" His face puffed as he spun on his heel, muttering about ungrateful workers. "You're leaving me in a hell of a bind, Katie." He stomped toward his office. "And, after everything I've done for you, too."

Katie rolled her eyes. "Worked me like a dog every weekend, that's what you've done. And all for less than minimum wage."

Renae was working and ran over. "You're leaving?"

Katie held up her left hand to show the ring. Renae sputtered, but a customer walked in, and she turned toward the door. "We'll talk on break."

Donette came on shift an hour later and got an earful as soon as she'd slipped on her apron. "Hey, ladies! What's up?"

Renae covered the distance immediately. "Katie ran off and got herself married."

"Married?" Donette spun around. Katie grinned and held out her hand.

"You weren't sick Sunday?"

"Nope. Flying back from Vegas."

"Vegas? This I gotta hear."

Ricky came out of his office and glared. "Did someone call a meeting?"

The three women hid smiles and studied their shoes.

"Get back to work." He stalked off toward the kitchen.

Donette whispered, "Margaritas. After shift." She shook a finger at Katie, "No excuses."

"I never saw it coming," Katie explained hours later as she poured the first margarita. Donette and Renae sat opposite Katie, hanging on every word as she walked them through the weekend. "He got down on one knee." Katie didn't mention the near date rape. *They'd never believe me.*

"Let's go to Vegas, Katie. Make me the happiest man on earth," Katie continued but didn't mention her empty checking account either. Instead, she launched into a description of Vegas. "It ain't Atlanta, Ya'll. The hotels are incredible." Katie flipped through pictures showing the MGM, Bellagio, and Venetian. "And, you never know what you'll see on the street. In one block, we saw an old man wearing a leopard leotard, a woman wearing a see-through blue hula skirt, and showgirls flouncing around in pasties!"

The pitcher of margaritas emptied as though it was water.

"Let me see that ring again." Renae yanked Katie's hand forward and examined it under the light. The old silver curled intricately around a single stone. "Is this a ruby? Garnet?"

Donette shook her head. "Damn, girl. How long have you known this man?" She appealed to Renae. "When was that political thing? The event where Katie met Prince Jack?"

"March, I think." Renae chugged from the salt-encrusted glass.

Donette made a show of counting the months on her fingers. "March, April, May, June…September. It's only been seven months!" She wiggled her eyebrows at both Katie and Renae. "You did good--landed a great guy."

Renae leaned back in her seat. "I hope you know what you're doing, girlfriend."

The three women hugged and promised to stay in touch.

Katie spent the rest of the week erasing her life in Atlanta. She sold her furniture to other residents, winnowed her belongings down, and packed up her decorating accessories and kitchenware. She hauled, pitched, and crated until she fell into bed exhausted each night.

On Saturday, Katie and Jack stuffed all the boxes and furniture into her car and the smallest moving truck she'd ever seen.

"No sense in spending the money on a big truck," Jack explained at her horrified expression when he pulled up to the curb.

They got into their first real argument over the last box on the sidewalk.

"There's no room, Katie. Leave it."

"Leave it? Everything I own is packed in a ridiculously small truck and one old car. How sad is that? Surely, we can fit in one more box."

Jack shot his hands toward the bloated car seats and the truck bursting at the seams. "We don't have room."

"All my summer clothes and photographs are in there. They're going."

"Fine. You figure it out." He kicked absently at her box and climbed into the van.

Katie emptied the trunk, piling everything on the sidewalk. She then began to reload, starting with the largest totes. She shoved, cussed, bent corners, and sat on the boxes to flatten them and make them fit. Neighbors milled about, pretending they weren't watching.

A young black man rested against a telephone pole. He'd grown up in the neighborhood with Katie, and although not exactly friends, they watched out for one another. He chewed the end of his cigarette, taking in all the details. "So, you married this guy?"

Katie wiped sweat off her face. "Yes, Vonte. You know I did."

"You just gonna let him sit in the truck?"

"It's okay, he doesn't understand."

"Oh, he understands just fine, sister." Vonte pushed away from the pole and thumped the side of the truck with the flat of his hand.

A startled Jack climbed out to help cram the last two boxes into the trunk. "You hold the boxes down while I lower the lid as far as I can. Take your hands out when I yell three, okay? One…two…three!"

Katie yelped as Jack slammed the lid.

"Whew. Made it!" Jack wiped his brow with broad, exaggerated sweeps.

"That's gonna explode when we open it!" Katie warned.

The trip took over five hours since the truck couldn't travel fast and needed gas every hundred miles. Katie had the honor of paying the bill.

Resigned to the fact her last paycheck would be gone, Katie bought fast food and Slurpees. "Enjoy every drop." She clunked her foam cup against his, "That's the last of the dough."

After they unloaded her stuff into Jack's small underground garage, Katie started to haul boxes inside. Jack stopped her. "Leave them there. You're just gonna have to pack it all up again."

"But ..." Katie stood in the garage, holding a tote. "I can't live out of boxes."

"You'll find what you need. It's only a few weeks."

Not wanting an argument after their long trip, Katie set the tote down.

What do I know about moving? She convinced herself Jack's logic made sense.

Chapter 8

Katie spent her first week in Savannah, lost. Despite GPS, the one-way streets were confounding, and she found something as simple as going to the grocery store stressful.

Jack complained daily, "I can't afford to pay for both of us.

"The groceries are higher, I'm paying for the cell phones, and even the gas in your car.

"You need to find a job!"

"It's not like I'm not trying, Jack," Katie defended herself.

His apartment became claustrophobic, and she ventured out daily, trying to find employment. A week later, a jubilant Katie met Jack at the door. "I have a job!"

"Really? Where?"

"The Blue Heron Bar and Grill," Katie rushed to explain. "You know the one I mean? It's three blocks from here."

When Jack said nothing, Katie talked faster, "I got lost again today, and as I was making a U-turn, there it was, 'Help Wanted.' I applied, and I start this Friday night."

"I don't want you waitressing. Men will be flirting and trying to touch you all the time."

"Like you did when we first met?" She meant it as a joke, but the humor was lost on him.

"You need to find something else."

He repeated it the next morning, and Katie called the restaurant to decline the job. "I'm sorry, but I've had another offer," she lied, not wanting to admit her husband had said no.

She applied at a nearby department store, but they only offered second-shift hours.

"We'll never see each other," Jack pouted, and Katie's list of potential jobs grew smaller.

Katie brightened her days with calls back home. The time passed quickly as she gossiped with Aunt Susan, Renae, and Donette. Embarrassed they may have been right about moving too fast with Jack, Katie glossed over her married life telling her friends, "Things are great!"

When the cell phone bill arrived, Jack was livid. "Twenty-minute calls to each of your friends? We can't afford this." He shook the bill in her face.

"Can't we get one of those unlimited plans?"

"That costs money, too, Katie" He sighed in disgust.

Shorter calls turned into less frequent calls as Katie nervously watched the clock, ending the conversations prematurely. The exception was her once a week call to Aunt Susan. On that, Katie refused to compromise. "She's the only other family I have, Jack."

Jack pursed his lips. "Fine. You need to find a job!"

I would if you weren't so damn picky, she bitched to herself.

Frustrated, Katie kept trying. She interviewed with several business offices, but her computer skills weren't strong enough. She was embarrassed to share the news with Jack.

"There's got to be something you can do, Katie. You can't sit around every day."

"I'm not sitting here." She popped off the couch as if to prove her point. "I'm applying, but nothing is working yet."

"Have you ever thought about adding highlights to your hair?"

"What's that have to do with a job?"

"If you fix your hair, wear a little more makeup, it might help with the interviews."

"It's not my hair. I don't have many skills."

Jack shrugged.

Confidence sagging, Katie added highlights to her light brown hair using a cheap, home-kit. She took more time with her makeup, too, playing up her eyes. *It can't hurt.* She spent the next day job hunting.

"Where'd you go today?" Jack asked as soon as he walked in the door. "You put forty miles on the car."

Katie rattled off a list of errands, a trip back home because she'd forgotten the dry cleaning, and three potential jobs.

"I asked you how you put forty miles on the car today?"

"I told you."

"No. You gave some flimsy excuses." He pulled her chair closer with her still sitting in it, putting them nose to nose.

Katie sat very still and looked straight ahead. She forced herself to use a soft, calm voice, "They're not excuses. I swear. I was just running errands."

Jack leaned in close. "Are you seeing someone?" Spittle flew.

Katie wiped her face. "No! I was right here."

Jack's face flushed, and he shoved the chair back, toppling her onto the floor. Katie held the back of her head in shock.

He glared down at her and then came to his senses. Dropping to his knees, he cradled Katie, stroking her hair. "Oh, my God! I didn't mean to do that. Are you all right?"

Katie looked at Jack out of the corner of her eye. *I've made a mistake.*

Feeling a lump under his fingers, Jack rushed to get an icepack, pressing it to her head. "I'm so stressed out. I shouldn't have taken it out on you. I know you're trying. Everything's gonna be fine." He kissed her head, her eyes, her nose. "We move into the house next week. It'll get better. This will never happen again, I promise."

She needed to believe him, needed to believe she wasn't re-living her parent's life, needed to believe he loved her. She nodded once, not trusting herself to speak.

Which allowed Jack to get in the last word, "Thirty miles or less a day on your car, would help a lot."

Once they moved, Katie's was optimistic their home life would improve. She loved the old house with all its nooks and crannies. It didn't matter to her that it was outdated, choosing to see its character and charm instead. She knew she and Jack would bring it back to its grand self.

In the interim, she hung the pictures from her apartment, laid out colorful rungs, and placed her knickknacks. It wasn't much, but the additions made it feel like home. She was particularly pleased with how their bedroom had turned out. Photo frames and trinket boxes were artfully displayed here and there. An overstuffed chair and her Grammie's pie-crust table filled one large corner. Katie added the amber candlestick and felt it was just the right touch.

Even Jack commented when he walked past, "Wow. That looks great there. The light from the windows makes the whole candlestick glow."

"Yep," Katie agreed. "Things are looking pretty good around here. Now we can plan our party."

"Party? What party?"

"You said we'd have a reception once we moved into the house."

"We don't have the money, especially with you not working. Maybe next month."

She suspected, from his dismissive tone, there would never be a party. "Well, when am I going to meet your parents." He didn't commit on that front either. And just like that, their shared moment was gone.

In between searching for jobs, Katie used her excess time and energy to scrub the old house until it gleamed. She bought clearance paint and tackled the office and dining room, determined to make the rooms brighter. YouTube videos explained how to repair plaster and strip wallpaper, and Katie eagerly followed instructions.

"God!" Jack said in disgust, coming in from work, and stepping over buckets and tools. "You're a mess." He sneered at her hair up in a clip, joint compound smeared on her arms. "Did you even look for a job today? You should take better care of yourself." He frowned and walked away.

Katie's face turned red, and she ran to scrub herself clean. When she came downstairs nicely dressed and wearing make-up, Jack smiled. "Now, that's the girl I married." He planted a kiss on her forehead. "I love the lipstick. You should wear it more often." He then invited her to take a walk with him through the neighborhood. He held her hand, waved to neighbors, and was more his congenial self.

Katie much preferred this Jack to the one who complained and insulted. She learned to clean up before he got home—exactly what he'd wanted.

During those first two months, Jack squeezed every paycheck until he had enough money to upgrade the outdated electrical system and add a security system.

"Cameras? We can't have a reception, and I can't call my friends, but we can put in security?" Katie couldn't believe it and followed Jack from room to room. "Jesus! You've got cameras in every room."

"We live in the most desirable neighborhood in Savannah. I want us safe. I make the money. I decide," Jack roared.

Katie stepped back from his temper, keeping her own anger in check until she saw the master bathroom. "In the bathroom? You've got to be frickin' kidding me! I'm not peeing on camera!" She fisted her hands on her hips. "This is bullshit, Jack!"

Jack was watching the installation, too, infinitely pleased with the progress. "We're not aiming it at the toilet, for God's sake. Anybody could climb the tree outside and get inside." He gestured to a tiny stained glass window over the tub.

"That's ludicrous. Neighbors would notice before anyone got inside."

"Not in the back." Jack strode to the window and cranked it open. "Look. Two big oak trees right here by the house."

Katie peeked out on their little closed-in yard. She acknowledged the trees were large and climbable. They shielded the back of the house, and while Katie still thought it was paranoid, she tentatively agreed with Jack's logic. "I guess I can see your point."

Standing underneath the soon-to-be-installed camera, Katie took in the angle. The toilet was private, but the glassed-in shower was clearly visible. She made a note to buy a curtain as soon as possible.

"Who's gonna track all this stuff?" Katie asked.

"There's software with this set-up. I can see the camera feeds on the computer downstairs, or on my phone. It's a safety thing, Katie. I'm trying to protect what's mine."

"Ours," Katie corrected. "You mean you're protecting what's ours."

"That's what I said," Jack answered. He turned toward her with a slight tick below his left eye. "There's no need to have some stranger watch us eating dinner or making love." He said it loud enough to make the technician turn around.

Mortified, Katie ran out of the room.

Jack gave a satisfied smile.

After the installation, Katie draped towels over the cameras in the bathroom and bedroom, sparking another argument.

"Damnit, Katie! The whole point is to be able to see the house and what's going on!"

"It's just me in here! What's the issue?"

"It's to protect you from anyone when you're here alone!"

"I cannot stay here," Katie huffed.

"What the hell is that supposed to mean?"

"It means, this isn't what I signed up for, Jack. Watching my damn miles, checking my phone, the stupid camera's, giving me crap about working, my hair, my clothes, everything!" She spun around to face him. "I'm not something you own." She pulled out a suitcase, throwing clothes into the bag.

Jack came over and dumped it all out. "Stop. You're not leaving."

"The hell I'm not." She re-gathered the clothing.

'I've never lived with anyone before and neither have you. We're both learning and need to work at this." He pulled her close, stroking her back. "Where would you go?"

It was a good question, and Katie didn't have an immediate answer.

"Don't leave," Jack said quietly, looking down into her face. "I need you."

Katie hesitated.

He made sweet love to her, showering her with affection. Flowers arrived the next day, and Katie decided Jack was right. *We just need to try harder.*

Chapter 9

As the new year rolled into place, Katie found a job at a daycare center and came home full of stories. "The kids are so stinking cute! The things they say are hysterical." She launched into yet another example.

As the weeks passed, Jack grew to hate her job. As Katie sat laughing about an incident in the boy's bathroom, Jack cut her off, "Taking care of kids isn't exactly tough, is it? You should try my job sometime. There's nothing 'stinking cute' about planning a city."

Katie leaned back in her chair. "Wow, Jack. Who said it had to be a competition?"

"There is no comparison. That's the point." He didn't talk to her for the rest of the night.

The next day, he grumbled further, "You never ever ask about my day anymore." He slammed away from the table and made a drink.

The drinking had increased since she started working, which made Katie nervous. She found ways to make Jack feel important and downplayed her job, concentrating on him and complimenting his every achievement.

It didn't matter. He just turned his focus elsewhere, "You never dress up for me anymore."

Embarrassed, Katie fiddled with her clothes. "What's wrong with this skirt?"

"It's old-fashioned. You're young, show off those long beautiful legs." He squeezed her thigh too hard.

Choosing sexier clothes backfired too. "I bet all those dads coming in and out like you, huh? All looking for a little something on the side," he accused.

Katie naturally denied such a thing was possible and showered Jack with compliments. He checked her phone more often, not even trying to hide the fact that he scrolled through messages and calls.

What am I doing wrong? She asked herself daily.

Weeks later, Katie was in the bedroom closet. They were close to completing their first do-it-yourself project and were headed out to dinner to celebrate. They'd renovated an upstairs laundry room and converted it to a new walk-in closet in the master bedroom. Katie stepped over screwdrivers and a caulking gun to go through her clothes one more time. "Jack?" She slid hangers across the fancy new pole and called his name again, "Jack? Have you seen my black skirt?"

"I threw it away."

She stepped out of the closet. "You what?"

"I threw it away." He sat on the bed, putting on his socks.

"Why?"

"I told you it was too long. It made you look like an old lady."

Katie stared at him in disbelief. "That was mine. You have no right…"

"I have every right to want my wife to look nice when we go out. You weren't listening, so I took care of it." Straightening the second sock, Jack stood and opened a dresser drawer. "I did, however, buy you a new one." He pulled out a bag and held up less than a yard of material. "You can wear it tonight."

She chose black slacks instead, defying him. He punished her by not speaking one word at dinner other than to order his meal.

The next day, Jack drove by the daycare building during his lunch break. He mentioned it during dinner. "Who was the man you were talking to near the swings today?"

The unexpected question left her floundering. "You were at school today? Why didn't you come inside?"

Jack glared, and repeated his question, "So, who was that man?"

"It was a dad, Jack--picking up his daughter. You could have asked me today. At the school," she said pointedly. "It would have been better than starting a useless argument at dinner."

Jack swiped his dishes from the table, leaving them in a heap on the floor.

Katie whispered to herself as she cleaned up the mess, "There was a crooked man, who walked a crooked mile…" *I can't do this. I need to leave.*

Before doing so, she tested a theory. The next morning, she parked her car at a nearby grocery store and walked to the preschool. Within an hour, Jack came roaring into the building, demanding to see Kathryn Werner.

Katie met him outside. "Is everything okay?"

"Why is your car at the Kroger? What the fuck is going on?"

Wide-eyed and seemingly innocent, Katie explained, "I stopped for donuts and decided to walk. It's a beautiful day. I planned to grab a few groceries after work. I'll get my car then. Is there a problem?" She forced herself to use a concerned tone, despite the fact she was raging inside. *He's tracking my car!*

"It was a stupid thing to do, Katie." Jack stomped off and moved her car to the preschool parking lot. "We'll talk about this later," he said as he peeled away.

She apologized to Jack during dinner. "I didn't think," she explained.

He rolled his eyes, as though it was a well-known fact.

"Everything has been so crazy the last eight months—moving to your apartment, the house, working." She continued, treading carefully, "I'm kind of a mess lately. I'm sorry. It's not fair to you. I think I'll go see Aunt Susan this weekend. It'll clear my head."

Jack raised his eyebrows. "You're leaving?"

"Just for a few days. I miss seeing Aunt Susan." Katie brushed her hands across his shoulders. "I'll come back better for it. You'll see." She gave him a come-and-get me-smile—anything to keep him off guard. She wasn't coming back.

Jack swept her onto his lap. "Maybe I'll come with you. It'll be a little get-a-way for us." He watched Katie intently.

"Sounds good, but we're planning to do girl stuff—nails, shopping, catching up on gossip. You'd hate every minute of it." She played her role to the hilt. "You and I will have our own reunion when I get home Sunday night."

Jack knew she was lying and watched Katie over the next few days. She added more clothes to the trunk of her car when she thought he wasn't looking. He scrounged through her purse, incensed to find cash, a copy of her resume, and the title to her car.

Jack stayed silent, making a few plans of his own.

Katie left work early on Friday, eager to get out of Savannah. She looked under the front and back bumper of her car, finally locating a GPS tracker, just like the internet had explained. Katie pulled the magnetic disk free and tossed it in the seat of the car, intending to throw it away halfway to Atlanta. She raced for the highway, eager to leave Jack behind.

When Katie pulled into the cul-de-sac with its matching cluster homes, she saw Jack's car in Aunt Susan's driveway. Panicked, she started to back out when Jack opened Susan's door, waving cheerily. With no choice, Katie pulled in and parked.

"Surprise!" Jack smiled. "I figured I'd join you. We'll all make a weekend of it!"

Katie sputtered a quick response.

Aunt Susan squeezed in beside Jack, grabbing Katie's hands. "What the hell is going on with you, two?" She shot a questioning look at Katie, swiveled her head toward Jack, and shook her head in confusion. "Get in here, Katie-girl, and give me a hug."

Jack joined the embrace, making eye contact with Katie over Susan's head. He pulled back his jacket to show a hunting knife, sheathed on his belt—something she'd never seen before. His right hand stroked the blade, while his left pulled Aunt Susan close. "We'll have to make this weekend extra special for Aunt Susan, won't we, Katie?" Jack's innuendo was clear, and Katie felt goosebumps break out on both arms. He caught Katie's eye again. *You do understand, right?*

She bobbed her head once.

Later, Jack whispered threats to Katie while they lay on Aunt Susa's pull-out couch. "I swear to God, Katie. I'll do it." He ran the tip of the knife between her breasts—a deadly caress that never broke the skin." I never liked the bitch anyway. You want Aunt Susan to live a nice long life, don't you?" The knife hovered just above Katie's belly button.

Katie nodded, afraid to breathe.

"We're never going to have this issue, again are we?" Jack pressed the tip of the knife and watched, fascinated, as a single drop of blood appeared.

Katie saw Jack's face change from anger to lust and knew he wasn't done meting out his punishment. Katie endured his love bites and bruising fingers for Aunt Susan's sake.

Saturday had the threesome traipsing across Atlanta, shopping, going to the park, and having lunch. Jack showered Aunt Susan with attention.

Aunt Susan giggled at Jack's compliments, "I didn't realize you were such a charmer."

Jack laughed, "There's a lot you don't know about me. We'll have to get to know one another better, won't we?"

Susan laughed and turned to find Katie. Katie had stopped walking and turned pale.

When Jack also turned around, his arm affectionately draped across Susan's shoulders, Katie gagged.

Aunt Susan hurried to Katie's side. "Are you all right?"

Jack's smile disappeared.

Katie shook her head as much at Aunt Susan as Jack. "Lunch didn't sit well with me. I think I need to lie down."

Back at the villa, Aunt Susan fussed over Katie, draping a cool washrag on her forehead, and feeding her stale, saltine crackers. "Poor baby. You never get sick."

Jack sat a few feet away, watching Katie intently. "It doesn't seem like Katie's getting any better. I think we should go home."

Katie felt nausea in her throat and tried to keep down a belch.

"Oh, no. The drive will make it worse," Aunt Susan protested.

"What do you think, Katie?" Jack looked her in the eye. "Wouldn't you rather be at home? It doesn't seem fair to ruin Aunt Susan's weekend, does it?"

"Jack's right, Aunt Susan. I may be coming down with something more serious. I sure don't want anything to happen to you."

Susan looked at Katie, looked at Jack, and crinkled her forehead. "Is there something going on here?" Her face then lit with excitement. "You're pregnant, aren't you?"

"God, I hope not," Jack and Katie said in unison.

At Aunt Susan's look of concern, Jack smoothed the situation, "We're not ready for a baby yet. If Katie has the flu, we need to be closer to home." He patted Susan's hand. "We'd hate for you to go down for the count."

Katie gagged again.

"We'll find a way to send Katie back here for a girl's weekend real soon. You'd enjoy that, right?"

Susan agreed, and Jack even pretended to make a date.

Jack drove directly behind Katie the entire four-hour drive. He kept her on the phone, laying out the new rules, "You will go to and from work only. You will not carry cash." On and on it went with Katie growing numb the longer he talked. He brought the knife to bed that night, placing it on their bedside table.

On Monday, Katie quit her daycare job to keep the peace and applied elsewhere. She found what Jack considered a more acceptable vocation as a home health aide with Comfort Keepers.

Jack took Katie to a fancy dinner to celebrate, toasting her new career. She soaked in the rare praise, praying this would work.

Although challenging, Katie loved her new job. Surprisingly, the more training she took—CPR, exercise therapy, massage--the better the pay, too.

Because her clients could be located anywhere in the city, Jack had to allow Katie more access to the car. They agreed she wouldn't accept any patients who lived more than thirty miles from Forsyth Park. Jack also insisted on having the patient names and addresses on his phone. "Just in case," he explained. But they both knew better.

In his mind, she'd be working with senior citizens who represented no risk. His assumption held true for more than two long, miserable years—Years in which he demanded more, gave less, and watched her every move.

Chapter 10

Katie packed her oversized tote, adding children's books for her Alzheimer's patient, Mr. Parker. Jack called out a reminder as he headed toward the door. "Don't forget Vicki's coming over tonight."

"Fine." Katie hated the sessions with the personal trainer—Vicki of the rock-hard abs, and enhanced boobs. The stupid woman came to the house once a week to put Katie through her paces. Katie had given up going to the gym a year before. It wasn't worth Jack's constant accusations of her flirting with the other men. Because image was vitally important to Jack, he needed Katie to look perfect too. So, he'd hired Vicki.

That night, Katie gnashed her teeth, determined not to complain while the She-Nazi made comments about Katie's inefficiency. "Do another set of lunges. That was pathetic."

Jack shared a conspirator's wink with Vicki.

Afterward, Vicki sidled up to Jack, rubbing against him and laughing too loud. He brushed a hand down Vicki's arm, stalling near her breast. The air vibrated with their sexuality.

When Vicki left, Katie had had enough. "Why don't you and Vicki run off together? She's obviously what you want."

He slapped her quick and hard. Usually careful to avoid harming Katie's face, Jack's lost his control, and she could feel her cheek swelling.

"You think I would align myself with such a woman?"

For some reason, the alignment reference made Katie think of tires, and she let out a small laugh. She regretted it at once and shifted backward as though that would make the sound disappear.

She babbled a quick excuse, "I'm tired. I don't think I heard you right. What did you say?"

Jack grabbed Katie by her hair and pulled her into the downstairs bathroom. Shoving her against the vanity, he used his other hand to grab her left arm, slamming her hand against the mirror. "You see that ring?"

Scared, she nodded.

He held her pinned against the sink. "We're together forever, Katie. Until death do us part." Katie and Jack's eyes locked in the mirror for several long seconds.

When she went to bed, the knife was on the nightstand again. It showed up from time to time, when Jack judged Katie to be misbehaving. Jack picked up the knife and sliced the strap on Katie's nightshirt. "Still nice and sharp." He ran his thumb over the blade; a drop of blood dropped on Katie's shoulder. He licked it off, never taking his eyes off Katie.

The next morning, Katie considered calling in sick. It wouldn't even be a lie since her sham of a life made her nauseous. If the patient were anyone else but Cassie, she would have made the call. Instead, she applied concealer, covering her bruised cheek, and headed to the kitchen.

Jack raised his eyebrows at the extra makeup but proceeded with their usual morning routine. "Coffee ready?" he asked while scrolling through the news. As he left for work, he leaned in for his customary kiss. "Let's have a nice dinner together."

Katie glanced at Jack, knowing precisely what he meant. *You'll be here when I get home, and we won't be talking about last night.*

As Katie joined the thousands of commuters, trying to bypass
Atlanta on the I285-loop, she had time to think about how much her life had changed in the three months since meeting Cassie.

Katie's boss, Cheyenne, had called in late June. "Are you feeling better?"

"I slept a lot at first, but I'm better."

Katie had taken a week off following a miscarriage. She'd been elated to discover she was pregnant, hoping a baby would help their marriage. Instead, Jack drank more and screamed about finances. She'd started bleeding after a particularly bad night when Jack literally dragged her up the stairs to their bed. Katie mentally swiped away the memory.

Unaware of Katie's thoughts, Cheyenne got to the point of the call, "Are you up to a new patient?"

"You usually assign. What's the deal?"

"Well, this one may be more difficult."

As the silence lengthened, Katie grew suspicious. "And…"

"She's young, Katie," Cheyenne paused, letting the words sink in. "She's twenty-four. Since you're just a couple of years older, we thought it may be a good fit."

"What's the catch?" Katie smiled. Cheyenne acted tough, but Katie knew better.

Cheyenne sighed. "It's more difficult when they're young, Katie. It's harder to stay detached. This girl—Cassandra--she's paralyzed from the waist down. Has been since she was sixteen. She was in a terrible accident and in a coma for more than six months. Her mother is the primary caregiver, and her father works from home, but the medical end of things is getting to be more than they can handle. Eight years have passed, and her organs are shutting down. There isn't going to be a miracle. You understand?"

"Yes, but the poor girl needs a friend."

Jack was less than pleased with the prospective new client, but he'd caught himself in a trap of his own making. Stretched thin by their mortgage and taxes, he'd recently asked if she could pick up extra hours.

Katie's potential new gig promised her two days a week.

"How far is the house?" Jack asked, pointedly.

Katie had done the research. "It's twenty-eight point four miles, just under the thirty miles you asked for."

He looked skeptical. "We'll see."

The next morning, Katie entered the Morrison's house wearing huge loopy earrings and a bright pink shirt. Seeing the young woman also dressed in pink, Katie pointed at their shirts. "Hey there, Cassandra. I see you got the memo about pink shirts, too?"

"Call me Cassie," she'd said with a lopsided grin.

Alike in age and taste, their kindred spirits recognized one another--one coming to the end of her physical life, the other slowly dying inside. Katie followed instinct and hugged Cassie. "I'm so glad to meet you." She was unfazed by Cassie's wheelchair, steroid-bloated body, or colostomy bag. Cassie beamed and hugged Katie back with surprising strength.

Cassie's parents, Bob and Julie Morrison, squeezed one another's hands. Julie had tears threatening; all her fears for her daughter's last days were so close to the surface, they were a tangible presence in the room. Bob draped a beefy arm across his wife's shoulder and planted a kiss on her forehead. "It's gonna be okay," he whispered. Katie heard him and shot them a reassuring wink.

Despite Cheyenne's continual words of caution, Katie latched onto Cassie with fierce loyalty. As the months passed, the two women grew inseparable and developed a routine.

"What's in your bag of tricks today?" Cassie always asked.

Katie, in turn, would dump out the contents of her tote. Gossip magazines, newspaper clippings, and lotions tumbled onto Cassie's bed. Katie would pluck something from the pile, tell a corny joke, and start their session. They laughed and talked as though they'd been lifelong friends.

So, when Katie walked into Cassie's room, following the confrontation with Jack, Cassie zeroed in on Katie's camouflaged face. "Oh, my God! What did you do?"

Katie made a lame excuse, "Workout last night."

"Vicki?" Cassie laughed and put her hands out in front of her breasts, remembering some of Katie's unflattering descriptions of the personal trainer.

"Yep. That would be the one."

Cassie frowned at Katie's short reply.

Katie pretended not to notice and told a joke instead, "You know why the gym closed down? It wasn't working out."

Cassie rolled her eyes and set her suspicions aside, needing time to think.

Katie spent three hours with Cassie, babbling and taking Cassie through a series of exercises to keep her leg and foot muscles from atrophying. A blood clot would be a death sentence. Katie turned Cassie from side to side, checking for unusual bruises, cleaning the colostomy site, and massaging her back. Cassie lay still, and Katie assumed she was asleep until Cassie blurted out, "You know what I regret?"

Katie's hands stilled. Cassie rarely grew melancholy. Although she didn't want to, Katie let the conversation unfold. "What do you regret?"

"I regret not doing more after the accident."

"Don't be hard on yourself. You had to learn how to cope with a whole new life."

"I don't mean that stuff. I was a cheerleader--a gymnast. I should have entered those Special Olympics, or coached. I was a good student. I should have tutored and made a difference. I've spent the last eight years concentrating on me."

"You did the best you could."

"I hope so," Cassie replied as she squeezed Katie's hand. "Don't get to the end and wish you'd done it differently. No regrets, Katie."

Cassie made direct eye contact, "You know why?"

"Why?"

"Because life is like toilet paper," Cassie paused dramatically. "No matter how long it seems, it always ends at the wrong time."

Katie's mouth fell open at the unexpected punchline.

"You're not the only one who can tell a joke," Cassie quipped.

As she left for the day, Katie's mood was remarkably better. Wanting to keep it going, she dialed Aunt Susan.

Recognizing the number, Susan answered with enthusiasm. "Katie-girl! How are you?"

"Hi!" Katie was already smiling. "I'm doing good. I'm leaving Cassie's and have time to catch up on the drive." Traffic was already backing-up, and Katie turned off the AC and rolled down the window. The two women launched into a non-stop conversation about anything that came to mind: the weather, books, music, politics. Katie even repeated Cassie's earlier joke. A half-hour passed quickly. "Whew," Katie let out a breath. "I'm almost home, so I've got to let you go."

"Great talking to you, honey. Tell Jack I say hello."

Katie snorted, "Yeah, right."

"What? You know how much I love that man." Aunt Susan gestured on her end, sending her always present, multiple bracelets jangling.

Katie smiled at the familiar sound—a long-distance hug from her aunt. "Here's my turn-off. I'll call you next week. Love you!"

Katie had almost forgotten the night before. Pulling into their driveway, her heart sank. Jack was home early and waiting by the door. She greeted him and went along with the game in which they both pretended their world was perfect.

"So, how's Aunt Susan?" Jack asked, proof he was still watching Katie's every move.

"She's doing great," Katie answered. There was no point in acting surprised.

"You are going to take a shower, right?" He wrinkled his nose in disgust. "You never know what those people may have on them." He shivered as though Alzheimer's or paralysis were contagious.

Katie dashed up the stairs, hoping Jack wouldn't be behind her, but instinctively knowing better. He considered it his right to watch her shower. If she opted for a bath, he would sit on the edge, watching her, or pouring water over her, or soaping her.

She'd questioned it once, early into the marriage, when she'd realized the bath routine never included words of love, or romantic overtures, or cherished looks.

Jack had been defensive. "Why wouldn't I want to see my beautiful wife? Most men don't care at all. You're damn lucky." He'd then proceeded to prove how lucky she was by dragging her to bed.

So, on this particular Friday night, Katie pretended she didn't mind him opening the shower doors to get a better look. Afterward, he held out a towel, encouraging her to walk naked toward him. He watched her body and not her face.

Katie considered that a good thing as revulsion shimmered across her skin, and hatred leaked from her eyes.

Chapter 11

A week later, Katie breezed into the Morrison's house as Bob and Julie were heading out. The three adults barely missed a collision at the door. Julie laughed and announced, "We're going grocery shopping. There's nothing to eat in here!" They were gone before Katie could reply.

Cassie rolled into the living room and agreed. "No kidding. We're down to carrots and oatmeal. Ugg. Let's order pizza. I want a big greasy slice with the works." She rarely had an appetite, so the statement came as a surprise to Katie.

"Okay, but I don't have any cash. Does the pizza place take debit cards?"

"How can you not have any money in that purse? You could have hundreds of dollars hiding in the bottom. How would you know?"

"Jack doesn't believe in cash. He says it's too easy to lose track of where we spend our money."

"So, what do you do if you want to stop and get something to drink? Put a dollar-sixty-nine on your debit card?" Cassie joked, but at Katie's shrug, she frowned heavily. "Fine. My treat!"

After lunch, Cassie sat by the window, fiddling with her lap blanket. Katie tried to make her smile by telling a joke, "Did you hear about the two guys that stole a calendar? They each got two months."

Cassie didn't respond.

Katie walked over and rubbed Cassie's. "What's up with you?"

"Homecoming's this weekend."

"Do you ever hear from your high school friends?" Katie gestured toward the groaning bookcases in Cassie's room. Dozens of photographs vied for space amongst the eclectic mix of nonfiction titles ranging from accounting to philosophy.

"Not as much anymore. I got to be too much work."

"That's not true."

"Yes, it is. After the accident, I was a celebrity. My friends took turns pushing me down the hallways, getting my books, hanging out. It was great for a year, but things changed."

"People don't always say or do the right things around someone who's disabled. Jerks."

"They didn't mean it. My girlfriends would be excited about a dance at school, and then stop talking mid-sentence, embarrassed because I couldn't dance. It bothered them more than it did me, but eventually, they quit sharing the important stuff—dates, driving, sex. Occasionally, one of them stops by or sends a text. And now it's too late." Cassie's eyes welled, and she wiped her face. "Do you think we could drive by the school today? I know it's silly, but I'd like to see the football field one more time."

"Absolutely." Katie glanced toward the driveway and groaned, "Oh, no. Your parents took the van." Not ever imagining the girls would want to venture out, Bob and Julie had taken the handicapped vehicle, out of habit.

"That's okay. We'll take your car. If you move your front seat all the way back, you can scoot me in. That's how we used to do it before we had the van."

Chewing her lip, Katie asked, "How far is the school?"

"Six or seven miles? Why?"

"Jack," Katie let the sentence hang, pursing her lips and thinking. "Oh, never mind."

"What? Tell me."

"Jack watches the mileage."

"What? Are you frickin' kidding me? Why would he care?"

"He worries and likes to know where I am."

"You mean he wants to know where you've been, don't you?"

The question startled Katie. "No, it's just that..."

"It's just that your husband is an asshole."

"Why would you say that?"

On cue, Jack called. Katie turned her back on Cassie and answered cheerily, "Hey! What's up?"

Cassie listened to Katie's end of the conversation.

"We're going to take my car to the high school, so Cassie can see the football field."

Cassie concluded Jack had asked questions because Katie launched into a detailed explanation.

"…It's only a few miles from here." Katie nodded several times. "I should be home by four or four-thirty at the latest. I'll call you when I leave." Katie hung up and sighed.

"See?" Cassie pointed at the phone. "Asshole!"

Katie snorted. "My friends Donette and Renae used to call men assholes too."

"Who?"

"Friends of mine, back in Atlanta. We worked at a restaurant together. According to them, all men were assholes--asshats if they tried to cop a feel as we went by." Katie laughed at the memory, distancing herself from Cassie's earlier comments.

Cassie didn't so much as snicker. In fact, her eyebrows were pasted as high on her forehead as they could possibly go. "I wasn't calling all men assholes. Just Jack."

Katie shook her head, ready to deny.

"Oh, come on, Katie." Cassie sighed in exasperation, finally fed up with the pretense. "I may be paralyzed, but that doesn't mean I'm deaf, dumb, and blind. You come in here with bruises you can't explain or some stupid story about how they got there."

Katie's eyes grew large.

Seeing the look, Cassie continued, "You try to cover them with makeup or loose clothing, but I've seen them." Cassie ticked off more examples, "You're not allowed to carry cash, he calls all the damn time, and now you're telling me he checks the mileage on your frickin' car. I'd have to be an idiot not to put two and two together."

Katie slumped on Cassie's bed. "You're right. It's a hot mess."

Cassie wheeled closer to the bed, not caring about the high school field trip anymore. She gripped Katie's hands. "Wanna tell me about it?"

Katie spent the next hour, emptying herself of all the secrets she carried.

Chapter 12

"I grew up in the heart of Atlanta. We lived in a run-down apartment building, in an area where crime was rampant." Katie made eye contact with Cassie. "Picture muggings, drugs, prostitution. Both my parents are long gone--victims of alcohol, heart problems, and self-centered choices. I've got no brothers or sisters. No family at all except for my Aunt Susan.

"She'd show up on Saturdays, knowing Mom and Dad would be hungover. She'd pull up in front of our building in her big 1979 Crown Victoria and honk twice. I'd rush out the door as fast as I could fly. She started each day with a joke. Usually, a bad one."

Cassie's eyebrows quirked, "Ah, so that's where you get it?"

Katie flashed a grin. "Probably. Anyway, she took me on field trips and introduced me to the city library. I loved that building. The only limit was my imagination and how many books I could carry." Katie showed an imaginary stack of books by holding one hand up to her chin and her other hand down by her belly.

Cassie grinned. "I used to do the same thing. Did you go to school? Sorry." She flinched. "None of my business. I've read about kids in the city and how they're not even in the system."

"Oh, I was in the system. Trust me. It meant Mom and Dad got a little more out of the state each month."

"Huh?"

"Welfare."

Cassie's mouth formed a perfect O.

"Dad was born with congenital heart disease. He had arrhythmias, shortness of breath, and couldn't do anything strenuous. He drank and smoked because he couldn't work. Mom stayed home supposedly to take care of him. We scraped by on housing allowances, government money, and side jobs they worked for cash."

Cassie nodded, getting a better picture of Katie's life.

Katie continued, "But, to answer your question, yes, I went to school, although there was zero help from home. My parents barked out threats, instead." Katie changed her voice, impersonating her mother's slurred speech, "Don't you be gettin' in no trouble." Katie cringed, almost feeling her mom's quick smack.

"God. Is it me or is it hot in here?' Katie stood and opened a window. She pulled in a few gulps of fresh air, taking in the Morrison's back yard. The gangly legs of the impatiens were a transparent green, and clusters of hydrangeas were browning. Winter was coming. *No more Cassie. Long nights with Jack.*

Turning away from the window, Katie picked up the thread of her story, "At the end of my junior year, my parents had a vicious, knock-down fight. So bad, in fact, my dad dropped dead of a heart attack on our kitchen floor."

"Oh, my God!"

"I didn't realize it until it was too late. I'd come home from school and heard my parents yelling. I slipped into my room. When the screaming got louder, I hid in my closet."

At Cassie's confused look, Katie gave a brief explanation, "It was an old habit—one I learned as a little girl. Anyway, on that day, I heard the heavy thud and my mom's screams. I stayed in the closet, assuming the fight had escalated. I heard sirens and knew the cops were in our apartment. They'd been there before, so I did nothing. The police found me later." Katie hung her head. "I stayed in the closet while my dad died. How could I do that, Cassie?"

"You were just a scared kid." Cassie wheeled close to stroke Katie's back. "What happened afterward?"

"Money was pretty tight. Mom cried all the time, drank more, and quit taking side jobs. We were in danger of losing the apartment, so I started waitressing at a nearby restaurant. Mom managed to climb out of her funk every other Friday."

Cassie frowned. "Why?"

"Payday."

"Oh. Your mom wanted money, right?"

"Exactly. I'd give her grocery money, which was stupid, because she ended up buying a bottle of gin or going to the bar. She cried if she didn't get any money and accused me of not caring. I just wanted her to be quiet," Katie flapped her arms, "and go away. I'd give her thirty bucks and never ask where it went. I forged her name on the state checks and paid the bills."

Katie was talking too fast and forced herself to slow down. "Less than a year later, Mom died too--stepped right out in front of a city bus. She was drunk at the time, so the coroner called it an accident, but I was never so sure."

"This is a terrible story. Did you go live with your aunt?"

"No. She's a lot older than my mom and not exactly healthy. She lives in one of those retirement villages, where you start off on your own and move into assisted living."

"Is she gone?"

"Aunt Susan? God, no," Katie laughed at the idea.

"Do you still see her? I'd like to meet this lady."

"Not often. She doesn't drive anymore, and Jack doesn't like me to make the trip to Atlanta."

Cassie rolled her eyes. "He probably thinks you'd use the trip to have a wild affair."

Katie blushed. "You're not wrong."

"Asshole," Cassie muttered and gave a quick shake of her head. "So, how'd you survive?"

"Weeks after my mom died, I found a ten-thousand-dollar life insurance policy, way back in a drawer. The money paid off the bills and funerals—well, cremations, and I stuffed the rest into a savings account. I begged my manager for more hours, and he put me on the catering crew. I was serving at an event when I met Jack."

"Did you wear a black bowtie?" Cassie jiggled her chest.

"Yep. I must have looked damn good too because Jack followed me with his eyes the whole night. Here's this good-looking guy…"

Cassie rolled her eyes.

"He *is* good looking." Katie pulled out her phone, clicked on a picture, and passed the phone to Cassie.

Cassie glanced at it and handed it back. "He's still an asshole."

"Well, at the time, he seemed perfect; handsome, smart, successful. He sent me flowers, drove back and forth from Savannah, and called me four or five times a day."

Cassie held up a hand. "Five times a day? Wasn't that creepy?"

"Not at the time. I was barely scraping by. Along comes this guy who promised to make my life better. Pretty naïve, huh?" Katie scoffed. "I grabbed the chance for a new life. It just never occurred to me a new life didn't necessarily mean a better life."

Cassie tilted her head, considering the words. "So, how long have you been with Jack?"

"We just celebrated our fourth anniversary."

"Four years? Jesus, Katie. Why have you stayed so long?"

Katie made eye contact with Cassie. "This mess didn't happen overnight, Cass. To go along with Jack's concerns about money, I quit carrying cash. To stay in our phone budget, I made fewer calls home. To keep the peace, I made sure my jobs were close to home. Before I knew what had happened, I was completely dependent. And after the miscarriage, I think I just gave up."

"Miscarriage?' Cassie's eyes grew huge. "You lost a baby?"

Katie hung her head and nodded. "It was a surprise—the pregnancy. I thought it would make things better. It didn't."

"I'm sorry. I guess Jack wasn't happy?"

"That would be an understatement." Katie's breath caught, "I'll never be convinced it was an accident."

It took Cassie a few seconds to connect the dots. "Jack?"

At Katie's nod, Cassie's anger returned and with it resolve. "Do you still have the money from the life insurance?"

"Yeah. It's still in an Atlanta bank, with a few branches here in Savannah. Funny," Katie tilted her head, "I never told Jack."

"Smart if you ask me. Gut instinct is real. My gut told me not to get in the car with all those kids that day."

"The day of the accident?"

"Yep. Seven teenagers crammed in a vehicle, speeding, and being stupid. No way that could end well. I didn't listen to the little voice and look at me now," Cassie ticked off her injuries, "kidney gone, spleen missing, intestines mangled, liver failing, paralyzed."

Katie started to sympathize, but Cassie slid her palms together a few times, and abruptly changed the topic, "You should go to one of those battered women's shelters."

Katie winced.

"What? That's what you are."

"Those places are supposed to be secret, but Jack works in zoning, he knows every property around Savannah."

"How much money do you have?"

"I've got a little over thirty-five hundred."

"Thirty-five hundred? What the hell are you waiting for, girl? You could get a ticket anywhere!"

"It's not that easy. I don't have a credit card, which means no ticket. Plus, I can't leave information like that behind—too easy to follow. And, if I ever leave, I'm not coming back. Ever. I need a vehicle, a place to stay, expenses."

"Still, Katie, it seems like enough."

"It's not. I've thought about it. A lot."

"We'll talk about it when you come next week." Cassie clenched Katie's hand. "You're a good woman, Katie. You deserve better."

Katie lowered her head to Cassie's. They sat that way awhile; one relishing the idea she had value, the other undone by the fact she still had something to offer.

Chapter 13

As Katie drove to the Morrisons for the next appointment, her jumbled thoughts meshed into a single, desperate word, "Run!" Her adrenaline pumped, and for a second, she considered it a viable option.

Logic stepped in. *I don't have my money. Jack will know. He's tracking me, even now.* She pulled into the Morrison's driveway and rested her head against the steering wheel. *God, I don't know what to do anymore.*

Katie winced as she slid out of her car and hurried, as best she could, to the Morrison's front door. They expected her to come and go without knocking, so she poked her head inside. Relieved to find the living room empty, Katie called out a quick greeting. "Hey, ya'll. It's me."

Hearing Bob and Julie's muffled 'hellos' from the kitchen, Katie limped into Cassie's room. Even now, she felt a little leap of joy to find Cassie still here, still living, intent on her computer screen, as usual.

Grimacing, Katie sat down slowly on Cassie's hospital bed. "Cass, I need your help."

"What's going on?" Cassie turned herself around, concern rippling across her forehead.

Katie lifted her shirt. A long, red welt rose between Katie's ribs, and angry black bruises spread in all directions.

"Jesus!" Cassie gasped. "What happened?"

"I think I've got a broken rib."

"No shit, maybe more than one."

"Jack doesn't want me to go to the hospital, but--"

"Of course not. Doctors would ask questions. Jack can't be the bad guy, right?"

Katie looked at her shoes.

Cassie shook her head in exasperation. "Never mind. You need help, regardless of what you think." Cassie pushed her wheelchair toward the door, mouth open, ready to call her parents into the room.

"No! You can't tell them," Katie yelled.

"Are you serious? You're going to protect Jack? He did this, right?"

Katie's face flushed. "I can't have a report, Cass. If I go to the police, who knows what will happen."

"What if your lung's punctured?" Cassie ran a hand through her thinning cap of brown hair. "What if there's more damage?"

Katie shrugged, and the simple motion brought tears to her eyes.

Cassie looked at Katie's face and made a quick decision. "Fine. We'll fake it and pretend you got hurt here." She barked out instructions, "Lay down on the floor. Over here by the desk. I'll throw a stack of books on the floor, and we'll say you tripped over them."

"No one will believe that."

"People believe what's easiest. You tripped and fell into the chair. End of story." Cassie pulled books out of the bookcase. "Get on the floor!" She tossed more books at Katie's feet. "You fell into the chair, got it?"

Katie had no time to argue. With surprising strength born out of need, Cassie knocked over the desk chair with a clatter and yelled, "Look out!"

At the noise, Julie flew through Cassie's door, shocked to find Katie on the floor and Cassie still in her chair.

"It's my fault. I'm so sorry," Cassie wailed. "She didn't see the pile of books on the floor. You know how she is," Cassie fluttered her hands, "all action and speed. She tripped over them and hit the chair. Hard." Cassie gestured to Katie, who was holding her ribs and moaning.

"Are you okay, honey?" Julie knelt on the floor, brushing Katie's white-blond hair from her forehead.

Katie held back tears. "I don't think so. My ribs…"

Julie lifted Katie's shirt. "Oh, my God! You're already bruising. Bob!" Julie ran to the bedroom door, calling his name again. He ran from the office, expecting the worst.

"Bob, get the van, Katie's hurt! We need to take her to the ER!" Turning back toward Katie, she asked, "Can you move?"

Katie answered by rolling to a sitting position. Bob stood in the doorway, gawking.

"Bob, hurry!" Julie's short, round frame didn't keep her from being formidable. Bob rushed to follow her orders.

Julie helped Katie to the side of Cassie's bed and gathered a bag full of Cassie's prescriptions and tubes. "Let us get Cassie in the van, and we'll be right back for you."

Katie sat dazed, not sure what had just happened or how the hell she was going to explain it to Jack.

Bob came back inside and helped Katie up from the bed. "Lean on me, honey. I'll do the work."

He buckled Katie in as though she were a small child. Being treated so carefully made Katie cry. Flustered, Bob climbed into the driver's seat, speeding toward the hospital, careening around corners and barely stopping at signs. Julie turned around to ensure Cassie's wheelchair was strapped in and patted Katie on the knee. "Should we call your husband?"

Katie gave a small shake of her head and took shallow breaths to keep the pressure off her ribs.

Cassie offered a plausible lie from the back of the van, "He's in meetings all day. Let's see what the doctor says first."

Hours later, the ER doctor at Savannah General slapped an x-ray onto the screen and tapped it twice. "You've got two broken ribs. They're not splintered, which is good. You need to take it easy and wait for them to heal." He wound medical gauze across her torso. "Leave this in place for three weeks, even in the shower." He scribbled out a prescription for pain meds and handed her an extra roll of gauze. "Re-wrap your chest loosely every day and make an appointment with your doctor."

Katie was silent during the ride back to the Morrisons. She went into Cassie's room to grab her jacket, hoping to make a speedy getaway, but Cassie was having no such thing.

Cassie shut the door and rolled around to face Katie. "What happened?" She asked it quietly, which was Katie's undoing.

Katie lowered herself to the bed. "I didn't have any clients yesterday and thought I'd work on the house. I was in an upstairs bedroom where we haven't touched a thing—pockmarked floors, molded wallpaper, old lights. You get the picture. Anyway, I was stripping wallpaper, with the music blaring and never heard the phone."

"Uh-oh. Jack called, and you didn't answer, right?"

Katie bobbed her head once.

At Katie's confirmation, Cassie muttered, "Asshole."

Katie ignored the comment. "Jack drove home from work. I heard him fly up the stairs and was climbing down the ladder when he came in the room—eyes wild and screaming about how I'd better not be seeing anybody." Katie's voice shook, "The next thing I know, he grabbed the broom and took a swing at me. I don't mean a little swing either. I mean a try-for-the-fences, home-run swing. You know the rest."

Cassie blew out a breath. "What's going to happen when you get home tonight?"

"I have no idea."

"I'm taking pictures." Cassie rummaged through her bag to find her phone.

"Thanks for trying to help me, but,"

Cassie shot her left hand in the air, cutting of Katie's sentence. "Stop. We have to document this." Cassie aimed the phone at Katie. "Can you lift your shirt?"

Katie followed instructions while Cassie took close-up shots of the bandage and the bruises. She lowered the phone. "Why do you stay with him?"

"We have good days, too, Cass," Katie defended herself, needing her one and only friend to understand.

"This isn't some random argument, Katie. It'll get worse, and then what?"

Katie scrubbed at her face. "I don't know."

Cassie persisted, "You're smart. You've got a job. Get the hell out."

Katie looked at her watch and cringed. "I've got to go."

Katie kissed the top of Cassie's head and scooted out of the room. Seeing Bob and Julie at the kitchen table, Katie veered in that direction. "Thanks for your help today. I'm sorry for any trouble I caused."

"Don't be silly," Julie chided.

"No big deal," Bob added. "You just take care of yourself."

Katie sobbed all the way home. She cried for herself, maybe for the first time. She cried for Cassie. She cried because Bob and Julie were the first real parents she'd experienced, and her relationship with them was fleeting too.

Pulling into a gas station, she fixed her makeup and tried to figure out what she was going to say to Jack. *Truth? Lie?* They all seemed the same, anymore.

She was at the stove when Jack walked in and gave her a hard squeeze, signaling he'd forgiven her for the day before. Flinching, Katie blurted, "I ended up in the ER today."

"What?" His face contorted. "Why?"

She recalled all the times Jack had convinced himself her bruises had come from somewhere else or simply didn't exist. If *he* didn't acknowledge them, they weren't real. Banking on that history, Katie told him the false story of tripping over Cassie's books. She showed Jack the bandages. "Can you believe it? Cassie's in a wheelchair, and I end up in the ER."

Jack raised his eyebrows. "You're lucky the Morrisons were home. We owe them dinner or something." His voice never wavered. His face never gave away any indication of the lie. As expected, the story was convenient and, therefore, true.

For the first time, Katie was genuinely afraid for herself. Whether it was Cassie's earlier comments or Jack's reaction didn't matter. *I'm in trouble.*

Chapter 14

The next morning Katie eased out of bed, grimacing with the effort. She dry-swallowed two Tylenol and unwrapped the bandage. Standing in front of the mirror, Katie turned sideways. A large, red mass smeared down from her underarm to her waist, with a tangled set of yellow and green blotches extending toward her stomach. More prominent than the day before was a vivid line matching the shape of the broom handle.

Jack followed her to the bathroom and stood behind her, taking in the damage. "Damn. That looks awful. Let me help you re-wrap your ribs."

Katie watched him in the mirror. *How can you act like you weren't involved?*

"It wouldn't be a problem if you took off today," Jack said as he tucked in the end of the ace bandage. "It'll be a little snug without today's hours, but we'll be all right."

She shook her head as much in reaction to Jack's incredible performance as in answer to his comment. "I'm scheduled with Mr. Parker today. He doesn't require much—a little straightening and spending time with him. If it were Gertie, that would be a different scenario. I'd be cleaning, running errands, and grocery shopping. Mr. Parker is more like babysitting."

Jack nodded and helped Katie into a blouse. He toyed with the buttons, taking extra time at her breasts, oblivious to her broken ribs.

Katie's phone beeped, and she gladly turned away from Jack.

How ya doing? Everything alright?

"Who's that from?" Jack asked, peering over Katie's shoulder.

"Cassie--wanting to know if I'm okay after yesterday." Katie clicked on a happy face and sent a cryptic reply. *'Thanx 4 ALL ur help yesterday. I'm sore but good. CU Monday!'*

Katie looked at the clock. "Oh, man. I'm running late." She exited before Jack could ask any more questions and painstakingly maneuvered down the stairs to the den. She shoved open the pocket doors and headed towards a bureau she'd lovingly restored.

She pulled out children's books and puzzles and shoved them in her oversized tote. Mr. Parker didn't always recognize Katie, but it didn't prevent her from finding ways to activate his old memories.

"You're gonna be late," Jack yelled from the kitchen.

"I'll make it!" Katie yelled back as she slung her bag over her uninjured shoulder. She hopped toward the door, trying to get her second shoe in place.

Jack shook his head at her hurried exit. "We'll go out to dinner tonight. No sense in you cooking with those ribs hurting."

Katie blinked once. She didn't want to go to dinner but wanted an argument even less. "Fine. I'll be home around four-thirty."

Katie pulled into Mr. Parker's single driveway, taking in the compact neighborhood. His tiny ranch home bumped up next to similar houses and owners-- all older and in need of some assistance.

Mr. Parker's niece, Nina, had moved in a few years prior. With her children grown and her husband off with another woman, it had been a good pairing of resources. It had been Nina who'd called Comfort Keepers asking for help on her two longest workdays.

Walking toward the house, Katie saw a post-it-note stuck to the front door. 'He's having a tough morning! Call me when you get here! ~Nina.'

Katie squared her shoulders and knocked on the door.

"Who is it?" Mr. Parker yelled from the other side.

Surprised he'd come to the door, Katie answered, "It's Katie, Mr. Parker."

"I don't know nobody named Katie."

"Yes, you do. I'm here two times a week, remember?"

At the silence, Katie tried a different tactic, "I'm a friend of Nina's."

"Nina's not here."

Jiggling the doorknob, Katie found it locked and fished in her tote for the extra key Nina had given her. Still talking through the closed door, Katie tried bribing Mr. Parker, "I brought you some puzzles and was planning on making soup."

Food got his attention, and Katie heard the lock click. She pushed her way inside before he changed his mind. "Good morning!" She took in his appearance. His gray hair stood at strange angles, unsure of which direction it wanted to go. His skinny frame barely held his sweatpants in place, and his t-shirt was on backward.

"Let's get you dressed and see about some breakfast."

His wary eyes told her he wasn't sure who she was yet, but he gave her a sweet smile, indicating he liked her well enough. "You're gonna make soup?"

Katie patted his arm and led him toward his bedroom. "I sure am!"

She pulled out her phone to text Nina and noticed she'd missed a call from her earlier. It explained the note. Katie sent a quick message: *I'm here. Everything's fine.*

Katie and Mr. Parker--she couldn't bring herself to call him Reginald--spent the day reading books and working jigsaw puzzles. When he zoned out from time to time, Katie straightened up the kitchen and did a load of laundry. She wasn't as fast as usual but managed.

When he seemed too quiet in the afternoon, Katie booted up a Motown station on Spotify. Mr. Parker perked up and clapped his hands to the beat. When the *Temptations* came on, he got up and shuffled his feet, swaying side to side, and copying the group's syncopated moves.

Katie laughed, soaking in a rare moment of joy.

Mr. Parker eventually wore down, and Katie settled him in his chair, knowing he'd nap for hours. She tiptoed out of the house, locking the door behind her.

Pulling into her own driveway, her heart sank. Jack was home early and waiting by the door. His beer bottle glinted in the late afternoon sun, and Katie groaned. Jack waved to several neighbors, making a show of welcoming Katie home.

Jack leaned in for a kiss. "I can't wait to take you out tonight. You're so beautiful." He turned her towards him, making intense eye-contact.

Katie fought the temptation to swat at the pheromones in the air. "Sounds good."

"You'll want to clean up first, of course."

When Jack opened the shower door, Katie closed her eyes. He eventually moved toward the sink, and Katie headed for the closet, anxious to hide her body.

Jack commented on her outfit immediately, "You should wear something sexier."

Katie touched her blouse. "What's wrong with what I'm wearing?"

"I thought you'd wear a dress tonight." He headed to their closet and emerged with a black mini-skirt, and a hot pink shirt.

"That's too tight with the bandages."

Jack turned and pulled out a low-cut dress.

Katie sighed. If she resisted, dinner would be miserable. Jack's disapproval would hang in the air like smoke, tainting the food and conversation.

Once they were seated, Jack scanned the patrons, hoping to see someone he recognized. Katie perused the menu for the least expensive entrée.

When the nearby tables were crowded, Jack presented Katie with a gold necklace. A single diamond was suspended in the middle. "For my beautiful wife," Jack said loudly.

Katie stared at the necklace. *Oh God. Not again.*

The neighboring customers beamed, and a few even applauded lightly. Jack basked in the attention, and Katie adjusted her face, pretending to be pleased.

The new necklace was obviously expensive. Katie decided it was in direct proportion to the broken ribs but couldn't imagine where Jack had come up with the money.

Jack helped her with the clasp, and she smiled all while cringing inside. Accepting the gift meant she condoned the behavior. If she refused, she invited his anger.

Jack watched for it the next morning. "Why aren't you wearing your necklace?"

"It's Saturday. I'm cleaning for God's sake. Hardly the place for fine jewelry, Jack."

"You don't like it, do you? And, after all the trouble I took to find you something special." He pouted, a little boy whose feelings were hurt.

"Of course, I like it," Katie lied. "It's beautiful. I don't want to catch it on something."

Jack barely nodded. "I can take it back to the jeweler."

A brave woman would have shouted, "Yes! Take the damn thing back!" Katie has long ago traded in bravery for self-preservation. "Don't do that. I love it," She said, instead.

As predicted, Jack's mood improved immediately. The chain glittered around her neck all weekend. She wore it to Cassie's on Monday as the damn thing was now required.

Chapter 15

Cassie spied the necklace immediately. "Is that a diamond?"

Fingering it, Katie blurted out, "Do you want it? It's yours."

"What?"

"Sorry. Nothing." Katie was sore and irritable. Jack had sensed her odd mood and been overly sexual the entire weekend—his way of assuring himself all was right in his world. Cassie didn't need to know those things.

"It is a diamond, right?" Cassie wheeled herself closer to see it better.

"Yeah." Katie pulled lotions out of her tote. "Let's get you oiled and massaged."

"Not so fast," Cassie said. "What did Jack say when you got home Thursday?"

"He was willing to believe I hurt myself here."

Cassie's mouth dropped open. "Really?"

"Sure. It got him off the hook."

Cassie continued her questions, "What'd he say? You're killing me, Katie!"

Katie pointed to the necklace. "He made up for it, of course."

"I don't get it."

"When Jack acts badly, I get presents." Katie listed examples, "Earrings after he literally ripped my clothes off a few months ago, a bracelet following a kick to the shin, and enough flowers over the years to open a florist shop."

Cassie shook her head. "Wow. This is how you live?"

"Yeah, Cassie, it is. You have no idea." Katie lifted the necklace away from her neck. "Getting a necklace? That's nothing, trust me."

Cassie raised her eyebrows. "Katie you've got to--"

Katie interrupted, "I don't want to talk about it, all right?" She moved across the room, away from Cassie's questions.

"We have to talk about it, Katie. You need to get out of there."

Running frustrated hands through her hair, Katie spun around to face her friend. "I don't know how, okay?" Her voice rose. "I don't have enough money. I've got no place to go. Do you get what I'm saying?"

"Yeah, I get what you're saying, or at least I'm trying to, so stop yelling at me!" Cassie turned stormy eyes toward Katie, "I didn't do this to you. Jack did. Yell at him."

Katie sagged on the bed. "I'm sorry. You, of all people. I didn't mean to shout at you."

"Oh, for God's sake, quit apologizing! I'm fine. I'm glad to see you've got a spine under all that perfection. You should try it on, Asshole Jack. Maybe he'd leave you the hell alone."

Cassie's face was flushed, and for some inconceivable reason, it made Katie laugh. "God, Cass. Why don't you tell me how you really feel."

Cassie gave a sheepish grin. "He pisses me off. You piss me off!"

Bob knocked on the door and opened it slightly. He pushed his bald head through, scanning the room. "Everything all right in here? I heard yelling."

Cassie caught Katie's eye, 'It's fine, Dad. I'm ranting, and Katie is telling me to shut up."

Bob noted Katie sitting quietly on the bed and Cassie breathing hard. "Maybe you should listen to Katie." He raised his eyebrows and closed the door.

Katie snickered. "Busted."

Cassie tried to stay mad but let out a chuckle, too. "God. I can't even have a good fight without them coming in to make sure I'm all right. It makes me crazy."

"They have your best interest at heart."

Cassie huffed. "Well, I've got *your* best interest at heart. So now what?"

Katie rolled her head on her shoulders. "You think I haven't tried to leave? I did, once. Jack figured it out, followed me, and ended up threatening my Aunt Susan. I run. He'll follow. He tracks my car, my phone."

Cassie squinted at Katie, "Okay. Then get your money and take a bus out of here."

"To where? As soon as I go to the bank, he'll know. If I ditch the phone, he'll know."

"How about a restraining order?"

"Seriously? Kick him out of the house? You think that would work? Hold him at bay?"

Cassie shook her head. "There's got to be a way."

"Well, I sure as hell haven't figured it out."

Cassie shook her head. "Fine. I don't want to fight. We're ruining our day."

Pushing the wheelchair to the mirror, Katie brushed Cassie's ridiculously short brown hair. "We should add some highlights. Maybe a little blond on the tips? Nothing crazy like mine." Katie touched her platinum head and winced.

Cassie made eye contact in the mirror. "Sounds good. I expect to see a Clairol box in your tote next time. But, just for the record, we're not done talking about you and Jack."

"Meanwhile, let's do your exercises." Katie lifted and pulled Cassie until she was lying flat on the bed. "Whew!" Katie wiped her brow and knelt at the end of the bed. Grasping Cassie's foot, Katie bent her leg at the knee and pushed it toward the abdomen.

"Seems stupid to do exercises. It's not like I'm gonna be modeling."

"You know why we do them, quit grumping."

"Yeah. Yeah. Gotta keep the muscles moving and oxygen flowing."

Afterward, Katie rolled up Cassie's sweatpants, examining each leg. Turning the left leg, Katie leaned in closer and squinted.

"What?"

"There's a little swelling here." Katie touched the area with her fingertips. "I'm not taking any chances. This could be a clot."

Cassie groaned.

"I know. I need to tell your parents."

When Katie entered the kitchen, Bob and Julie took one look at Katie's face and stopped talking. Julie jumped up from her chair. "What is it?"

Katie explained the situation. Julie turned to go to Cassie, but Katie stopped her. "It wasn't there on Thursday. Let's take pictures and send it to the doctor so they can start a blood thinner."

Bob and Julie headed toward Cassie's room. Katie sat at the table, staring at the wall. She laid her head on her arm, already grieving her only friend. Noting the time, Katie waved goodbye from Cassie's bedroom door. "Keep me posted. I'll be back in a few days!"

Bob and Julie barely nodded.

In need of a friendly voice, Katie called Aunt Susan.

Susan answered immediately, "Hello! Katie-girl!"

"Hi!" Katie felt her spirits lift. "What news do you bring?"

"Well hell, Katie, you called me."

Katie chuckled, and the two women talked over one another. They both stopped to catch their breath, and Susan asked a few polite questions, "How's Jack? You two doing all right?"

Katie gave a vague response. "You don't want to hear about us. Same ol' same ol'."

"What the hell is going on with you, Katie-girl?" Susan asked, not for the first time.

Katie pretended not to hear. "I'm almost home. Love you!"

"Love you more!" Susan answered, but frowned as she hung up the phone.

Chapter 16

A few weeks after Thanksgiving, Katie drove to Fleming to see Cassie as scheduled. The blood clot emergency had been averted, thanks to a few days in the hospital, but new problems continued to crop up.

Bob and Julie met Katie at the door, practically sharing the same physical space. Their eyes were blood-shot, hair mussed, and all color leached from their faces. They motioned Katie inside, whispering, "She had a pretty bad night. She's still sleeping."

Katie peeked in on Cassie, noting her pallor wasn't much different than her parents. Katie winged a quick prayer toward the ceiling, pleading for less pain--a little guidance.

She headed for the kitchen and poured herself a cup of coffee. She'd been in and out of the house for months and followed their request to make herself at home. She joined Bob and Julie at the table and waited for them to start the conversation.

"She's in more pain. Last night was bad," Bob stated, ending his sentence with a long sigh.

"It was," Julie agreed. "She was in bed, clutching her stomach and crying. God." Julie wiped a shaky hand across her face. "She's been through enough. I can't stand it anymore."

Katie patted Julie's hand. "There's no reason for her to suffer. Have you called the doctor?"

Bob nodded his approval. "That's what I said."

Julie frowned at him, shaking her head furiously. Bob made eye contact with Katie, silently asking for help.

Katie acquiesced, "The doctor said he'd increase the morphine anytime. It would ease her pain."

"Do you understand what that means?" Julie wailed.

"I do. It means we're closer to our goodbye." With tears in her eyes, Katie stood and coaxed Julie into standing too. She reached for Bob, and the three melted together, swaying and holding one another. Julie choked on a sob, and Katie slid backward, allowing Bob to embrace his wife. Katie left them to their anguish and slipped into the bathroom to splash water on her face. Heading back toward the kitchen, she paused in the doorway. The couple had gathered their emotions and stood united.

"Do you want me to make the call?" Katie asked.

They nodded, and Katie left the room to take care of business. Afterward, she checked on Cassie, who was just waking up. She shared a weak smile with Katie. "Hey, girl. What's in your bag today?"

Katie didn't have as much on hand as she would have liked but pulled out a bottle of nail polish. "Spa day?"

Katie painted Cassie's toenails an obnoxious color expecting a smart-ass comment from Cassie. When there was nothing but silence, Katie shared a joke, "Have you heard of the new website conjunctivitis.com?"

Cassie crinkled her forehead. "No."

"It's a site for sore eyes."

The joke fell flat. When Cassie fell asleep, Katie stared out the window, watching the wind whip the dead flowers in Julie's garden into a frenzy. *What am I going to do without Cassie?*

Bob knocked on the door and ushered in a nurse. An IV pole followed with a drip bag already attached and ready. Katie leaned across the bed, "I'm heading out. You're gonna be higher than a kite in an hour, giggling, not making sense, sleeping."

Cassie grinned.

"I'll be back in two days." Katie exited quickly.

She made it a mile before the tears came. "Goddammit!" Katie smacked the steering wheel. "It's so unfair!" She sobbed and cussed as she made her way through snarls of interstates. She railed at God, the fates, life. "Why do you have to take the good ones?"

Once home, Katie curled up on the couch and stared at the ceiling. Jack came home to no dinner, and she didn't even care.

"What's going on?" Jack asked. "Are you sick?"

"They put Cassie on more morphine. She's dying, Jack."

"She's been dying all along, Katie. You couldn't save her. You've been through this before."

"This is different. She's my best friend." With that, the tears came again.

He squeezed her shoulder and went to make a can of soup. "Want some?" he called from the kitchen. Not hearing an answer, he went back to a now darkened living room. Flicking on the lamp, he noticed Katie hadn't budged. "Are you going to be all right?" He brushed her hair away from her forehead.

"No. I'm not. I just want to lie here and do nothing."

Later, Jack helped her to bed, stroking her back, and not pushing sexually, for once. "We'll get through this."

Here's the man I once loved. He didn't show up often but, for now,

Katie snuggled into him for comfort, hoping there were no strings attached.

The next morning, Jack let her sleep and made the coffee, which was too strong even by his standards. He left Katie a sweet note and headed out to work. He called during his lunch break. At her groggy hello, his patience evaporated. "Are you still in bed?"

"Uh-huh."

"You need to get up, take a shower, get on with the day. It'll help you get past this funk."

Katie scrubbed her face and stretched. "You're right. I can't believe I slept so long."

"Think of all the energy you'll have for later."

Katie closed her eyes. "What a fool," she whispered.

"What'd you say?"

"Nothing."

Jack repeated himself. "Get it? Plenty of energy for later?"

"Yep. I get it, and I'm quite sure I won't be tired later."

Jack called again at two. "You up and moving?"

"Yep. Busy cleaning."

He called at five to say he was on his way. "Let's not talk about Cassie tonight, okay?"

Katie's one day of sadness and dejection was evidently over. Ending the call, Katie muttered things she'd love to say to Jack. She pounded the couch pillows back into shape. "We wouldn't want to talk about anything in Katie's world, now would we? God, no." She slammed the soup dishes into the dishwasher. "Can't be unhappy, can you, Katie? That would mean Jack didn't have a good day." She threw the dishtowel across the room. "You need to be sexy," she wiggled her hips, "and make Jack feel better. Cassie's right, you are an asshole." The mention of Cassie had Katie's face crumbling.

When Jack walked in the front door, Katie gave him a welcoming but false hug.

Dinner was routine with Jack doing most of the talking. He noticed her silence. "Why are you so quiet?"

"I'm still sad, I guess. You haven't even asked how I'm doing."

"We said we weren't going to talk about it, remember?"

Later, she sat beside him on the couch while he flipped through channels stopping when there was sufficient female skin showing. Eventually, Jack pulled Katie toward the bedroom.

Ahhh. Here is where I pay my dues. Jack was kind and put up with my bad mood. Now, I get to show him how grateful I am for his consideration.

She opted for a shower, not surprised when he joined her. Water sluiced over their bodies. Jack took over the soaping and scrubbing, running eager hands across her chest and over her thighs. Katie winced as he rubbed her still sore torso.

Once in bed, Jack rose over her and commanded, "Open your eyes. I want to see you."

Katie hated this part the most. Between Jack and the security cameras, there seemed to be a thousand spider eyes watching her physical reactions. Because Jack often reviewed the tapes, she'd learned to show only pleasure. Jack was too egotistical to concede it might not be real.

Having cleaned up the sheets, she padded toward the bathroom to clean herself as well. Looking at the mirror, her image reflected abject sadness. "You deserve an Academy Award for that one, Katie-girl." She turned away in shame.

Chapter 17

Katie juggled her schedule, asking another aide to check on her beloved Mr. Parker. She regretted the change, but, with his faded memory, he wouldn't notice. She drove to the Morrisons instead. Bob held Julie's hand as they brought Katie up to speed.

"We've already had to increase the morphine."

"I've taken a leave of absence from work." Bob hung his head and stared at his coffee.

"There's not much time."

"You've done everything humanly possible. That girl in there," Katie pointed towards Cassie's room. "has had eight more years because of you. You gave her the care and hope she needed." Katie's voice shook, "She's funny and gifted and my best friend." A sob escaped.

Julie and Katie dissolved into tears, sniffs, and hiccups. Bob patted both ladies on the back. It made Katie laugh, breaking the intensity of the moment.

"Whew." Katie shook herself free. "Enough of that. I'm gonna need your help. I promised Cassie, we'd color her hair, put in some blond tips. Do you mind?"

Bob and Julie answered in unison, "Who cares?"

"Good. Do you have an extra big bowl, a pitcher, and some old towels?"

While Julie and Bob scouted out the requested items, Katie pushed Cassie's door open, and the two women made eye contact.

"Hey." Cassie's voice was as weak as her smile.

"Hey, yourself."

On cue, Cassie asked, "What's in your bag of tricks today?"

Katie made a big show of digging in the tote, mumbling to herself as she walked toward the bed. "Where is that thing? Here it is!" She yanked out the box of Clairol Summer Blond.

Cassie looked askance. "You're kidding, right?"

"Nope. One blond bombshell coming up."

It wasn't easy. Bob and Julie helped with the preparations. They rolled Cassie from side to side and spread plastic across the bed. Katie filled the pitcher with water, laid out towels, and emptied the box of Clairol.

"This better be worth it!" Julie shook her head at the paraphernalia.

"Blonds have more fun," Bob quipped as he left the room. He missed Katie's grimace. She could have argued all day and night that blondes do not have more fun.

Katie mixed the solution and began painting the tips of Cassie's thin hair. "We're gonna highlight an inch or so, and perhaps a streak here and there. Ready?"

Cassie chatted while Katie applied the color.

While they waited the allotted fifteen minutes, Cassie and Katie lay next to each other on the bed. They talked about TV shows, the latest Hollywood gossip, and any non-death related subject which drifted across their minds.

Unexpectedly, Katie asked, "Did you know a recent survey shows that six out of seven dwarves aren't Happy?"

Cassie grunted and punched Katie lightly on the arm.

The door was open, and Julie and Bob found a million reasons to wander past.

"Time's up!" Katie announced.

Katie dragged Cassie closer to the edge of the bed. "I've got towels down, and the bowl is underneath your head. I'm gonna pour water over your head to rinse." Katie splashed, and lathered, missing half the time.

"Ow. Shit. It's in my eyes!"

"Don't be such a baby!" Katie grinned and dried Cassie's eyes.

"I'm pretty sure we ruined all five towels." Katie gathered them up and brushed at her jeans. "And, there's hair everywhere." She'd added layers to Cassie's basic cut. "Time to dry!" Katie wielded the hairdryer, hoping to God she hadn't screwed this up. "Ready?"

Katie handed her the mirror, and Cassie sucked in a surprised gasp. "You should be a professional!"

Bob and Julie came in to admire the new hairdo. "She's gorgeous, isn't she, Bob?"

"My princess has always been a looker." Bob sat down next to Cassie. Julie joined him, bookending Cassie, and stroking her hair. Understanding they needed time, Katie carted the messy load of towels to the laundry room. She sat at the kitchen table, waiting.

Julie and Bob shuffled in. Bob patted Katie on the back. "You did good in there." He thumbed a gesture at Cassie's bedroom. "You made her feel special."

"She wants to see you again." Julie stroked Katie's hair absently.

"Really? I figured she'd be tired." Katie started to rise, then sat back down, thinking better of her actions. "If you'd rather have your own time together, I understand."

"No," Julie said, "she's better when you're here." She laid her head on Bob's shoulder.

At a loss for words, Katie pulled two Cokes out of the fridge and went back to Cassie's room. Surprisingly, Cassie had pulled herself into the wheelchair. Her face was creased in pain, and sweat stained her shirt.

Katie plunked down the cans and ran across the room. "What the hell are you doing?"

"I wanted to sit up, have a real conversation without lying in bed waiting to die, okay?"

Katie sensed the fire still burning inside Cassie and changed tactics. "Fine. Last time I color your hair. It makes you bitchy."

Cassie snorted. "Now who's being bitchy?' She pushed herself to the door and closed it, working her way back to the bed. The trip across the room and back had her sweating more. She made a face at Katie. "Don't you say a word. I don't want to hear it." She patted the still damp bed. "Sit. I've got something to share with you."

Cassie opened the drawer of her bedside table and pulled out a red folder. She laid it on her lap and peered at Katie. "I need you to listen to what I'm about to say without interrupting."

Not sure what was going on, Katie nodded

Cassie opened the folder and pulled out documents, laying them on the bed next to Katie. Puzzled, Katie looked at a birth certificate, driver's license, medical records, high school diploma, a social security card, and an envelope.

"I've been thinking about this since you came in here with those broken ribs," Cassie explained. "I started sneaking into the den, making exact copies, and gathering this stuff." She let out a breath. "I want you to take these original documents and make a new life."

Katie shook her head.

"I'm serious, Katie. My birthday would be in February, making me twenty-five. You just turned twenty-seven. In a year or so, when no one would suspect, you could leave, get out of Savannah. With this stuff," she pointed to the papers, "you could create a whole new life—one without Jack."

Katie was still shaking her head.

Cassie lowered her head. "I've got a week, maybe two. I don't think I can stand the idea of me slipping away and you living with Asshole Jack the rest of your life."

"I can't do it, Cass. I wouldn't even know how. No one can ever be you, but you."

"You can do this. You have to believe. I could go on living through you."

Katie picked up the papers, looking at each one. "We have the same middle name, Anne. That's nice, isn't it?"

Cassie said nothing, unwilling to give in to Katie's misdirection.

"What's in here?" Katie held out the envelope.

"The pictures I took of your ribs, my testimony, and," Cassie paused, "Nine-hundred and sixty-seven dollars."

Katie shot to her feet. "I can't take your money. Are you crazy? How'd you get nine-hundred dollars anyway?"

Cassie puffed herself up, making Katie smile. "I've got money—social security, but it's still my money."

Katie's eyes widened. "Oh. Wow. I didn't think about that."

"I give the money to my mom and dad to pay expenses, but once or twice a year, I cash a check, keep out the cash. That way, I can buy my own things when we're out, or take Mom and Dad to dinner. It makes me feel human—less of a burden. Anyway," she held out the bills, "this is what's left."

Katie tapped the envelope on her leg. She latched onto the driver's license lying on the bed. "Seriously? How'd you get one of these? I know you didn't pass the driving test."

Cassie snatched it away. "If you look at it, smart ass, you'd see it's a state ID. I made my mom take me to get it when I turned twenty-one. I wanted to go to a damn bar and have a damn drink without my parents."

"How'd that go?"

"I got thoroughly sloshed and barely remembered a thing!"

"Did you get lucky?" Katie asked.

"I have no idea." Both women giggled.

"At least you didn't have to worry about drinking and driving."

"Ok, that's it!" Cassie grabbed the papers. "You can't have these. I was gonna give them to someone nice. I thought it was you, but nope. It's not."

Snickering, Katie snatched them back. "Stop it, brat! I need to think about it."

"There's no time, Katie. What if something happens to me?"

Katie took Cassie's hands in hers and gazed long and hard into her eyes. Seconds ticked by until Katie gave a slow nod.

Cassie squeezed Katie's hands in return. "You've got to hide them and start making a plan." She put the papers back in the folder. "There's some doctor reports, in here too--evaluations after the coma, and therapy sessions. I figure you're going to need a real driver's license, and those documents will help explain." Cassie's face crumbled, "You can tell the license bureau you've had a miracle."

Katie clenched Cassie's hand. "I did. I met you."

"Then you'll give some real thought to leaving?"

"I will, but for now, let's get you back in the bed."

"No way, it's wet as hell!"

They both laughed, and Katie experienced a feeling she'd not had in years. Hope.

Chapter 18

The folder was a red beacon; pulsating, and full of danger. Katie wracked her brain the whole way home, trying to think of where to hide the papers. Jack always inspected her bag and car. The same with the bureau and desk in their den. She needed a place he wouldn't look--someplace in plain sight.

She stood in their closet, evaluating possibilities. Jack went through her clothing, shoes, and accessories regularly, looking for anything new or out of place. *I bet he doesn't do that with his clothes.* Katie began to push the documents into the sleeve of one of Jack's summer suits when other papers fluttered to the floor

Katie frowned as she picked up three receipts with "Kane Brothers" in the heading. 'Refund for unused materials' was written on each one. They totaled eight thousand dollars paid to Jack—precisely the amount she and Jack had paid Kane Brothers Construction for the kitchen remodel earlier in the year. It was news to her. The project had emptied their savings, and they'd cut out all extra expenses to rebuild their account.

Dots started to connect: Jack's job at the city zoning board, his responsibility in setting up bids for new construction. Enough money to buy a diamond necklace. "Is he taking bribes?" Katie clamped a hand over her mouth. She glanced at the ceiling. *Has he added cameras in here?*

Seeing no evidence of added surveillance, she put the receipts back in order and carefully replaced them in the suit jacket sleeve. "I'll figure it out later." Jack would be home soon, and she was out of time.

Desperate, she pulled a boot box down, lifted the tissue paper from beneath the shoes, slid in Cassie's documents. Katie replaced the box precisely as it had been on the shelf. It would have to do for now. She hurried downstairs to start dinner.

Ten minutes later, Jack walked in the door, pulled her into a hug, and wiggled his fingers down her pants. Katie concentrated on not slapping at his intrusive hands.

Katie spent the following day doing what appeared to be mundane tasks. She started a load of laundry, wiped off counters and worked her way toward their office. In that room, the cameras faced the desk, making the computer screen invisible.

She sat down at the computer and started a search for Kane Brothers Construction. Several stories popped, listing their latest endeavors. There were coincidences that Katie couldn't ignore. She wished she could print the data to share with Cassie. *Too many pages*, Katie told herself. Jack would notice them in her tote. *Can't email them either. There's no way Jack isn't tracking my mail.*

She committed the site name to memory and went to fold a load of laundry before going back to the office. When Jack reviewed the footage later—and she knew he would—he'd see Katie playing on the computer in between chores.

Carting the laundry upstairs, she hurried toward their closet. She exited with her purse after tucking the Kane Brothers receipts inside.

Standing by the copier, Katie took papers out of her messy tote; the joke book, comic strips, and a newspaper clipping. She always carried such things for her clients. Mixing in the Kane Brothers receipts, she made copies and crumbled the whole mess down inside her tote.

She erased her search history, then realized a blank computer log would make Jack suspicious. She quickly accessed a few sites on Alzheimer's, as though she'd been researching for Mr. Parker. Seeing a link for the Traveling Vietnam Wall Memorial, Katie clicked on that as well. Macy's had an enticing ad, so she opened it, scrolling through several items.

She glanced at the clock and, finalizing her act for Jack, jumped up from the chair. "Crap. I've wasted an hour!" She snagged her purse and headed upstairs, carefully replacing the receipts in Jack's suit

After dinner, Jack rummaged through Katie's bag. She watched him out of the corner of her eye. He pushed the papers aside, more intent on checking the zippered compartments. Katie released the breath she'd been holding. Jack went to the office, and she smiled when he called out, "You were on the computer a lot today, weren't you?"

The next morning, Katie performed for the cameras again. As she was heading out the door, she gawked at her shoes. "These don't even match!" Taking off the shoes, she jogged upstairs and headed straight to the closet. With little time to spare, she removed the papers from the boot box, shoved them in her tote, and put on matching black shoes. She stopped in front of the full-length mirror in their room and fluffed her hair. "Much better." She ran out the door before she gave anything away.

Once at the Morrisons, Katie went straight to Cassie's room. "Hey, girl. How you feeling?"

Cassie's response was immediate and animated, "I'm doing pretty good today!"

Katie wondered briefly if it was morphine talking or Cassie's last rally. Not liking either answer, she said nothing.

Cassie didn't notice and launched into conversation, "So, have you thought about what we discussed?"

"A little. I don't know where to go."

"Why not Atlanta?"

"Jack would look there immediately."

"So, what are you thinking?"

"I can't go far, not enough money, remember? Although," Katie paused for effect, "thanks to you and the money in my savings account, I've now got over forty-four-hundred dollars. So,

I do have a nest egg going." Katie winked at Cassie. "If this works, I want to find a small tourist town with steady business. You and I are going to open a bookstore called *Inklings*. It'll be stocked with local artists' work, and paperbacks for tourists."

Both women sat picturing the scene.

"Oh my God, how could I forget?" Katie ran for her purse. "I need to show you something. You won't believe what I found."

Katie pushed Cassie towards the desk where she could access the computer and typed words into the search engine. "I found papers Jack was hiding." Katie pushed Cassie closer to the keyboard and pointed. "Click on that link."

Cassie frowned at the news story, *Kane Brothers Leads the Way*.

Katie yanked out the copies of the receipts from her purse, waving them in front of Cassie. "Look at these! Kane Brothers Construction paid eight-thousand-dollars to Jack."

"I don't get it."

"We paid eight-thousand to have our kitchen remodeled." Katie shook the receipts at Cassie, "They pay the money back to Jack, and then get a county job. I think Jack's taking bribes. Look at the dates."

"March of this year. So, what?"

"Wait." Katie scrolled through the online news story. "Here it is. In April, the Kane Brothers were awarded a four-million-dollar job at the library. See? Jack gets money in March, and The Kane Brothers get a job in April. Jack's had more money to spend lately." She fingered her gold necklace. "That could land him in jail, right?"

"It'd be hard to prove, but you have information that might keep him away." Cassie printed out the Kane Brothers' information. "Kind of reverse blackmail. Good thinking."

Katie grabbed the stack of papers from the printer. "I've got to get all these documents somewhere else."

"Safe deposit box?"

"No way. How would I explain a bank key?"

"How about a post office box?"

"I'd still have a key to explain."

"Tell Jack my parents need you to pick up the mail." Cassie tilted her head, considering the idea further. "Yep, that's the answer.

Nobody here has a mailbox. It's some city ordinance thing. We have to go to the post office to pick up the mail. So, *you* get a post office box here and tell Jack it's ours. It's even a reasonable story--my parents need you to pick up the mail because they're afraid to leave--which is hardly a lie."

Katie pursed her lips. That might work."

"Cool. We have a plan starting here." She squeezed Katie's leg and stuffed the printed pages, receipts, and identification papers into a large padded envelope.

"Wonder what a post office box cost?" Katie asked.

Cassie picked up her phone and typed in "Fleming Post Office." When the website popped up, Cassie pushed the phone number, waited for a connection, and started asking questions. "How much does it cost to rent a Post office box? Forty-eight dollars? And that's good for how long?" She winked at Katie. "A year. Okay. Good."

Katie dug in her tote. "Shit. I've only got six-dollars and sixty cents."

Cassie opened the manila envelope and pulled out fifty dollars. "See? I'm helping already. Done."

They high-fived—conspirators against Asshole Jack.

Katie left early and hurried toward the local post office in Fleming. There, she rented a post box and locked the papers away. Threading the new key onto her existing key ring, she acknowledged Jack would find it, but also knew better than to keep it hidden.

She barely beat Jack home. He came in, right on time, automatically reaching for her breasts first, and then pulling her into a kiss. She pretended to play, slapping his hands away. "Stop, you're going to make me burn dinner!"

Jack opened her purse and pawed through the contents. "What the hell is this?"

Feigning disinterest, Katie glanced over her shoulder. "What?"

"This key?" He held it up where it glinted in the kitchen light.

Katie swallowed once. "It's for the Morrison's post office box." Katie filled in the fake story. "They gave me their extra key today."

"Why a post office box? Don't they have a mailbox?"

"I guess no one in Fleming does. Some city ordinance thing."

Jack whipped out his phone, typing furiously.

"What are you doing?" Katie asked, as her heartbeat increased.

"We'll see, won't we?" He googled information and found Katie's story to be true. Next, he entered the stamped number from the key into the search engine. The USPS website listed a phone number, an address to return the key, and not much else. Jack put the keys back in Katie's purse, digging in the bottom once again, in case there was anything else he'd missed.

Chapter 19

Katie talked nonstop through breakfast. "…and I'm not even close to being done with our Christmas shopping."

"Keep it in budget." Jack raised his eyebrows, waiting for Katie to agree. At her subtle nod, Jack changed the topic, "Where are you headed today?"

"Gertie's. Poor thing, I haven't been to see her in weeks due to the extra visits to the Morrisons. I'll check on Cassie afterward." Katie loaded her tote and headed out the door.

Gertrude Taylor's rheumatoid arthritis was so crippling, she could only manage the simplest of tasks. At Katie's knock, she opened the door immediately. "Katie! Come in!"

"Oh, my!" Katie laughed and patted Gertrude's snarled hair. "Let's see what we can do here." She tugged at knots and teased it into the old-fashioned style Gertrude still wore. Katie started a joke, "So, these two ladies are havin' lunch together."

Gertie giggled too early. "And what happened?"

"One pointed across the room at two old women and said, 'That'll be us in ten years.' Her friend says, 'You idiot! That's a mirror!'"

Gertie howled. "You always make me laugh, Katie."

Katie helped Gertie with grocery shopping, errands, and cleaning. Three hours disappeared quickly. Afterward, Gertie pointed toward a stack of mail. "Look at all of these Christmas cards I've received. I can't write anymore, or I'd send a few myself."

"Oh, Gertie, I never thought of that." Katie plopped down in a kitchen chair. "Get out your address book. I'll help you. I'm going to the post office anyway."

An hour later, cards in hand, Katie hugged Gertie. "Merry Christmas!"

Katie drove toward Fleming, unsure of what she'd find. Bob and Julie were unusually quiet. Katie hugged them and headed toward Cassie's room.

"Hey, beautiful."

Cassie, looking small and vulnerable, offered a small smile.

Katie walked towards the bed, already opening a jar of cream. "I've got to go back to the post office," Katie chatted as she massaged Cassie's calves. "There's no postage on the envelope I put in the box, and I'm afraid a post office employee will remove it. Then what?"

Cassie shook her head. "You've got bigger problems than that, I'm afraid."

"What do you mean?"

Cassie pulled herself into a sitting position. "I was thinking things through last night. There's no way you can get a driver's license once I'm dead."

Katie grimaced.

"I am dying, Katie." Cassie let out a sigh of regret, but continued, "I looked it up on the internet. Once the death certificate is filed, my social security number will be frozen for a minimum of six to nine months. I've never had any credit history, so it seems like closer to the six-month mark. It's all about identity theft. Anyway, you won't be able to use the social security number for a while. Do you understand?"

Katie slumped on the bed. "So, this isn't going to work?"

"It can, but you've got to go get the driver's license soon. This week."

"This week? Can't it wait until I make my move?"

"Nope. You can't take the chance. A driver's license is critical. You'll need it for everything: rent, bank accounts, job."

Katie popped off the bed to pace. "How am I supposed to do that? I can't go to the DMV. Jack will know."

"You've got to use a different car. One Jack can't track."

Katie shook her head, trying to think. "I know. But how?" She did another lap around the room, then stopped abruptly. "Mr. Parker. I could use Mr. Parker's car. His niece, Nina, likes me to drive it once in a while anyway."

"Ok. Good. It's something Jack's accustomed to, right?"

"Yeah. She likes me to use it once a month or so." Katie frowned, "Why would I need to take Mr. Parker's car to the DMV? Jack tracks my phone, too. He'll know where I am."

Cassie frowned. "Try this, his niece needs to renew the license plates, but she's out of time. Holidays. Work. Whatever. Anyway, Nina needs you to do this favor for her. Got it?" Cassie kept talking. "You take his car to the license place…"

"And Mr. Parker. He has to go too."

"Fine. You and Mr. Parker take his car to the license bureau. Jack will see that your car's parked at Mr. Parker's house. He'll then see you're at the DMV, by your phone's location."

Katie nodded, seeing the plan more clearly. She twisted her hair around a finger, thinking through the pitfalls. "Let me borrow your phone. I'll call Nina and put things in motion. It screws up the story if my phone shows I called her first."

When Nina's phone switched to voicemail, Katie launched into her story. "Hey, Nina. It's Katie. My phone is out of juice, so I'm calling from my friend's phone."

Cassie nodded encouragement, waving her hands to keep Katie talking.

"I need a favor. Can I borrow your uncle's car on Friday? I'm scheduled to see him anyway. My check engine light's on, and I need to run a thousand errands. I'll take him with me, and it'll be like an adventure. Call me when you get off work. Thanks!"

When Katie hung up, Cassie gave her a high-five. "See? We've got this!"

"I'm glad you think so. Now, I've got to get the papers back from the post office. Shit. Where can I hide them 'til Friday?"

"You'll need proof of address and some of the money, too."

At Katie's confused look, Cassie explained, "New Driver's license. Driver's test."

"Driving test? Are you kidding me?"

Cassie shrugged. "Brand new license means test and fees." She directed Katie to her desk, "Open the middle drawer. There's a recent social security pay stub. Take it as proof of address.

Katie opened the drawer and stuffed the paper into her tote. "Fine. One more thing to hide."

Cassie was relentless. "Go to the post office, and get the envelope. Drive it to Mr. Parker's. Hide the envelope at his house, so the documents are where you need them on Friday."

Katie smiled. "Great idea. I've got to go right now, or I'll never have enough time. Wish me luck!" Katie yelled, already on her way out the door.

"Bring the license next time. I wanna see how I look!" Cassie laughed, infused with energy now that a plan was falling into place.

Katie drove to the post office, mailed Gertie's stack of Christmas cards, and retrieved the envelope. She headed straight to Mr. Parker's, kissed him on top of his messy head, and hid the envelope way back under a couch cushion when he wasn't looking. Alzheimer patients were notorious for moving items to unusual locations. She doubted Nina would look there either. She turned on a movie, locked him safely inside, and skidded out of his driveway.

Katie drummed her fingers on the steering wheel, willing Nina to call. Sometimes, prayers are answered, and her phone came to life, announcing an incoming call.

Nina had no problem with Katie borrowing the car. "He'll love seeing the Christmas displays!"

Chapter 20

Friday morning arrived, and Jack naturally questioned Katie's day, "So, where are you going again? You ran through your schedule so fast, I lost track." He sipped coffee and waited.

Yeah, right. You enjoy questioning me, you bastard. Katie's forced herself to be pleasant. "I'm taking Mr. Parker to get his license plates and registration today. They expire next week, and Nina forgot to renew them online."

"So, she naturally asks you to take time out of your schedule to fix her mistake." Jack slapped his coffee cup on the table, and Katie went on high alert. "You've got to stop letting people walk all over you, Katie."

His comment was laughable, but Katie kept a straight face. "I'm scheduled there anyway. Nina likes me to drive his car occasionally. Otherwise, it just sits."

"Why can't she drive it, or better yet, sell the thing?"

"She works all day and takes care of Mr. Parker every night. The car will probably go to her when he passes away."

"So, it's an asset?"

Katie shrugged.

Jack nodded once, now admiring Nina's tactics. "You'll be home at the normal time?"

"Yep." Katie scooted out the door, afraid her face would betray the lie. She was early to Mr. Parkers, which worked out well since his shirt was fastened wrong, and he couldn't find his shoes. Retrieving the folder from the couch cushion, Katie rushed Mr. Parker out the door. "Mr. Parker and Cassie are out for the day."

"Out for the day. Out for the day," he repeated.

Katie continued calling herself Cassie in hopes Mr. Parker wouldn't create a problem at the DMV. That's all she needed—him to unexpectedly have a lucid moment and call her Katie.

She held his hand as they worked their way through the line. Jack called, and she fumbled her papers and phone. The waiting area was noisy, confirming her story. Mr. Parker wandered away, and Katie yelled his name. "Mr. Parker! Over here. Come stand by me." It was enough to convince Jack, and he hung up satisfied.

When her turn arrived, Katie laid out the necessary documents: Cassie's state, I.D., birth certificate, social security card, and paystub. "I'd like to get a driver's license, please."

The clerk tapped in the name Cassandra Anne Morrison. "This is your first license?" She frowned. "Nothing from another state?"

Katie launched into her story, "I was in an accident and spent eight years in recovery. To go from a wheelchair to a driver's license is a wish come true." Katie beamed.

The clerk smiled, "Wow. Good for you. Let me set up the testing. It'll just take a minute."

Mr. Parker tried to pull away again. Katie handed him a set of keys. "Can you tell which one of these is for the house?"

He fiddled with the keys, studying each one.

Katie shrugged at the clerk. "My uncle has dementia, and I help take care of him."

"He drove you here?"

"God, no!" Katie laughed, coming up with a quick answer. "My cousin dropped us off." Katie pointed at the Walmart across the street. "She walked over there to do some shopping."

The clerk nodded. "You're all set. You'll take the Rules of the Road test first." She pointed towards a door. "Afterward, come back here." She winked in encouragement.

Katie pulled Mr. Parker along with her. She gave him a form and a pen. "Can you fill this out, Mr. Parker?" As he sat puzzling over the paper, Katie answered questions concerning speed limits, road signs, and how to handle a spin. Fifteen minutes later, she let out a relieved breath when she heard the test results. "You only missed one. That's good."

Katie paid the thirty-two dollar fee and went back to the license area. She waited for the clerk who'd helped her earlier.

The woman checked the exam. "Great. I'll set you up for the driving portion."

"The what?"

"The driving portion. You'll drive with an officer to show you can properly handle a vehicle."

Katie leaned in closer. "Umm." She looked around nervously. "I can't leave my uncle by himself. He'll wander away. Can he ride with us?"

The clerk frowned and went to find her supervisor. They agreed that due to extenuating circumstances, Mr. Parker could sit in the back seat, so long as he remained quiet.

Minutes later, a uniformed police officer called her name. "Number 132--Morrison."

Katie hurried over. Seeing his badge, Katie thought of the laws she was breaking—fraud, impersonating Cassie, identity theft. Sweat popped out on her forehead.

The Driving instructor tucked his clipboard under his arm. "Nervous?"

"Yes."

"Don't worry. It only takes about ten minutes." He shot a puzzled look towards Mr. Parker.

"Sorry, he has dementia. I can't leave him alone. The supervisor said it's all right if he rides in the back."

The instructor frowned. "I'm not sure. Don't you have someone else with you?"

"We did." Katie rolled her eyes. "My cousin dropped us off to go shopping. She was supposed to be back by now. Please don't make me wait in line again."

The instructor glanced at the twelve people waiting and agreed. "Fine. He sits in the back and can't help you."

Katie buckled Mr. Parker into the back seat and climbed behind the wheel, gripping it so hard it was a wonder it didn't crack. She drove the route, used her signal, backed up, and manipulated a nearly perfect example of parallel parking.

Mr. Parker abruptly asked, "Can we get a toy at the store today?"

Katie looked in the rear-view mirror, "Sure we can, Uncle Parker."

The officer smiled. "You passed. You can go get your license."

Katie took the eye test, waited for her picture, and paid out another nineteen dollars. At ten minutes before noon, she was as legal as a person using a false name could be.

With the driver's license in hand, a jubilant Katie made two more stops. She coaxed Mr. Parker into a local post office, where she made a photocopy of the license to show Cassie. She mixed it with other items in her tote and re-mailed the license and documents to her PO box.

Next, she headed to a satellite branch of The First Bank of Atlanta and deposited the remaining cash from Cassie into her savings account.

Once back at the house, Katie propped Mr. Parker in his favorite chair and read him *The Night Before Christmas.* He recited some of the passages--proof old memories were still in his head.

He was so pleased with himself, Katie read it a second time. He had, after all, unknowingly helped through a scary day.

Chapter 21

The following Tuesday, Katie headed to the Morrisons. She let herself into the house and called out a greeting. No one responded, and she heard Julie crying in their bedroom, and Bob's muffled voice consoling. Katie tiptoed to Cassie's bedroom, shocked to find her slumped in her bed. Katie hurried over to pull her into a sitting position, propping her into place. "I leave for a few days and look at you--slouched on the bed, hair a mess," Katie jested.

Cassie rallied at the sound of Katie's voice. "Did you get the license?"

Katie dug out the copy from her purse and waved it triumphantly in the air. "Look how good you look." Katie handed over the paper.

Cassie studied it in earnest. "You changed my eye color."

"I had to--yours are brown, mine are green. Lucky for me, the lady never even compared the information to the State I.D."

Cassie smiled. "This is great, and you're right, I look fantastic all things considered." Surprisingly, tears sprang to Cassie's eyes. "I wish I could run away with you, and we could be friends forever."

Katie reached in and hung on to her friend while they both grieved. Grabbing tissues, Katie handed a pile to Cassie. Once they'd regained their composure, Katie gave Cassie a present. "Merry Christmas!"

Cassie took her time opening the gift, savoring her last moments. She pulled a filigreed music box free of its container. "It's beautiful." She opened the lid, and the timeless chorus from Mariah Carey's "Anytime You Need a Friend" filled the room.

Katie leaned in to hear it better, and for a moment, the tiny mirror caught their heads together. Their eyes found each other. "I love you, Katie."

"I love you, too. You're the best friend I could ever have."

Katie slipped out when Cassie fell asleep and called Aunt Susan on the way home.

Susan answered at once, "Hey there, Katie-girl."

"Hey, back at you."

Aunt Susan heard the ache in Katie's voice and pounced. "What's going on, sweetie?"

"Oh, Aunt Susan, I'm so sad." Katie filled in the gaps from their last conversation about Cassie. "I'm losing her, and she's the only friend I have."

"I'm so sorry, baby. Losing someone you love is hard. Why dont'cha come see me? Then I can give you a proper hug."

That was Katie's undoing, and the sobs came. "I will." She sucked in air loudly. "Christmas Day. I promise." A hiccup escaped.

Katie tried to listen to Christmas carols after she hung up, but they felt pretentious. She jabbed the radio off and lowered her window, letting the chilly air whip through her hair. The oaks lining the streets were bare of leaves, their skeletal branches jutting skyward. The Forsyth fountain was shut down and covered—no longer jetting water into the air. It added to Katie's depression.

At seven a.m. on December twentieth, Katie's cell phone vibrated across the nightstand. Seeing the Morrison's number, Katie braced herself and answered, "Is it Cassie?"

"She passed away last night. We were with her the whole time." Bob's voice caught.

They spoke for a few more seconds with Katie stumbling for the right words. "I loved her so much. I love you and Julie too."

Jack had been brushing his teeth when the phone rang and stood in the bathroom doorway, listening. Laying the toothbrush on the dresser, he crossed the room and sat beside Katie. He patted her back and pulled her closer.

Katie stiffened, waiting for the "I told you so," or even some sexual comment. When they didn't come, and Jack simply held her, she was grateful. Sometimes, he was strong enough to be the man she needed.

Jack tipped her chin up, brushed her hair back from her face. "When's the funeral?"

"Day after tomorrow. It's not like they haven't had time to prepare. They're going to do the last respects and service in one day." She wiped her tears.

On the day of the funeral, Katie dressed more carefully, choosing a modest black skirt and a plain blouse. She pulled her hair into the elegant chignon she used to wear and minimized the makeup.

At the church, she waited behind a group of young adults who had formed a circle around the Morrisons. Katie recognized most of them as older versions of the photographs Cassie had placed around her room—friends from high school who'd drifted away. *They'll feel bad about that,* Katie sympathized, knowing guilt to be a withering emotion.

The group thinned, and Katie moved forward. When Bob and Julie saw her, their composure crumbled, and they opened their arms. Katie walked into their welcoming hug full-force, and the three rocked as they had so many times in their kitchen.

"I'm so sorry," Katie's voice cracked.

Julie pulled Katie closer. "We could never have gotten through it without you."

Katie embraced them both once more before moving toward an empty seat. As the music began, Cheyenne, Katie's boss, slid into the pew. She bumped hips with Katie, so she'd make some room.

"I'm gonna be late for my own funeral someday," Cheyenne whispered.

Katie skootched and leaned in for a hug. "You're right, but I'm glad you're here now."

A slideshow whirled on a screen near the altar, and Katie sat mesmerized, getting to know the little girl her friend had been. She watched in amazement as Cassie turned cartwheels, and rode daredevil style down the street, pedaling fast, with both hands in the air. There was a shot of her with new braces. Another of her dressed in a purple dress ready for the eighth-grade dance. That one got Katie, and she swallowed a sob. Cheyenne dug for Kleenex.

The priest stood. "Our reading is from Psalms Chapter 139, verses 13-14. For you created my innermost being, you knit me together in my mother's womb. I praise you because I am fearfully and wonderfully made; your works are wonderful. I know that full well."

Afterward, Julie climbed the stairs toward the altar as if working her way towards the very gates of hell. She stepped on a stool behind the lectern, wiped away tears, and opened the Bible.

In a voice, stronger than Katie expected, Julie explained, "I'm reading from Matthew and the story of Jesus and the children. 'So, the disciples came to Jesus and asked, "Who is the greatest in the kingdom of heaven?" He called a little child and had him stand among them. And he said: "I tell you the truth unless you change and become like little children, you will never enter the kingdom of heaven."'"

"Cassie gave us that--a short kingdom of heaven right here on earth. She brought joy to us every day. The greatest compliment any of us can give Cassie is to be like her—selfless, fun, and full of life regardless of circumstances."

Julie viewed the congregation and ended her eulogy, "God bless Cassie. She's at peace and no longer in pain. I hope we can find the will to move forward without her." With a fresh slew of tears streaming down her cheeks, Julie staggered back to her seat.

The congregation concentrated on their shoes, their knees, their hymnals, anywhere but Julie, unwilling to look grief so fully in the face.

Bob shuffled forward, pulling at his tight collar. Katie instinctively understood his speech would be the hardest. She gripped Cheyenne's hand hard enough to leave half-moon circles from her nails.

Bob cleared his throat twice. "Julie and I are blessed. We are. We had twenty-four years with an angel." He pulled out a handkerchief and wiped his face. "We were given a miracle when she was born and watched her grow. Even after the accident, she was so strong--so willing to give life another chance." He sniffed into the microphone. "She never complained. Isn't that amazing? She was a joy to us. She still wanted to be a young woman, listening to crazy music, getting her ears pierced half-a-dozen times, and doing bizarre things with her makeup."

A few relieved chuckles drifted through the sanctuary.

"She wanted to fix her hair and be pretty." His eyes found Katie, and he pushed his lips together and nodded a few times. "I wanted to say something profound, but I keep picturing my little Cassie tucked in for the night. We'd say our prayers, and then she'd beg me to tell her a story." Bob stepped back a foot or so, licked his lips, and gathered himself. "Because I can't get that picture out of my mind, I'm going to borrow a few words from Winnie the Pooh. "'If there is ever a tomorrow that we are not together, there is one thing you should always remember. You are braver than you believe, stronger than you seem and smarter than you think. But the most important thing is, even if we're apart, I will always be with you in the heart.'"

They were the perfect words for Cassie. And Katie.

Chapter 22

Christmas day arrived quietly, and Katie turned the carols up to chase away the sorrow. She smiled as she and Jack opened presents, but her heart was elsewhere. Needing to find her center, Katie drove to the only sanctuary she knew—Aunt Susan's. It was a tradition, and one Jack allowed if Katie called him during the drive and checked in once she arrived.

Katie's mood improved the closer she got to Atlanta.

Aunt Susan answered the door wearing a white cashmere jogging suit, matching jewelry, and at least four bracelets. When Aunt Susan opened her arms, Katie stepped gladly into the circle. "Merry Christmas, Katie-girl."

Aunt Susan moved toward the couch, patting it in invitation. Katie fidgeted with her coat buttons. As the coat came off, the dam inside Katie broke, and she sobbed, "I miss Cassie so much already."

Aunt Susan rocked Katie and comforted as only a loved one can. "Lord, girl, I've lost my share of friends." Aunt Susan closed her eyes for a second. "I'm still losing them, to the point I dread answering the phone." She kept her arm around Katie's shoulder. "I can tell ya I've learned a few things along the way."

Katie turned to look at her aunt. "I'll take any advice you have."

"Allow the grief, or it will grow into an awful black sickness inside. Try writing Cassie a letter and sharing the thoughts you have inside. I've had luck with that one over the years."

Katie thought about the hundreds of things she wished she could still say to Cassie.

Aunt Susan let the silence spread for several minutes then tapped Katie's knee. "Enough of this seriousness. What did Adam say to his wife right before Christmas?" Susan's eyes twinkled as she delivered the punchline, "It's Christmas, Eve!"

Katie bumped shoulders with Aunt Susan. "You and your dumb jokes."

"Life goes on, Honey. You either laugh or cry. You," she pointed at Katie and raised her eyebrows, "need to laugh." Aunt Susan stood abruptly. "Let's make cookies!"

They destroyed the tiny kitchen when Aunt Susan snuck up behind Katie and smeared batter on her nose. "Take that, brat!" Susan wielded her spoon as a shield.

Katie retaliated by flinging flour in Susan's face, ruining her impeccable makeup. Swordplay with spoons and spatulas ensued with utensils clanking, and items knocked off the counter. Katie grabbed a towel by both ends, quickly swirled it together, and let loose with a sharp *thwack* right on Susan's butt. Aunt Susan dropped her spoon, and the look of shock on her face had Katie howling in delight. The cookies burned, and their mouths were tired from laughing.

After cleaning up, Katie stood looking out the window. Aunt Susan joined her, rubbing Katie's shoulders. "Are you going to be all right?"

"Maybe not today, but I will be. Losing Cassie? It's changed my perspective."

"Are you referring to you and Jack?" Aunt Susan cocked an eyebrow. "You know how I love that man."

Katie laughed at the old line. "Liar. You don't like one hair on his head."

Her aunt shrugged her bony shoulders. "What can I say? I have good taste."

As the new year unfolded, Katie worked to get out of her funk. Although Mr. Parker and Gertie afforded Katie good days, the rest of the week felt as though she was slogging through mud.

Cheyenne called the second week of January. "I know you're still hurting Katie, but other people need your unique gifts."

Katie reluctantly agreed to take on Amanda Stokely, a thirty-nine-year-old lady who'd suffered a stroke. The Stokely home was only ten minutes from Fleming and the Morrisons, and Katie couldn't ignore the convenience. Working with Amanda would allow Katie to zip to the Fleming post office and check on her precious documents. She couldn't guarantee they'd stay in her box unless she cleared it from time to time. Until Amanda came into the picture, Katie had been wondering how she could pull off that feat without making Jack suspicious.

On the way to her first meeting with Amanda, Katie warned herself not to get too attached. *Losing friends is an emotional train-wreck.*

Within five minutes, Katie knew she'd fall in love with this woman, too. Comparing the picture on the mantle to the woman she was talking to in the kitchen, Katie noted the differences: Amanda's once manicured nails were cut short, and the blond highlights in her hair had grown out showing darker roots. The left side of her mouth had slipped into a semi-frown—corresponding to her limp arm, and unresponsive left leg.

Amanda's two girls, aged six and nine, were shy around Katie, but still wanted their Momma's attention.

"Look at my drawing!"

"Watch me twirl, Mommy!"

Amanda's overwhelmed husband, Dan, never finished a sentence. "The kids' are making me--I don't see how Amanda--" And he was off to investigate a ruckus in the living room. "Girls stop fighting! Or--"

"Whew! Busy place." Katie grinned. "I bet you had things running like clockwork."

Amanda agreed, "I did. Not having control of anything in my life," she used her right hand to lift her left arm, and then let it drop uselessly to her side, "is almost worse than the stroke."

Katie rubbed Amanda's shoulder in sympathy. "We'll get you back to normal. I can come on Tuesday and Thursday morning. We'll work through breakfast, get those cute little monkeys off to school, and tackle housework."

Amanda slurred a grateful, "Thank you," and used her right arm to wipe off a counter.

Jack took Katie to dinner to celebrate her new assignment. "You'll make that lady's life better," he said as he toasted Katie. Jack's moods were mercurial, and Katie concentrated on clinking her glass.

A nice dinner out naturally required sex. Katie's hands twisted in the sheets when Jack grabbed her hips hard enough to leave finger-sized bruises. "Look at me, Katie," he demanded.

After his orgasm, he fell asleep quickly while she lay awake, thinking about an exit plan. *Cassie would want me to keep moving forward.*

She worked a trip to the post office into her next appointment with Amanda, explaining her day to Jack, "After I'm done at Amanda's, I'm going to stop in and see the Morrisons."

"Why? Cassie's not there anymore."

"Exactly. It's been a month, and the cards and calls quit coming. They need to know I'm still here for them."

Jack shrugged. "Suit yourself."

By the time the Stokely family finished breakfast, and Dan had pushed the girls out the door, Katie was sweating. "Good Lord! Lunches, homework, braids, missing shoes!" She turned wide eyes toward Amanda. "How do you moms do it every day?"

The two women cleared the chaos in the kitchen and were working their way toward the living room when the physical therapist arrived. It signaled Katie's exit. She yelled out, "Bye! I'll see you on Thursday."

Katie drove to the Morrisons and sat in their kitchen, looking through the picture album Julie laid on the table. Katie commented on Cassie's banged up knees and missing front teeth.

An hour later, Bob and Julie walked Katie to her car. "Thanks for coming. It meant a lot."

Katie squeezed them once. "I'll try to stop by from time to time."

Checking her watch, Katie high-tailed it to the post office. Weeks before, she'd made a tiny slit in the pad to her makeup compact and inserted her post office box key. Jack was used to seeing the compact in her purse. Even if he opened it, the key would remain hidden. No way could Katie keep the ring visible after Cassie's death.

Katie cleared her box of advertisements and opened the manilla envelope. Just seeing the documents made her feel close to Cassie and filled Katie with resolve. She locked up the papers and drove away thinking, *Don't waste this gift, Katie.*

Chapter 23

In February, Katie's phone blipped, reminding her to make her annual OB/GYN appointment. She called and sat through three minutes of awful music.

When the receptionist got on the line, she took Katie's information and announced, "We're booking into September already." Katie heard furious typing in the background. "You're also due for updated lab work. It's been more than six months since the miscarriage. Are you feeling okay?"

Katie answered quietly, "I am. I haven't thought about losing the baby in a long while." Saying the words out loud brought the memories temporarily to the surface.

"You have plenty of time for another child. You're young. You'll be twenty-eight this year. Correct?"

"Yes," Katie answered, stiffly, resenting how easily this woman had dismissed the loss.

The woman continued, unaware of Katie's distress, "Doctor Swisher has a note in your file requesting a mammogram. It may seem early, but with both parents deceased and so little medical history, she wants a baseline. If you schedule it a few days prior, or even the same day, the doctor could read the results during your visit."

A possible plan burst into Katie's head—*this might be it*—Katie's brain crackled with excitement. *The timing is right.* Katie remembered Cassie's warning that she needed to wait six to nine months before making her escape.

"Let's book all of them back to back. I'm there anyway." Katie fist-pumped the air. *Yes!*

She purposely picked a payday Friday, giving her an excuse to go to the bank beforehand and get some cash. Security cameras would pick her up at the bank and the medical parking lot. But inside the medical center? She didn't think so.

The complex had been an old Georgia mansion, renovated with a new wing added for lab and diagnostics. Katie doubted there were cameras in the original section but needed to double-check before getting too excited. She remembered reading a news article about the careful restorations. The builders had promised to keep the foyer/lobby as close to the original as possible, showcasing the home's rare Bubinga woodwork and carved staircase. It had been big news as Southerners love their history and don't appreciate unnecessary modernization.

Katie wrote down the information; Mammogram 9:15. Lab work at 10:15 and the Ob/Gyn exam at 11:00. With careful planning, she could disappear for hours, and Jack would be none the wiser. She wouldn't have to answer her phone either since all doctors' offices demanded their patients, "Silence cell phones."

Katie circled September 6th on her calendar. Twice. She had months to put all the pieces into play.

She stopped by the medical building a few days later, walking up to the desk in the lobby. "Good morning. I'm hoping you can help me." Katie gave a warm smile. "I made appointments last week and never wrote them down. Can you verify if I have the right date?" As the receptionist logged into her computer, Katie leaned across the desk, watching the security camera feeds.

They showed the parking lot, the diagnostic wing, hallways, the double staircase, and the bank of elevators behind the desk. As she'd hoped, there was no video of the small, ornate foyer, or the tiny restroom just inside the door. *This could work*. Katie began to plan in earnest, not only on how to disappear but how to ensure Jack would leave her alone--forever.

On an unusually windy March afternoon, the power went out at home, and Katie sprang into action. She'd been hoping for such an opportunity. She went to the electric box and hit the breakers for the security cameras, the outside lights, and a bathroom. Turning off just the cameras would be suspicious if Jack came home.

She jumped when her phone rang, reverberating against the old stone walls in the basement. Katie looked at the screen. It was Jack, and she answered quickly.

"The power's out here at work. How about there?" Jack's voice sounded unusually loud.

"It's off here, too. I was heading to the box to see if it was just us."

"The box? You mean the breakers? Why?"

Katie made up what she thought would be a plausible response--one Jack would believe. "I was gonna flip some of those switches."

"For the love of God, Katie, don't touch anything. The power's out across the city. Wait for the electric company to fix it."

"Okay. I'll light some candles."

"That sounds sexy. I'll be home early if the electricity doesn't come back on."

She played the sex card, which always worked in distracting Jack. "That sounds nice. Candles, a storm, and the rainy afternoon." She scurried upstairs, yanking candles out of the pantry.

"Yeah?"

"Yeah," she purred.

"Well, in that case, I'll be home early whether the power is on or not. See you at four."

Katie grimaced and entertained a recurring fantasy in which Jack would be in a one-car deadly accident on the way home.

"Stop it," she said out loud, feeling awful for allowing herself to think such things. "You're better than that, Katie."

With less than an hour, she lit the candles and ran to the office. Easing open the bottom drawer, she carefully scanned each item. Sure as hell, a paper clip was balanced on top of the hanging folders. Noting its exact location, she set it aside and thumbed through files.

Mixed in with years' worth of electric bills, she found what she was looking for, "Ah-ha. A different bank account. I had a feeling."

She carefully removed the statements, pulling an electric bill partially out of the file so she'd remember where the papers had been hiding. She traced her finger down the columns. *Looks like ol' Jack has taken in another three thousand since Christmas.*

She stacked the papers on the printer and prayed for the power to return. When the lights flickered and stayed on, she punched the copy button, willing the damn machine to go faster. She set the original papers and paper clip carefully back in place. Rolling the copies, she stuck them down inside her frilly purple umbrella in the hall closet.

Remembering the breakers, she rushed to the basement to flip them back into the on position. She was bent over, looking in the fridge, when Jack walked in the door.

"No, no. Don't move. I love that position."

Katie gritted her teeth and commanded her face to relax.

Chapter 24

With a probable escape on the horizon, Katie devised ways to accumulate more funds. She'd read items returned on a debit card were refunded as cash instead of credit if done within two days.

With some trepidation, Katie experimented. She did their regular grocery shopping but left several items in a plastic bag in the pantry. As usual, Jack skimmed the receipt. Nodding in satisfaction, he tossed it in the trash. Later, Katie retrieved it and put it back in her purse.

The next morning, she slipped into the pantry, shoved the bag of groceries into her tote, and headed to the store. Katie plunked her items on the counter and held her breath.

The woman at the service desk scanned the receipt, and the groceries and handed Katie four dollars and fifty-six cents. No questions asked.

Katie rushed home, hid the cash down inside an instant potato box, and logged in to their bank account. Sure enough, only her purchase from the day before showed and not the refund. She checked the next day to be sure.

Repeating the process when she could, Katie managed to squirrel away almost forty-five dollars a month. When errands took her near a branch of her bank, she'd park far away, leave her phone in the car and deposit her carefully acquired funds.

With her account growing, it was time to think about a destination. *Where can I go?* She dreamt of a quiet town, a little off the beaten path--a place where she could blend in seamlessly.

Researching at home was too risky. Using her phone was obviously out of the question. She attempted to sneak in a little study time while at her clients' homes.

"Gertie, can I use your computer?" Katie called from the living room, where she'd been vacuuming.

"That old thing? With these hands," Gertie held up her twisted fingers, "I haven't touched it in years. But you can try."

At the ninth upgrade message, Katie pushed back from the desk in frustration. "You're right. This thing's a mess!"

Mr. Parker couldn't have cared less about Katie being on his computer, but he couldn't remember his Wi-Fi password. She considered texting Nina but decided it would seem strange.

Amanda's speech and motor functions were returning, thanks to all the therapy, and the two women had become friends. Amanda wouldn't care if Katie used the computer, but she'd likely ask questions Katie couldn't answer.

Katie sat in her car, the only place she could be assured of privacy. "I can't go north. Myrtle Beach is too expensive." She'd been to Birmingham, Alabama once—the only vacation her parents had ever taken. "Jack would remember that, though." She continued talking to herself, "I'd love to skip all the way across the country, but there's not enough money. That leaves south. Florida? Louisiana?" She wasn't sure.

On a drizzly afternoon, Katie headed to the library. Dodging the puddles, Katie ran up the wide, stone steps, flung open the doors, and stood still, momentarily filling her senses with the sight of bookcases and the smells of dust jackets and old paper. She located a sitting area full of magazines, and a bank of computers. Knowing Jack would see her location at the library, Katie pulled out her phone, sending a quick text. I'm at the library spending a rainy day with books!

Silencing her phone, she slipped it into her tote and got busy looking at maps. She read statistics and researched apartments and the cost of living. After an hour, she'd narrowed her choices down to a tiny, tourist town named White City, Florida. It was three-hundred miles down the coast, and as far as her money would take her. Toggling through data, Katie was pleased to find the town had plenty of shops and restaurants. *I should be able to find a job.* She researched a few property management companies, too.

She clicked "Print" and headed toward the printers when she caught sight of Jack coming through the door. His head swiveled left and right, searching for her, and her heart hammered. *Should have known he'd show up here, Katie.* Taking a quick left into a stack of books, she pretended to be reading the titles, when he found her.

"What the hell are you doing?"

Even expecting his voice, Katie still jumped. "Jack? What are you doing here?"

"I could ask you the same question. I've been calling you!"

"Sorry." She rummaged in her tote and pulled out her phone. "I turned it off. Library. Gotta be quiet," she whispered and winked, praying he'd buy her innocent act.

"Why are you here?"

"Hanging out. I had nothing else going today." Conscious of her precious research sitting on the printer, Katie selected a slim autobiography off the shelf, slipping her phone in the empty space. *No problems here. No sir. Katie's just looking at books.*

"You've got an e-reader. You can download books all day long."

"It's not the same as being able to look at the covers and turn pages." She thumbed open the book in her hand, letting the pages ripple. "They're like magic, and –"

Jack cut off her sentence, "I've told you to leave your phone on no matter what." Looking at his watch, he sighed. "I took off for lunch. We may as well grab a sandwich. The Ghost Café is close." He took hold of her elbow and steered her toward the door.

With no choice, Katie followed him, hoping her phone would go undetected among the autobiographies. As Jack started toward his car, Katie held back. "We need to drive separately, Jack."

At his look of disapproval, Katie explained, "You've got to go back to work, right?"

He nodded his head. "And you'll be headed home?" His eyebrows rose, waiting for confirmation.

"I've still got to go to the post office for stamps, but then, yeah, home."

She trotted toward her car, irritated to see he waited inside his own vehicle with the engine running. When Jack saw her pull out of her parking spot, he edged into traffic. He waved her forward in his rearview mirror, indicating she should follow directly behind him.

Katie chewed a fingernail off as she worried about her research still at the library. She made herself smile, though, since Jack kept checking his mirrors.

As they were finishing lunch, Katie played her ace in the hole. Dropping the remainder of her sandwich on the table, Katie dug in her tote, opening one section after another. "Oh, my God. I left my phone at the library."

Jack took the tote out of her hands and checked the cavernous inside pocket to assure himself the phone was indeed gone. Whipping out his own phone, Jack clicked his GPS app. He zoomed in on the dot, assigned to Katie's phone. "Yep. It's still at the library."

"Oh, man. I'm sorry. I'd better go." She kissed his cheek before he could protest.

Once inside the library, Katie bee-lined to the bookshelf where she'd hidden her phone. *Please be there.* Finding it, Katie let out soft, "Thank you, Jesus!" She ran to the printers, but there were no print outs in any of the trays. Panicked, she dug through a nearby trashcan.

"Miss?" A librarian approached. At least Katie thought he was a librarian--tousled hair, glasses, and an air of authority. "Miss, is there something I can help you find?"

"My papers. I printed them and then got busy. They're not here!" Katie moved through the area at top speed, looking under the printers, on chairs.

"Today? You printed them today?" The man asked.

Katie nodded and continued her search.

"We can't leave papers in the printer long due to privacy issues." He smiled and pushed his glasses up on his nose.

"Are you serious?"

He pulled out five manila folders with numbers printed in wide black marker. "Which computer were you using?"

Katie swiveled her head toward the computer bank. "Four. I was on number four."

Mr. Save-the-Day Librarian handed over her printed materials.

Katie scanned them quickly, assuring herself they were all there. "Oh, thank God!"

"Glad to help, but you owe two-dollars and thirty cents. Ten cents per page." He blushed. "Sorry."

Katie dug in the bottom of her tote and carefully counted out the amount. Her phone vibrated. Jack had called, and then immediately texted. *Did you find ur phone?*

Stuffing the research down inside her tote, Katie hurried toward the exit. Once outside, Katie called Jack back, "I found my phone. I must have dropped it on our way out the door."

"You're headed to the post office, then home?"

"Yep." She gritted her teeth over having to reconfirm what she'd already said.

The rain had allowed her to carry her umbrella where Jack's bank information had been hiding.

Stopping at the post office, Katie read through her research one more time, memorizing the data, and imagining what her new life could look like. Katie mailed the printed pages and Jack's nefarious bank statements to her PO box. And bought the damn stamps.

Chapter 25

As spring turned to summer, Katie continually replayed her escape, mentally mapping out what she would do day one, day two and three. She'd literally have the clothes on her back and whatever she could hide in her tote. With that in mind, Katie began to make subtle additions to her bag.

Knowing money would be tight for her, she replaced old makeup in her tote with newer, fuller bottles. She even switched the compact but kept the old pad with her post office key safely tucked inside.

Coming home from Gertie's, Katie made a big show of rubbing her eyes and taking out her contacts. "The entire house was covered in dust today." Katie's contact case and a bottle of rinse went into the tote, "Just in case," Katie explained to Jack.

She complained about the cleaning agents at Amanda's. "The woman sprays Lysol all the time. It makes my eyes burn." Katie slipped her glasses into the bag.

"Mr. Parker keeps the house at eighty degrees. He's always cold, but I sweat my ass off when I'm there." A hair clip and hair bands were added to the purse a week later

Jack pawed through the extra items shaking his head at the jumbled mess.

Katie used her next free day to calm her mind, planting showy pansies along the front walk. Summer had turned green and gold, and Katie hummed as she dug. Lifting the plants out of their plastic containers, she eased them into the soil and watered each one. She was struck by the symbolism; that she, too, hoped to remove herself from her contained life Savannah and be replanted in Florida.

Their next-door neighbor stopped along the low, ornamental fence, forgetting the dog she was supposed to be walking. "Hi, Katie! You're not usually home during the day." Mrs. Donohue was widowed and lonely. She walked the dog three times a day in hopes of running into a neighbor and having a conversation.

Katie unfolded her legs and rose to meet her at the fence. "I'm in between assignments today. Lucky me." She lifted her face to the sun. "You and Buster out making your rounds?" Katie scratched the happy dog behind the ears.

"Oh, my goodness! What did you do to yourself?" Mrs. Donohue pointed at several yellow bruises under Katie's bicep. "Working in the yard?"

Katie nodded, thankful the old woman had supplied an easy excuse. Had she looked closer, she would have seen they were shaped like fingerprints—Jack's, to be exact. Pinching was a common punishment, and under the arms was the usual choice since the area wasn't easily visible.

Oblivious, Mrs. Donahue shared the local gossip, asked Katie if she had news worth repeatin', and ambled away.

Katie went back to weeding and thinking. A week earlier, she'd gone to a pawn shop near a discount store she shopped in occasionally. She'd gladly traded in all the apology jewelry Jack had given her over the years for look-a-like pieces, praying Jack wouldn't notice the difference. Between the groceries returned for cash and the pawned jewelry, she had a little over fifty-two-hundred dollars in her savings account.

She didn't know if she had enough money, how she would get a vehicle, or if she'd make it out of Savannah. Too many things could go wrong. *And then what? There is no plan B.*

A slamming car door startled her back to reality. Jack was home early, and Katie winced. She'd been having fun playing in the flower beds and hadn't had a chance to shower. Jack hated her working in the mulch and dirt.

Mrs. Donohue watched from her porch.

"Assholes!" Jack flung his suit jacket over his shoulder, already zeroed in on Katie's location.

She scrambled to her feet. "You're home early. Is everything all right?" She brushed at her hands and knees before Jack noticed.

"They're cutting the budget, maybe some layoffs."

"Is your job in jeopardy?" Katie smoothed his shirt.

Jack knocked her hand aside. "They wouldn't dare."

Mrs. Donohue frowned but called out a greeting, "Hello, Jack! Any chance you can help me get my patio furniture from the shed?"

"Sure." Jack smiled. "I'll do it this weekend." He turned back to Katie. "Nosy bitch," he muttered.

Katie turned toward Jack. "What?"

"She's always watching." He stomped into the kitchen and yanked a beer out of the fridge. Twisting the top, he drank deep and tossed the cap in the sink.

Katie followed him inside, snatching off her shoes.

Jack never broke stride in the conversation. "And, to make matters worse, there's an audit scheduled. Got to get more efficient, and account for every last fucking dime. How the hell am I supposed to get any work done with less help and stupid auditors added to the mix?"

Katie nodded her head. *Ah. Here's the real problem. Jack needs to cover his tracks.* She wondered if the audit might work to her advantage. *Could I make an anonymous tip? Tell them about the Kane Brothers? Jack goes to prison, and I receive a free get-out-of-jail card.* Without meaning to, Katie smiled ever so slightly.

Jack pointed the beer bottle at her face. "You think this is funny?"

"God, no." She backed away. "You've got nothing to worry about, because you're so good at what you do." She opened and shut cabinet doors to keep busy and avoid eye contact.

Jack took long swallows of his beer and watched her make dinner. He switched to two fingers of whiskey, and Katie went on high alert. When he graduated to a full tumbler of whiskey, she slid biscuits in the oven, hoping the carbs would soak up the alcohol.

He kept pouring drinks all evening. By nine, he was slurring and talking loudly, "Stupid people. Can't they see cutting jobs and wasting time on an audit makes us work slower?" He gestured wildly, and the last liquid in his glass threatened to spill.

"Watch it!" Katie called out, unwittingly drawing his attention back to her.

He corrected the glass and sauntered over. "Maybe you can make me feel better." He ran his hands over her chest, raising his eyebrows. "Take my mind off work?" He pulled her close, rubbing his thighs against hers.

Already worried about his mood and the amount of alcohol he'd consumed, Katie followed him up the stairs. Unfortunately, the five or six drinks proved stronger than Katie's less than enthusiastic approach to sex.

"Jesus, you could at least try a little harder, Katie," he sneered. He continued ramming himself at her until she'd had enough and rolled aside.

"This isn't working." She sat on the edge of the bed, rubbing her legs.

"And, whose fault is that?" He rolled out of bed, his face puffed and blotchy.

"Mine. It's my fault." Katie stared at the floor.

He grabbed her chin, "Is that sarcasm I hear?"

"No. I said it's my fault, and it is."

"Damn straight it is. Look at you." He landed a kick below her knee. "Dirt under your fingernails. Old nasty clothes. No wonder I can't stay excited." He shoved his arms into a shirt. "I need another drink."

Katie didn't dare rub her leg and sat ramrod straight on the edge of the bed until he left the room.

When Jack slammed their door, she shook her head back and forth. Jack was a snake, shedding his skin, growing larger, and deadlier each year. Katie could feel hate filling her up inside. Starting at her toes, it worked its way up her spine and into her throat.

I'm not going to make it to September. Sorry, Cassie, but I've got to get out of here now. Katie stood, intent on getting dressed and making a fast get-a-way. Jack's inebriated state was an advantage. *All I have to do is get down the stairs, out the front door and go.* She grabbed her tote and pulled out the keys. As she pulled a shirt over her head, her rational mind began listing reasons she should stay. *Jack can track the car. The bank isn't open.*

"Shit." Katie sat back down on the bed. She rubbed her hands up her face, scrubbing at her forehead to push away the headache and frustration. She pulled in a long breath, releasing it slowly and willing the emotion away. *I have to survive until September.*

The next morning, Katie pretended nothing was wrong. She'd do anything to reach her goal. "Fourth of July is coming up soon," she said casually. "We should have a party. Invite your co-workers. Show them you're not worried about restructuring or an audit. They'll look to you as the leader."

She stroked his ego, well aware it took the pressure off of her. *It's a dangerous game you play, Katie.* She pictured herself as a marionette responding to the strings Jack pulled.

Unaware of her philosophical thoughts, Jack grunted and agreed with her suggestion, "Maybe a party would be a good idea."

Katie nodded her head. "Let's do a cookout."

Chapter 26

Katie caught herself brooding about Jack and her tender knee. She picked up her phone instead.

"Katie-girl!" Aunt Susan's voice rose with excitement--a balm to Katie's frayed emotions.

"What's going on with my favorite niece?"

"I'm your only niece."

"Well then, that makes you my favorite," Aunt Susan cackled on her end.

The women brought each other up to speed since their last call. Aunt Susan mostly expounded on recent doctor visits. "I swear that's all us old people do—make appointments, give blood, and pee in cups. Tell me what you're up to. I need a burst of youth."

"We're thinking about having a Fourth of July party. I wish you could be here."

"I'd never survive the trip, or Jack, dear. But your party reminds me of something. Did you hear the joke about the Liberty Bell?"

Katie rolled her eyes. "No."

"It's a great joke. It cracked me up!"

Katie groaned but could feel the hate from the night before banking its fire. Glancing at the clock, Katie began her good-bye. "I best be letting you go. Love you!"

"Love you more!"

Katie's mood was lighter, and she started creating the Fourth of July invitations. Imagine Dragons was singing "Believer" as she toggled through internet pictures, pasting stars, and fireworks into her word document. Katie sang along to the song and thought of Cassie.

She sent the invitations along with Jack the next morning. He called at noon, "Almost everyone is planning on coming to the party." She heard the pride in his voice.

Katie suspected his co-workers were coming out of a desire to see their century home versus spending time with Jack, but she congratulated him instead, "That's wonderful!"

July 4th started off perfectly. An occasional cloud drifted across the sky, and a welcome breeze kept the sun's intensity and ever-present humidity low. A constant loop of bees buzzed the stone patio as they dipped in to sip the wine condensation from the sangria pitchers. Katie watched them fly drunkenly toward the hydrangea bushes planted along the back fence.

Appetizers were warming in the oven, and big metal tubs were full of ice and packed with beers. Katie had wrapped white lights around the base of each of the two old oak trees, standing sentinel in the small, square backyard. Card tables were adorned with bright red tablecloths, and pots full of miniature carnations.

Jack was in a great mood. He whistled as he cleaned the grill. "Everything looks great, babe. Inside and out—very festive."

Katie beamed. They'd had two good weeks, and he'd helped her with the cleaning and getting the yard ready. They'd asked one another's opinion and planned the event as a team. She walked toward Jack. "I can't believe every single person is coming."

"Well, you were right. They need an excuse to get together, and the atmosphere at work is better ever since you invited them to our party."

Jack giving Katie credit was unusual. Mixed with his earlier compliments, she was thrown for a loop. "Did you just compliment me?"

Jack looked confused. "Yeah, why wouldn't I?"

"It's kinda unusual."

"No, it's not. I say nice things all the time. For instance, I couldn't live without you."

At her shocked expression, Jack grinned and pulled her in for a quick kiss. He released her with a playful push, "Now back to work, Mrs. Werner." He turned back toward the grill.

Katie watched him out of the corner of her eye. *If this is how things were all the time, I'd stay. I love this old house. I love my job. I could even love this Jack.* Cassie's voice interrupted Katie's thoughts, and she heard her friend warn, "Tigers don't change their stripes."

Noting the time, Katie headed inside to take a shower. Jack was naturally right behind her. He yelled from the closet, "Hurry! "They'll be here soon. I need to clean up, too."

He laid out a mini-skirt, tight top, and black heels on the bed. As she dried off, Katie noticed the display and balked. "Come on, Jack. That'll be uncomfortable. I'll be yanking on the skirt and trying to keep my balance on those heels."

He made a puppy dog face. "But you look so beautiful. You'll be the best-looking lady here tonight. What's wrong with me showing off my wife? Wear them for me?"

She shook her head. "Those heels? On our patio? I'll be tripping over myself all night."

"Please?" he begged, tipping her face up towards his for a kiss.

She'd failed this argument more times than she could remember. If she didn't wear the suggested outfit, his mood would plummet and ruin the evening. Sighing, she agreed and hurried to finish her hair and makeup.

An hour later, Katie admitted the party was a tremendous success. Jack operated the grill, taking orders, and flipping burgers. He received a lot of back-slapping and compliments on the house and the holiday decorations. "We sure needed this," several commented as the night waned. There was a lot of shop talk and an overwhelming consensus that their bosses were idiots.

Katie agreed sweetly as she gathered trash and freshened drinks. She'd been right about the shoes. They did occasionally get stuck in the cracks between the pavers.

Jack watched Katie throughout the evening, and at one point, she caught his eye. She smiled, sharing their success. He gave her a thumbs up.

On Katie's next round through, Jack glared at her and turned away.

What? What have I done now? She thought through the last twenty minutes trying to determine what had affected Jack's mood. She couldn't come up with anything and concentrated on their guests instead.

It was near midnight when the last person left. Katie toed off the shoes and ran a sink full of water. Jack sidled up behind her, running his hands up under her skirt and nuzzling her neck.

Katie laughed and pushed his hands away. "Stop! We'll never get this mess put away if you do that."

He drew her backward toward a kitchen chair, settling her on his lap.

One too many sangrias had Katie giggling and not thinking clearly. She was still riding the high of their successful evening and enjoying Jack's company.

Jack stroked her rib cage. "I noticed you talking to Mike for a long time."

It sounded like a conversation, and Katie responded, "I think I spoke to every single person, tonight. My mouth is tired." She snickered again.

"No. You spent more time talking to Mike than anyone, even bent over to pour him a drink and give him a nice long look down your shirt." Jack's caress had stopped being gentle.

Uh-oh. Her mind raced, trying to remember Mike and any conversation they'd had.

"I saw you flirting with several men, although Mike seemed to be your favorite."

"I wasn't flirting. I promise I was just playing host." She tried to slip away.

Jack held her in place. "I've told you over and over, you're mine."

"I didn't do anything and wouldn't. You have to believe me."

Jack's eyes turned to slits, and his whiskey breath filled the space between their faces. "You will not embarrass me again."

Before Katie could react, Jack twisted her around and yanked her down across his knees. Wrenching her skirt up, he yelled, "You are my wife! No one else touches you." His hand came down repeatedly as he spanked her into submission.

Jack's breathing changed, and Katie was sickened by his excitement over her subservient position. She cried, not out of pain, but shame. With her head hanging down toward the floor, her tears dripped off her face and onto the tile. She watched them land, each one a reminder of a year she'd lost and the indignations she'd suffered.

Knowing it was required, Katie apologized, "I'm sorry, Jack. It'll l never happen again.'

Jack hauled her to their room and slung her on the bed, tearing into her with primal lust.

Later, she lay awake and counted the days until her get-a-way. *Sixty-five.*

As August neared, it was increasingly difficult to keep up pretenses. Jack sensed something amiss and scrutinized her moves more than ever. He lifted books off the coffee table, reading the inside flaps. "Why are you reading this? It sounds like garbage."

He listened to the conversations she had with Aunt Susan and Cheyenne. If she drifted off, he reeled her back. "What are you thinking about? You seem to be daydreaming more."

Katie walked on eggshells daily.

Unfortunately, Katie's schedule lightened, giving her too much time at home, and putting her in Jack's crosshairs more often. *I've got to fill my days, or I'm going to make a mistake.* She still had a month to go.

"I was thinking about picking up another client," Katie mentioned casually as she and Jack were having breakfast. "I only have one morning with Amanda now that's she's improving. Add in a half-day with Gertie and two days with Mr. Parker, and there are almost two full days in my week with nothing scheduled."

Jack raised his eyebrows and waited.

"I'm going to check with Cheyenne's rotation. The extra money would be nice."

Jack was noncommittal. "We'll see."

When Katie asked Cheyenne about potential clients, she was disappointed to hear the response. "We're covered, for now, Katie."

"Can you put me on the substitute list?" Katie tried not to beg.

"You don't normally like to be called on short notice. Are you sure?" Cheyenne asked.

"Yep. We could use the extra money."

"This is not what we agreed to!" Jack screamed, when Katie shared the news. "I'm supposed to wonder where you are every day?" He grabbed Katie's arm. "I don't think so."

"I'll…I'll know the address and time frame the night before," Katie stammered.

"You'd better, Katie."

When she went to bed that evening, the comforter was turned down, and there, on her side of the bed, lay the knife. Katie hadn't seen it in well over a year and trembled.

When Jack came into the bedroom and picked up the knife, Katie stopped breathing. *This is it.*

He took it out of the sheath and held it up toward the light, turning it, twisting it, admiring it. He slid the knife back into its case, laying it carefully on the nightstand.

Climbing into bed, he pulled Katie close and whispered. "You and me forever, right?'

She kept her eyes on the knife and answered in a small voice, "Yes, Jack."

He rolled away and fell asleep while she stared at the ceiling.

She was on her very best behavior for the next few weeks.

Chapter 27

Katie woke up thinking, *September 6! Today is the day*. She'd expected to be nervous but was surprisingly calm. She put on a lightweight, eggplant-colored sweater over a sleeveless white blouse.

It was payday Friday and would be normal for her to make their standard, two-week withdrawal; Jack's $300 payout, $80 for gas in both vehicles, $100-weekend money, and her measly $20 allowance. The $500.00 would keep her going until she could get to her bank.

She dared not take more, or it would alert Jack. He verified as much as they worked through their morning.

"You're going to the bank today, right? The usual amount? Errands, groceries that kind of stuff?" Jack stood at the counter, scrounging through her tote. He came across her usual mishmash of miscellaneous items, including her precious compact. When he placed it and a tube of mascara on the counter, Katie froze.

She made herself concentrate on the iPad but watched him as he unzipped the little interior area assuring himself there were only tampons hidden inside. A pair of tweezers rattled around on the bottom, mixed in with six or seven pens and various post-it notes. A few coupons were loose, and her grocery list was half crumpled inside a couple of empty plastic bags. Jack replaced her makeup items and zipped her bag closed. Katie let out a breath and answered his question.

"Yep, in fact, I've got to leave early. I have my mammogram at nine-fifteen, then the lab work, and then my Ob/Gyn appointment."

Jack's eyebrows rose. "With Dr. Swisher, right? The female doctor?"

"Yes," Katie answered and swallowed her irritation. He knew dame well Dr. Swisher was a woman, as he'd insisted upon such. Katie stayed silent. She couldn't afford to be combative this morning.

Jack glanced meaningfully at Katie. "You want me to come along?"

"Come along? You mean to the doctor's offices?"

Jack nodded.

"No. I do not want you to tag along." Katie shook her head from side to side, fast enough to have her hair flying around her face. "It's embarrassing enough without you sitting in the chair."

She thought about how he insisted on going with her to the dentist or clinic. He followed her into the examination rooms, exuding charm and giving the impression of the caring partner. Katie had seen the wistful expressions on the faces of other female patients and heard their whispered comments.

"Isn't that nice?"

"I wish my husband would come with me, and actually care."

Katie would silently seethe. *You have no idea.*

Jack interrupted her thoughts. "Two women, one of them naked while the other pokes inside? Sounds sexy to me."

Katie gagged on her coffee, quickly disguising it as a cough.

"No way. Not happening."

He shrugged. "Your loss. Tell me again why there are so many appointments today. It seems weird."

"I swear I've explained this to you a hundred times." *Easy girl.* She softened her tone, "Because I'll be twenty-eight I a few weeks, they scheduled me for my first mammogram. I figured, without much family history, it made sense."

Jack nodded, accepting the information. It matched what she'd told him previously, and what he'd researched on the internet. "And the lab work? What's that all about?"

"Jesus, Jack." Katie bowed her head. She ran a hand across her abdomen. "It's been over a year since we lost the baby. They want to do blood work to ensure things are still all right."

He turned to the sink and rinsed his cup. "Oh. I remember now."

Satisfied all was in order, he grabbed his briefcase and headed toward the door. "Call me when you're finished. Maybe we can have lunch. You should be done around noon or twelve-fifteen, right?" This was another test. Jack watched her face to see how she accepted the potential change in her schedule.

Katie's mind screamed, *Lunch? Oh my God, now I've only got three hours!* She couldn't panic and worked at smiling and putting the right inflection into her voice, "That sounds about right. It depends on Doctor Swisher. She's usually running behind, but twelve-fifteen seems a safe bet. We haven't had a lunch date in a long time."

She followed Jack to the front door and kissed him goodbye, not in the least sorry it would be the last time.

Conscious of the security cameras, she went through the rest of the morning as casually as possible. She completed a few chores, added a few items to her grocery list, and killed a half an hour. To anyone looking at the video feed, it would appear mundane, and even a little boring.

As Katie backed out of the driveway, she took a long last look at the house. She'd loved it from day one. Looking at the gleaming windows, the Victorian color scheme, and the carefully tended landscape, Katie felt a pang. She'd poured blood, sweat, and tears into bringing the house back to life. She committed it to memory and pulled away.

At the bank, she left her sweater on and buttoned up to the top. She filled out a withdrawal slip, waited in line, and chatted with the cashier, leaving a vague memory of a pleasant woman out running errands.

Although the medical complex wasn't far from Forsyth Park and the bank, the drive took twenty minutes due to all the one-way streets and traffic. Katie sang with the radio, happier than she'd been in years.

She parked halfway down an aisle, wanting to make sure the parking lot cameras had her in sight. It was nine a.m., and she was right on schedule for someone who had a mammogram at nine-fifteen.

Katie popped down the visor and used the tiny mirror to apply a little lipstick. She shook her head at the irony. She hated Jack's constant scrutiny but was counting on such surveillance today.

She repeated a phone number in her head as she walked toward the entrance. *330-555-1818. 330-555-1818.* Once inside the building, she headed straight for the tiny reception desk.

"Oh My God. I locked my keys and my phone in my car! Can I use your phone to call my husband?" Katie reached for the phone, not giving the woman a chance to say no.

The woman shrugged her shoulders. "It's a local call, right?"

Picking up the receiver, Katie smiled. "Nine to get out?" The girl nodded and turned away to assist the next person.

When the dispatcher at the local cab company answered, Katie launched into her practiced speech, "Hello. I'm going to need a ride. Can you pick me up at the Cooper Primary Medical Complex?" She rattled off the address. "Right out front, under the archway?"

"Yeah sure," the bored dispatcher said. "When?"

"As soon as possible, please."

"Okay, give us about ten minutes."

Katie ended the call but pretended she was still speaking to her husband. "I locked the door just as I saw the keys on the seat. They must have slipped out of my purse." She paused as if listening to a question. "Yeah, I'll be out front."

Katie hit the redial button, calling the cab company again. She turned her back to the receptionist and walked a few feet away, careful not to get too close to the camera near the elevator.

Katie changed her voice a little, "So, can you pick me up at Cooper Medical Complex in twenty minutes?"

The dispatcher sounded surprised, "That's weird. We had a call from there not two minutes ago."

"Huh," Katie answered, feigning disinterest. "Can you pick me up out front, please?" If the receptionist was listening, Katie needed it to sound like one continuous conversation.

In reviewing her getaway plan weeks ago, Katie had decided a single cab would be too obvious if the police got involved. A second taxi would make it appear more routine. It was all about perception. They might not follow such a lead for days, giving her precious time. She'd hoped to use Uber, but without a credit card, she couldn't set up an account. The cab was the only choice she had.

Katie hung up the phone, waved at the receptionist, and headed toward the family restroom in the lobby. Taking the second stall, she removed her sweater and shoved it into the tote. Fishing out the hair bands, she scraped her hair into a ponytail and twisted it into a quick knot at the back of her head. Anyone who had seen her earlier would hopefully remember a dark purple sweater, and long, loose hair.

She heard someone come into the bathroom and froze. Whoever it was entered the adjoining stall, and Katie breathed again. Not Jack. She spun her wedding ring around her finger. *Throw it away? Keep it?* She decided she'd be less noticeable married.

Once the other person was gone, Katie popped out of the stall and hurried to the sink. She removed her contacts and scrubbed off most of the makeup she traditionally wore. The rest of the alterations would take place later. She shoved her glasses on her face, hurrying.

She pulled out her wallet, removing the debit card and her license. She put the cards and two-hundred dollars in her front pants pocket and zipped the remaining cash inside her tote.

Looking around quickly, she pulled out the plastic bags she'd put in the purse days before and shoved her tote down inside. She twisted the tiny bit of plastic left at the top. The tote was distinguishing with all its colors and sheer size. Getting rid of it here would be too coincidental. She wanted the police and Jack to wonder what had happened? Where's her purse? Has anyone used her credit card? Had she been kidnapped?

Katie wiped her billfold with a damp cloth and shoved it to the bottom of the trashcan. She put her phone on vibrate only. Turning it off would alert Jack. When Jack checked on her whereabouts via GPS, and she was sure he would, the phone would show her "in" the building. If the items were found later, so much the better. She wiped the phone clean, trying to remove fingerprints and make it look intentional. Wrapping it in dozens of paper towels, Katie shoved it toward the bottom of the trash can, covering it thoroughly so it wouldn't vibrate to the surface.

Head down, she made her way toward the entrance just as the cab pulled under the portico. Katie tossed her car keys in the outside trashcan and ducked into the backseat as fast as she could. "Hey! How are ya?" She slammed the door and clicked her seatbelt into place.

The cab coasted. "Where to?"

Katie rattled off the address she'd memorized. "957 Hidden Lake Court."

It was ten minutes after nine. If things went as planned, she had at least a three-hour head start.

Chapter 28

The cabbie plugged the address into his GPs, but his face was puzzled. "Hidden Lake Court?"

Katie pointed to the stoplight. "Whoops! It's green, make a right toward the highway." She smiled encouragingly--anything to keep him moving.

He pulled through the intersection, and she let out a long breath.

"I never heard of no Hidden Lake Court," the driver insisted.

"It's further south. Below Middleburg, near the mall."

He caught her eyes in the rearview mirror, and his eyebrows went up. "That's a haul." He smiled, though, thinking of the fat fare and upcoming tip.

"I know. My car broke down this morning. I can't get hold of my husband and just want to go home." Katie shook her head—exasperated, frustrated by the day, and playing her part to the hilt.

Katie settled in, looking out the window, a clear sign she wasn't in the mood for conversation. The cab ride was a little over fourteen miles and cost Katie $30.00 with the tip, but it was worth it to get out of downtown Savannah. After paying the fare, she walked toward the broad steps of the big old house as though she owned the place.

In reality, Katie had no idea who lived there. She'd found it using Google Earth and had chosen it because of its proximity to her bank and shopping.

Once the cab rounded the corner, Katie retraced her steps and turned the corner as well. It was three blocks to her destination, and her vulnerability had her senses heightened. She walked quickly, watching her feet, glancing at signs, and making her way to a small branch office of First Bank of Atlanta.

Once inside, Katie filled out a withdrawal slip and scooted up to the first available cashier.

"Oops. You didn't write in the amount." The teller's name badge listed her as Bethany.

"I need to determine the balance first." Katie smiled easily. There were no problems here.

"We'll need your ID, please."

Katie pulled her driver's license out of her pocket and handed it to the teller. *Hurry*, Katie silently begged.

Bethany studied the picture and read the information. "The name on the account is different than the one on the driver's license. The address isn't the same, either."

"The account is under my maiden name, Follings. I never got around to changing it."

The teller nodded slightly and directed her to one of the desks in the lobby, "Angela will help you."

Summarily dismissed, Katie had to do as she was told. She snatched one of Bethany's cards.

Angela seemed friendly but spent five minutes grilling Katie and asking security questions. *Dammit! I can't afford a stall right now.* Katie smiled sweetly and answered anyway, providing the supervisor her complete name, "Kathryn Anne Follings-Werner."

Next, she rattled off her Social Security number, address, pin number, last deposit amount, favorite pet, and on and on it went until Angela was finally convinced of Katie's identity. As Angela walked Katie back to the cashier, Katie snagged a few of Angela's business cards, too.

Katie asked for a certified copy of her last statement. "I'm going to need it to show financial status." She'd researched and learned certified reports could be used as identification.

After Bethany printed, signed, and date stamped each page, Katie handed her a withdrawal slip listing the entire amount of $5254.28. "I'll be closing this account."

At Bethany and Angela's concerned looks, Katie announced, "I'm buying a car today. And moving! It's been a crazy week. New job. New apartment. My friend from work…," Katie gushed about the car, finding a bank closer to home, and on and on she went until their eyes glazed, and they handed over the money. She loaded several of the withdrawal envelopes with the cash and stuffed them down inside the plastic shopping bags. Katie forced herself not to run out the door.

Although it felt like days had passed, she'd left the medical complex less than an hour before. Katie needed to get settled quickly but couldn't afford any mistakes. She made a deliberate left out of the bank, walked two full blocks, and crossed the street. She worked her way back to the Motel 6 she'd found on the internet and stood at the side of the building, taking in the angle from the bank. Deciding the security cameras weren't aimed in her direction, she slipped inside.

The stale lobby was empty except for Katie and the desk clerk. He was college-aged and appeared to be doing homework. He looked up at Katie through long, dark hair.

"I need a room for the night."

"Single or double?"

Katie hesitated until she understood he was referring to the beds and not occupants. "Uh, the single is fine."

"All right. Then it will be seventy-five dollars and twenty-seven cents, with tax."

Katie extracted cash from her front pocket.

He punched numbers into his calculator and asked her to sign the registration—something she hadn't considered since she'd never purchased a motel room in her life. She signed as Patty Stanford, the first name which popped into her head.

Katie hoped the clerk wouldn't ask for ID. If he did, she was prepared to open her plastic bags, search in her tote, and…w*hat?* She had no idea. *Run?*

Luckily, the motel employee didn't ask. He handed over her change and the key and never made eye contact again.

Katie made her way to room twenty-seven. Locked in the room, she stood with her back against the door slowing her heartbeat and stilling her trembling hands

You got the money, Katie. It's gonna be all right. Keep moving. Stick to the plan.

Although she'd love to hightail it out of town, there were still two critical steps: purchasing a vehicle and changing her driver's license. The current one still listed the Morrison's address, and she couldn't have any roads leading back to them.

Yanking the curtains closed, she pulled her tote out of the plastic bags and shook out her purple sweater. *I need every item of clothing I own.* She hid the bulk of the money in several places: behind a picture, under the microwave, and between two dresser drawers. She couldn't risk being mugged, losing her purse, or someone breaking into the room. The rest she put in her pocket and headed back toward the alley and a nearby Dollar General.

Katie picked out the items she'd kept as an ongoing list in her head for months; hair color, scissors, and sunglasses. She found a different purse, t-shirt, shorts, three pairs of underwear, a plain pair of tennis shoes, and one oversized sleep shirt. They even had $3 flip-flops, thank the Lord! She bought breakfast bars, a half-liter of Diet Coke, toothpaste, and trail mix. She parked her loaded cart in front of a locked, glass case displaying cell phones.

The only cashier was busy checking out customers, and Katie tapped her foot, excruciatingly aware of every passing minute. The clerk finally noticed Katie and radioed in for 'assistance out front.'

A manager mosied out of the office and removed the $39.99 flip-phone Katie indicated, out of the case.

She explained that Katie would need to pay for the phone separately, and then added the unwelcome news that there was a $10.00 activation fee, and the charger wasn't included either.

Katie handed over $66.33, then waited while the woman called the phone company and read the serial number to activate the phone.

The clock ticked off more minutes--six, seven, eight.

Once the phone was initialized, the manager turned to Katie and suggested she buy extra minutes fo the phone. "This phone only comes with thirty minutes of talk and text."

"Seriously?" Katie let out a sigh.

After listening to the options, Katie chose a twenty-dollar card giving her an additional one-hundred twenty minutes for the phone. She took her place in line, unloading all her purchases onto the conveyor belt.

"That'll be one-hundred-twenty-six dollars and thirty cents," the cashier announced, and Katie winced.

As Katie left, she glanced at the information board by the exit. It was jammed with items for sale, babysitting ads, and public notices. There was also a transit map showing all Savannah bus routes and schedules. Although she'd memorized it long ago, Katie glanced around to make sure no one was looking and pulled the map off the board. Stuffing it down in one of the grocery bags, she hurried out the door.

She did math on her way back to the motel. *I've spent more than two-hundred dollars already.* A headache began to pound behind her eyes.

Glancing at her watch, she noted the time; eleven-fifteen. Spying a McDonalds, she hurried inside and splurged on a chicken wrap.

You want fries with that?" the cashier asked out of habit.

"Why not?" Katie answered. "It may be the only meal I have today."

Back at the motel, she climbed the stairs two at a time, fiddled with the key, shoved through the door, and slammed it behind her. She'd made it. *Phase one is complete.*

Tossing all her purchases on the bed, Katie sat at the little corner table and inhaled her meal. Crumbling up her trash, she rummaged through the store bags and pulled out the box of hair color.

"Blonds Do NOT have more fun," she announced to the face in the bathroom mirror. Eager to wash away the white-blond Jack had insisted upon, she pulled out the mixing bottle.

Chapter 29

Jack called Katie's phone again. When it went to voicemail for the sixth time, he slammed his fist on his desk. It was eleven-fifteen, and she should have at least checked messages between appointments.

He pulled up the GPS apps for the car and her phone, his fingers tapping impatiently, waiting for the damn circle to find her location. The maps showed the vehicle in the parking lot of the Cooper Medical Complex, and her phone inside the building. "Something's weird." Signing into their bank website for the second time, he reverified the amount and time of her earlier withdrawal.

"I'm taking an early lunch," Jack yelled out to his assistant. Grabbing his keys, he drove straight to the medical complex. He found her car and parked next to it, noting nothing out of the ordinary. Jack checked his watch and headed toward the building. Not entirely sure where mammograms were performed, he stopped to ask directions from the same receptionist Katie had spoken to earlier.

The woman directed him toward the diagnostic wing. Other patrons stepped out of his way, instinctively aware of his intensity. Once his turn came, he oozed charm and flashed his sexiest smile at the receptionist. "My wife and I must have our times mixed up. I was supposed to meet her after her appointment, but now I'm not sure of the time. Can you tell me if she's finished yet? Kathryn Werner?"

The woman smiled back, taking in his handsome face. "Do you have your ID? Privacy laws being what they are, I can't give out patient information." She shrugged an apology.

Jack pawed through his wallet, seething. *Little bitch! Asking me for ID as if I'm not who I say I am.* He pulled out his driver's license, never dropping his smile. The girl checked his name against the authorized list on file and reviewed the appointment chart. She crinkled her forehead. "I'm sorry. Your wife never checked in today."

Jack turned, heading back toward the lobby.

The receptionist called out, "Her appointment was at nine-fifteen if that helps."

Jack didn't answer. He pulled out his phone and hit redial.

In the nearby restroom, Katie's phone vibrated among the used paper towels, and the screen announced, "Incoming Call from Jack."

He stabbed the elevator button and stood with his nose a millimeter away from the doors. When they opened, he was inside immediately, pushing buttons again. He turned left toward the OB/GYN office, having made the trip before when Katie had first needed such exams.

Jack repeated his concerns and asked whether his wife had completed her check-up. As before, the receptionist informed him Katie had never checked in for her appointment. He spun in a half-circle, ready to race off when he remembered the lab tests she'd scheduled. He turned back to the desk. "Could you possibly call the lab department? I don't know where it is, and I'm starting to get nervous. She was supposed to have blood work today too." He ran his hand down his face theatrically.

The administrator took pity and dialed the lab. After asking questions, she looked at Jack. "I'm sorry Mr. Werner, she's not been there either."

He pounded the counter once. "Dammit."

Katie sat on the bed with her head saturated with hair coloring solution. She wore nothing but her underwear, so she didn't get anything on her clothes. Spinning her wedding ring on her finger, she decided to hide it in the zippered compartment of her new purse. She hated to sell the beautiful, old ring--not because of Jack, but because it had been in his family for a long time. *If I don't need it, I'll return it to Jack's mother. Someday.*

Jack narrowed his eyes. The situation was serious, and he needed to play his part differently. Aware of the receptionist and patients watching him, Jack sank down in a chair and called Katie again. Instead of hanging up at the voicemail, he left a message and did so loud enough so the people in the waiting area could hear. "Hey, sweetheart. I'm at the medical building, and I can't find you. Your car's here, but none of the offices have seen you today. Call me back as soon as you can. I'm going crazy, worrying. Love you!"

He thanked the receptionist, who was smiling again and hurried out to the parking lot.

He bent over, looking underneath her car for a clue—her keys or her phone. He unlocked the car, looking under the seat, in the glove box, and trunk.

Finding nothing out of the ordinary, he called Katie's boss at Comfort Keeper. "Hey, Cheyenne. It's Jack. Jack Werner?"

"Jack? Is everything okay?"

"I'm checking to see if there was some sort of emergency at work today. I can't reach Katie, and thought, well, with her clients and all—" He left the sentence hanging--the epitome of a caring husband, who understood some patients were nearing the end.

Cheyenne wasn't fooled. She'd observed Jack and Katie for years. Katie was too skittish not to suspect Jack was the cause. Cheyenne had received enough complaints over the years to know he was in constant contact and called Katie while she was with patients.

Cheyenne adjusted her considerable bulk in her chair, interested in the call. "No, we haven't had anything come up today. Katie's had this day scheduled off for months. It's unusual for Katie not to check-in, isn't it?"

"Yeah, she always takes my calls."

"I know." Cheyenne let her implication hang in the air. "Now I'm worried, too. Let us know what's going on, okay? Or, have Katie call us later. Promise?"

"I promise," Jack replied, eager to end the call. "I've got to go."

His hands shook with silent rage. *Fucking bitch ran off.* He stood staring in the parking lot, imagining Katie laughing as she drove off with another man. *She wouldn't dare.* Jack's fingers curled into fists as he noted the time--eleven-forty. She hadn't been gone long. All he had to do was find the little traitor.

He called his office next, "I'm taking the rest of the day off."

"Is everything all right?" His assistant asked.

It's none of your fucking business, Jack seethed but made himself answer casually, "I'm meeting Katie after her appointments. I'll use my personal time." Jack hung up, not waiting for a reply.

Katie watched the clock, waiting for the dye to do its stuff. In the interim, she transferred her personal items to her new purse and clipped her license and debit card. She put one-half of each inside her new tote to be disposed of tomorrow or the next day. The other half of the cards were shoved into the McDonald's bag, mixing them with ketchup and food. Finally, she took the PO box key out of its hiding spot in the compact and attached it to a metal loop inside the purse. She couldn't lose the key. It was her entire future.

Chapter 30

Jack raced home and watched the security tapes. He hit the slow-motion button and watched Katie from the time he went to work until she left for appointments. Playing it back twice, he looked for anything suspicious. There was nothing.

He frowned as he watched himself go through her purse. That would seem strange to the police. *And I will be calling the police if I don't find her soon.* He decided he'd tell them he had been looking for the checkbook.

Next, he systematically went through her closet. Nothing was missing. Her shoes were in order, carefully arranged the way he liked. He rushed into the bedroom, opening the jewelry box. Hastily moving items around, he quickly determined anything worth any money was all still there. He shoved his hands through his hair. "Where are you?"

Katie washed and dried her hair. "Shit." Natural Instincts Caramel Crème' had sounded like the right choice, but looking in the mirror, Katie worried the color was too light. *I haven't changed it enough.* There wasn't a thing she could do about it now. She took out the scissors, took a deep breath, and started cutting.

Jack whipped out his phone again.

Aunt Susan's sugary voice came on the phone after six rings. "Hello?"

"Aunt Susan, it's Jack."

The sweetness melted away, "Oh. Jack. Is everything all right?"

Jack scowled at her disapproving voice. *I wonder what lies Katie has told her.*

"Jack? Are you still there?"

"Yeah. Is Katie there, by chance?"

"Katie? Well, no. Goodness, I haven't seen her in months. I talked to her on Monday. I haven't seen her, although I wish I could."

Jack gritted his teeth and closed his eyes, willing himself to stay pleasant. "Well, I can't seem to find her today."

"What?"

"I said I can't find her."

"Well, where is she?"

"I don't know. That's why I was calling you. Katie had appointments this morning but never showed up for any of them. I wondered if she came to visit instead or said something to you on the phone?"

"Well, I'll be. Did you call her?" On her end, Aunt Susan gave a satisfied smile. She loved antagonizing Jack. Susan knew Katie was unhappy and suspected Jack was the cause. She crossed her fingers, hoping Katie had left him. *Oh, Katie-girl. I hope you're safe.*

Like every other frickin' person that day, Jack promised to call if he found Katie. He headed for his car, intent on visiting Katie's clients. He scrolled through his phone, finding the first one, Mr. Parker. The man had dementia or something. Jack couldn't remember and didn't care. He plugged in directions and started driving.

Jack rang the doorbell four times before Mr. Parker answered. The old man's clothes didn't match, his pants were unzipped, and his thinning hair stuck straight up from his head.

Jack explained who he was and why he was there, but the light never reached Mr. Parker's eyes. He stood in the doorway, unsure. "Katie? Do I know Katie?"

Jack asked more questions.

"Leave the mail on the table." Mr. Parker shuffled away.

Frustrated, Jack pulled the door shut and got back in his car. "Jesus! What a waste of time—man's fucking wearing diapers."

He pulled up his phone for the next address--Amanda Stokely.

When Amanda answered the door, Jack barely introduced himself before launching into the reason he was at her house.

Amanda narrowed her eyes and listened to his explanation. At Katie's name, she brightened. "Katie?" She slurred slightly. "I love that woman. She's a huge help, but no, I haven't seen her since yesterday."

Jack left without saying goodbye.

Gertrude Taylor was last. Jack knocked on the door and couldn't hide his disgust at the bent old woman who answered the door.

"Katie's husband? Oh, I'm so glad to meet you. She's an angel that one." Gertie lifted gnarled fingers to shake Jack's hand. He recoiled.

He explained the situation, but Gertie hadn't seen or heard from Katie either. As a last resort, he drove by the other addresses Katie had temporarily worked at during August. They turned out to be dead ends. Out of options, Jack drove home, still calling Katie's phone and fuming.

Katie watched the afternoon news, flipping through local channels, and holding her breath. *Nothing yet, thank God.* She stroked her new hair absently, wondering what to do to fill the time. She pulled out the pad of paper from the motel drawer and began to outline what still needed to happen.

As she wrote, Katie realized she needed dishes, linens, and a few personal items. It would make her story of starting over, more believable. She added 'household stuff' to her list.

Reading through what she still needed to complete, Katie sighed heavily. *God, there's so much that can still go wrong.*

Jack looked at the clock. 'It's fucking six?" He slammed his glass into the sink, not caring that it shattered. "I need to speed things up." Grabbing his keys, he headed toward the local police station. He marched in, already talking, "My wife is missing! You've got to do something."

The officer at the front desk barely acknowledged Jack, "I'll be right with you. Have a seat." He inclined his head toward the row of dejected chairs guarding the wall.

Jack chose one far away from the people already seated. Eyeing their shabby shoes and street clothes, he turned himself sideways. After ten minutes, Jack approached the desk again. "Officer, I have an emergency!"

The policeman rolled his eyes. He peered over his glasses and took in Jack's appearance, nicely dressed, hair mussed, face flushed. "Let me finish this form, and I'll be right with you."

Jack stood ramrod straight at the counter.

A second officer strolled in, read the paperwork, and glanced at Jack. The first police officer leaned sideways in his chair and addressed the other people who were waiting patiently.

"Sorry, folks. this man seems a little desperate. Be right with you." He caught his partner's eye and made a face.

Jack launched into his story, "My wife is gone and has been for hours. Her car's still at Cooper Medical. Her phone says she's there, but she's not. The office closed at six. I've called her boss and her clients. No one's seen her. Something's wrong."

"Whoa. Whoa. Whoa. Slow down."

"How long has she been gone?"

"Nine hours."

The first officer leaned back, tipping his chair onto the rear wheels. "Nine hours isn't so long. Hell, my wife can spend that long at the mall."

The other officer grunted.

"She's not at the damn mall. She doesn't even shop!" Jack shook his index finger at the officer, with each word he spoke, "You're not listening."

The first policeman raised his eyebrows. "You need to settle down."

The second officer stepped forward, and the two presented a formidable front.

Jack put his hand down and slowed his speech. "I'm telling you she was supposed to be at the doctor's office, but she's not."

"Your wife is still at a doctor's office?" The second officer checked the clock and frowned.

Jack sighed. "No. She was supposed to be at the doctor's office but never showed up."

"None of this sounds like an emergency," the first officer commented nonchalantly.

"Why are you so upset?" the second policeman asked.

"I'm upset because her car is in the lot, but no one has seen or heard from her all day. She didn't show up for any of her appointments. She had one at nine-fifteen, ten-fifteen and eleven. I've been there, asked around. She never showed up for any of them."

"All those appointments? Is she sick?"

"No. It was all routine visits."

"But her car is there?" the second officer asked, needing further clarification.

"Yes! I've already said that. I'm telling you she's gone. The first twenty-four hours are crucial, right?" Jack was breathing hard again, and the officers paid more attention to him.

"You watch too much TV. Twenty-four hours isn't always true for adults."

The second officer asked, "Does she have a mental condition?"

"Jesus Christ. No!"

"A medical condition? Diabetes? Handicapped? Pregnant?"

"No! She's healthy. Why in the hell would that matter?"

"Well, we can speed things up if there's a mental or medical necessity. Faster than the twenty-four hours you mentioned." Sarcasm dripped.

"I'm telling you she's gone."

They watched his agitation grow, and the officers double-teamed him.

"Are things okay at home?"

"Nothing wrong with leaving, right?"

"Does she have a boyfriend, maybe?"

"She better fucking not," Jack mumbled under his breath.

"What was that?" The first officer leaned forward. "I didn't quite hear you."

"I said, I hope not."

"Hmm. I thought you said something else." The first officer made eye contact with his partner again.

The people waiting in the row of chairs leaned forward, listening intently. This confrontation was far more interesting than counting floor tiles or staring at the wall.

Jack shouted, "We aren't having problems!" Spittle flew as he ticked a list off on his fingers. "She's never late. She always checks in, and always goes where she's supposed to."

Both cops raised their eyebrows at the last comment and stared at Jack.

"Let's start with having you fill out a questionnaire. Do you have an actual photo?"

Jack dug in his wallet, pulled out an older, folded picture of him and Katie. His hands shook. *These jerkwads are wasting my time.*

Katie sat on the bed, packing and re-packing her new tote. She'd read every pamphlet in the room and loaded her extra phone minutes. Wandering the shrinking room, she checked the clock for the hundredth time. She hadn't anticipated interminable waiting.

Jack stormed out of the police department and called the local TV station. They always bragged about their hometown pride and how they were there for their viewers, often airing small stories to endear them to their viewership. The station was interested in Jack's story. "Can you get here soon? Bring a picture."

Jack agreed and sped toward the station. After waiting a nerve-wracking two hours, a harried reporter hustled over to do a quick interview. A triumphant Jack opened the gallery on his phone and showed them a recent picture of Katie.

"She's a pretty woman," the journalist commented. "We'll need to upload this to our IT guy."

Right or wrong, Jack understood the implication. A good-looking woman garnered more interest. The technician, Georgio, enhanced the picture and added an image of the medical building. Jack stood directly behind him, breathing the same air.

Georgio scowled. "Look, man, you're making me nervous. How 'bout you wait over there?" He pointed toward several fold-up chairs on the outskirts of the set.

Jack reluctantly sat down.

Katie wandered to the bathroom. Locking both arms on the vanity, she stared long and hard at herself, taking in the shorter hair, the bangs, and different color. "You can do this, Katie. I mean Cassie." Katie gently bumped her head against the mirror. "You are Cassie." Thump. "You are Cassie." Thump. She opened her eyes and looked at herself again. "Maybe I should go by Anne or Annie. That'd be easier since it's my middle name too." As the more familiar name rolled off her lips, she smiled and climbed into bed.

Katie turned on the news at ten, half-tuned into the weather, and a traffic accident earlier in the day. At 10:27 p.m., she bolted straight up in bed, shocked to see her picture with the words: "Possible Disappearance in Uptown Savannah."

The newscaster gave a fifteen-second explanation, "Kathryn Follings Werner, aged twenty-eight is *possibly* missing. Although her car is located at a local doctor's office," a picture of Cooper Medical Complex appeared on the screen, "she never signed in for any of her three scheduled appointments. Foul play isn't being ruled out at this time. She was last seen wearing a purple sweater and black pants." Katie's picture filled the screen again with a number to call the TV station with information.

Katie was instantly nauseous. "Oh God."

Jack watched the newscast and erupted, "Fifteen seconds? That's all I get? Jesus! The fricking commercials are longer!" Jack left the station, still muttering under his breath. At home, he laid in bed, staring at the ceiling and fumed over Katie's disappearance.

An hour later, Katie sat up with a start, eyes darting around the unfamiliar room. Hearing tires crunch on the loose gravel in the parking lot, she slid her hand under the motel pillow and pulled out her new scissors.

Headlights stabbed through the thin curtains, making her heart accelerate. She eased from the bed and stood behind the door, gripping the only weapon she had. *I'm not going back.*

A car door slammed, and Katie counted to ten, then twenty, squinting hard and evaluating every noise. Watching the clock, she waited for the minute hand to turn over, convinced she'd hear Jack's angry fists banging on her door.

Further down the row, a different door thumped shut, and she let loose the breath she'd been holding. It was just her overactive imagination—probably a result of the earlier broadcast.

Keeping the scissors nearby, Katie curled up in the lumpy corner chair. "There was a crooked man, who walked a crooked mile. He found a crooked…" She repeated the rhyme one more time, calming down, and grateful she'd survived day one.

Chapter 31

Saturday morning turned out to be unseasonably warm, and Katie was grateful. It meant she could wear her new shorts and flip-flops. Cramming all her earthly belongings into her new tote, and the plastic bags from Dollar General, she checked to make sure the motel room contained no evidence.

The five inches of hair she'd cut the night before had been carefully gathered into paper towels and every inch of the bathroom scoured. She stuffed the plastic grocery bags with the price tags, the box of hair color, and her original tote. Satisfied she'd covered her tracks, Katie munched one of her breakfast bars, took a last swig of the Diet Coke, leaving the containers as the only trash in the room.

She walked back toward the business area, shoved the trash into a nearby container, and waited at the bus stop for her next ride toward freedom. Paying the three-dollar fare, she found a seat toward the back. Despite her semi-disguise—hair, glasses, clothing—she was terrified she'd be recognized after last night's news story. She didn't make eye contact with anyone.

To take her mind off Jack and his evident pursuit, Katie thought of her bookstore *Inklings*. She didn't care what anyone else said about libraries and bookstores disappearing. There was still something magical about holding a book in your hands. She pictured her store: an adult area full of classics and the latest bestsellers and a separate children's area. She'd have small-sized furniture, stuffed animals, and cozy rugs, begging a child to curl up with a book. She wanted a turnstile full of postcards and a section with local recipes and history. Coffee. She definitely wanted to serve coffee so customers would wander.

The bus shuddered to its last stop, ending her daydream. She was south of Georgetown, on the outskirts of Savannah. It was less than thirty miles from home, but as far as the Savannah bus lines went. From here, she'd need new transportation.

Katie had done her homework and knew there was shopping, another branch of First Bank of Atlanta, and a small city motel. Entering the bank, Katie walked up to the first available teller. "I'm interested in opening an account."

The woman, Alicia, directed Katie toward a desk where a financial planner was waiting. Katie plucked Alicia's business card off the counter before moving toward the cubicle.

Katie started a dialogue immediately, "I'm in a hurry this morning, but I'd like to come back and talk about opening a checking account with direct deposit."

The young man rattled off all the options, as he'd obviously been trained. Afterward, he handed her a brochure and one of his business cards. "We're open at eight a.m. Monday through Friday. Ask for James when you come back."

"I will. Thank you." She pocketed his card, giving her a total of four from First Bank of Atlanta. She hoped it would be enough.

She crossed the street to the City Manor Motel. The faded blue paint was peeling, the roof sported a full layer of green-gray moss, and the parking lot asphalt had long since crumbled. They rented kitchenettes by the week, though, which meant no problem with cash, and no questions asked.

Jack shoved his way out of bed at 6:30 a.m. Sitting at the end of the bed, his brain woke with a single purpose—find Katie. "I know I'm missing something." He rummaged through the dresser, then the closet, pushing hangers out of the way, and checking all pockets, Katie's other purses, and even her shoeboxes, looking for any clue, any evidence of another man.

Tossing the last two boxes in the corner, he growled, "I will find you."

He pawed through the jewelry box again, slower than he had the night before. He held up a thick gold chain. "Would you leave this behind?" Fingering the necklace, a ghost of concern floated across his brain. *Maybe something has happened to her.* He dismissed the notion and pulled out the jewelry drawers to look underneath.

Remembering his hidden papers, Jack hurried over to his suit jackets and extracted the Kane Brothers receipts Katie had found months prior. "Shit. These have to go." He shook his head in frustration. His plans for mild extortion were disappearing fast thanks to the ongoing audit at work and now, Katie. He shoved the receipts down the front of his pajama pants.

Once downstairs, Jack logged into the office computer, performing for the camera and unknowingly emulating Katie's actions. He had every intention of going back to the police and assumed they'd want to search the house, watch the video footage, etc. If he turned the cameras off, it would be questioned.

He opened the middle drawer, hiding his lap, and extracted the papers from his pants. Mixing them in with a few documents from his desk, he made a big show of pawing through files. He pulled out papers from Katie's employer, the bank, and the doctor's office and put them in a folder, along with his own secrets. He added a picture of Katie, taking it out of the frame on his desk. He knew the cameras would show an image of a sleepless, worried man.

Checking the time, Jack went back upstairs to dress and was in the car by 8 a.m. Driving past the medical complex, he saw Katie's car still parked there and drove toward the police station. He ripped up the Kane Brothers receipts as he drove, shoving them into a trash can outside the police station. *No one will look there.*

Jack headed straight toward the front counter, ignoring the crying woman already in line. Naturally, a different cop was sitting at the desk, and Jack released a heavy sigh.

"Can I help you?"

"Yes," Jack barked the word. "I was here last night to report my wife missing. No one took me seriously. She's still gone. Her car is still at the doctor's office, no phone calls, no contact whatsoever, and I need someone to help me!" He took a deep breath, not wanting to seem overly agitated.

"You were here last night?"

"Yes."

"Filled out paperwork?"

"Yes."

"Ok, let's start with your name, and I'll see what's going on."

"Jack Werner."

The officer carefully wrote it down on a pad of paper, verifying the spelling.

Jack read the officer's name, *Wells,* and committed it to memory as this woman was seriously pissing him off.

The officer dug through the pile of unfiled reports from the night before. An impatient Jack, leaned across the counter, reading upside down.

"Hey, buddy, step back from the counter." She pushed away from the desk and placed a hand on her hip, where she wore her gun.

Hands in the air in mock surrender, Jack stepped back. "I'm just trying to help."

"I don't need your help."

Another person walked into the lobby, and officer Wells pushed the intercom button, "We need an officer to the front desk."

A policeman pushed through the door, and Jack couldn't help but notice the crew cut, and a muscular body packed into the uniform. It screamed ex-military, and Jack backed away.

Wells greeted the officer, "Sergeant Darrow."

"You okay out here?"

"Mostly," Wells answered. "We're backed up a little."

Darrow motioned the next person in line forward.

Officer Wells relaxed and shuffled through papers again. "Ahh, here we go." She smiled at Jack, pleased to have found the form. "Missing wife. Kathryn Werner, right?"

Jack crossed his arms and nodded.

"Missing less than twelve hours at the time of the report. No mental or medical problems. Do you have any newer pictures of Kathyrn? The one from last night is folded."

Jack handed over the one he'd taken from the frame.

"Oh. I recognize this lady from the news last night. You shouldn't have done that."

"You guys weren't doing anything." Jack gestured wildly, and his voice grew louder, "My wife is gone, and I needed some help before she gets too far away."

"What makes you think she's far away?"

"I don't know where she is." Jack waved his hands around again. "Gone? Disappeared? Kidnapped? Jesus, I sure as hell don't know the right words."

"I'm going with what you said. You said you didn't want your wife to get too far." Wells turned to Sgt. Darrow, "That is what he said, right?"

Darrow nodded and tapped the report. The Friday night officer had written: "*Husband seems angry, not concerned.*"

Darrow took over the conversation. "Well, now it's been a full day. We'll send an officer to the medical building." He read the report. "2012 white Honda. Go on home until we check out the medical complex. Then, we'll get your full statement, okay?" Darrow verified Jack's address. "My partner and I will be at your house soon."

Jack had no option but to leave the building.

Darrow went back into the office area, looking for Lieutenant Hopkins. Spying him filling his coffee cup with black sludge, Darrow called out, "Hey! We've got a missing person report."

Hopkins groaned, "Those things never turn out to be true."

Chapter 32

Katie could see a motel employee in the back room. His chin rested on his chest, and a television droned in the background. She rang the desk bell to get his attention.

The manager, or whoever he was, shuffled out of the backroom, and they were both surprised. He was younger than she'd expected, and she was classier looking than most of his clientele. He admired her openly, and Katie tucked her chin, mumbling about a room for a couple of days. He rattled off the nightly charge.

Katie agreed and watched him ring up the total.

"That comes to a whopping one-hundred-forty-eight dollars and eighteen cents." He gave her bare legs a quick appraisal.

Katie didn't want his attention and yanked out twenty-dollar bills.

"Passing through?" He glanced at the registration. "Anne?"

She hadn't practiced the next lie and stammered a bit, "Annie. And no, I just got a job at the First Bank of Atlanta." She pointed toward the bank across the street. "I need a place to stay until I find an apartment."

"Really?" He pulled the word out longer than its two syllables.

Shit, Katie thought. *That's all I need is him asking me out.* She frowned, trying to look unappealing.

He pointed to his name badge. "My name's Chad. Can I show you around?"

Katie shook her head. "Thanks, but I wanna get settled first.

Maybe in a couple of days, who knows?" She didn't want to encourage but didn't want to offend either. *He might come in handy.*

Taking the room key, she headed out the door before he asked more questions. She needed to be safely tucked away before noon. There was little doubt she'd be on the news again.

Once in the room, she stood taking in her temporary digs. The walls were dingy at best, and she could see a sag in the mattress. The kitchenette consisted of a three-foot counter with two stools tucked underneath. She opened and shut the door to the microwave twice, shaking her head. "That's the tiniest microwave I've ever seen." A mini-fridge and grimy coffee maker rounded out the appliances. Checking the cabinets, Katie found them all empty. "Great. I need to buy paper products, too."

She poked her head in the bathroom, noticing old white tile with grout the color of mud. A rust ring, in the bottom of the sink, was evidence of a constant drip from the faucet. Katie jumped when she caught her appearance in the mirror over the sink.

She laughed at herself and pulled back the shower curtain, happily surprised to find the area sparkling clean. She put away her makeup, moisturizer, contact case, and other personal items and tucked the few clothes she owned into the nightstand.

Finding a half pad of paper, Katie made a list of items to hold her through the weekend: basic food and drink, plastic ware, and paper plates. Grabbing her purse, she headed out toward the little corner grocery store. She spent another $40.63 and mentally subtracted it from the running total she had in her head.

Jack drove home and waited for the cops, who took their sweet-ass time and didn't show up until nine-thirty.

Officers Darrow and Hopkins both had their hands on their hips when Jack answered the door. He assessed their tightly packed uniforms and matching stance. *Jesus! They even have the same haircut.*

In turn, they looked around the enviable neighborhood and carefully tended yards. Detective Hopkins introduced himself. "I'm Lieutenant Hopkins. You remember Detective Darrow from earlier?"

They pushed their way inside the house, noting details as fast as their eyes could scan. Spotting the security camera by the front door, Hopkins pointed and asked, "Are these in every room?"

Jack glanced at the camera. "Yep, except for the master bedroom closet and guest room."

Jack's cell phone rang, and he answered quickly. The TV station that had run the story on Katie asked if there were any updates and whether she had family nearby. Hopkins and Darrow listened to Jack's end of the conversation.

"No family. No updates. No calls or signs of Katie anywhere. The police are here now."

"We'll rerun the story at noon," the reporter said. "Do the police have anything to add?"

Jack covered the receiver and asked. Darrow and Hopkins shook their heads no.

"Not at this time. I've got to go."

Hopkins went back to his questions about the cameras. "What kind of footage do you have? Twenty-four hours at a time?"

"No, this system runs in a seventy-two-hour loop."

"Can we review them?"

"I've watched them three times. She didn't do anything weird. She did exactly what she always does."

His wording caught their attention. "What do you mean? Do you watch her every day?" Darrow asked.

"Well, I review the footage. Make sure things are running smoothly, no surprises."

"Hmm, "Hopkins frowned. "We still want to take a look. Maybe we'll see something you missed."

"Fine." Jack stood in place.

"We need to keep moving, Jack. Let's have Office Darrow review the film while you show me the rest of the house. I'll take notes and get your statement as we go. Sound good?"

Jack led them to the office and loaded the software for the cameras. He stood watching the pictures intently.

Hopkins cleared his throat. "So, you were going to show me around the house?"

Jack walked Hopkins through each room downstairs and then headed up the stairs to the bedrooms.

Poking his head into the guest room, Hopkins asked, "Nothing out of the ordinary?"

"No."

The policeman slowed down when he and Jack entered the master bedroom, noting two cameras in the corners. Hopkins raised his eyebrows but said nothing. "And you say nothing's missing?" He worked his way to the closet, noting Katie's side held less clothing than Jack's. Hopkins used his pen to move a few blouses aside.

"Nothing. I've checked the dresser and emptied all the drawers. There's not so much as a pair of underwear missing."

Hopkins wrote down a few things, hiding his notebook from Jack's curious eyes. *Husband is obsessive. Cameras in all rooms. Seems to know every item his wife owns.* He peeked in the trash can, noting a few items, indicating it hadn't been emptied. "Let's see how Darrow is doing with the tapes, and we'll head over to the medical center."

Jack nodded, then turned to answer his phone. Another TV station had picked up the story and wanted to ask a few questions.

"Not now," Jack barked. He agreed to talk later, "After we get done at the doctor's office."

Hopkins rolled his eyes. "Great. Now the reporters will be there. You need to let us handle this, Jack. No more interviews. No more talking to reporters. Do you understand?"

Hopkins jogged down the stairs and stuck his head in the office. "Anything?"

"No," Darrow answered, "nothing abnormal. No calls, no stuttered movements."

"Alright. We've got to go. We need to get to the medical building before the news stations." Hopkins jerked his head toward Jack. "He just shared that little tidbit with a reporter."

Darrow moved away from the desk. "Great. That's just great."

"Why don't you ride with us?" Hopkins suggested.

Jack hesitated. "Maybe I ought to drive myself. If I get out of the back of a police car and reporters are there…."

Darrow and Hopkins raised their eyebrows.

"You should have considered that before telling the media where we're heading."

"We'd rather you ride with us. We could use the time to finish your statement. The medical office closes at noon, right?" Darrow looked at his watch for emphasis.

"I guess that makes sense." Jack glanced at his watch too. It was ten after ten.

Katie slapped together a quick sandwich and chugged milk straight from the jug. She put away the rest of the food and noting it wasn't quite ten-thirty, decided she had enough time to buy some clothes. "One outfit isn't going to cut it. And, I need a suitcase too," *It'll look weird to be staying at a motel without luggage.* She headed out to the nearby Target she'd seen earlier.

Chapter 33

Jack slouched in the back of the police car, answering questions.

"Does Katie have family nearby?"

"No, just her Aunt Susan in Atlanta. She's in one of those retirement places."

"Are the two of them close? Does Katie go see her? Call?"

"We don't get there often, but Katie calls her at least once a week."

"We're gonna need her name, address, phone."

"I called her yesterday. She hasn't heard from Katie." Jack pulled out his phone and rattled off the requested information, while Officer Darrow added to their notes.

"We'll need to interview her anyway. Could Katie be staying with a girlfriend?"

"No. She doesn't have any close friends, just a few people she works with."

Officer Darrow caught Hopkins' eye. No friends. No family. Surveillance. The less than flattering picture of Jack was growing.

They pulled into the medical lot at ten-twenty-seven.

"Shit," Darrow muttered, pointing at two news vans.

"Yep." Hopkins turned to glare at Jack. "There they are."

The reporters hurried over, cameras running and audio on high. "Are you here concerning Kathryn Werner?"

"Do you suspect foul play?"

The two officers barreled through the group, with Jack between them, and headed straight toward the front door. They showed their badges, scaring the girl at the desk half to death.

Hopkins flashed the picture of Katie. "Have you seen this woman?"

Darrow interjected, "Were you working yesterday?"

She stammered, "No. I only work on Saturday mornings. Megan was here yesterday."

"Can you get your boss up here, please?"

The news reporters had followed them inside. Jack slid toward a clump of fake trees near the staircase, trying to be inconspicuous.

Hopkins stayed in reception, waiting for the supervisor, and moving the media outside.

"I'll go up to the doctor's office. Come on, Jack." Detective Darrow marched toward the elevator.

The doctor's assistant's eyes grew large when she saw the police uniform. She pointed at Jack, "He was here yesterday looking for his wife. What's going on?"

Darrow took a brief statement, writing down Katie's appointment time and confirming she'd never shown up or called. He noted the time Jack came in, and what questions he'd asked. Darrow repeated his actions at the lab and mammography station.

Meanwhile, Hopkins met with the supervisor. She called in extra security guards to handle the press and loaded the surveillance tapes from the day before. Friday's receptionist, Megan, was heading into the office to see if she could identify Katie or remember anything.

The entire group, including Jack, hunkered around the security screens watching the film.

"There she is!" Jack's voice screeched as he pointed at the screen. They all watched Katie park and walk inside. Other patients came and went. A taxi pulled in and left. A community van unloaded two elderly women. Another taxi parked under the portico. It wasn't particularly notable, but Officer Darrow wrote down the name of the taxi company. They were all watching for the bright purple sweater, long blond hair, and the big bag Katie carried. They fast-forwarded through the tape, never seeing Katie exit the building.

Darrow rewound the tape to the taxi frame. "I can't see the passenger." They switched to the back entrance and picnic area used by doctors and staff. There was no sign of Katie.

Turning to the supervisor, Hopkins asked to see all maintenance personnel. "We need access to all closets and rooms in this building."

Darrow and Hopkins explored all three floors to no avail, even searching the back entrance and courtyard.

Darrow walked footpath leading between the lunch area and an employee parking lot--a natural shortcut created over time. He shook his head. "There's nothing here. Besides," he pointed toward the camera mounted on the corner of the building, "we would have seen her on the tape."

Katie bought jeans, khakis, underwear, another bra and six pairs of socks. With the weather turning cooler, she purchased a few long-sleeved shirts and a thick wool-lined jacket on sale. A pair of casual shoes went in the cart, and she bit her lip over waterproof hiking boots. She took the shoes out of their boxes, conserving space.

She chose hygiene items, mumbling to herself about needing household accessories to complete her story. Unwilling to buy too many things, Katie chose a clock radio and an oversized coffee mug. Katie smiled at the mug featuring *Maxine* asking 'My update Status? Is Alive good enough?'

A thick blanket, a pillow, and one pillowcase were piled precariously on top of the clothes. Katie was thrilled to find a cheap suitcase and an overnight bag combo. She stuffed the smaller case under the cart and pulled the larger one behind her as she and the cart wobbled drunkenly toward the checkout area. Two cheap books, a notebook, pens, and the local newspaper were added to the cart along the way.

She laughed with the clerk. "How am I gonna cart all of this stuff out of here?"

"You've been busy!"

"You can say that again. Let's put the clothes in the suitcase." Katie unzipped it and loaded the bags.

She reluctantly handed over $258.18. Even with most of the clothes and shoes shoved inside the suitcases, the other items filled three massive store bags. Attaching the smaller suitcase to the larger one, Katie ran the bag handles through her arm to her elbow and half-jogged toward the motel.

She spilled into her room and leaned against the door, breathing hard. She dumped the bags on the bed, automatically turning on the TV. The news would be on soon.

There was a light knock on the door. Katie froze, then made herself look through the peephole. *Chad--not Jack.* She fastened the safety chain and opened the door.

"Hey there. Do you have everything you need?" Chad asked as he peered in through the three-inch opening. "Been shopping, huh?"

"Yeah, I'm kind of jazzed up about the new job and getting my own place."

"I get off at three today. Wanna get a bite to eat?"

"Thanks, but I grabbed food while I was out. I need to go over my notes for work. So, not today, okay?"

"Do you even have a car? I didn't see one in the parking lot?"

"My car's junk. Totally unreliable." Katie rolled her eyes dramatically. "My brother dropped me off this morning and is gonna help me find something tomorrow," Katie lied.

Chad left, hope still in his eyes.

Katie locked the door and pushed a chair under the knob. She ate ravioli out of the can and watched her story unfold on the news. She was fascinated to see Jack get out of the back of the police car and walk with two policemen toward the medical building.

Reporters yelled out a few questions, but the cops gave the standard, "No comment," and then entered the building.

"Breaking news" rolled across the bottom of the television screen. "Kathryn Follings Werner disappeared from Cooper Medical Center Friday morning. The police have been questioning employees and reviewing camera tape. They had few clues until a few minutes ago." They cut to a scene of an employee opening the locked dumpster area. Police and maintenance personnel wore gloves as they dug through the trash. There was a dramatic pause, and the camera zoomed in closer.

"Hey! I got something!" A janitor waved a billfold in the air.

Darrow pushed his way through the crowd, ignoring questions yelled from reporters.

"Is that Kathryn's wallet?"

"Do you suspect foul play?"

Opening the wallet, Darrow pulled out the grocery cards Katie had purposely left behind. Seeing Kathryn Werner's name, he held both arms out. "Move back! This is a crime scene."

Hopkins whipped out an evidence bag, and Darrow carefully dropped in the wallet. Katie's cell phone was found a little further down in the trash, and the media went crazy.

Katie watched open-mouthed. It was far more dramatic than she'd ever dreamed. She'd been gone less than thirty hours, and things were ramping up quickly. She needed to get out of town soon. Unfortunately, she had three important things to take care of before hitting the highway.

Chapter 34

Working the patrol car in between the reporters and the dumpster, Hopkins hit dispatch on his shoulder radio, "We've got a real missing person here. I need another officer at the medical center ASAP. Send a crime team to dust for fingerprints and secure the scene. Tell the chief I'll call him in a little bit."

The janitor, who'd found the billfold, happily swayed by the dumpster, a fifteen-minute hero, hoping for more.

Jack was shocked. He'd been sure Katie had run away. Officers Darrow and Hopkins watched his face, as confused as he was as to what had happened.

As soon as the crime squad arrived, Darrow and Hopkins barked out orders.

"I want this site secure. Barricades, whatever you need, but keep those reporters back."

"Check the car for prints and get a tow truck here to impound the car."

Hopkins rattled off the next task. "We need warrants for phone records, credit cards, financials, and the Red Cab Deluxe Company. Hospitals need to be called too."

Darrow agreed. "I'll call the DA on the way to the precinct. You're staying here, right?"

"You bet. I'll interview the receptionist as soon as she gets here. I want to watch the tapes again, too. Take Mr. Werner with you. Finish the list of family, friends, neighbors, clients—whoever has any contact with Katie. We need Jack's fingerprints too. Oh, and his permission to open Katie's phone. We don't have time to wait for the damn phone company."

Darrow steered Jack toward the patrol car. "Come on, Jack, let's get you out of here." Jack sat in the front seat this time.

Hopkins took a big breath and called the police chief, "We're gonna need a task force immediately. We're working on subpoenas and should have them in front of a judge in an hour. We need to check local hospitals too."

Police Chief Greer, a skinny man with a nose too large for his face, yelled into the phone, "Goddammit! How many officers do you need?" He glared at the TV.

"Two? Maybe three?" Hopkins answered.

"We don't have the budget for that! I can give you two, maybe."

"We got a wide area to cover in a short period. Plus, the employer, neighbors, clients, and family. She's been gone more than a day."

"How'd this get so out of control? Why'd you wait so long?" Greer pounded his desk. "This thing has been all over the news already."

"The husband was acting strange. We didn't consider anyone else."

Greer sighed. "I'll see who's available since the media are flapping their jaws non-stop."

Back at the police department, Darrow got Jack's signature of release and wrote out a complete list of contacts. "Her parents are both dead. Correct?"

Jack nodded.

"No cousins? No girlfriends? College roommate?"

"No other family and Katie didn't go to college. We don't have time for socializing."

"How about your side of the family? Any reason to believe she could be visiting them?"

"She'd never go there. We barely speak."

"We need their numbers anyway."

Off to the side in his notes, Darrow wrote, "Katie is completely isolated."

Chief Greer barreled into the office. "I've got two guys with Hopkins at the medical center. That gives us one more here, Jenkins."

"Got it."

Darrow pulled Tyler Jenkins into the conference room. "Call all local hospitals, check on a Kathryn Werner or Jane Doe from yesterday to today. Track all information here," he pointed to a whiteboard, "and try the D.A.'s office again. We need those records!"

Turning to Jack, Darrow announced, "I'm gonna get your prints and take you home."

"Home? What if you find her?"

"We'll keep you posted every step of the way." Darrow's phone rang, and he read the screen, already turning toward the door, he motioned Jack to follow.

Hopkins was on the phone, "Did you file the warrant?"

"Jenkins is still trying to get ahold of the prosecutor. What's going on there?"

"Nothing in the car. Locks aren't forced. The receptionist recognized Katie. Said she used the lobby phone to call her husband. She doesn't remember seeing her after that."

"Jesus. This is a mess. Can we verify the phone call?"

"Add it to the warrant. Come get me when you're done. We need to go see the aunt."

Darrow drove Jack home, barely stopping the car to let him out at the curb. At the courthouse, Darrow ran into the district attorney and propelled him toward the judge's chambers. The only available judge listened to their story and signed the requested warrants.

Darrow called Jenkins. "Pull those records and keep me posted."

Leaving the television on, Katie spread out the classified section of the paper she'd bought earlier. "I need a truck. No one will be looking for me in a pickup, especially Jack." She circled four possibilities and pulled out her new flip phone. She asked questions with each call, "How's the body? How about maintenance? Leaks? Accidents? Original tires?"

Katie scribbled notes, and dollar amounts across her notebook. She circled the ad most in line with her budget. The Dodge Dakota was listed at $1900 and had what the owner called a "ding" in the passenger door. Katie hoped it meant she'd get the vehicle cheaper. Without wi-fi, she couldn't do any research and wasn't willing to use any of her precious minutes or data anyway. She pursed her lips. *Chad's interest might pay off after all.*

Walking into the motel office, Katie stroked her ponytail and smoothed her shirt. Chad's eyes followed her hands.

"Can I use your computer, Chad? I'd like to check out the Kelly Blue Book site. See if any of these cars I'm looking at are priced correctly and get some tips."

Chad happily ushered Katie into the cramped office, shoving paperwork and, what looked to be his own bills out of the way. Katie slid into a yellow plastic chair and accessed the internet.

Chad leaned against the doorframe, watching until the phone rang, and he turned away.

With Chad gone, Katie opened a new page and left it open to show a 2013 Nissan Sentra. She exited the office and, seeing Chad still on the phone, mouthed, "Thanks! You helped a lot."

He waved back and gave her a thumbs-up sign.

Armed with new information, Katie headed back to her room and called the truck owner again. "I forgot to ask if you have the title?"

Sensing a potential sale, Rob, the owner, talked faster, "Yep. It's here at the house."

"And how about the odometer reading? It needs to be notarized," Katie stated, grateful to have read that piece of information as a subtopic in Kelly's Blue Book.

"The Odometer form has already been taken care of," Rob assured, smugly. "We're ready to go on this end."

Katie arranged to see the truck the next day and wrote down the address. Checking the map she'd snatched from Dollar General, she calculated the distance between the motel and Rob's house. "Less than five miles."

She pulled out the ratty, motel phone book and called a local cab company, confirming they picked up passengers from *City Manor Motel.* She didn't schedule the ride, as it would be odd to call an entire day ahead.

Chapter 35

Tearing into the medical complex, Darrow braked beside Hopkins. "Ready?"

"Yeah. I'm sending these guys," Hopkins jabbed his thumb over his shoulder at two other officers, "to the victim's neighborhood. We'll see if they turn up anything." He jumped in the car, rubbing his chin in aggravation. "This doesn't feel right."

"What?"

"The whole thing. It doesn't feel like a mugging or abduction, or any damn thing."

Darrow agreed. "Let's wait to see what the warrants and interviews tell us."

While other reports continued to work the dumpster angle, investigative journalist, Bruce, and his camera operator, Dave, watched the police car screech to a halt. When the lieutenant jumped inside the squad car, Bruce raised his eyebrows. "Wanna see where they go?"

Dave shrugged. "Up to you, man."

Bruce considered for just a few seconds. "Follow them. The boss has been giving me shit all morning, screaming we need a new angle."

Hopkins checked his watch. "It's almost two. It'll take what? Three and a half hours to get to Atlanta?"

Darrow nodded.

Hopkins pulled out his phone. "We need to speed things up." He called Jenkins to see if any data was back yet.

Jenkins, who was the department tech geek, had stressed himself through an entire bag of potato chips, waiting on information. He was happy to have at least something to report when Hopkins called. "Cell phone calls and credit reports are coming in now, sir."

"Good. Send it to me on the car's computer. I want feet on the ground, questioning Katie's clients and neighbors." He hung up before Jenkins could answer. Turning to Darrow, he asked, "What's the aunt's number? I want to call and make sure she'll be home."

Darrow raised his butt off the driver's seat to reach the notebook in his back pocket. He tossed it to Hopkins. "Turn to the last page." Concentrating on getting out of the city, he didn't notice the white van keeping pace and following behind.

Bruce and Dave stayed four or five car lengths behind the police car all the way into Atlanta. Bruce spent his time Googling different versions of Katie's name—Katie, Kathryn, Werner, and Follings--across the internet, Snapchat, Instagram, Facebook, and Twitter. "There's nothing about this woman. It's weird."

When Darrow and Hopkins pulled up in front of Susan's villa, Bruce and Dave parked a block away to bide their time. It gave Bruce a chance to search the address. His research gave him Susan's full name, which sent him back to Facebook. "Finally. It seems this lady, at least, has some kind of life." He scrolled through dozens of pictures Susan had posted and found one of Katie. "Hah!" He yelled and pointed towards Susan's house, "This is Kathryn's aunt."

Susan Garrison had been eagerly waiting for the police and waved them inside as soon as she heard the doorbell. She'd tidied the living room and applied fresh makeup.

"We know your niece's disappearance is upsetting, but we have questions. It's easier to ask in person." Darrow and Hopkins quickly scanned the open floor plan.

Susan followed their line of sight. "She's not here. I promise."

She set out a plate of store-bought cookies. She'd zapped them in the microwave, making them as warm as the Cokes she'd pulled from the pantry. "I'm worried and scared. I love Katie as if she were my own daughter." She sank into the couch and gave background, "My sister and her husband both died when Katie was still in high school." She continued with details about Katie's life, the restaurant, and meeting Jack. "…and before I knew it, they'd flown to Vegas and gotten married."

Darrow took careful notes while Hopkins asked the questions. "When did you last see Katie? When did she call you? Did you hear anything odd in her voice? What can you tell us about her relationship with Jack?"

"Is he a suspect?" Susan's voice grew louder, "Tell me what you know."

"We have no suspects. We're just following leads," Darrow answered smoothly.

Susan let out a sigh. "Well, we never talked much about her marriage or Jack."

Aunt Susan told them Jack had called the day before. "He never calls unless Katie is here. And even then, he hardly ever lets her visit." Susan gave away other tidbits. "He watches her phone, makes her keep our calls to under thirty minutes. I'm tellin' ya'll, he's done something to her." Susan stood to pace the room.

Hopkins pounced on the statement. "Did you ever see evidence that Jack hurt Katie?"

Susan frowned. "No, it's just a feeling I have. I don't think things have been good between them for a long time."

"How about Katie's friends?" Darrow asked.

"Once she got to Savannah, she didn't seem to have any friends Jack approved of--at least none I can recall." Susan silently congratulated herself on her wording.

"Does she have a good relationship with her in-laws, Fred and Sylvia Werner?" Darrow asked.

"Jack never introduced Katie to his parents." Susan shook her head, obviously disapproving of yet another thing about Jack. "Katie found them on her own, drove to their house and met them a few times. Other than that, I couldn't say."

Hopkins joined the questioning, "Do you think there could be another man in her life?"

"Goodness, no! The only other man she loves is Mr. Parker," Susan paused, anticipating their reaction.

Both officers looked up quickly. "Mr. Parker?"

Susan laughed, "Yes, he's eighty-three and has Alzheimer's. Katie adores him."

The officers frowned simultaneously.

Darrow scanned his notes. "Orphaned during high school. No known friends." He'd scribbled in the name *City Palette* once Susan recalled the name of the restaurant where Katie had been a waitress. He'd circled a sentence about Jack's parents with a question mark behind it. *If she'd gone there on her own already, maybe she'd do it again.* He wrote Jack's name off to the side, added the word controlling, and underlined it twice.

Both men gave Susan their cards and made her promise to call if she remembered anything else, or if Katie contacted her in any way.

Darrow drove well above the speed limit, while Hopkins called the station. He put the phone on speaker, so they could both hear the results of the interviews with Katie's clients, her employer, and neighbors. The story never changed. Katie was well-loved and still very much missing.

Meanwhile, the reporter sat in Susan's living room, gobbling up the leftover cookies. Bruce had no trouble expanding the picture Susan painted. The hints were juicy, and he asked questions as his partner filmed. The camera zoomed in on Susan's craggy face and caught the glint of tears as she made an emotional plea, inviting anyone to come forward with information.

Bruce hopped back in the van, already talking to Dave, "We've got a chance to make the ten o'clock news. Think we can shoot down into Atlanta and get some video of the apartment? The restaurant? It's a hell of a story."

His partner eyed his watch and nodded.

Once there, Dave filmed the old brick restaurant. Apartments were housed overhead, with rickety fire escapes clinging to the side. Dave adjusted filters to show the shadows, leaving little doubt this area of the city was not experiencing a re-birth.

Bruce was ecstatic to find out about Renae, who'd worked with Katie years before. He set up a quick interview.

Renae cried when they asked if she'd heard from Katie. "Not in years. Once Katie got married, the calls came less and less." Renae was all too happy to tell them about the whirlwind romance, and Vegas wedding. "I told Katie it was too fast."

Bruce and Dave hurried out to get footage of Katie's old neighborhood. Daylight was fading, making the crowded buildings and streets seem dingier. They filmed an abandoned car sitting on blocks, trash cans overflowing, and people of varying colors hanging out on corners.

"Talk about your Cinderella story," Dave said as they raced back to Savannah.

"There's no way Katherine Werner just walked away." Bruce edited and uploaded his notes and the video. This story was a thing of beauty, and he had an exclusive.

Chapter 36

By 9:33 p.m., six people crowded into the tiny conference room at the police station. The smell of stale coffee and sweat permeated the air. Chief Greer scribbled notes and columns across the top of the whiteboard anchored across one full wall. *Facts. Interviews. Ideas?* "We need to work this case, people."

Hopkins read the columns and nodded. He took the pen out of Greer's hand and filled in the blanks:

Time of disappearance approx. 9 am Friday Cooper Medical Complex

Car in the lot, no other fingerprints except the husband.

Wallet and phone found in the trash

"Jenkins, you get anything on the credit cards? Banking?" Hopkins stood poised, ready to write down the latest information.

Jenkins read his report, "Nothing new on the credit card. Katie isn't even listed as a co-owner of the card. She has a debit card only. She withdrew five-hundred dollars from their checking account yesterday. The husband, Jack, says the amount matches their regular payday withdrawal. There is, however," Jenkins hesitated for effect, "one other savings account in Kathryn's name only."

Hopkins spun towards Jenkins. To date, Katie had nothing in her name, not the cars or house. "Where?"

"First Bank of Atlanta"

"Activity?"

"A few small deposits here and there. One transaction pending yesterday. Nothing else for weeks."

"So, what happened yesterday?" Hopkins asked, clearly annoyed.

"Well, that's the shit of it. Being Saturday, it shows pending. Nothing else."

Hopkins created a new column--*To Do* and wrote *Savings account for Katie* underneath the header.

Greer took center stage, again, "Jenkins, I want you monitoring those accounts every hour."

Jenkin's rolled his eyes at the room. "Yes, sir. I won't be able to do much 'til Monday, but I'll keep looking."

Hopkins addressed the next item. "Life insurance?"

"There's a half-million-dollar policy on Jack one small policy on Katie—just ten thousand."

"Shit. Living in one of those old houses on Forsyth Park, I figured we'd follow the money." He rubbed away a growing headache. "How about phone records?"

"There were no calls made by Katie yesterday. She did, however," Jenkins rolled his eyes again. "receive seventeen calls from Jack."

"Seventeen? He made seventeen calls to her?"

"Yep, one right after another. He's fuckin' obsessive." Jenkins flushed. "Sorry."

"You're not saying anything we're not thinking."

"He made four other calls. One to his workplace, one to Katie's employer, the aunt, and the TV station."

"Okay. Tell me about the neighbors. Who canvassed them?"

A young black woman, who Hopkins didn't recognize, raised her hand.

"And you are?" He turned his head sideways, listening intently.

"Thomas, Sir. Jayla Thomas." She stated clearly and with a fair amount of pride.

"Ok, Thomas, what'd you learn?"

"Nobody saw anything unusual. No one seems to know Jack well. He waves and socializes occasionally, but generally keeps to himself. Katie is well-liked. Their next-door neighbor, Mrs. Donohue, says Jack helps her from time to time but is convinced

Jack mistreats Katie. The lady said she "notices" things." Jayla bracketed her fingers in the air, emphasizing the word notices. "Anyway, she claims to have witnessed bruises, and a little slap a few months ago."

Jenkins interrupted, "I checked local hospitals. There's nothing. Zilch. Nada for a Kathryn Werner or Jane Doe for Friday or Saturday."

Thomas pressed her point, "We should consider previous medical records."

Hopkins wrote it on the whiteboard

Darrow stepped in to handle the next part. "How about work? Who talked to the boss?"

Randy Fairchild, who was anything but with his dark hair and roly-poly body, spoke up, "Cheyenne McMathews is the supervisor at Comfort Keepers. Katie's worked there for four years. Always on time. Clients love her. The boss stated the husband called yesterday. He also drives by the office occasionally. I didn't get the impression McMathews cared for him. She said Katie tended to look drained on Mondays. I pushed to get more detail, but she didn't have anything to add. I got a list of Katie's patients from McMathews and tracked them down." Fairchild thumbed through his notes.

"Talked to Mrs. Gertrude Taylor. She thinks Katie's a saint. She didn't like Jack, who stopped by yesterday. Talked to Mr. Reginald Parker, the man's got dementia. Bad. He smiled at Katie's name but never said a word. His niece, Nina Parker, says Katie is a godsend. Amanda Stokely said she and Katie were just ending their sessions, but that Katie is an excellent caregiver and always pleasant. She clearly didn't care for Jack either, after he stopped there yesterday, too. She has no ideas as to Katie's whereabouts.

"The Morrisons—Bob and Julie—hired Katie for six months as an in-home assistant for their daughter, Cassandra. They lost their daughter last year and were still pretty broken up over her death. Bob and Julie couldn't say enough nice things about Katie. They even pulled out pictures of Katie and Cassie together."

The room grew quiet as the officers took in the last sentence.

Randy continued, "I met with a few other clients Katie had visited over the summer. They were all temporary gigs, and none of them have seen or heard from Katie."

Hopkins scrubbed at his face and glared at the room. "What are we missing?"

Darrow stood to add more detail. "Hopkins and I talked to the aunt, Susan Garrison. She made a few insinuations about Jack too. Otherwise? Nothing."

Hopkins remembered another angle. "Get in touch with the in-laws." He gave the order to the room at large. Hitting the table with his hand, he yelled, "No one walks into a doctor's office and simply vanishes."

Greer flashed him a smile, appreciating the fist to the table move.

Jenkins muttered into his lap. "The only one acting weird is the husband."

All heads nodded.

"Okay, so we agree the husband is obsessive, but is he our only suspect?" Hopkins ticked events off on his fingers, "Jack makes an insane amount of phone calls trying to find her. He goes to the doctor's office, the lab, and the mammogram department. He goes to see all her clients and even manages to get the story on TV. He has the life insurance and the banking accounts--not her. He doesn't act like a guy who harmed his wife."

"Maybe he's covering his tracks?" Jenkins asked

"Maybe she left him," Thomas offered.

"What else do we have? What does that leave?"

Jenkins chimed in, "The cab company? I watched the video you sent twice today. I got the supervisor on the phone, but he was vague. He said he was at home and didn't have the routes in front of him. He made noises about requiring a warrant due to privacy issues."

Hopkins wrote *cab company* on the board too. "We need more information." He pointed to the board. "Jenkins start adding to the warrant reports. Get the DA back on the phone. We need access to all medical records." He paused, made eye contact with the female officer, and snapped his fingers twice. Remembering her name, he yelled out, "Thomas. Help him get that as soon as possible, and report to Darrow."

Jayla smiled, pleased he'd remembered her name.

Jenkins scribbled and nodded.

"Ten o'clock news is on," Fairchild announced, and they turned as a group toward the tv. Mouths opened, and eyes widened at the breaking news story and the additional details concerning Kathryn Werner.

"How the hell did they get those interviews?" Greer shouted and spun around to glare at Hopkins.

Hopkins' ears turned a bright shade of red. "We must have been followed."

They all quieted down to watch the broadcast

Katie was glued to the TV, too.

The reporter recapped the earlier story showing the medical center, her car, the wallet. Added information rolled, and Katie watched footage of her old apartment move across the screen. She swallowed twice when the interviewer asked Renae questions, but when Aunt Susan's face filled the screen, Katie's frame folded in on itself. She perched limply on the bed, concentrating on every word. Her hands covered her mouth, and tears slipped down her cheeks as Aunt Susan made eye contact with the camera.

"She's exceptional. Please, if you've seen her or something suspicious, call the police. Katie, wherever you are, I love you. Stay safe."

Katie reached toward the screen, laying her palm against Aunt Susan's face--making invisible contact. Katie rocked herself, fully understanding she couldn't call or see Susan for a very long time.

After the broadcast, Darrow shrugged. "Well, they did some groundwork for us."

Thomas spoke up, "What the aunt said about Katie staying safe seems odd, doesn't it?" She narrowed her eyes, thinking it through.

A whole new discussion with Jack being the prime suspect started up again.

Thomas stood with hands on her hips. "I still say Katie left. If Jack's as big an asshole as everyone is saying, I sure as hell wouldn't stick around."

Hopkins didn't argue. "Jenkins call the D.A. and add the cab company and medical records to the warrants. I want the rest of you back here by 8 a.m. sharp. We can't do anything else tonight."

Jenkins saluted smartly and picked up the phone.

Chapter 37

The investigative team shuffled into the precinct office Sunday morning, heading for coffee and their own cubicles. Thanks to the warrants, new information was tricking in through downloads and attachments.

Thomas commandeered a corner cubby to access medical records, and, hopefully, get Katie's doctor on the phone.

Fairchild and Jenkins—an utterly opposite mix; one short, one tall, one brown, one neon white-- looked at banking in more depth. Unfortunately, the bank servers were all updating before the workweek began, and they couldn't access a thing. Hopkins and Darrow drove off to see the owner of the Red Cab Deluxe company.

The morning segment of *Savannah Live* aired the Kathryn Werner story, and Katie groaned aloud when her picture flashed on the screen.

WSVA, the station which had first aired Katie's disappearance, had pulled their best investigative reporter, Lindsey Shepard, into the mix. The waspish woman was notorious for alluding to the suspicions police and lawyers couldn't express. She raised her voice, made subtle references, and demanded resolution. "Where is Kathryn Werner?"

"Shit." Katie watched Lindsey's eyebrows do calisthenics across her forehead and worried the disappearance was turning into a bigger story than she'd ever intended.

She hoped her quasi-disguise was enough to fool the public, the police, and an overly interested Chad. She had more reason than ever to buy the truck today and get herself out of town.

Katie called the local cab company and watched the clock, needing to be done with this next phase before Chad came back on duty. His interest in her could potentially ruin her plan.

Katie was at the motel curb when the cab pulled up at nine. She hopped into the back of the car and rattled off the address. Looking out the window, she noticed an apartment complex along the route. With bright red flags fluttering in the breeze, a sign advertised, "Furnished Studio for rent. Immediate occupancy." She scribbled the name on a scrap piece of paper. *This could be the icing on the cake.*

The driver slowed as he turned into a quiet street with a row of ranch houses.

Katie yelled from the back seat, "No! Don't stop. Go around the block."

The cabbie looked in the rear-view mirror, confused.

"Sorry. I'm trying to buy a truck. If the owner sees me get out of a cab, he'll know how much I need it and want more money."

The cabbie gave a half-smile. "Can't look desperate, right?"

"Exactly, even though I am," she confessed.

The cabbie gave her a conspirator's wink.

"There's a spot. Park there. I'll walk back and see if I can make a deal. Can you wait?"

The driver nodded and yelled out last-minute encouragement, "Good luck!"

Darrow and Hopkins pulled into the Red Deluxe Cab Company parking lot just after 9 a.m. They were directed to a corner office, tucked as an afterthought into the garage. The owner, Caleb Robinski, ambled in, shoving papers off chairs and gesturing the officers toward the seats.

He listened to their story, nodding when they got to the missing woman. "I saw something about that on the news. What's it got to do with Red Cab Deluxe or me?"

"Two of your cabs showed up at Cooper Medical Complex yesterday. We need information on those pickups."

Caleb rubbed his stubble-covered chin. "I'd have to go look those up, but it seems to me there may be some privacy issues." He stayed stubbornly in his chair, not accessing the computer, and certainly not looking through any paperwork.

Detective Darrow sighed and pulled out the judge's orders. "We got a warrant."

It was all legal, but Caleb took his time reading the order, enjoying their annoyance.

Hopkins had had enough. "It's in order. You can see we've covered the bases. A woman is missing. Pull up the damn records." He narrowed his eyes, took out his notebook, and wrote down Caleb's name. He leaned across Darrow to see the cheap brass nameplate to ensure he spelled Robinski correctly.

Caleb got the message and scrolled through reports on his computer. "Here we go. Two calls to Cooper Medical. Denny picked up a client. Tom waited, but no one came out, so he left."

"And where did Denny go with this customer? Was it a man? Woman?"

"957 Hidden Lake Court." Caleb frowned. "I have no idea where that is. Twenty-five- dollar fare, though, so it was a long ride." He stood up abruptly and opened his door, yelling out to the garage, "Is Denny here?"

One driver answered, "Yeah, I saw him by the coffee machine."

"Get him in here!" Caleb slammed the door.

Hopkins nodded his approval. "So, two calls, but only one fare?"

"Yeah. Denny will know more." Caleb drummed his fingers, anxious to get the cops out of his office as fast as possible.

Their cruiser in the parking lot wasn't doing him any favors. He looked out the window and cussed, "Goddammit! The news people followed you." He pulled the curtain closed.

Darrow shrugged. "Bound to happen, everyone's trying to find this woman."

Hopkins pulled out his phone and typed in the address Caleb supplied.

Katie was talking with the truck owner. He'd been waiting just inside the door when she knocked. "Are you Anne, the woman who called?"

Katie nodded.

"I didn't see you pull in. Where's your car?"

"Oh, I got a ride from my brother. He'll be right back. You're Rob?"

He nodded moved toward the truck, not paying attention to her answer. He already saw dollar signs. Katie walked around the vehicle, running her hand along the frame where rust peeked through. She frowned and leaned back to get a better look at the bashed-in passenger door. "This is more than a ding, Rob."

"Well, I did have a fella hit me months ago. Neither of us wanted to fight over the insurance and deductibles. I mean, the truck's twelve years old."

"That's what I'm worried about."

"It runs great. Tires are in decent shape." He kicked one for emphasis.

Mirroring Rob, Katie kicked the tires too, sucking in her breath over her jammed toe. To cover herself, she bent down to look under the truck for fluids—a tip she'd read on Kelly Blue Book, yesterday.

Rob dug in the glove box, pulling out receipts for oil changes and the tires he'd purchased three years prior.

Katie crouched to look at the tires again, running her hands across the tread. "How many miles are on these?"

"A little under twenty-four thousand," Rob mumbled low under his breath.

"I don't know, Rob. I'm afraid it's too old and banged up." She eyed the rust around the wheel wells. "And there's what? A year left on these tires? It makes me nervous."

Rob waxed poetic about the truck, "I loved this truck. In fact, I bought a newer one just like it." He pointed at a new silver Durango in the driveway. He started the older truck, revving the engine for emphasis.

"Can we take it for a test drive?"

Denny opened the door to Caleb's office, pushing his skinny frame through. "You want to see me?"

Hopkins took over. "You had a rider yesterday--a pick-up from Cooper Medical. Went a long way. Hidden Lake Court?"

"I remember. The lady said her car had broken down, and she needed to get home."

Darrow took abbreviated notes.

"Can you describe her?" Hopkins demanded

Denny didn't answer right away.

"A lady disappeared from Cooper Medical Center yesterday. It may have been your rider. Anything you can give us will help." Darrow smiled to disarm Denny.

"The one on the news?" Denny perked up. He could work this angle, maybe even get on the news himself. He suddenly remembered all sorts of details. "She didn't say much, kinda stayed slumped in the back. I figured she was pissed about the car. She had on nice clothes--white shirt and black pants."

"Can you remember anything else about her appearance?

"White lady, maybe thirty years old. She wore glasses. Her hair was pulled back tight in one of those ponytail things—blond, maybe." He glanced off to his right, trying to remember more.

Darrow and Hopkins gave each other questioning looks.

Denny rambled on, not noticing. "Decent enough neighborhood, but took some time getting there. Traffic was heavy. She paid cash, which was good. She even said thank you. Most people don't give a rat's ass. Don't even so much as say goodbye."

"Did she go inside? It was a house, right?" Hopkins asked.

"Yeah, one of those older ones with a big porch and lots of windows on top. What do they call those things? Dormers, that's it." Pleased with his vocabulary, Denny kept talking, "I kinda watched her in the mirror for a few seconds. Not a bad looking woman. Ya know how it is." He had the good grace to blush.

"But did she go inside?" Hopkins leaned forward, pushing for information.

"I'm not sure. I wanted to get back to the city. She walked right up the sidewalk and headed for the porch. Seemed like it was familiar. After that, I turned the corner and was gone."

Hopkins and Darrow stood.

"Thanks."

"You've been a big help."

"You think it's the missing lady?" Denny asked.

"Maybe." Darrow shook Denny's hand. Hopkins was already halfway across the garage, phone out, calling the station. As the detectives exited the building, two reporters yelled out questions. "Did Katie take a cab? Is there evidence of a possible kidnapping?"

Darrow and Hopkins answered in unison. "No comment."

Denny waited until the cops were gone and sauntered out, ready to share his story.

Chapter 38

Hopkins finally got through to Fairchild and had him on the phone. "I want you to go see Jack. I want a new face, another police officer, putting pressure on him."

"I'm already on my way. Greer had the same idea."

Hopkins gestured to Darrow to drive and dialed Jenkins next. "Add this new stuff to the whiteboard: Cab driver Denny, possible appearance changes for Kathryn, 957 Hidden Lake Court."

Darrow purposely took a few wrong turns. Hopkins raised his eyebrows at the missed directions.

"News. Watching for news vans," Darrow mouthed.

Hopkins nodded and let Darrow handle the navigation.

Katie and Rob drove the truck around the block, and she tensed as they passed the still waiting taxi, but Rob didn't notice. She covered herself by flipping on turn signals, the wipers, radio, and the air conditioner. The last one was a necessary feature in Savannah, particularly today, with the temperatures already teasing ninety.

When she tested the turning radius and brakes, there was a strange sound. Katie whipped her head toward Rob. "What's that noise?"

"It hasn't been driven in a while. The brakes are just a little stiff," Rob assured her.

"And the vibration I feel in the steering wheel?"

Rob shrugged. "Same thing. It's just reacting to the brakes."

Katie wasn't so sure and looked at Rob suspiciously.

"You drive it every day, all those things will disappear. We ain't driven this thing in over three weeks--ever since we got the new truck."

As Katie drove back to Rob's house, the vibration and noise stopped. She needed this truck badly and had to believe Rob. "Would you take fifteen-hundred?"

Rob acted offended, "No way. I've had three other calls this morning. Maybe eighteen-fifty."

"Fifty dollars? Come on, Rob. There's got to be more wiggle room here."

"Eighteen-hundred." He sounded less sure.

"I'll give you seventeen-hundred. Cash. Right now."

"Eighteen-hundred." Rob reiterated.

"Nope. Seventeen-hundred cash. That's my best offer."

When he hesitated, Katie put the truck in park, opened the driver's door and climbed down. Rob popped his door open and ran around the hood. "Okay, I'll take your offer. I'll get the title, and we'll do the deal."

Katie jogged back to the cabbie. "I bought myself a truck!" She stunned him with her full smile. Katie paid the ten-dollar fare, and feeling magnanimous, threw in a five-dollar tip.

With the light Sunday traffic, Hopkins and Darrow made good time and pulled up to the house on Hidden Lake Court at 9:45. The street was filled with similar Sears Catalog homes from the 1940's—cottages with asphalt siding and scorched lawns.

They climbed the wide porch stairs and rang the doorbell twice. When there was no answer, Hopkins walked the perimeter while Darrow peeked in the garage. "One vehicle inside, but it's got a dust cover draped over the whole thing."

The officers split up and began knocking on doors. No one seemed to be home. At the sixth house, a woman, still wearing her robe, answered. "That's the Lockheed's place," she told

Hopkins. "They're on vacation. Somewhere down in the Florida Keys."

Hopkins wiped his sweaty face and radioed Darrow.

Hopkins asked the woman rapid questions. "Have you noticed anything unusual? Any strangers coming and going?"

The woman squinted. "No. Me and my husband, Paul, have been getting their mail and picking up the newspapers. Paul took their garbage out a week ago, Friday. Why?"

Darrow jogged up the porch steps and joined them at the door. He introduced himself, "Officer Darrow, and you are?"

"Ruby Smythe."

"Well, Mrs. Smythe, we've had a report of a stranger on their porch and wanted to check it out." Darrow didn't mention Katie, the cab, or that they were out of their jurisdiction. Hopkins didn't correct the oversight, either.

Ruby pushed open her door and angled her head toward the house as though she would see the stranger lurking in the bushes.

Darrow smoothed her anxiety, "Don't worry, ma'am. We've checked the windows, the doors, and even the garage. The house is secure."

Hopkins nodded. "But keep an extra eye out if you would."

Ruby nodded vigorously. As she watched the officers walk away, she was already punching in the number to call her husband at work. She eyed Nettie Paulzer's house across the road. Ruby couldn't wait to call her too.

Darrow and Hopkins cruised the neighborhood aimlessly. "Why'd Katie come here?"

Rob handed Katie the certified odometer form and title, jingling the keys toward her face. "It's all yours."

Having never seen a title, Katie turned it over, carefully reading the fine print on the back. "Oh, wait. It says you should have a witness for your signature. Is anyone else home?"

Rob's wife came out and quickly signed her name. Rob took off the plates and fixed a hand-made temporary tag in place.

"What if the police stop me?" Katie fretted

"As long as you have the title, you'll be okay. I wouldn't wait long to get new plates, though." Rob and his wife headed inside, absently waving goodbye and eager to spend their cash.

Chapter 39

As Katie accepted the signed title, Darrow and Hopkins drove through the business area near Hidden Lake. Spotting a First Bank of Atlanta branch, Hopkins pointed at the building through the car window. "Coincidence?"

Darrow shook his head. "Not likely." Darrow eyed the area and pulled into the nearby Motel 6.

The young clerk studied Katie's photo and nodded. "The face looks familiar. But the hair's wrong. She was wearing glasses too, so it's hard to say."

The information matched the cab driver's description, and both officers leaned in closer. The hotel clerk pulled the register. "Here it is. Patty Stanford."

Hopkins made an immediate phone call to Fairchild. "You with Jack?"

"Yes. We're going through the story again."

"How is he?"

"Not good."

"Jack's standing right there, isn't he?"

"Yep." Fairchild took a step back from Jack, who was eavesdropping.

Staying cryptic, Hopkins asked one-worded questions: "Upset?"

"A little."

"Angry?"

"Definitely."

"Good. Ask Jack if he or Katie know anyone who lives in Middleburg? Family members or clients at 957 Hidden Lake Court?"

Fairchild lowered the phone. Hopkins stayed on the line, listening as Fairchild relayed the questions to Jack.

"No. I've never heard of Hidden Lake Court." Jack's voice crept up an octave, "Why?"

"Possible sighting out in Middleburg."

"I have no idea." Jack's lips thinned. "Where'd you say it was?"

Fairchild rattled off the address again.

Jack committed the answer to memory. *I'm coming, Katie.*

Fairchild turned his attention back to the phone, "Sorry, Lieutenant, but Jack says he's never heard of the address."

Hopkins offered another piece of information, interested to hear how Jack reacted, "We've also got a possible check-in at a motel. Ask Jack if he knows a Patty Stanford? A woman, kind of matching Katie's appearance, checked into a Motel 6 here on Friday."

Fairchild ran his hands through his unruly hair, already dreading Jack's response.

"What the hell? We don't know anyone by that name." Jack's ears turned red at the thought of Katie with another man at some sleazy motel.

Katie drove off in her new truck, free and happy until she noticed the gas tank light. "Crap. I didn't think to look at that." She stopped at a gas station near the highway and ran inside for a bottled water as well. "There goes another forty-one dollars." Checking the time, she headed toward the post office in Fleming. From this end of Savannah, it was less than fifteen minutes away.

Darrow and Hopkins drove to the local police precinct. The Middleburg officers had no reports of suspicious activity but were able to corroborate the name of the owners of the house on

Hidden Lake Court. "Couple by the name of Stan and Lou Lockheed."

The Middletown cops agreed to contact the homeowners and, in the meantime, share any footage from traffic surveillance cameras around Motel 6.

As it turned out, none of the cameras were operational. "Sorry, man," the officer assigned to work with Darrow and Hopkins admitted, "All the damn budget cuts mean we can't keep up with maintenance."

Hopkins and Darrow left the Midtown precinct, lobbing questions back and forth as they drove.

"Is she calling herself Patty?"

"Did she leave with someone? Coerced?"

"Why'd she come to Hidden Lake Court?

"Dammit!" Hopkins slapped the dash.

Jack peeled out of the driveway and headed south, unaware Fairchild had only gone a block and was watching the house. Fairchild called Hopkins, "Looks like Jack's heading your direction."

Katie emptied the PO box for the last time. All of Cassie's documents, the evidence against Jack, and her research were intact. Blowing out a breath, she tapped the papers together. "I hope this works."

Hopkins and Darrow drove back to Hidden Lake Court. They were parking by the curb when Jack drove past. Three pairs of eyes stared at one another.

Darrow turned to Hopkins. "If Jack did something to Katie, why would he drive here?"

"It's screwed up. I can't tell if there's been foul play or not. Did Jack hurt her, or kill her in a fit of rage? Come here to throw us off track?

"No way. We got cameras showing Katie walking into the medical center. Some woman, I'm assuming it's Katie, took a cab out here."

"Shit, you're right." Hopkins rubbed his eyes. "I'm tired and not thinking straight."

"We need to review. Let's head back to the office."

Hopkins called Jenkins on the way. "Talk to me. Have you pulled the updated bank records?"

Jenkins scratched at his neck in frustration, "No. The servers are still down for maintenance. No transactions are showing. I can't see shit 'til tomorrow."

"Did Thomas find anything on the medical end?"

Jenkins and Thomas were sitting side by side, and Jenkins reached over to grab paperwork. "She just got hold of the Ob-Gyn. There's no other doctor listed in the file." Jenkins fumbled through papers and looked at Thomas for affirmation. She nodded.

Jenkins scratched his neck again, leaving long red marks. "Ob-Gyn does blood work and basic stuff. No other visits except for…" He trailed off, in his signature way of being dramatic.

"Get to the point!"

"Well," Jenkins continued, "there was one trip to the ER back in November of last year. Two broken ribs. Katie tripped and fell at a client's house." Papers rustled. "Here it is. She fell over some books and crashed into a desk at the Morrisons."

"Yeah. Sure, she did."

"There was the miscarriage and a broken front tooth earlier in the year. Says here Katie slipped on the icy porch."

"Probably bullshit as well. We're on our way back. I know we're missing something."

Jack drove the streets around Hidden Lake court—a predator, circling, and watching for prey. *Why here? Who the fuck was Patty Stanford?* Jack made the circuit again. Maybe something would jog his memory.

Back at the precinct, Hopkins paced in front of the whiteboard. Jenkins read previous dates of injury, and medical data while Darrow wrote down the details.

"Add the cab information, Hidden Court, and the Motel 6 from this morning," Hopkins directed while continuing to wear a path in the linoleum.

Officer Thomas entered the room, and the men eyed her fresh Starbucks coffee jealously. Jayla smiled and sipped slowly, enjoying her moment.

Darrow added notes about Katie's appearance change and stepped back to study the timeline. "Does she have a lover? Is she being blackmailed? Is Patty Stanford the same girl? Jenkins run that name through the computer."

"Nah." Hopkins shook his head. "I think Thomas is right, Katie wanted to get away."

Thomas agreed, "Can't blame her for that. I still say Jack's the key. Maybe he knocks her around? We've got a broken tooth, notable bruised, two busted up ribs. Maybe she's had enough, works out a plan to get out of town?"

Jenkins couldn't resist jumping into the conversation. "Maybe she was having an affair. You said she took a cab, changed her appearance. Then she ends up at a motel where she meets her lover, and they drive away in his car?"

Thomas offered another scenario, "Maybe Jack suspects something and follows her to the motel and offs his wife?"

"Then why would he drive back to the area? We saw Jack this morning--on Hidden Court, right Hopkins?" Darrow asked.

"Yeah, we did. He didn't seem to care if we saw him. Looked me dead in the eye. If he did something to Katie, he probably wouldn't go back to the scene."

Jenkins hung his head. "We've got no proof of anything."

Jack's eyes were scratchy, and his head was pounding. He couldn't put the pieces together. With his stomach complaining about a lack of food, Jack pulled into a convenience store. He bought an overcooked hot dog, and, on a whim, a pack of Marlboro cigarettes and one cheap lighter.

He'd never smoked in his life but hoped it would calm his nerves. Coughing and choking, he tossed the partially smoked cigarette on the ground, grinding it into the asphalt with enough force to disintegrate the filter.

Spying the Motel 6 down the block, Jack jogged toward the building and shoved his way into the dingy lobby. He yelled out questions before the door had a chance to close.

"Dude, I already answered the police questions." The young man leaned away from Jack.

Jack held up a picture of Katie. "This is my wife. She's missing. Do you understand? Did she check in here, or not?"

"Maybe. Same as I told them, it looks kinda like the lady who was here Friday."

"Was there anyone else with her?" Jack's eyes bulged. "Did you see her leave? Did she get in a car?"

The young man stammered, "I swear, I never saw her again."

Jack stared at the young man for a few seconds more, trying to intimidate him into saying more. When the clerk remained quiet, Jack slammed back out of the lobby, walking the perimeter of the motel.

He even opened the dumpster. No sign of Katie or any of her personal items surfaced. He went back to his car and sat in the parking lot, eyeing the motel and trying out another cigarette.

Chapter 40

Jack returned to Hidden Lake Court and noticed several neighbors had congregated in the street. After parking, he walked toward the group, waving as he approached. "Sorry to interrupt," he gestured toward the big empty house a few doors down, "but my wife is missing. She took a cab here yesterday, and I have no idea why. Did any of you see a woman around that house?" He made his voice shaky, "Please. Is there anything you can tell me?"

"Are you talking about the missing woman on the news? A fiftyish man asked.

When Jack nodded, the man leaned over to shake hands. "I'm Wayne."

The circle of neighbors opened to allow Jack access. "Well now, we'll get the story firsthand," Ruby Smythe said excitedly.

Jack asked more questions, "Do you know the people who live there? Did you see anything?"

"That's the Lockheed's place," Wayne supplied.

"They're in Florida. Don't see how they can afford a vacation," Nettie another older woman commented.

"The man drives a ratty car, and hardly ever mows the grass," Ruby added, going into gossip mode.

Jack rolled his head back on his neck. "We don't know the Lockheeds. Please, I need to find my wife."

The three re-focused on Jack's concerns.

The Middleburg police tracked down the Lockheeds, who were understandably distressed that a strange woman might be inside their home. "We have no idea why the woman would go to our house." They gave permission for the police to check their property.

News vans entered the street, having eventually wrangled the address from Denny, the cab driver. Seeing their cameras, Jack rushed back to his car and left before they could ask him any questions. They filmed his car speeding away.

Sharks smelling blood, reporters spilled into the street, eager to talk to the people in this neighborhood and get an angle on what had happened to Kathryn Werner. The news teams drew the attention of remaining neighbors who streamed out of houses eager to be a part of a story. Ruby and Nettie talked over one another, spitting out details as fast as their tongues could fly.

"That was the lady's husband," Nettie gushed, as she pointed at Jack's retreating car. Cameras swung to capture the action.

Ruby shot Nettie a withering look and elbowed her way forward.

The reporters were still in place when the local authorities pulled into the neighborhood. Cameras filmed the police inspecting the perimeter and entering through the front door.

When the officers exited the Lockheed's house, reporters shouted questions,

"Is there any sign of a break-in?"

"Did you find anything suspicious?"

"Is Kathryn Werner inside?"

Both officers shook their heads and drove away.

Just after eleven a.m., Katie parked her new truck in a remote corner of a nearby strip mall and walked back to the *City Manor Motel.*

Chad jogged out of the office, "Hey! Whatcha been up to?"

Katie mentally congratulated herself on hiding the truck. "I went to see a car with my brother this morning. It's not bad, but he wants us to sit on it a few days--see if the price comes down."

Chad nodded. "Nissan, right?" As predicted, he'd followed Katie's open link on Kelly Blue Book.

"Yep, a little older, but in pretty good shape, if I can ignore the rust by the back door."

"You should take me for a ride if you get it." Chad wiggled his eyebrows.

"Maybe. I at least owe you coffee since you let me use the computer."

Chad strutted beside her as they headed toward the lobby.

Katie fed a dollar into the vending machine. "Black or with cream?"

"Black."

She carried his coffee to his desk, passing the hot cup from hand to hand. The news was on in the background, and Chad angled his head to see the story.

Reporter, Lindsey Shepard, was in her element, demanding updates, "Where is Kathryn Werner? She didn't just walk away."

"You see this?" Chad asked.

"What?"

"The story about the woman who's missing?"

Katie froze, watching Chad out of the corner of one eye and the TV with the other.

All the stations in Savannah, even the tiny ones, were now carrying the story, and speculation was high. Reporters insinuated she'd married up, had a prestigious home, and a job she loved.

The broadcast switched to the interview with the cab driver.

Katie swallowed hard and made herself answer Chad,

"I saw something on the news last night." She stuck her face down in her purse, on the pretense of looking for more change.

"You look kind of like her," Chad commented, studying Katie more closely.

Katie pushed her glasses up on her nose. "Hardly. She's blond and beautiful."

"I think you're beautiful." Chad colored and added, "You've got the same green eyes."

"Lot's of people with green eyes, Chad." Katie clutched her purse tightly and pivoted on one foot, ready to bolt toward her truck if Chad pushed the issue.

Chad shrugged and turned back toward the TV. "The husband looks like a sleazebag. I say he did something to her."

Katie let out her breath and watched the repeat footage of Jack getting out of the back of the police cruiser. "You're right. He is creepy." Katie plopped quarters in the vending machine, needing coffee and caffeine for herself. Hot water sloshed down the shoot and splashed into the waiting cup, making her jump.

She switched topics, "Hey, I saw an apartment for rent today. Ashley Commons, on Harris Trail. Know anything about them?"

Chad frowned. "They're kinda old."

"I can't afford much until I get some regular paychecks, and hopefully a raise." Katie walked across the room, effectively taking Chad's attention away from the television. "I certainly can't stay here. I'll be broke in a week." Katie spun out the lie. She had no intention of moving into a nearby apartment.

"I get off at five. I could go with you and take a look."

Thinking ahead, Katie kept her options open, "Sounds good, but I think they'll be closed by then. I need to look at it this afternoon, but I'll keep you in the loop." She gave Chad a wink. "Maybe you could put in a good word for me?"

"Sure, I can." He'd cut off his left arm if she asked.

"Do you have a business card or something?"

Chad dug one out of the register drawer, and Katie hurried away.

Fifteen minutes later, Katie banged back into the motel office, talking to Chad immediately, "Well, the apartment manager can show it to me today at twelve-fifteen, but I can't get ahold of my brother. Is there a local cab company?"

"A cab?" Chad's forehead creased. "You can't go over there in a cab."

"I don't have a choice until I get a car." Katie plopped down on a hard, plastic chair and adjusted her shorts. "The manager said he has two other showings today," Katie whined as she ran her hands up and down bare thighs.

Chad followed the movement. "You could take my car."

"I couldn't. That's too much." Katie feigned surprise despite the fact she'd been hoping for such an offer. She couldn't let Chad see her truck, and the apartment manager needed to remember her in a different vehicle, as well. It wasn't much, but she hoped the little deceptions would help hide her real intentions.

They argued back and forth until Chad pressed his keys into Katie's hand. "I insist."

Jack was home well before noon. He poured a drink and stood in living room nursing the Jameson as he watched the latest news broadcast featuring footage of his car racing away. *Shit.* All eyes were on him.

The Savannah officers hunkered around the TV in the conference room watching the noon news, too. Most of it was repeat information except for Jack Werner racing away from the house in Middleburg.

"There's nothing else we can do until tomorrow," Darrow announced firmly. He had a suspicion Hopkins would stay all day picking through each minute detail.

Chapter 41

Katie drove through the cracked parking lot of Ashley Commons and entered the rental office right on time. The manager wiped the remnants of his greasy lunch onto his pants and offered a limp handshake. "You here to see the studio?"

At Katie's nod, he lumbered to a cabinet and pulled out a set of keys. "Follow me." He didn't bother to hold the door for Katie. "Had several people looking at this unit."

She rolled her eyes behind his back, recognizing a sales job when she heard one.

The apartment was dated, but not horrible. A tiny table and two chairs crouched in the kitchen, while a lumpy couch shared the living room with a cheap set of end tables.

"Wow. This is considered furnished?"

"It doesn't take much to fill a one-bedroom place."

"True. How about the bedroom?" Katie peeked inside. "No furniture?"

"We've found people prefer their own mattress and box spring." The manager continued in a conspiratorial voice, "You never know what's happened in a bed."

Katie took a step backward. "How much is the rent?"

"Five-hundred, including water and trash. We require a two-hundred-dollar deposit, and the first and last month's rent would be due this Friday, provided the background check is clear." The manager stuck his left index finger into his ear and then examined it for treasure.

Disgusted, Katie turned away, talking over her shoulder, "I just got a full-time job at First Bank of Atlanta."

The manager wiped his finger on his shirt. "You got anyone to verify that? It *is* Sunday."

Katie handed over the four business cards she'd picked up at both bank locations: Branch Supervisor, Angela, who'd grilled her on the security questions, James, the finance consultant, and tellers Bethany and Alicia. Katie pointed at Angela's card, "She's the boss."

The manager noted the same bank, the same logo. Katie hoped it was convincing enough. He frowned, trying to decide. "Is there anyone we can call now?"

She handed over Chad's card. "Well, this is where I'm staying. It's across from the bank branch here in town, where I'll be working." She injected pride in her statement, praying it would be enough to convince this man. Katie tapped Chad's name. "He already confirmed my employment when I rented a room." Katie held her breath.

The manager squinted, rubbed his chin, and slowly shook his head. "I don't know."

Desperate, Katie let her purse fall open where her cash was visible.

The manager noticed the stack of bills. "Let me make a call. I think we can work this out." He really didn't care. The deposit was non-refundable. If she didn't stay, or couldn't pay, he'd start over and be fine.

"Today? Can we work it out today?" Katie needed this to fall into place. An address was vital to her plan.

"Yeah, if he can verify the job." He took out his phone, dialing Chad's number.

"City Manor Motel," Katie heard Chad answer.

"This is the Manager of Ashley Commons. Got a young lady here, goes by Anne Morrison. She says someone named Chad Richardson can verify she works at The First Bank of Atlanta?"

Chad swallowed once before giving an answer that wasn't quite a lie. "Yeah, she's staying here until she finds her own place. I can verify that."

The manager smiled. "Thanks. I'll keep your card as a reference."

Katie, eager to avoid more questions, announced, "I'll take it! For six months, anyway, then maybe I can move up to something bigger." When Katie pulled crisp green bills out of her purse, it sealed the deal for a man used to receiving bounced checks. Katie filled out the application form and handed over Cassie's Social Security card.

The manager scowled. "You said your name was Anne. This says, Cassandra."

"My middle name is Anne." Katie pointed to the social security card, proving her point. "I don't go by Cassandra."

The manager shrugged and logged into the computer to start the preliminary background check. He frowned at the credit number. "This shows you've only got a six-hundred score."

"No kidding. I don't have any credit." She opened her wallet, "See? No credit cards."

The manager scrolled to the next credit report page, saw no overdue bills, or delinquent payments. "You'll be paying the entire amount on Friday, right?" He raised his eyebrows, waiting for confirmation.

When Katie nodded enthusiastically, he filled out the lease agreement, stamped the date and handed it to Katie with the receipt of deposit. This was the last piece of the puzzle before she could move on to her final destination--an address different than the Morrison's.

Katie shook his slimy hand; grateful she'd never see him again. She sped out of the parking lot, ever conscience of time.

Making a quick stop at a CVS near the motel, she purchased a box of address labels and whiteout.

When Katie returned to the motel, she went straight to the lobby and laid Chad's keys on the counter.

He popped out of the back office. "How'd it go?"

"Thanks to you, I got the apartment!" She waved the lease papers at him.

"So, dinner?" Chad raised his eyebrows.

"Well, umm…" Katie slid away. "Sounds great, but maybe later this week? I need to call home. I'm so excited! I might have a car and a new apartment tomorrow. I owe you more than I can say." She gave Chad a long, hard hug, on purpose. "We'll practically be neighbors. Maybe I'll make you dinner at my new place, later in the week." She didn't wait for his reply and angled toward her room.

The hug and the idea of them alone in her apartment had the teasing edges of a fantasy forming. "I'll look forward to it," Chad called out, feeling good about his place in the world.

Katie let herself into her room and let out a whoop. "It's working!" She ate the rest of her food staples, leaving half a bag of trail mix and one breakfast bar for the morning. "Get to work, girl!"

Sitting at the kitchen counter, Katie began making alterations to her paperwork. First, she carefully changed the date on the lease from 9/8 to 8/8. Next, she pulled out her bank statements and compared the address section to the address labels she'd purchased. They didn't entirely cover, but it was close. *The whiteout should take care of the rest.*

Ten minutes later, Katie bounced back into the lobby. "Can I use the computer one more time, Chad?" Even though she hated to do it, she let her tank top slip, showing cleavage.

Chad naturally agreed and followed her inside the office.

Without even asking, she made a copy of the bank statements in case she messed up. "I want to make labels with my new address. I'll need them for work tomorrow" She sat at the computer, pulling up templates.

Chad didn't consider whether making labels made sense or not. He was angling for a better view of Katie's chest. The lobby bell rang, and Chad reluctantly turned away.

Katie printed out a sheet of labels with the Ashley Commons address. Spying Chad's gas bill mixed among the papers on his desk, she snatched it up and added it to her pile. *It might be just the insurance I need.* She waved at Chad, who was registering a new guest.

Back in her room, she carefully placed the printed labels over the address field of the bank statements. "Shit." The last page had gone on crooked. Pulling out the extra copies she'd made, she found the correct sheet and tried again. Her tongue stuck out a tiny bit as she carefully put it in place. "Whew! Got it!" She dabbed whiteout lightly at the few letters still showing on the side of each label, blowing on them and holding them up to the light. She did the same to Chad's gas bill.

"I need to make copies of these again, so the label doesn't show." *I can't keep using Chad's office.* She frowned until she remembered seeing a copy machine inside the door of CVS.

Avoiding Chad, she ducked around the back of the motel and beelined toward the pharmacy two blocks away. She made copies and then copies of the copies until the bank statements looked older, and the label was no longer visible.

Katie snuck back to her room and spread out all her paperwork. She piled Jack's bribery information on one pillow, and Cassie's documents on another. The last stack held the documents necessary for Katie's new life: truck title, lease agreement, and the data she'd compiled for White City, Florida. She'd memorized the information months before but poured over it once again. It had more significance since she was heading there tomorrow.

At five p.m., Katie turned on the news, anxious for updates.

Lindsey Shepard happily showed footage of the house where Katie had been dropped off by the cab driver. The reporter had done her research. "There is no connection between Kathryn Werner and the Lockheeds. Local authorities contacted them in Florida and verified the couple has never heard of or seen Kathryn Werner. No business dealings. No shared friends. No Christmas cards exchanged."

The screen flashed briefly to the officers exiting the house and shaking their heads, confirming there was no evidence of Kathryn having been there.

"Why would this well-loved woman end up at an unknown home in Mid-Savannah? Was she invited with a false claim?" Lindsey expounded on ideas and suspicions.

Katie fell back against her bed in disbelief. "I picked a house where no one was home?"

The constant news feed was problematic, though. A dull headache was building, and Katie massaged her temples. G*et the driver's license changed, Katie. It'll be all right.* To truly start over, she needed the license to show a new address. She needed to register the truck too. *An accident? A ticket? Everything would unravel.*

Jack sat in his chair, drinking whiskey and watching the news story, too. He dreaded going to work tomorrow and decided to call his boss, Barry.

"Good God, Jack. Did you find Katie? The story's all over the television."

"No, and I don't know what to do." Jack's voice broke, surprising them both.

"The police will figure it out soon. If you need time off, I understand."

Barry's response was unexpected, and, like everything else currently happening in his life, it threw Jack for a loop. "Thanks, but I think I'm better off working. I'm going crazy here. I wanted to run it by you first. I don't want a lot of questions. Hell, I don't know how to answer them anyway."

Barry considered the problem. Human nature would have the office workers gleefully discussing the details. "You're right. It's going to be a zoo at the office. Why don't you come in at ten instead of your regular start time? It'll give me a chance to have a meeting and calm down the troops."

Jack spent the rest of the evening, considering his next move in his search for Katie.

Katie fell into an exhausted sleep but woke with a start an hour later. She couldn't chance leaving the truck, with its temporary license plate, at the strip mall. She'd be towed. She relocated the vehicle to the street closest to the motel, and hauled her earlier purchases down the stairs, filling the passenger seat and floorboard. She'd done all she could.

If the police followed her route to Georgetown, they'd lose time looking for Anne Morrison, working at the bank, driving a Nissan Sentra, and leasing an apartment nearby.

Chapter 42

Katie rose early on Monday morning. She left the television off. Today was going to be tricky enough without the added stress of the news.

She showered, leaving her hair loose again. She put in her contacts and stowed the hated glasses. Scrubbing down the counters, and emptying the trash, she took one last look at the room to ensure she hadn't left any clues, even swiping the hotel notepad where she'd taken notes on the truck.

She headed out well before Chad was scheduled, driving aimlessly and munching on her leftover trail mix. Checking the time, she headed toward the driver's license bureau.

She chewed off one remaining fingernail as she drove, hoping she was making the right decision. She concluded, months before, it would be far easier to register a vehicle and change her driver's license in Georgia. If she waited until she got to Florida, she'd have to wait a minimum of thirty to sixty days to prove residency. That was too long to leave clues lying about in the open.

By 9 a.m., bank records were being downloaded at the police station. Jenkins poured over them, cursing under his breath because "The fricking internet is so slow." He drank his third cup of coffee and scowled at anyone who wandered past.

"I need to update my address," Katie announced as she handed over the driver's license showing Cassie's name and home address. She laid the lease and altered bank statements on the counter as well.

The woman glanced briefly at the license and then Katie. She verified the new address and scowled. "This lease is barely a month old, and the bank statement is only a few days old. Do you have any other proof of address?"

Katie dug in her purse, pulling out Chad's altered gas bill. "Here's a utility bill. Will that help?"

The clerk squinted at the earlier date and began typing.

Katie let out a relieved breath. "Can I register a title here too?

The clerk pointed to a door. "Go outside and down the sidewalk. It's the third door down." She leaned sideways and gestured the next person forward.

By nine-thirty Monday morning, officers were arranged around Jenkins. Fairchild rested a hip on a nearby desk and dribbled cookie crumbs all over his pants. Greer stood with his skinny arms folded menacingly across his chest. Rookie Thomas pushed her way forward.

"Anything?" Darrow asked.

Jenkins addressed the crowd, "The old savings account we found? She opened it up more than ten years ago. She never took it out of her maiden name and has been making small deposits to it for years, but a lot more in the last year. Our girl's got herself almost fifty-three-hundred dollars. Bet old Jack doesn't know about that." Jenkins smacked his lips in satisfaction. And…" Jenkins stopped to sip tepid coffee.

"Knock it off!" Greer and Hopkins yelled simultaneously.

Jenkins leaned back in his chair. "She emptied the whole damn thing Friday."

Katie waited behind four people, watching the clock and trying to stay calm. When her turn came, Katie handed over the $3.50 required for the clerk to go outside and copy down the VIN from her windshield. Katie paid out another $23.00 for the title transfer fee and concentrated on writing Cassandra Anne Morrison on the back of the new title.

"How do you want to pay the taxes?" the clerk asked Katie.

"Taxes? I thought that was only at dealerships."

"It starts over with each new purchase. It comes to one-hundred-nineteen dollars."

Katie handed over her precious cash. "Is this where I get the plates too?"

"No, you have to go back to the license bureau."

Katie let out a long sigh.

Jack squared his shoulders and walked toward his desk. Conversations stopped as his co-workers watched his progress. One brave soul walked over to shake his hand.

Darrow and Hopkins walked into the First Bank of Atlanta Branch in Middleburg just past ten a.m. They drew immediate attention when they asked to speak to Teller #103 and were ushered into a side office.

Teller Bethany entered the room, and Darrow briefed her on the situation.

Bethany listened with her eyes wide, and her mouth hanging open. "I sent her to Angela when she didn't have a license or debit card. We have to get supervisors involved when such situations happen." Bethany licked her lips several times. "I don't know anything else."

"Angela?" Darrow asked, waiting for clarification.

"Angela Krebs, Sir. She runs this branch."

Darrow and Hopkins paced the small room waiting for the supervisor.

Angela entered and took charge, "You have questions about Kathryn Follings?" Angela sat down and straightened her jacket, ready to conduct business. "I saw her on Friday morning."

"Finally," Hopkins huffed out a breath and sat down too.

Turning to a new page in his trusty notebook, Darrow asked questions, "So, the account was emptied? Completely closed?"

"Yes, Sir. It's unusual, so I remember it well. She had no driver's license, no other ID, so I took her through a list of security questions. She answered them correctly, her signature matched, so
we honored her request."

"How much money did she have?"

Angela started to protest, but Hopkins pushed the warrant across the table, tapping it once. Angela left to verify the amount. When she returned, she plunked a copy of the withdrawal slip onto the table. It showed $5254.28

Darrow and Hopkins made eye contact. The amount matched what Jenkins had found.

"Was there anyone else with her?"

"Not that I recall."

"Did she seem nervous or scared?"

Angela thought about the question. "Not scared. Nervous. She never quit talking."

"Any idea where she went?"

"I'm sorry, I don't. I had another client waiting."

"We'd like to watch the surveillance tapes from Friday morning."

All three trooped to a row of computers and watched Katie walk into the lobby. "White Shirt. Black pants. Just like the cabbie said," Darrow noted.

Hopkins agreed, "Yep. Hair pulled back. Glasses."

Darrow and Hopkins sat in their cruiser, outside the bank, mulling over the possibilities.

"This seems to be Katie's destination on Friday. She took a cab to a local neighborhood and walked up to a strange house."

"Setting a scene? Trying to throw us off?" Darrow asked.

"If so, it worked." Hopkins let out a sigh and picked up the thread of his thoughts. "She goes to the bank and removes all her money."

"She didn't seem to be under duress," Darrow added. "No one else was with her. The cameras show her walking out of the bank without even looking around."

Hopkins listed additional facts, "She goes to a motel and registers under a false name."

"Katie wanted to disappear."

"Probably, but we need to know for sure. Where'd she go? How'd she leave the area?"

Katie handed over the growing stack of documents and another $48.00 for license plates. She'd been at the license bureau for an hour and a half and was numb to time and money.

Finally done, she stood in the parking, holding her new license plates. She had no tools and was befuddled as to what to do next. A woman heading toward the driver's bureau saw Katie's deflated face and took pity. "I've got a wrench. I'll help you."

With the plates in place, and an enthusiastic thank you to the woman, Katie shoved the title and registration into the glove box. The truck made a grinding noise when Katie turned the key.

Assuming she'd tried to re-start an already running engine, Katie's face turned red. More eager than ever to get away from this place, she turned right and headed toward I-95. If she drove hard, she'd be in White City, Florida, in six hours.

Jack had been listening to the whispers floating around the office for almost an hour. His co-workers had found numerous reasons to walk past his office, gauging his demeanor. Jack walked out of his office and took in the group of cubicles, and the heads tilted together. One by one, they became aware of his staring at them, and the office grew eerily quiet.

"Look, I understand you all have questions, but things were fine Friday morning. "By noon, Katie was missing." He shoved away from the wall. "I don't know where she is. The police don't either. My being here doesn't mean I don't care."

He nodded a few times. "I can hear the things you're saying."

They looked guilty and glanced away.

"Staying home is making me nuts. I need to stay busy. Can you understand that?"

No one answered.

"I didn't do anything to my fucking wife!" Jack stomped to his office and slammed the door. The whispering resumed immediately.

The numbers on the report Jack was reading blurred together. *God damn bitch.*

Hopkins and Darrow drove aimlessly through the business area in Middleburg. "She doesn't seem to have an accomplice or lover," Darrow said randomly.

"She didn't have another car either, or why take the cab?"

"What are you thinking?"

Pointing at the bus stop blocks from the Motel 6, Hopkins replied, "I think she took a bus as far away as she could go."

Darrow nodded. It made sense. "Has she done anything wrong at this point?"

Hopkins pursed his lips. "No, except for the false name at the motel."

"Nothing wrong with leaving."

As Katie neared the highway ramp, the impact hit. She pulled over and rested her forehead against the steering wheel. "We did it, Cassie." Wiping away happy tears, Katie pulled into a Taco Bell to grab some lunch.

Darrow Googled bus routes while Hopkins ran to grab two coffees. Hopkins handed over one of the cups. "Anything?"

"Routes are circling the entire Savannah area with stops toward Georgetown, Isle of Hope, Montgomery, Garden City etcetera. She could have headed anywhere."

"Hmm." Hopkins pointed toward a Chevron gas station diagonal from the bus stop. "Think they have any cameras?"

"Why bother? She obviously left on her own."

"I wanna be sure."

Darrow and Hopkins walked into the gas station, and Hopkins pointed at the two cameras outside. "Do those cameras work?"

The clerk nodded.

"We need to call the local police again. We've got no authority here," Darrow reminded Hopkins.

When the assigned police officer from Middleburg arrived at the gas station, the group watched the video from Friday and saw nothing. "Load Saturday's tapes," Hopkins ordered.

"Is that her?" Darrow pointed at a woman on the screen.

"Zoom in!" Hopkins barked. The picture grew grainier, and Hopkins squinted. "Same build. Ponytail and glasses."

"Yep. She's changed her hair color and cut it too." Darrow noted the time and location.

The officers watched the footage closely. The woman kept her head down and boarded bus number 5621. The facial features matched the picture Jack had supplied.

"Ok. We've seen enough." Hopkins motioned Darrow and the local officer outside.

The Middleburg officer looked at his watch. "Are we done?"

Hopkins answered. "She didn't look coerced. There's no crime here."

As the officer turned to leave, Hopkins called out, "Hey, no use in saying anything to the press about this until we finish our report, right?" He waited, hoping to God the man got the point.

The officer nodded once. "Sounds good to me. This one's from your office, not ours."

Darrow waited until he was alone with Hopkins. "What gives?"

"I'm giving Katie more time. We tell Jack the bare basics—she left on a bus. Period. We write a thorough, time-consuming report and share those details with Jack later in the week. Katie gets another three or four days under her belt."

"You think Jack will do something?"

Hopkins shrugged, "I don't want what seems to be an escape becoming a crime scene."

Katie jumped back in the truck, ready to hit the highway. The engine made the grinding noise again, and Katie hung her head. "Dammit, Rob! You sold me a piece of crap, didn't you?"

Chapter 43

Katie had been driving an hour--singing to the radio and moving quickly down the highway. Glancing at the speedometer, she yipped, "Seventy-seven miles per hour!" She braked and frowned immediately. "What's that sound?" She stabbed off the radio, listening intently. The sound disappeared. The steering wheel vibrated a little, and the truck kept pulling to the left.

The vibration grew more substantial, and Katie slowed the vehicle in the breakdown lane. The sound of metal grinding on metal was unmistakable.

She yanked out the map she'd snatched from Dollar General. "Where am I?" Katie craned her neck and squinted to read the mile marker. Locating it on the map, she saw the next town, Bluff Creek, was less than five miles away. Katie checked the odometer. "I've only gone sixty-eight miles? Frickin' fantastic."

Katie pulled back on the highway, fighting the steering wheel to keep the truck in the right-hand lane. "What's that smell?" She lowered the window and inhaled. "Something's burning!" She checked the mirrors as fast as possible, lifting herself up off the seat to see behind the tailgate. Seeing nothing, she kept going. "Come on, you stupid truck!"

Nearing the exit, Katie slowed down, and the grinding and the smell intensified. "Oh, God. There's smoke!" She coasted off the highway into an Exxon station on Route 341 and ran inside.

"My truck's smoking! Ya'll have a mechanic here?"

"No, ma'am," the clerk answered, leaning sideways to see her truck, "but there's one down the road a piece— Ginos. Most folks around here use his garage."

"How do I get there? That truck's not going much further."

He pointed out the window, "Take this road about a mile. Make the first right. Gino's is on the left-hand side."

Katie babied the truck, gripping the steering wheel, which was shaking hard enough to make her upper body quake too. Once at Gino's, everyone was busy or at lunch. She signed in and watched the hour hand switch over to 1 p.m. Wandering to the window, she noted ominous gray clouds were building. Katie shook her head. *Of course it would rain.* It fit the day.

A mechanic approached the waiting room desk, wiping his hands on an already filthy rag. It didn't matter. Nothing was going to remove the staining of grease and oil, which permeated his hands. He read off her name, "Anne Morrison?"

Katie crossed the room quickly. "Are you Gino?"

He nodded. "Says here you've got trouble with your truck?"

"Yes. It's making a grinding noise, and I even saw smoke!"

"Pulling?"

"Yes, to the left."

"Sounds like you've got a burned-out wheel bearing. If it's smoking, the damn thing's probably seized up."

"What does that mean?" Katie asked, trying not to whine.

"Means you ain't going any further until we fix it."

"Oh, God." Thunder crashed, and rain lashed at the window.

"My son's finishing another truck, then I can get yours up on the rack--see if we can save the bearing. I doubt the rotor's any good either. If we change the rotor, gotta change the brake pads, too." He rubbed his right ear leaving a line of grease.

Befuddled by his shoptalk, Katie asked, "It's just the one wheel thing, right?"

"How many miles are on it?"

"Ninety-three thousand."

Gino shook his head sadly. "I wouldn't chance it. If one bearing's bad, the other one's right behind it. Means it hasn't been greased up and taken care of." He raised an eyebrow.

Katie put her hands up in the air, "Not on me. I just bought the damn thing."

"No kidding? Bad luck for you."

"Do you have all those parts?"

"If you had an F150 or Silverado, we'd be in luck. A Dakota, though?" He lifted a shoulder and grimaced.

Katie twisted her hair around a finger. "So, this isn't going to be done today?"

"No, ma'am, it's not."

"Any guess on cost?"

Gino tilted his head, considering. "I'd have to write it all down to be sure, but wheel bearings, including labor, will be around a thousand. Rotors and pads for the front? Add another two-fifty."

"So, the best case is a thousand, and the worst case is twelve-fifty?."

"There about. Gotta figure tax on parts and disposal fees. Maybe another hundred dollars."

Katie dropped her head into her hands. "I'm going to be sick. How long will this take?"

"If I order the parts today, they'll be in by tomorrow afternoon--Wednesday morning at the latest. Should have you back on the road late Wednesday afternoon or Thursday."

"Is there a cheap hotel around here?"

"There's a Travelodge and a Holiday Inn back by the highway." Gino looked at her and saw genuine tears forming. "You have anyone you can call?"

Katie shook her head.

"You're travelin' alone?"

Lightning flashed, and Katie hesitated. *How much information should I give?* Noting his gray hair and wedding ring, Katie answered,

"Yes. I'm moving to Florida. This," she gestured wildly toward the truck, "is gonna make a serious dent in my finances."

"If you're interested, they rent cabins and campsites in Old Bluff Creek. It's not far, maybe a half-mile at the most. They're not ritzy, but it would be cheaper than a motel."

"What's the name?"

"Connelly Rentals. Don Connelly—a friend of mine-- rents them. There's a brochure on the rack." Gino pointed toward the wall closest to the door and asked for her keys.

Katie handed them over and trudged toward the display. She read the slick ad and called the number listed.

"Connelly Rentals and Construction. Don speaking."

"Umm. Hi. I'm wondering if I could rent a campsite or one of those cabins by the creek?"

"Well, now, it depends on when you want it." His voice was smooth as old whiskey.

"Today. My truck's at Gino's garage, and he's telling me it could be a day or two."

Don scratched his head. "Well, we're pretty booked up for the weekend, but let me see what's available." Computer keys clicked in the background. "You're in luck. We've got two campsites open and one small cabin."

"How much are they?" Katie asked as she watched Gino drive her truck around the parking lot.

"It's seventeen dollars per night to camp, but they're primitive," Don warned, "No electricity. Just a fire pit and picnic table. The communal bathroom is nearby. It's thirty dollars per night to get the full luxury of a cabin, complete with electricity and a bathroom," Don chuckled to himself.

Communal bathroom? No electricity? Katie hung her head. "I'll take the cabin."

Don took down the information and gave her instructions on how to find his office. "We'll have the cabin cleaned up for you. It's available 'til Friday."

Katie hung up, calculating expenses. She stood by the desk until Gino finally noticed and came out again.

"You get ahold of Don?"

Katie nodded. "Will my truck hold up long enough for me to go back to the Walmart by the highway? I need some supplies."

"No way. That wheel seizes up? You'll be stranded. The damn thing could catch fire."

"How am I gonna get to the cabin?" She gestured toward the window, where rain still fell in steady drops.

Gino's eyes widened. "Well hell. I didn't think about that." He grabbed the phone, punching in numbers. "Don? It's Gino." He rolled his eyes and answered Don's questions. "We're all doing fine. Listen, a lady just called to rent a site from you."

"Yep-- a lady named Anne." Don leaned his chair back on two legs, ready to talk, "Sounds like she's stuck." He left it as a question, interested in any details Gino offered.

"She is. She's also by herself and could use a little help."

Katie cringed.

"Any chance you could get her out to the creek? I don't want her to drive this truck anywhere until I get it fixed."

Katie shook her head vehemently.

Gino held up his index finger. "If she has to wait on Vinnie or me, she'll be sittin' her 'til after five."

"Sure." Don landed the chair back on all four legs, happy to be part of the action. "I'm free, and if my Maggie gets wind I'm sitting here doing nothin', she'll make a to-do list up quicker than you can blink." Don laughed. "Give me ten to fifteen minutes."

"Sure thing. Thanks, Don."

When Gino turned back toward Katie, she looked ready to crumble. "Why did you do that? I can't drive off with a total stranger. He could be a psycho, an ax murderer!"

"Don?" Gino chuckled. "I told ya I've known him all my life. He wouldn't hurt a fly. You'll be fine and a lot happier with him than hangin' out here."

Katie's nerves snapped. "You should have asked me first."

Gino put up his hands in mock surrender. "Sorry. I was trying to help. Why dontcha fill this out the best you can, and we'll see about getting you back on the road, okay?"

Katie nodded once. *Calm down, girl.* She took the clipboard and began writing down answers. She peeked at her new driver's license to write down the false address. Gino filled in the rest, scribbling in a quick estimate. She took a business card off the desk. "Can I call tomorrow and see how things are going?"

Gino nodded as he turned to answer the phone.

Katie went to the parking lot, grateful the rain had stopped. Luckily, most of her clothes were already in the suitcase. She shoved her precious papers inside and zipped it closed just as a white Jeep pulled in and honked.

An older man unfolded long legs and stepped out with ease.

"You, Anne?" He asked.

She nodded once. "You're Don?" He wasn't what she'd pictured in the slightest.

"Yep. Hop in, and I'll get ya away from here." Don sauntered around his vehicle and opened the passenger door with a flourish. He smoothed what was left of his once blond hair and turned a genuine smile toward Katie. "Time's a-wastin'"

Gino, still on the phone, waved to Don through the window.

Halfway to Don's jeep, Katie stopped, spun around, and ran back to her truck. Don and Gino both frowned as they watched her.

Katie pulled out a book and held it up triumphantly. "Can't leave without one of these!"

Don talked non-stop as he drove, "We got two restaurants here in this section of town; Tipsy McQue's, a sports bar with good food, and Joe's Shack which isn't much to look at but will make ya think you've died and gone to bar-b-que heaven."

He kept the monologue rolling as they drove another block. "If you need food or supplies, the General Store's the place to go. Skinny Tom will take care of you."

Katie nodded, taking in the old-fashioned main street with its wooden buildings and brick sidewalks. It was a completely different picture from the business area near the highway. Katie's head turned to watch window displays as they cruised past something called The Blue-Sky Market.

"It's a quiet little town, isn't it?"

"This time of year, it slows down, but it's busy as all get out March through August. During the summer, every cabin, campsite, and motel are booked solid. Tourists come here to get away from the bigger city feel of Brunswick, or the resorts further down in Florida."

Katie tried to image it but couldn't.

"We need to stop by my office to fill out the paperwork." Don pointed toward a small Building. *Connelly Rentals* was neatly lettered above the front door. Window boxes tumbled over with pansies, and a bench held a place on the sidewalk.

After filling out a receipt and accepting Katie's hundred-dollar payment, Don handed her change and a one-page map of the town. "Since you're gonna be here a few days, figure you need to know the area." He circled the wooded area outside of town. "Your cabin's back here along Fancy Bluff Creek. Nice and secluded." Remembering she was alone, Don turned and asked, "Are you gonna be all right out there by yourself?"

Katie smiled at him. "I'm getting used to being alone."

It was an odd statement, but Don didn't ask questions. He'd talk to Maggie about it later.

"Anyway, there's a path here." Don made another circle on the map. "It takes you into town without having to walk the road all the way back."

Map in hand, they headed back to the Jeep, and Don turned onto a side road. Katie, who'd never been in the woods, was amazed by the canopy of trees growing thicker as they drove. The cabin was the last in a row of five and boasted one large room.

Don unlocked the door, showing her inside. "Couch opens into a bed." He opened a closet showing her the linens. "The kitchen is functional, but there's no heat out here in the woods. You get cold, you light yourself a fire." He pointed toward the stone fireplace. "There are logs on the porch and matches in the kitchen."

Katie nodded. The cabin was roomier than the motel rooms she'd been staying in, which was positive. She carried in her suitcase and waved to Don as he drove away.

Checking her phone, Katie was surprised to see it was only a little after 2 p.m. Her stomach grumbled, and she found half a breakfast bar in her purse. She nibbled it as she wandered the area around the cabin. The rocks and mud made short work of her flip-flops, and she changed into her new hiking boots.

Standing in reverence of the trees, she marveled at their size, the silence. She followed Fancy Bluff Creek—a tiny spit of water near the cabin which grew wider the further she walked. Pausing beside the bank, the seriousness of her situation hit home. She hadn't gone far enough. Jack would find her. *What the hell am I gonna do now?*

Chapter 44

Late in the afternoon, after a lengthy lunch, Darrow and Hopkins consolidated the notes from the whiteboard and met with each officer involved in the investigation. Near the end of the day, they consulted with Chief Greer and laid out the evidence.

Greer considered the data, rubbing his chin as he read the report. "I agree. There's no crime here. We'll do a press conference tomorrow. Call Mr. Werner. Give the guy some time to come to grips with the findings."

Katie passed the little path Don had mentioned and remembered she needed supplies. She headed back to the cabin to take inventory. Thankfully, the cabin had dishes, cookware and utensils. There was a microwave but no coffee maker, and she frowned. With a list forming in her head, she followed the trail toward town.

A bell over the door announced her arrival at the General Store. A fifty-something man with sparse hair and a rail-thin body looked up and waved. *Skinny Tom*, Katie told herself and smiled. She picked out sandwich supplies, breakfast bars, a liter of Diet Coke, and a tiny jar of instant coffee. At the counter, a flashlight caught her eye, and she tossed it in the basket, too.

"A stranger in town attracts attention," Skinny Tom quirked an eyebrow as he rang up her purchases.

"I'm staying in one of the Connelly cabins," Katie answered his unspoken question.

"Are ya now?" He waited, hoping for more information.

Katie remained silent.

"Well then, that'll be Twenty-six dollars and ninety-five cents."

Katie paid the bill, pocketed the nickel, and high-tailed it out of the store. She had no idea if Savannah news channels reached this far.

At 4:30 p.m., Jack rushed into the police station.

Whether by design, or long-ingrained habit, Darrow and Hopkins took turns sharing information with Jack.

"There'll be a press conference tomorrow. We wanted you to hear the facts first,"

"Jack, there's no foul play where Katie is concerned."

"We've followed her route from Friday to Sunday."

"We can't find anything suspicious." Darrow offered Jack a look of apology. "It appears Katie left on her own."

Jack pushed up and out of his chair. "No way! She wouldn't do that."

"She called the cab."

"She checked herself into a motel."

"She voluntarily left the area."

Jack's ears turned red. "How do you know that?"

Darrow shrugged.

"You'd rather she be safe, right?" Hopkins stood and leaned a hip on the corner of the desk. The silent threat calmed Jack down.

Darrow smoothed the tension, "Nothing wrong with a grown woman leaving."

Jack sat back in his chair. "I don't believe it. Can I get a copy of the report?"

"Because you're the one who reported her missing as next of kin, and since there's no crime, you can. But, I have to warn you, it will take weeks to get through our system. That's expedited. Trust me. You can probably get a summary report in three or four days. How's that sound?"

Jack gave a terse nod.

"Alright, we'll give you a call."

Both Darrow and Hopkins watched with satisfaction as Jack stormed out of the office.

Katie made her way back to the cabin, jumping at shadows and animal noises. The woods were beautiful but also an unknown entity. She'd never been so alone in her life. She locked the cabin door, closed the drapes, and forced herself to calm down. She rubbed her arms, marginally aware the temperature was dropping.

Jack parked the car and was headed toward their house when Mrs. Donahue called out from her own front porch. "Oh, Jack, there you are. I'm so worried about Katie. Have you heard anything?" She wrung her hands, waiting for his reply.

He swallowed his first response, which was to tell her it was none of her fucking business. He gave a small shrug."Not yet." He wasn't about to give her any details.

He stood in the foyer, picturing Katie. He saw her messy purse by the door, her coming out of the kitchen to greet him. "Where are you, Katie?" He asked the empty kitchen. His stomach growled, but he ignored it, pouring a whiskey and Coke instead.

Jack polished off three drinks, the rest of the lunchmeat in the fridge, and three small, limp carrots. He headed toward their bedroom to change his clothes, replaying Officer Darrow's snide voice from earlier. *It appears Katie left on her own."*

Standing in their closet, Jack stripped off his tie. As he did so, his sadness ebbed, and anger rushed in to fill the void. "Bitch!" he roared, only to have his tortured voice bounce back at him from the small space. He fingered her shirts and sweaters, moving hangers first left then right. "You liked your silly nursery rhyme. How about this one?" Jack softly sang, "Come out, Come out, wherever you are."

He then systematically tore and shred every article of her clothing. He sat laughing among the ruins and finished his drink.

Katie carted in the logs, dumping half of them in the fireplace. She'd never made a real fire as their fireplaces in the old house had been converted to gas. She located the matches and wadded up some paper towels and went to work. Ten minutes later, she wiped away frustrated tears. "Dammit!" The logs were too big and a little damp.

She scrounged the campground, looking for twigs, but the few sticks and leaves she found were wet from the earlier rain. Empty-handed, she tried again. The fireplace sputtered and smoked but never made a flame. She unzipped her suitcase and threw on extra clothing.

The light was fading, and she put her flashlight together and made up the couch-bed. She sat down to read, but her mind wouldn't settle. Turning off the lamp, she lay looking at the ceiling and wondering if she could still salvage her plans.

With no city lights, the cabin sunk into impenetrable darkness, and her palms began to sweat. She tensed at the unfamiliar noises; rustling in the leaves outside, an owl taking flight. The flue to the fireplace expanded with a pop, and she screamed. She flicked on the lamp. "And that's staying on," she said out loud just to hear her own voice.

She clutched her flashlight under the blanket. If the electricity went out, she wanted to make damn sure she wasn't sitting in the dark. Flicking the flashlight on and off, she chanted, "There was a crooked man," Click. "who walked a crooked mile," Click. "He found a crooked sixpence beside a crooked stile--"

She repeated the familiar song to herself until she fell into a restless sleep. Her fears and anxieties turned into hellish dreams of being chased and falling from a rocky cliff.

Chapter 45

Early Tuesday morning, Chief Greer stood on the steps to the Savannah police department and held a press conference. "Kathryn Werner's disappearance is no longer being investigated as a kidnapping or a crime. The woman appears to have left the area of her own free will. There are no suspects, and we will be closing the case as such. If new information comes forward, we'll review it at that time."

Reporters interrupted one another as they shouted questions at Greer.

"Has your office heard from Kathryn?"

"What about the empty wallet?"

"Were there any calls on her cell phone?"

"How can you be sure Kathryn is okay?"

Greer repeated himself, "All evidence points to the fact Kathryn Werner left on her own. There is no evidence of foul play." He turned and walked back into the building.

Katie read pieces and parts of the news while standing outside the General Store and using their guest Wi-Fi. Hurrying back to the cabin, she played out possible scenarios. On the one hand, it was good the police were out of the picture, but on the other, she worried about Jack. He's been publically embarrassed, and he'd never give up so easily. *And here I am, only seventy-five miles from home.*

She walked the length of the creek and ended up sitting on the damp bank, watching the ripples. She replayed the last five days of running and trying to stay a step ahead of the police and Jack.

It had been frightening and nerve-wracking at times, but also full of new experiences and freedom. She closed her eyes and listened to the breeze sifting through the trees, allowing herself to remember why this new life was so important. As pictures of her life with Jack spun through her head, she watched the years pass and saw her world get smaller and darker. She stood up, announcing with more courage than she felt, "You've come this far, see it through."

Jack spent a miserable morning at work. His co-workers issued him various apologies.

"Hey, man, so sorry."

"I can't believe Katie would leave."

Jack grunted and closed his office door.

Aunt Susan called the office, "Oh, Jack. I saw the news. I can't believe Katie would do such a thing."

For once, Jack agreed with the old woman.

Katie needed to verify where she stood financially and walked back to the cabin, collecting sticks and twigs along the route. "I am damn well going to have a fire tonight."

She deposited her kindling in the smoke-stained fireplace and dug through the overstuffed suitcase and myriad of bags until she located a legal pad. Dumping out her tote, even Katie was surprised by the amount of junk she'd accumulated in the last few days. She smoothed out the crumpled receipts, ready to do business. Starting at the beginning and wrote down $5754.28.

The minus column was significantly longer. Friday's costs for the cab, Motel 6, fast food, and her purchases at Dollar General came to $279.21.

Saturday had been even more expensive as she'd purchased new clothes and supplies, rode the bus, bought food, and paid for two nights at the *City Manor Motel.* She subtracted another $449.99.

Sunday was the real whopper thanks to the truck and the deposit on an apartment she'd never see again. "I spent almost two-thousand dollars on Sunday!" Katie circled the new total and dropped her forehead into her hands.

She started to add up Monday's expenses, then stopped abruptly. "This is stupid. All that matters is what I have left." Crumbling the receipts, she threw them in the fireplace.

Counting cash, she shook her tote to find all the change. She had $2741.14. "God. It's not going to last. I'm not going to make it."

She called Ginos at 10 a.m. The news was bad.

"Sorry, Ms. Morrison. We're gonna have to do the bearings, rotors, and brakes. I'm cutting expenses where I can, but it looks like it will come in around twelve-hundred."

Katie groaned. "Any idea as to when you'll be done?"

"Parts are still coming in. Hopefully, we'll have ya up and runnin' tomorrow afternoon, but you probably need to make plans 'til Thursday morning. Sorry," he said again.

Katie ended the call and flopped on the couch. *By the time I leave here, I'll be lucky if I have $1500.* The cheapest studio apartment she'd found in White City was $500 a month with first and last month's rent due at signing. If she stayed with her current plans, she'd have $500 to her name. It didn't sound bad until she added in gas for the truck, food, a deposit, and money for utility bills. She'd have to get a job immediately and then admitted renting an apartment might not be so easy until she had a job and a few paychecks to show for herself. *Where do I live during that time? How much will it cost? Can I sleep in my truck?* She scrubbed at her face for the hundredth time in two days. "I can't live like this. It's killing me!"

Unwilling to sit and worry, Katie headed back toward town. She bee-lined to the Blue-Sky Market and fell in love. There, the exotic smells, mixed with vibrant colors and a cacophony of sound, felt like conversation. Katie eagerly lapped up the interaction as it chased away her loneliness.

Although she could hardly afford to be an impulsive shopper, Katie couldn't resist spending ten dollars on a silly, glass tree frog at Junkalicious. He caught her eye and made her feel better. For years she'd been unable to buy anything for herself without Jack first approving the purchase. Peering inside her bag, she smiled at her frog as she made her way back to the street.

Spying Joe's Shack--which was precisely that—Katie veered in that direction. She'd barely eaten in days, and her mouth watered as soon as she walked in the door. She eagerly ordered the "Joe Momma" special.

Katie didn't know what else to do with her day and returned to the shopping area. She entered the first storefront she encountered. Hungry for human contact, she struck up a conversation with the man behind the counter. "Drift Away--it's an imaginative name. I would have come in here based on the name, even if I hadn't seen the amazing bench in your window." Katie fingered several carvings and crouched to get a better look.

Isaac grunted and kept working. Muddy brown eyes observed her through shaggy bangs.

"Are you the artist?"

Isaac grunted again.

"You're talented. If I had more money, I'd buy the piece with the four branches you turned into rolling waves and surf."

He permitted a small smile.

"It's nice to meet you. What's your name?" She held out her hand to shake.

He ignored the gesture. "Isaac." He watched her as she wandered through his store. She paused at what he considered his best pieces, which pleased him.

"See ya later, Isaac." She waved goodbye and wandered further down the street. She stood on the sidewalk peering through the display window of the Crested Iris.

A red-headed lady opened the door. Wearing ripped jeans, and a flowered shirt, Katie guessed her to be around forty. The woman gestured Katie toward the door, "Come on in, you can see better from the inside."

"Oh no," Katie blushed and shoved her hands into her back jean pockets. "I'm just looking. Well, admiring."

"You can look all ya like and smell all the flowers too. It's allowed. I know the owner, Maggie." She pointed to her chest, "Me. I'm the owner!" She belted out a boisterous laugh.

Unable to resist, Katie hurried through the open door and inhaled deeply. "Heaven will smell like this." Katie lifted a vase, watching the colors swirl. "Oh, this is beautiful."

"That's carnival glass. I picked it up at Tanja's Antiques. I use local talent when I can."

Nodding, Katie added, "I saw a small piece in Drift Away with three random holes. I pictured it with pretty flowers tucked inside."

Maggie raised her eyebrows, appreciating the young woman's creativity. "Nice idea. I'll take a look. Are you here on vacation?"

"No. This is an emergency stop."

Ahh, Maggie thought, t*his must be the woman Don mentioned last night.* Maggie could talk a mile a minute, but she was smart enough to know when to be quiet. She waited and was rewarded with a detailed answer.

"My truck broke down and is at Gino's. I'm coolin' my jets until it's fixed."

Maggie poured a cup of coffee and handed it to Katie as though they were old friends. "Been through a rough time I take it?"

"An understatement, to be sure." Katie sipped the coffee, not even aware she'd taken the cup. "I recently ended a bad marriage. I was heading to Florida. But now? The repairs on the truck? I'm not sure what I'm going to do." Katie's face turned red. "Sorry. I'm blathering, aren't I?"

"Seems to me you need someone to talk to, right? Small towns are good for that. People got a way of listening."

Katie shrugged.

"You're at a crossroads and never saw it coming." Maggie took a big sip of coffee, eyeing Katie over the top of her cup. "You're staying at the cabin on Shore Drive?"

Shocked, Katie stepped back, sloshing her coffee. She licked coffee off her hand and asked, "How'd you know that?"

Maggie laughed. "Connelly rentals. I'm Maggie Connelly. Don's my husband. See? That's a small town for you."

"Don's wife?" Katie squinted at Maggie, seeing the fine wrinkles around her eyes and mouth. Katie adjusted her initial estimate of Maggie's age and put it closer to fifty. Katie handed back the cup. "Thanks for the listening ear and the coffee. I made instant this morning, and it may have been the worst cup of coffee I've ever had."

Maggie smiled. "Stop in anytime--" She cocked her head, waiting for a name.

"I'm Anne. Annie to my friends." If Katie hesitated just a bit, she couldn't help it. Lying about something so ingrained as your name wasn't easy.

"Well, Annie, I hope to see you again." Maggie wondered if the girl would end up staying. If so, Maggie would find a way to introduce Annie to her son, Nick. Maggie sensed strength beneath the shadows she'd seen in the woman's eyes.

As Maggie watched Annie walk away, her face tugged at Maggie's memory. She felt sure she'd seen her somewhere before. *That girl's hurting, no doubt.*

Slightly shaken that Maggie knew more than she should, Katie kept walking. *Annie. Annie. Annie,* she repeated in her head, trying to get more accustomed to the name.

At 4 p.m, Jack called the police station and asked for Sgt. Hopkins. "Is the summary report ready?"

"We're still working on the details. It's going to be a few days yet."

Jack's boss, Barry, knocked on the office door. Jack waved him in and finished his conversation with Hopkins. "So, you're saying I may not get the police report 'til Thursday?"

"'Fraid so. We'll call you as soon as it's completed. " Hopkins ended the call without saying goodbye.

Jack let out a long sigh.

Barry closed the door. "You look awful."

"I know. I can't sleep, can't eat." Jack scrubbed at his face. "I have so many unanswered questions."

"I can understand that. You still want to finish out your week?"

Jack nodded. "Absolutely. I'd go crazy with nothing to do." He pictured himself in the closet the night before, surrounded by pieces of Katie's clothing. "I need to stay busy."

Jack watched the news and fielded phone calls. The first from Mrs. Donohue, who offered to bring him dinner, which Jack naturally refused. *No way is she coming over here.*

The second was from his mother, "Your father and I saw the broadcast this morning, Jack. I 'm so sorry. We didn't know Katie well, but she was always sweet and sincere." Sylvia Werner paused. "We told the police that when they questioned us on Saturday. I hated to admit we'd only met her a few times."

Jack rolled his eyes and balled his fists. Here was the censoring he was used to; his mother's not so subtle way of telling him he'd not handled the relationship well. He poured himself a drink and unplugged the phone.

Katie did a happy dance when the fire sputtered to life. The kindling and wadded up receipts had helped. She made a tuna sandwich and fiddled with the dials on an ancient radio in the living room. Her disappearance barely made the broadcast.

Tired and anxious about her circumstances, she sat on the cabin's porch and watched the night descend. The woods grew darker and deeper. It was less frightening now that she was more familiar with the area.

A tiny curve of a moon, climbed through the tops of the trees, working its way upward until it held a tenuous place in the vast, dark sky. Katie understood the feeling.

Chapter 46

On Wednesday, Katie fixed herself a leisurely breakfast, grateful not to be in a rush. Afterward, she wandered the trail around the cabin. She wished for a good cup of coffee but soon forgot the desire as she watched the sun caress the tops of the trees with gold-tipped fingers.

Back at the cabin, she eased off her new boots, cringing at the raw blisters on the back of each heel. Between yesterday and today, she guessed she'd walked five or six miles. She slipped on tennis shoes and limped to the General Store. The old bell over the door tinkled again. Skinny Tom made eye contact. "Morning, can I help you?"

"Good morning. Band-Aids?"

"Left-hand side, toward the back."

The group of old men gathered around a scarred table in the corner, couldn't resist the draw of a possible story. One of the retirees called out a question, "You stayin' out at the Connelly's cabins?" He was the oldest and obviously used to taking charge.

"How'd you know?" Katie's shocked face delighted the group.

Skinny Tom answered, "The whole town's got the dirt on you and your truck. We've had all kinds of reports: Gino, Don, Maggie. Even Issac mentioned you, and he ain't got two words to say--ever."

"You by yourself?" another retiree asked while tugging on his overalls.

It was a seemingly innocent question, but Katie understood they were fishing for information. She decided to lay some groundwork and see if it triggered any recognition. *I could be stuck* *her*e. "Hmm. How should I answer?" She wiggled her left hand in the air, showing a bare ring finger, "I recently ended my marriage and was heading to Florida to start over. The truck has messed up my plans."

"Well now, ya might like it here. We got some fine young men, too." The last and youngest of the men eased his bulk back in his chair. "My son, Blake, comes to mind."

Katie shook her head. "I'm not interested in finding a young man, or woman either, for the record." Taking in the table of old-timers, she added, "No, I think experience is better--someone who's been around the block and understands how to treat a woman." Her wink had the three old men sitting taller.

Skinny Tom flicked his ever-present towel at the group, as though brushing away an annoying fly. "You old geezers wouldn't know what to do. Now me, on the other hand…"

His statement had the old men sharing surprised looks and whispering among themselves.

"Can't believe Tom said that."

"He ain't looked at another woman since Martha died."

"Yep, been what? Eight years?"

Tom blushed, and Katie gave him a wink too. She paid for the Band-aids and left the store. She'd drawn attention, but not too much. No one had put the pieces together.

She called Gino's and left a message. As she headed back to the cabin, her mind was in a whirl. *Get real, Katie. There's not enough money to go to Florida. Even if you get there, find a place, and an immediate job, there'll be no paycheck for at least two weeks. It could be a month before you can get an apartment.* Her breath hitched.

Leaning against a tree, she let loose the dam inside. She bent at the waist, with her hair hanging down, and sobbed. "I can't go back. I won't go back."

Swiping at her tears, she angled toward the water. As she walked, she considered the pros and cons of staying in Bluff Creek. *It's probably cheaper. It's not far enough from Jack. I've already met people. I need more reconnaissance.* With the last fact in front of her, she decided she'd have lunch at Tipsy McQue's. *Who knows? Maybe they're hiring.*

Later, when Katie entered the restaurant, she was assaulted by sound; muted conversations, glasses clinking, and music. The dark, paneled walls were covered with pictures of Cork, Guinness, and The Republic of Ireland football team. She took a corner seat at the bar.

"You the girl stranded in town?" the server asked as she polished a long, smooth bar.

Katie nodded and studied the menu quietly.

Picking up the sad vibe from the girl, the bartender offered up a joke, "So this giraffe walks into a bar,"

Katie looked up. "Are you talking to me?"

"Yes. I'm telling you a joke."

"Oh."

"So, this giraffe walks into a bar. Why the long face, the bartender asked?"

Katie smiled.

"Get it? Giraffe? Long face? Okay, here's another one. A woman and a duck walk into a bar. The bartender says, 'Where'd you get the pig?' The woman says, 'That's not a pig, that's a duck.' The bartender says--"

Katie provided the punchline with a tentative smile. "I know, I was talking to the duck."

The bartender grinned, impressed the girl knew the joke.

The two women high-fived one another and shared a laugh. *God, when's the last time I told a joke?* Katie felt her world tilt back to center.

The woman smiled at Katie. "Heard about your truck. That sucks."

Katie nodded once and rolled her eyes.

"I'm Colleen, by the way." She worked her way down the bar, filling orders and making small talk.

Katie ordered a sandwich and a drink, taking in the flow of the restaurant.

Colleen never stopped moving. Even her close-cropped, red hair stood at attention, ready to take off in any direction. She spat out sarcasm as easily as chewing gum and kept her co-workers laughing.

Giggling as Colleen sent yet another insult zinging across the bar toward some poor waitress named Lorraine, Katie sensed she'd made a friend.

"You come back and see us," Colleen called out as Katie paid her bill.

"Be careful what you wish for," Katie replied, earning a quick smile from Colleen.

While Katie was at Tipsy's, Jack called the police station again.

"We might be done late tomorrow," Darrow said, "You want me to call you?"

Darrow was more pleasant, but Jack still hated him.

Aunt Susan called Jack asking about Katie, "I wish I'd sensed something, don't you?"

"Yeah," Jack agreed, keeping his thoughts to himself. *If I'd have sensed something, the little bitch would never have left the house.*

Vicki, Jack's personal trainer, called too. Hers was a much more interesting conversation as she offered to do anything to help. Jack pictured her sculpted body. *I could use a physical release.* It'd been days, and he needed to feel better. He made arrangements to meet her that night.

Katie walked through town again. *Talk to me, Cassie. What should I do?* Katie peeked in the windows of Tanja's Antiques and waved at Maggie, who was watering her flower boxes. *Can I live here? Will Jack find me?*

She resisted the Blue-Sky Market, knowing she'd buy something else she couldn't afford. She headed to the cabin, hoping to calm her mind with a book. After re-reading the same page for the third time, she tossed it aside. The questions refused to be silent.

Katie's phone rang—the first call she'd received. Panic had her hands trembling. *What if it's Jack?* The idea didn't make sense, but she couldn't help herself. "Hello?" she whispered.

"Ms. Morrison?"

Thank God. Gino. "Yes, this is Annie."

"We'll be done with your truck later today. I'll drive it out to the cabins since you've got no transportation. Six o'clock sound good?"

"Perfect. Thank you so much!"

"Don't thank me yet. You still gotta hell of a bill to pay." Gino Chuckled, "Came in at one-thousand-twenty-six dollars and forty-seven cents--pretty much where I said."

Lower, actually. Nice man. Nice town. I could have ended up in worse places.

As Jack walked in the door, the phone rang. His dad was on the line, and Jack wondered briefly how long it had been since they'd had a conversation.

"Are you all right, Jack?"

It was ironic that Katie's disappearance had them talking. They'd barely had a conversation since the night Jack had demanded his Grandmother's ring for Katie.

"Your mother wants to know if you'd like to come to dinner sometime this weekend?"

"We haven't had dinner together in years. I think the time has come and gone." Jack found one clean glass and gulped water.

Fred waited a few seconds before responding, "You're probably right. We wanted to tell you we're sorry." Fred put little emotion into his statement.

"Sorry Katie's gone," Jack snapped, "or sorry we don't have any kind of family?"

"Goodnight, son." Fred Werner ended the call.

Jack flung his glass across the kitchen and watched it shatter against the wall. He grabbed his keys, anxious to connect with Vicki.

Gino rattled down the lane and pulled up in front of Katie's cabin. Gino's son, Vinny, followed behind in a primer-coated car. Standing on the cabin porch, Gino handed over receipts, warranties, and the keys to Katie's truck. She, in turn, carefully counted out cash.

"Should be good as new. You can get yourself back on the road, huh?"

Katie tilted her head. "We'll see. You ate up my funds, Gino. Florida's probably out of the picture now."

"You thinkin' of staying, or goin' back home?"

"I'm never going back. Might be Bluff Creek's got a new resident."

"You hear that, Vinny?" Gino yelled toward the car, "She might be stayin'." He shook Katie's hand. "Good Luck, whatever you decide."

Katie climbed in the truck and headed to the McDonalds by the highway. There, she could get full Wi-Fi. For the first time in six days, her disappearance wasn't mentioned. With no sordid details, the story was no longer interesting.

Katie returned to the cabin and sat on the porch. Staring at the woods, she wished she had someone to talk with. The temperature dropped, and she ran inside to snag a blanket off the couch. Hunched in the porch rocker, she worried she'd left too many clues.

As tree frogs warmed up their voices for their nightly serenade, she remembered a quote from Desmond Tutu, "Hope is being able to see the light, despite all of the darkness." She snuggled deeper in the chair, hoping Bluff Creek would be her light in the darkness.

Chapter 47

Katie woke up ready to take the next step. She went back to the General Store to buy food for the next few days and gather more information. Her reservation for the cabin was almost expired, and she may not have anywhere to stay. Remembering the blanket and pillow she'd purchased during one of her shopping trips, she felt marginally better. *I can sleep in the truck if necessary.*

She walked her bag of groceries over to the old men gathered around the table and quirked her eyebrow at the partially finished jigsaw puzzle. "Seems to me ya'll meet here daily and have been for a while."

"I'm Jarrod," The oldest one pointed at his chest in case there was any confusion. His bald head was as wrinkled as his face and permanently tanned. "Jarrod Jones. I used to do maintenance at the resort."

A second man held out a pudgy hand. "I'm Craig Struthers. County Sheriff for twenty-five years."

Katie winced at his profession and forced herself to shake his hand, "I'm Annie."

Not to be outdone, the third retiree piped up, "I'm Thaddeus James Lucas. Thad to my friends. Retired mechanic. That your Dodge Dakota out there?"

Katie nodded. "Yep. Fixed up and running again."

"Well now, you need anything--" Thad trailed off as Skinny Tom inserted himself between Katie and the table.

"How long ya here?" Skinny Tom asked, bringing Katie's attention back to him.

"It depends. I'm a bit stuck, thanks to the truck, but I love this little town. The people are wonderful." She smiled fully into his face, making Tom blush. She leaned around him to include the retirees. "All of them. I even had a fun conversation with Colleen at Tipsy McQue's. Maybe I should stay."

Their tongues tripped over one another.

"What?"

"You thinking of moving here?"

"Do you work?"

"I need a job immediately," Katie answered. "And a place to rent. Someday, I'd like to open a store here."

Her statement settled it as far as they were concerned--a young woman, having trouble and wanting to move to their town? Their brains could be seen going into high gear.

"Circle K is hiring," Thad offered.

"She can't work there! Crazy people coming in at all hours," Craig admonished.

"How about the resort? I've still got some pull there." Jarrod tugged on his overalls.

"Really? Maybe I'll check it out. I was sort of thinking about serving food. Is Joe's Shack hiring?"

They laughed at her question, "Joe? You can't work for him."

"He's mean as a snake. Besides, his wife, Linda, helps him out, and they're always hiring nieces and nephews. Keeping it in the family."

"How about Tipsy McQue's?" Katie wondered.

"If you're gonna stay around here, you gotta call it Tipsy's. Otherwise, you sound like a tourist."

"Good tip. What do you think? Are they hiring? I used to work for a catering business years ago. I know how to serve food."

Craig, always blunt, asked, "But can you deal with half-drunk men?"

Katie scoffed, "I think you'd be surprised. I can handle myself."

"I bet she can," Jarrod said, and Thad nodded in agreement. The three men talked and argued among themselves.

"I still say she should go to the resort."

"She says she used to be a server. How 'bout the Rotisserie, up by the highway?"

Tom touched her arm. "I'm not sure whatcha got in mind, but there are a few rentals in town." He led her away from the group, walking toward a bulletin board tacked up behind the door.

The bell rang, announcing new customers, and a noisy family of five walked inside. The mom held two sets of little hands and sent out instructions. "Look with your eyes, not your hands!" Dad carried a miniature version of himself straddled across his hip.

Tommy pointed Katie toward the board. "There are a few rentals listed there," he said and turned to greet his newest customers.

Katie squeezed behind the door and began reading. The local church had a food pantry, and she filed the information away, hoping she wouldn't need to ask for handouts. She cocked her head sideways, reading the ads. She was intrigued by an apartment over the General Store, of all places.

Not aware she was there, Nick Connelly crashed through the door and smashed Katie against the wall.

Katie yelped and put her hands up to shield her face. She bent her head and squeezed her eyes closed, ready to take the blow.

Craig Caruthers had been on enough domestic dispute calls over the years to recognize a woman used to taking a beating. He stood up, ready to help, while the rest of the people in the store stayed in place, their mouths hanging open.

Katie jerked her head around, convinced Jack had found her. It took a long two seconds to realize she was looking at a stranger. Rust-colored hair, taller. Wiry, not muscular. *Not Jack. Not Jack.*

Nick reached toward Katie. Her eyes were huge, and he noted they were greener than any he'd ever seen. "Are you okay?

She couldn't stop herself and flinched. "Sorry. I'm so sorry."

"Why are you apologizing? I crashed into you."

Katie's face turned dark red. Squeezing past Nick, she mumbled, "It's my fault." Before he could stop her, she fled toward the cabin, forgetting the truck in her hurry.

Nick stood with his mouth open, and his hand still outstretched to help her. He turned to face the store. "What just happened?"

Katie sat in the corner of the cabin, her hands over her ears. "There was a crooked man, who walked a crooked mile..." It took ten minutes, but she calmed down. *I have to go back. There's no way around it.* She walked back to town, took a big breath, and re-entered the store.

Skinny Tom looked up when the bell rang and rushed to her side. "Are you okay?"

"I am. That guy took me by surprise." Her eyes silently begged him not to pursue the conversation.

"You can say that again," Skinny Tom said. "We haven't had that much excitement in years, right boys?" He raised his eyebrows--a silent warning--they'd better not ask a bunch of asinine questions.

Thad chimed in, "That's for damn sure."

"Got my heart pumping," Craig added.

Jarrod harrumphed. "We could use more stimulation, instead of sitting around playing cards."

Craig smirked as he laid his card on the table, "Rummy!"

Katie gave a small appreciative smile and went back to talking to Skinny Tom, "Is the apartment over this store still available?"

"So, you're serious about staying?"

All conversation stopped as the old men listened.

"Maybe. If I had a place to live, it would be a start."

"Well, I can let ya see it," Skinny Tom said as he pulled out an enormous ring of keys. "It's been vacant awhile. The Connelly's rent it out, but they won't mind if I show it to you.

He reluctantly left Craig in charge of the register and walked Katie through the storeroom to a back entrance and staircase.

"The apartment's big, about half the size of the store. My office and a storage room are up here too." He pointed at another door at the top of the wide landing.

"Who was the guy who crashed into me anyway?" Katie asked, changing the subject.

"That's Nicky. He just moved back from New York. He's still clipping along at city speed, which is why he crashed through the door instead of walking in like normal folk." Tom made a big show of jiggling the lock. "Don't worry about him."

Katie quietly waited for Tom to open the door. "Wow." Katie was right on Tom's heels. "It *is* big." A large living room faced the street with two windows, letting in plenty of southern light. "There's furniture!"

"Well, that can be put in storage. I imagine you've got nicer stuff." Tom patted the old green couch, and a plume of dust rose and danced in the sunlight.

"Actually, I don't. I'm starting over from scratch." A well-loved chair, coffee table, and two end tables completed the living room ensemble. Old wood flooring still gleamed here and there.

A thick half-wall with a spacious countertop separated the living area from the kitchen. Katie imagined a couple of stools pushed underneath, eliminating the need for a table. "There's plenty of cabinets." Katie trailed her hand along the countertops, picking up dust as she went. There were appliances, which was good. She peeked out the window over the sink and saw an alley below. "Is the alley lit at night?"

"Yeah, it's lit. The door at the bottom of the stairs has two deadbolts, too. You'd be safe here," Skinny Tom added.

Katie squeezed his shoulder as she walked through the kitchen. Double doors revealed a deep pantry. She opened and closed the doors twice. "Extra storage. Nice."

"Yeah, Don added as much as he could."

Katie entered a good-sized bedroom, pleased to see there was indeed another large closet. The double window here faced east, and she relished the idea of waking to the sun each day. A small second bedroom and full-sized bathroom completed the place. "How much is the rent?"

"I think Don said he was getting four-hundred."

Katie frowned, already doing the math.

Watching her face, Tom added, "It includes water and trash." "Any little bit helps."

"You'd have to be adding internet."

"That's not going to happen for a while. None of it matters if I can't find a job. I think I'll go check out Tipsy's."

They locked up, and Tom kicked Craig out from behind the counter where he'd been eating a donut. "Go on back to your corner, ya freeloading S.O.B."

Craig grinned at Katie and licked the icing off his lips.

Katie waved goodbye to the entire store. "Wish me luck!"

As the door shut, the retirees hammered Tom with questions.

"Did she like the apartment?"

"What's she talking 'bout?"

"Wish her luck about what?"

"A job," Tom answered. "She wants to stay here."

"Where's she wanting to find a job?" Thad asked.

"Tipsy's, I think. At least that's what she said."

"Well, when will we know?" Craig demanded.

Tom flicked his towel at the lot of them. "Hell, I don't know. You got nothing but time anyway, old man."

"Old man, my butt. I'm two years younger than you."

And with that, the old men were back to arguing and talking over one another.

Chapter 48

John Giovanni, the lone police officer in town, walked into the General Store and grinned at the raised voices in the corner. "What are you guys arguing about this time?"

"New girl in town," Thad answered.

"Her name's Annie. Wants to move here and is looking for a job," Jarrod clarified.

"I say The Rotisserie is the place to look, but this yahoo," Craig jabbed a finger at Jarrod, "wants her to go to the resort."

"We don't get many new people here. Is that her truck outside?' Giovanni asked.

Thad answered, "Yep, Dodge Dakota."

Giovanni walked to the window and wrote down the license plate number. He could hear the old-timers still debating where this Annie should work. If they were interested, he was too.

Katie wandered down the street, trying to calm her nerves. She craved all of it--the apartment, the town, the new life. She found herself entering the Crested Iris. A motion detector chimed, and Maggie poked her head out from the storage room where she'd been stripping thorns off roses.

"Hey, Annie! Be right there." Maggie came out, removing her gloves, "How you doing?"

"Fine, I guess."

"Still checking out our Bluff Creek?"

"Yep, all sorts of things, including the apartment over the General Store."

"This I got to hear." Maggie pulled Katie toward a stool at the counter. "Coffee?"

Katie grinned and nodded.

Maggie poured two big mugs and added cream without asking. She plopped down beside Katie. "So, you're thinking of staying?"

"Well," Katie plucked out her two front pockets, "I'm outta funds. So, here I am." Katie spread her arms. "I guess we'll call it fate."

"Fate or damned good luck. This is a nice town—a good place to start over." Maggie drifted off, thinking about her son, Nick, and Annie.

"….and, I need to talk to Don about another night."

Maggie shook her head, embarrassed she'd been daydreaming. "What'd you say?"

"I need to talk to Don about renting the apartment. As of tomorrow, I'm out of places to stay since he's kicking me out of the cabin."

Maggie hopped off the stool. "He'll do no such thing." She yanked her phone out of her back pocket, ready to give Don a piece of her mind.

Katie laughed and pulled Maggie's arm back down. "I'm kidding. There's already another reservation. Maybe it's just as well. It's forcing me to choose." Katie gulped coffee. "I need a job!"

"Yep, you do. Whatcha have in mind?"

"Tipsy's first and then maybe the resort." Katie walked her coffee cup back to the sink. "I need to change my clothes and get myself psyched up first."

Katie drove to the cabin, talking to herself the whole time. 'God, I hope I'm not making a mistake."

Freshened up, Katie walked into the restaurant. She waved to Colleen, who was cutting up limes and lemons for the bar.

"Hey! Annie, right?"

Katie didn't remember sharing her name yesterday. "Yep, and you're Colleen."

"You know why blond jokes are so short?"

Katie smiled. "No, why?"

"So brunettes can remember them." Colleen pointed at her own red shock of hair, "Me on the other hand? I've got no such trouble."

Katie snickered and ordered a Diet Coke.

"No lunch today?"

"Not this time. I'm hoping to talk to your manager."

"You got complaints already, girl?"

"No. I need a job."

Colleen considered her more thoroughly. "Ah, thinking of staying." She nodded twice. "Colin owns the place. Colin McQue." Colleen let out a shrill whistle, "Colin! Got a girl here wants to see you."

When Colin stuck his head out of the office, Katie was momentarily taken aback. She'd visualized a barrel-chested, red-haired man to go with the name. This man was easily pushing sixty years old, lean as a pole, and sporting a full head of bright white hair.

"You Annie?" he asked, blue eyes twinkling.

Katie sputtered out her Coke. "How'd you know?"

"My phone's been ringing for the last hour, wanting me to hire some new girl called Annie." He ticked off names. "Heard from Maggie, Jarrod, Skinny Tom, and Giovanni."

"Who's Giovanni?"

"Police chief. He ran the plates on your truck out there," Colin pointed out the window. "Appears you're not on America's Most Wanted List, and I should hire you. Come on back."

Katie swallowed around the sudden lump in her throat.

Once in the office, Colin got down to business. "Do you have any experience?"

"I used to work for a catering crew." She didn't want to say a restaurant. The news from Savannah was still too fresh.

"So, you can handle the work? We get pretty busy on the weekends."

"Can't be any busier than catering for hundreds of people," Katie said with a smile.

"What's your schedule like?"

"I'm completely at your disposal. No commitments, no kids, and nothin' but time."

"Know any jokes?"

At Katie's puzzled look, Colin continued. "You gotta be able to swap lies and tell jokes if you're gonna work here."

Katie blinked. Just that morning, she'd looked up a few jokes on her phone, hoping to forge a friendship with Colleen. So, she offered the first one that popped to mind, "An amnesiac walks into a bar. He spies a beautiful blond and asks her, 'Do I come here often?'"

Colin barked out a laugh. "You'll do. 'Fraid I don't have a lot of hours to give you since the season's over. In fact, they're all the crap hours."

"I'll take them."

"You don't know what they are yet."

"It doesn't matter. I'll take them."

Colin cocked his head at her and repeated, "You'll do. Be here tomorrow afternoon, one to six. I can give you five dollars an hour, and the tips are yours."

Katie popped out of the chair. "I'll be here!" She ran out the door to tell Colleen but then spun back around. "Don't I have to fill out an application?"

"Let's try things out a few days. If it's working, we'll make it official."

Katie ran out and then back in again, "What should I wear?"

"Jeans are fine. We'll supply the shirt." He studied Katie a second, taking in her lean but firm frame. "Medium?"

She nodded, and Colin laughed. "See ya at one."

Katie danced her way to the bar. "I got the job!"

Colleen high-fived her and announced, "We got us some help startin' tomorrow!"

A short, blond woman walked over and introduced herself, "I'm Lorraine. Do you have any experience? We need help!" Her eyes were hopeful.

"I'm a little rusty, but I can hold my own," Katie assured the woman.

The other barkeeper checked Katie over from the sidelines and pretended to be uninterested. "I'm Mark. What time do you start?"

Colleen wasn't fooled and shot him a scowl. "Back to work, lover-boy."

"See you tomorrow!" Katie rushed out, eager to sweet talk Don into renting her the apartment.

The Connelly Rental office was locked. Katie sat on the bench outside. A half-hour passed, and she was about to give up when she saw Don drop Maggie off at the Crested Iris. He kissed his wife goodbye. *They must have had lunch together. Isn't that sweet?*

Maggie saw Katie and held both her hands out, asking a silent question, "Well?"

Katie flashed a smile and thumbs up. Maggie pushed a bewildered Don toward his office. The scene convinced Katie she'd made the right decision.

Katie and Don sat at his desk as he searched through desk drawers and files for a rental agreement. "You've seen the place, right?"

"Yes. Tom showed me this morning. I hope that's all right."

"Fine with me. Skinny Tom's got keys to all the locks in the building." Don found the form and flourished it triumphantly. "The rent includes water and trash. You gotta haul the trash down to the dumpster, though."

"How much is the rent?" Katie fumbled with her tote.

Don watched her. *Poor thing. She's scared to death.* "Maggie and I talked it over at lunch. We'd rather have some rent come in versus none at all." Don patted Katie's nervous hands. "How's three-fifty sound?"

"Really? Tom thought four-hundred."

"You'd rather pay more?" Don chuckled and pretended to write in the new amount.

"No! Three-fifty would be great."

"Okay then, it's a deal. The electric's in my name. You'll need to switch it over this week. We require a two-hundred-dollar deposit and the first month's rent. Can you swing that?"

Katie pulled out crumbled bills. "So, you need five-fifty?"

"Whoa. Hang on there. First, you shouldn't be carrying around that kind of cash, and second, we haven't even filled out any paperwork."

Katie blushed. "Sorry. I'm excited about having my own place."

Don couldn't help feeling protective. "Let's at least do a quick background check."

Katie handed over Cassie's social security card.

"Cassandra?" Don frowned at the full name on the card. Seeing the middle name, Anne, he nodded. "Anne suits you better. And you shouldn't be carrying this around either," He gestured with the social security card.

Katie fidgeted on the edge of the chair while Don typed information into a website. She suspected Don would be more thorough than the manager at Ashley Commons.

Don frowned. "This says the social security number is flagged as deceased."

Katie dropped her head in her hands and groaned, "I can't believe it's still showing incorrect information. I've spent months convincing the social security office I'm very much alive." She dug in her wallet and placed her driver's license on the desk in front of Don. She pretended to take her pulse too. "Yep. I still have a heartbeat."

Don narrowed his eyes, wanting to believe.

Katie rushed on with more of an explanation, "All our finances were in my husband's name. They tell me it has to do with no credit, no job, no utilities, or loans in my name, for our entire marriage." She shook her head sadly. "Stupid of me. I just didn't know."

"Not stupid," Don consoled, "Naïve maybe, but not stupid. On the plus side, you're not delinquent on loans, you haven't racked up debt, and you're not wanted by the police. I guess we're gonna have to trust each other, aren't we?"

Overcome, Katie offered her thanks, "That means a lot. Can I rent the cabin one more night?"

"No need. Maggie's already at the apartment, cleaning as though the hounds of hell are after her. Give her a couple of hours, and the place is yours." He checked his watch. "Say six?"

After the two of them completed the paperwork, Don handed her two keys. "This gold key opens the back door to the store. Keep it locked, or Skinny Tom will have our butts. This one," he held up a small silver key, "is to your apartment."

Katie took the keys and burst into tears.

Don stood and patted her on the shoulder. "It'll be okay. I know you're scared."

Katie sniffed, "I'm not scared. I'm happy!"

"Aw hell," Don pulled her up and gave her a hug, "Welcome to Bluff Creek."

Chapter 49

Jack called the police department on Thursday morning, asking for Darrow. He was forwarded to a voicemail and wasted no time in getting to the point, "I'm calling about the report for Kathryn Werner. It's been four days."

Unable to stall anymore, Darrow called Jack late Thursday afternoon, "The report is ready if you want to pick up a copy."

Jack left work early and rushed to the precinct and was ushered into Darrow's small, windowless office. Darrow was on the phone, distracted and harried, "I'll be with you in a minute," he mouthed to Jack, indicating he should have a seat.

Jack flopped down in a hard chair, flipping his phone back and forth between his hands.

Darrow finished his call and focused on Jack. "Sorry about that. You're here earlier than I expected. As we explained, all we can share with you right now is the summary" He shuffled folders on his desk, and opened what was obviously a case file. He pulled out the top three sheets.

Jack saw other papers were underneath, including hand-written notes, post-it notes, and several paperclips holding pages together. Gesturing toward the folder, Jack asked, "So, what's the difference between what I'm getting today and what's in there?"

Darrow rolled his head on his shoulder, tired of the day, tired of Jack. But he remained professional and explained, "This is more detailed," he turned a few pages of the file, and Jack glimpsed what looked like a photo. "everything said in interviews, downloads, warrants, stuff you don't need right now. It needs to be reviewed for accuracy. The main information," he held out the top pages, " is what you're looking for—a synopsis of the investigation."

Jack reached for the papers, but Darrow pulled back. "These are the originals. Like I said, you're here earlier than I expected. I need to make copies." He walked to his door, looking for an assistant. Seeing empty desks, Darrow sighed. "I'll be right back."

As soon as Darrow left, Jack sprang into action, opening his phone's camera app and snapping a picture of the real report's first page, turning quickly to the first post-it notes, and the page where he'd seen a photo. Jack was done in less than ten seconds and sat back down, pushing the phone into his pocket before Darrow returned.

"Here ya go," Darrow said as he re-entered the office. "I just need you to sign a release form, and we're good to go."

Two minutes later, Jack ran out with the manilla envelope clenched in his fingers.

Once at home, he settled himself in his den with a bottle of whiskey and his new Marlboro habit. Reading the summary, Jack concluded it was more a timeline, chronicling details in succinct order: His first verbal report listing Katie as missing on Friday night, the car verified at the medical center, searching their house, the doctor's offices, and finding her phone and wallet in the dumpster.

Jack flipped through pages quickly, already well aware of how much time had passed and what happened when.

A list of witnesses was next, and he scanned names, seeing only a few unfamiliar names: the Motel 6 clerk, the cab driver, and the neighbors from Hidden Lake Court. No new names, no men, nothing. "Fuck."

He poured another drink, and opened his photo gallery on his phone, scanning the pictures he'd managed to snap. Expanding the image, he read about the bank account and zoomed in on a post-it note, which read, "$5254.00 withdrawal"—something Darrow and Hopkins had failed to mention. "You had five-thousand dollars? Little bitch. Keeping secrets and making plans."

The next page, in his photo gallery, referenced a camera #3217 outside a Chevron station, in Middleburg. *A woman resembling Kathryn Werner in body style, and overall appearance boarded a city bus, unescorted, and uncoerced*, the report said. *Could not identify as 100%.*

"Bus? What fucking bus?" Jack's hand shook as he shuffled papers in the file, looking for the bus number. That particular detail was missing

The last picture on his phone was a surveillance photo, Grainy, and black and white, Jack enhanced it and could see Katie with darker hair, glasses, and wearing some kind of cheap-ass t-shirt.

Jack screamed, "I will find you, Katie."

Needing to release the black rage building inside him, Jack called Vicki. She happily agreed to meet again and met Jack at her door wearing a black thong and seamless plunge bra. She'd slathered on oil, and Jack caught the scent of coconut.

Primal lust pumped through his veins, and he kicked the door shut. He had Vicki stripped and on the foyer floor before she knew what had happened. Enjoying his energy and need, Vicki gave as good as she got, not caring that Jack bit her shoulder or left finger marks on her hips. It was a hell of a ride. Afterward, she lay on the foyer rug, stretching like a contented cat.

Jack was enjoying the aftermath, too, until Vicki opened her mouth. "That was fantastic. With Katie gone, maybe we can do this at your house next time. I'd love to get naked on the widow's walk."

Jack narrowed his eyes, seeing Vicki as an opportunist. Rolling to his feet, Jack got dressed without saying a word.

Vicki sat up, watching him. "You leaving already?"

In answer, Jack walked out the door, pulling it closed with a definite click.

"What a dick!" Vicki grabbed her clothes and headed to the shower, humiliated, and thinking she didn't know Jack at all.

Katie pulled her truck up behind the now-closed General Store. Opening the door to the apartment, she was greeted by a bouquet of fresh flowers on the counter. Katie read the note. "Welcome to your new home! ~Don and Maggie."

Katie wandered the rooms, noticing there was no overhead lighting in the living room or bedrooms—something she'd missed in the light of day. She frowned, unwilling to be in the apartment at night, in the dark. The uncovered widows made her feel vulnerable and naked, too. She peeked down on Main Street, looking for Jack. *What if he shows up here?* She eyed the only door to her apartment and shivered.

She went to her bedroom, shoved open a window, and stuck her head out. Seeing a small parking lot and the alley behind the store, Katie gauged the drop. "I need one of those fire ladders."

The idea satisfied her, and she hauled her suitcases and bags up the stairs. She didn't have much; some clothes, personal items, a few household articles, and the groceries she'd bought earlier. She couldn't even put away her clothes because she had no drawers or hangers. She grabbed her keys and headed back toward the highway. *If Bluff Creek is going to be home, it's time I decorate it to my liking.*

Katie pulled into the twenty-four-hour Walmart, ready to knock out her list. She found the safety ladder first; not even caring that it cost almost thirty-five dollars. She plopped it in the cart and, on a whim, grabbed a small tool kit.

Because she couldn't afford a real bed, she opted to buy a blow-up mattress. She agonized over two: one had a softer cover for fifty-one dollars, and the other was more basic for forty-four dollars. Deciding to save her pennies, she chose the lesser of the two. "I'll make up for it with bedding," she said aloud, not caring who heard.

After choosing a comforter/sheet set and one more pillow, to go with the one she already had, she moved toward the furniture section. Considering the build-it-yourself night tables, she decided she'd done enough work at the house on Forsyth Park to be able to put one together with a fair degree of confidence. She then changed her mind. *I can't be buying furniture.*

Walking away, she consulted her list, "What's next?" *Hangers. I need hangers.* She spun toward the correct aisle.

She splurged on two lamps: a multi-faceted glass lamp for the living room, and a more basic one for her bedroom. She ran off to get light bulbs before she forgot.

Looking at a canvas print of wildflowers, she nearly talked herself out of that as well, but gave in at the last minute. *I don't want bare walls. It'll feel like a prison.*

Two hardcover books went into the overflowing cart. They were on clearance, which made them impossible to resist.

A second cart was necessary as she loaded up with essential dinnerware, glasses, utensils, silverware and a few pieces of cookware. "And I need a coffee maker," she reminded herself.

The rest of the money she was willing to part with went toward paper products and enough cheap food to last two weeks—easy meals and things she could stretch like spaghetti, soups, peanut butter, and eggs. *No way can I afford to eat out.*

It took a long time to tally up the two carts, and despite buying everything on clearance, the bill totaled $399.81. She cringed, mentally adding up money. *I've got to live, eat,* she consoled.

Driving back to the old section of town, Katie was surprised to see all the streets dark. *It's not even ten-thirty.* She shook her head at the idea but was comforted to see soft lights spilling out of the windows of homes instead.

That changed when she pulled in behind the General Store. Here, one meager spotlight illuminated the door. She shut off the truck, peering into the shadow, and breathing hard.

Backing as close to the door as she could without ramming the building, she propped the storeroom door open, flinging her bags and boxes inside as fast as possible. Sweating and nervous, she locked her truck and slammed the storeroom door closed. "No way am I going back out there tonight."

Supply boxes for the store were stacked high, and the single lightbulb cast shadows in all the corners. The freezer motor let out a long whine, and Katie ran up several stairs before she came to her senses. Easing her way back down, she re-checked the door.

She braved the steps, unlocked the apartment, and turned on all the lights. She made herself look in every closet, and even yanked the shower curtain back. Convinced she was alone, she carted items to the apartment. After several trips, a three-foot pile of bags was stacked in the living room.

"First things first." Katie dug through the pile until she found the ladder. She carried it to the bedroom, reading instructions as she went. "Clamp steel handles to the window ledge." Katie fiddled with them until they felt secure. "Unfurl ladder with safety stabilizers against the wall." Katie let the fourteen-foot ladder loose, watching it open like a Slinky.

She leaned out the window, looking for anyone lurking. "I said I wasn't going out there, but I need to know I can do this." She took a deep breath and kept reading the instructions, "Test ladder for support." Katie pulled on the clamps one more time and clutching the ledge, she backed out the window. Her legs shook, but she made herself stand on the rungs, even bouncing once. When the ladder held, she climbed to the bottom, counting the seconds. "Five seconds down." She ran to the alley, still counting. Allowing a few seconds to get inside the truck and start the engine, Katie announced, "I should be able to drive away in about twenty seconds."

She rushed back to the ladder and hauled herself inside, disgusted she hadn't brought her keys. Tugging the ladder behind her, she left it directly below the unlocked window, ready to be unfolded at a moment's notice.

Needing noise interaction, anything to drive the fear away, she located the radio from an earlier shopping trip and found a classic rock station. Music blared as she tore into the rest of her bags, eager to see her purchases again.

After putting away the food, Katie hung up her clothes, counting just seven items, minus what she was wearing. She thought about the closet full of clothes back in Savannah, but then remembered Jack had purchased them. She nodded at her few pieces of clothing, "Good enough for now." Socks and underwear were folded into piles on the closet floor.

Thinking about what she would do if she had to run, Katie packed a change of clothes and a few makeup items in the carry-on suitcase, she placed it by the door.

"I'll put that in my truck tomorrow." *I should set aside some cash, too,* she told herself, overwhelmed by having to have a plan A, B, and C for everything right now.

Plugging in the mattress pump, she watched her double-sized bed get bigger. Bon Jovi sang, "It's My Life," and Katie joined them, belting out the chorus as she hung the landscape print, and made up the bed. As the last pillow was tossed artfully onto the comforter, Katie admired the results, "This is perfect."

It was past midnight, but she didn't care. She piled her new dishes in the sink, ready to wash them, but when she turned on the faucet, water sprayed in all directions. "Yipe!"

It was too late to call Mr. Connelly, so she headed for a shower. As she stepped under the water, she remembered she hadn't purchased any towels. "Well, that's just great." Katie dabbed at her wet skin with the sweater she'd worn all day. She mentally created another shopping list. Her eyes began to blur, and she dragged herself to bed.

She'd overfilled the mattress and kept rolling toward the edge, but eventually fell asleep. She dreamed of falling through empty, black space. As she was about to hit the ground, Jack appeared, arms open, ready to catch her.

Chapter 50

Katie was up before eight and wanting a cup of coffee badly. Unfortunately, it was another item she'd forgotten to buy. *Great. A coffee maker, filters, a mug, but no coffee!*

A fist pounded on her door, and Katie pivoted, ready to run for the bedroom ladder.

"Are you in there, Annie?"

Hearing Skinny Tom's voice, Katie opened the door. "I'm here. What's wrong?"

Tom stepped back, and his face flushed. "Your truck's practically parked in the back room." He shuffled his feet. "I got nervous."

She opened the door wider to allow him inside. "Sorry. I got home late last night. The store was dark, my apartment was dark, and I kinda freaked out. It won't happen again."

"Bluff Creek's safe. Quit worrying."

Katie said nothing. Tom understood her too well.

Seeing a multi-colored lamp, and some of her personal items in the living room, Tom commented, "The place is looking good. Do ya need anything?"

"Coffee! If I can have a cup of coffee, I'll bake you something."

Tom pretended to consider the offer. "Cookies? I get cookies if I give you coffee?"

"Anything!"

"Well, come on, then."

Tom and Katie stood shoulder to shoulder, waiting for the store coffee machine to warm. "I'm glad you decided to stay," Tom said to break the silence.

"Me too." Katie fidgeted from foot to foot, willing the coffee to hurry up and get done.

"Ya need help moving stuff inside?"

"I hauled it all in last night."

Tom handed her a steaming cup of coffee. "Keep that back door locked, ya hear?"

Katie held her cup up in salute. "Yes, sir!" She spun towards the storeroom. "See ya later!"

Tom shook his head. "That woman's gonna take some getting' used to."

Katie left a message for Don about the sink and killed time fussing with her books and adjusting the few items she owned.

On Friday morning, Jack's boss, Barry, called Jack into his office and closed the door. "Jack, I know you've had a hell of a week, but I need to talk to you about the audit."

Jack's eyebrows lifted, and he tilted his head, waiting.

"After two months, the team's finally winding down." Barry ran a hand through his gray hair and took a deep breath before continuing, "The auditors have a list of questions concerning your department, zoning permits, and construction bids."

"What are you saying? Am I under investigation?"

"No. They need to tidy up a few loose ends and get more detail. I've set the conference room up for later this afternoon."

Jack had no choice in the mater and left Barry's office, forcing himself to remain calm.

Another knock on her door, had Katie checking the clock. It was 9:30 a.m., and she opened her door, expecting Don. She was shocked to see the guy who'd smashed her behind the door in the General Store. Panic set in. "What are you doing here?" she demanded and instinctively took a step backward.

Recognizing her face, Nick's neck turned red, but he recovered quickly. "You called about the sink leaking."

"I called Don. Why are you here?"

"Ahhh. I see you haven't been clued in yet. I'm Nick Connelly. Maggie and Don are my parents, and I come with the rental end of things."

Flustered, Katie gestured him inside.

What the hell happened to this girl? Nick wondered.

"Well, I'll, uh, let you get to it." Katie went to the bedroom and closed the door.

A half-hour later, Nick had fixed the faucet. "It's good as new," Nick called out. Taking in the few dishes, and the lack of anything on the counter, he asked. "Do you need anything else?"

Katie opened the bedroom door and came halfway to the kitchen, keeping her distance. "No, that's it. Thanks."

Nick saw the air mattress on the floor. "You got more stuff to move in? I've got some time if you need a strong back."

"Nope. I'm afraid this is it."

He scrutinized her bedroom. "You don't even have a bed."

"Nope, not yet."

Nick's head swiveled toward the living room. "Or a TV."

"I've got my books." Katie pointed at the stack on the coffee table.

"No TV? That's crazy." Nick frowned and placed his business card on the counter. Pointing at it, Nick explained, "I'm easier to get ahold of than my dad. Call me if you need anything." Still shaking his head at the lack of a TV, Nick let himself out and headed for the General Store. There was more to this story.

Once Nick was gone, Katie washed her dishes and put them away. They barely filled one cabinet. Sighing, she headed back to Walmart to buy towels, washcloths, and coffee. She doled out another $36.17 and didn't give in to the temptation to purchase more things for the kitchen.

Unsure what else to do with herself, Katie showed up at Tipsy's a half-hour early.

"Watch it, girl, you're making us look bad," Colleen teased. She handed Katie her new work shirt and pointed her toward the bathroom to change.

Katie spent her first day acclimating herself to the restaurant and multiple storage areas. She snickered at the liquor supply stored in a massive vault with a safe-like lock. "Jeez! Kinda serious, huh?"

"An Irishman and his liquor?" Colleen winked, "You can never be too careful."

Katie hauled and rearranged food staples—oldest to newest--in the freezer. Lorraine ran through the kitchen, harassed, as usual, and Katie bussed tables when she could.

"New girl gets bathroom duty!" Colleen laughed. Katie didn't.

A few hours into the shift, Mark snuck an unauthorized break outside. Colleen threw open the back door, making him jump. "Dude, we don't pay you to smoke. Annie's running circles around your sorry ass. Get in here!"

Mark made a face and stubbed out his cigarette. "You can tell who's the boss' kid."

Katie's mouth flopped open. "You're Colin's daughter?"

"Yep. Have been all me life." Colleen put brogue into the statement.

Katie felt foolish for not putting the pieces together sooner.

Catching Katie's eye, Mark grinned. "Know how to get a redhead to change her mind?"

Colleen's shot Mark a murderous look.

Katie couldn't resist and took the bait, "No. How?"

"You wait ten minutes!"

Within a nano-second, Colleen quipped, "Why is a banana better than Mark?"

Katie's eyes grew large. So far, the jokes had been tame.

Colleen snorted, "Get your mind out of the gutter."

Lorraine swung through the kitchen. "Big family of six just walked in. But, tell me, why is a banana better than Mark?"

"A banana has a-ppeal!"

"Oh, you're hysterical. Haha." Mark rolled his eyes but got back to work.

By 4:30 that afternoon, Katie was exhausted. Her head hung heavily on her neck as she leaned against the sink. She was convinced she'd run every plate, glass, and piece of silverware through the dishwasher. She filled the soap dish and slammed the door, running a hand across her forehead and leaving a line of suds. She leaned against the counter and sighed.

Lorraine snickered. "Get used to it, honey. They're all long days around here." She handed Katie a towel, "Wipe your face. You look ridiculous."

"I did move into my apartment last night," Katie called out in defense. She was happy, though. To work and joke with people without the constant strain of Jack's presence was a novelty.

Late in the afternoon, Jack found himself sitting on one side of the long conference table. The three auditors faced him across the polished oak.

"Mr. Werner, we have a few questions we hope you'll answer before we finalize our report." The first auditor picked up a stack of papers and tapped them together.

The second auditor pushed his glasses up on his nose. Addressing Jack, he said, "There seems to be an unusually high number of construction bids granted to two local contractors who's estimates were toward the higher end of the scale. We need to review your parameters used in determining who received building contracts."

The third auditor said nothing, which was unsettling.

Jack cleared his throat. "Is there a list of contracts in question?"

The first auditor split his stack of papers neatly in half, handing four pages to Jack.

Jack's eyes grew large. "All of these?" He scanned them quickly. At least forty contracts were being questioned, with more than two-thirds awarded to Kane Brothers Construction. Jack fidgeted once in his chair and willed himself to sit still. "I don't think we're going to get through this in a day."

The middle auditor agreed. "This may take most of next week, maybe two. You'll want to gather your notes and get the files together. We'll reconvene at ten o'clock on Monday."

The third auditor had saved the best for last. "No paperwork leaves the office, Jack. We'll be watching."

Jack's weekend plans of following Katie's possible routes evaporated.

After work, Colleen handed Katie twenty dollars. At Katie's questioning look, Colleen explained, "You get part of the tips today. You bussed tables, and kept things running." Katie accepted it gratefully and headed toward home. *Home.* She bounced happily on the truck seat, but then Jack's face filled her mind. She drove with caution, scrutinizing each car and driver she passed.

Chapter 51

Jack spent Saturday morning in his home office. He turned off the cameras temporarily and shredded the hidden bank statements in his desk. Next, he called each of the Kane brothers to set up a meeting, "Let's meet in person and not do this over the phone."

Sipping coffee, Katie re-figured her finances. Rent, the deposit, and two trips to Walmart had made another significant dent. She was slightly nauseous when she counted out the remainder of her money--$703.36. "I'd have less if I'd gone to Florida," Katie comforted herself.

She paced the living room twice and walked toward the window to look down on the street below. "And I need some damn curtains too." Scrubbing her face with both hands, she flopped on the couch.

She closed her eyes, thinking through what she absolutely had to do before her first paycheck. *Put the electricity in my name, open a checking account, and get a few more basics for the apartment.*

"I need another job!"

She missed Aunt Susan terribly and almost gave in to the temptation to call. *Not yet.* Katie told herself. *It's too soon.* It made her sad, and with nowhere else to sit, she ended up on the couch again.

Looking at the clock, Katie realized fifteen minutes passed. "Quit feeling sorry for yourself, Katie. Get moving." She grabbed her keys and all the paperwork she thought she'd need and drove toward a branch office for Georgia State Bank in the business section of town.

Less than an hour later, Katie was the proud owner of a checking account, ten temporary checks, and a debit card, arriving in three days. She'd deposited $400 in the bank to cover the next month of rent and electricity and hid $200 under the passenger floor mat of her truck. If Jack showed up, she needed to be able to run. The rest of her cash went into her tote to cover expenses until she got her first paycheck.

Katie called the electric company and set up the utility in her name. They required a fifty-dollar deposit, and she happily read off her new bank account number and authorized them to electronically collect the deposit. She called Don next, surprised when he answered the phone.

"Oh, hi. It's Annie. I was going to leave a message."

"Well, you got the real thing instead. Everything all right?"

"Yep. Your son fixed the faucet this morning."

Don nodded, happy to have Nick home. "It's good to have him here to help again."

"Tom said he just moved back from New York?"

"Yep. Ran off for a few years, thinking the city would do him good. He had some lofty ideas he got to try out, but you can't shake off the hometown roots--ya know?"

"Hmm," Katie answered noncommittedly. "I called to tell you I transferred the electricity to my name. I opened a bank account today, too. You won't need to worry about me carrying all that cash."

"Good girl. You hide all them documents. too, okay?"

She smiled at his advice. "Yes, sir."

Jack met the three Kane brothers at a local sports bar. To anyone noticing them, they were simply four guys eating snacks and watching the football game. Jack told them about the audit, and they took the news better than he'd expected.

"We've seen that happen before."

"No big deal if you covered your tracks."

"We made cash payments from separate accounts, a little here and a little there. We wrote it off as marketing. We have accountants and audits, too."

All three brothers eyed Jack.

Scott, the oldest, leaned forward. "You were careful, right?"

Jack answered quickly, "I deposited the money into a separate account, right about the time I'd have gotten my bonus from work anyway."

"You should have left the transaction as cash," Scott admonished. "It's harder to track. You should close that account. Not now, or it will look suspicious.

Ronnie, the second brother, issued a soft warning, "We don't want anyone knocking on our door. You understand, Jack?"

Tim, the muscle of the group, stayed silent.

They spent another hour discussing ways around questions, giving tips, and coaching Jack. They naturally left him to pay the bill.

It wasn't quite noon, and Katie wasn't scheduled to work until five. She had no idea what to do with so much time. She headed toward the General Store and was disappointed to find the old-timer table empty.

With nothing else to do, she traipsed in and out of all the specialty stores at the Blue-Sky Market, pestered Isaac about his carvings, and once again drooled over the piece resembling an ocean wave. Katie stood on tiptoes and peered through the window of the empty commercial space next to Tanja's Antiques. She could fully envision it as her future bookstore. *It won't be happening anytime soon, that's for damn sure.*

Since it was next door, Katie walked into the antique store. The cashier was about her age, so Katie struck up a conversation, "You're young to be working in an antique store. I always assumed antique stores were for retired people."

The woman laughed and pushed her long, brown hair behind her ears. The move made her pixie-like face stand out, and Katie was charmed.

Well," the woman answered, "a little old lady owned it—my grandma. She named it after me. I'm Tanja." Her eyes turned wistful. "I spent every summer here, helping Nannie run the store. She taught me about furniture and china and crystal perfume bottles. It was a magical place, and I fell in love. When she died, the store came to me. I never dreamed that was her plan, but here I am," Tanja's voice held pride.

"I wouldn't mind having a little store of my own someday. Not antiques, though, so don't worry. I won't be competing. I'm Annie, by the way."

"I know. The whole town's talking about the new girl."

Katie had picked up the same china pitcher three times during their conversation. She turned it over, frowned, and set it back down.

"You like this?" Tanja put the small vase into Katie's hand again.

"No. I love it. The bright red roses, the gold plate around the rim. It's calling my name."

"You've got a good eye. That's Bavarian china signed by Findley Rosenthal."

Katie blinked. "I have no idea what you just said."

"It's rare to find a piece without any chips."

"Is that why it's twenty-seven dollars?" Katie pouted.

Tanja laughed. "Where do you want to display it?"

"On my kitchen counter." Katie playfully ducked her head and closed one eye, waiting for Tanja to scold her.

"You want to put a rare piece of china on your kitchen counter?"

Katie nodded.

"Just because it looks nice? Annie, you're my new best friend!"

"But I can't spend twenty-seven dollars."

"Oh, you're a wheeler-dealer, huh? Twenty-five?"

"No, I mean I really can't spend any money right now."

Tanja nodded and set the vase down. "Are you all moved in?"

Katie's eyes grew large. "How did you know?"

"I told you. You're big news."

"Hardly," Katie scoffed. "But yeah, I'm moved in, although I still need a hundred things. I'm out of money until I get paid. Is there a thrift store around here where I can get the stuff I still need--cheap?"

"Did you say you want to go to a thrift store?" Tanja pretended to fan her face. "My God. You *are* my new best friend."

Maggie strolled in, at that moment, and caught the end of the conversation. "Now you've done it. Tanja will be dragging you to the Goodwill Store every free hour you've got."

Tanja nodded her head hard enough to have her hair flying around her face.

"See?" Maggie asked.

"Seriously, what are you doing tomorrow afternoon?"

Katie spread her hands. "Absolutely nothing. I don't work until Tuesday."

"Wrong." Tanja made a game buzzer sound. "You're going shopping with me!"

Maggie laughed. "I warned you, Annie."

Katie worked six hours behind the bar at Tipsy's Saturday night. Her back hurt, her feet were sore, and she felt vulnerable out among the customers. Her head swiveled toward the door every time someone new walked in the restaurant.

"You looking for someone, *A Chara*?" Colleen asked. "You got a hot date tonight?"

Me?" Katie flushed. "I just got here, remember? And, What's A Chara?"

"It means friend. We take care of our friends here, understand?" Colleen gave Katie a pointed look.

Katie nodded once and began cleaning the bar top in earnest. Later at closing, Katie accepted $46—her portion of tips. It eased her financial worry a tiny bit. Katie waved goodbye to Colleen and Mark and headed for home.

She watched every car along the route, peering into windshields and still expecting Jack.

Chapter 52

Sunday morning found Jack in his office again. He drank his third cup of coffee, trying to develop a reasonable approach to tomorrow's meeting with the auditors. He swiped the dust off his desk and spent hours creating an official list of pros and cons for choosing construction companies to complete county jobs. His vision blurred a few times, but he made himself finish the document, adding a much earlier, fictitious date to the footer at the bottom. He researched the companies he'd bypassed over the years, so there'd be a believable explanation as to why Triple C or Kane Brothers Construction were chosen over lower bids.

He tossed a ready-made dinner in the microwave, hating this new aspect of his life. *If Katie hadn't left, frozen dinners wouldn't be necessary.* It was one more thing to resent.

With no opportunity to bring Katie back home, and the auditors breathing down his neck, it was going to be a long week. Jack mixed himself the first of several drinks.

Katie didn't know the last time she'd had so much fun. She'd shown her list to Tanja, who had taken off like a shot, scouring the aisles of the Goodwill. It was an education, as Tanja gave a running monologue, "Oh my God, would you look at these!" She held up a set of salt and pepper shakers. "These are leaded crystal!" She dropped the set into the cart.

Katie sidetracked to the clothing area, finding another pair of jeans, shorts, and one more bra. When Tanja caught up to her, Katie played off the clothes, not wanting to admit how desperate she was, "These are all name brands!" Katie wheeled the cart back toward the household aisles.

She and Tanja found the right sized curtains for the bedroom and living room. When Tanja threw curtain rods in the cart, Katie grinned. "I would have forgotten those."

They found a plethora of accessories; a dish rack, two wine goblets, ice trays, measuring cups, a cutting board, and two paring knives. Tanja even made Katie try on hats, and they each picked out a book.

"I had no idea," Katie said, still wearing her silly hat and loading her truck. The whole experience had cost $47.08. "I'm never going to Walmart again."

"That a girl! You got any wine to go with those goblets?"

Katie shook her head.

"Well, stop at the liquor store. We've got some celebrating to do." Tanja saw Katie purse her lips, and added, "My treat. I made a new friend today."

Katie fretted. Her lack of things would be painfully noticeable, and she was afraid Tanja would ask questions. *Let it go, Katie. See what happens.* As they entered Katie's apartment, Katie did, however, close her bedroom door.

Tanja took in the kitchen and sparse living room. "Let me guess. Bad relationship just ended, right?"

"Pretty much."

Tanja nodded, opened the wine, and made a toast, "To two fabulous women."

Katie clinked her glass, and they spent an hour getting better acquainted. They even hung up the curtains in the living room. Katie felt some of the stress of running and hiding ebb. Katie hadn't experienced such natural camaraderie since her Atlanta days with Renae and Donette, a whole lifetime ago.

As a slightly tipsy Tanja walked home, Katie rested her head against the door and decided she was calling Aunt Susan. It had been ten days, surely it was safe now.

"Hello?" Susan barked into the phone.

"Aunt Susan?"

"Oh, my God! Katie? Where are you? Are you all right?"

"I am. I can't talk long, but I had to hear your voice."

"What happened?"

"I left Jack, and I'm trying to start over. He'd have never let me simply walk away."

The women spent ten minutes talking as fast as humanly possible. There was a lot to discuss: Katie's get-a-way story, the media, the police, and Jack.

"Reporters are still calling here from time to time, hoping I've got new information," Aunt Susan said, "And I'm getting damn sick and tired of it, too."

"I can't tell you where I am yet, just in case, but soon. I'm making a new life. I've made friends. I have a job and my own apartment. I'm happy, Aunt Susan."

"I can hear it in your voice. Be careful, Katie. Jack's still a loose cannon."

"I know. I need more time. And then I'll make it right." Looking at the minutes left on her phone, Katie reluctantly ended the conversation, "I'll call you again soon."

"I love you!"

"I love you more."

Katie hung up and bawled.

Jack showered early Monday morning, taking even more care than usual with his appearance. He was prepared to defend himself and convinced the questioning would go quickly.

Renewed following the conversation with Aunt Susan, Katie woke up Monday morning and started baking.

"As promised!" Katie marched into the store and handed Skinny Tom a plate full of chocolate-chip cookies. He made a big show of smelling them and set the plate as far away from the retiree table as possible. "These are mine, so ya'll keep your hands off!"

"How come he gets cookies?" Craig grouched.

"He gave me coffee in my time of need."

"Well, I can fix your truck anytime," Thad offered.

"That ain't nothin' You'd screw it up anyway. Me?" Jarrod continued, "I'll carry your groceries upstairs next time."

Craig leaned back on two legs of his chair. "Hell, I'll shoot all you bastards and save Annie the trouble."

Katie grinned. *Where else could I find these priceless men?* "Since you're all willing to help, maybe I'll make you a plate of cookies too."

"Each? We each get cookies?" Craig thunked his chair back down, waiting for her reply.

Not willing to lose Skinny Tom as an ally, Katie shook her head. "I think you'll have to share."

Tom grinned and ate one of his warm cookies.

Katie waltzed out the door, pleased with how things were going.

Jack sat, listening to the auditors outline their concerns. He said nothing unless asked a specific question. He knew the ruse--get him talking, and he'd give away more than intended and hang himself in a noose of his own making.

Although she wasn't scheduled, Katie headed toward Tipsy's Monday afternoon. She walked in as Colleen slammed the phone down in disgust.

"Dammit." Colleen fumed. "I hate days like this! Lorraine has to leave early to take her mom to the doctor. The nursing home doesn't keep up with things, and her mom's got another urinary tract infection. I could handle being one server down, but the other girl, Lisa, called in sick, too." Colleen threw her towel. "I have to be home by three for Josh."

"Who's Josh?"

"My son."

Katie swiveled her head toward Colleen. "You have a son?"

"I do, and he's the most amazing little boy in the world." Colleen pulled up a picture on her phone and showed it to Katie. "He just turned eight."

Katie recognized Down's Syndrome features. She smiled. "He's special."

"Damn straight he is."

Katie didn't ask any questions, which earned her big points. Colleen cocked her head and filled in the blanks voluntarily. "His dad hit the road three days after he was born. Said he couldn't handle a child like *that.* Asshole. We weren't married, so I sent him on his way. Been Josh and me ever since. Well, and Colin. He adores his grandson."

"Your mom's gone?"

"Yeah." Colleen sighed. "She died before Josh was born. Cancer."

"My mom's gone, too. I'm sorry. Is there anyone else to help with Josh?"

My brother, Conner, and his partner, Shane, but they're down in Tampa running Tipsy McQue's Two."

"Wow. I didn't know there was a chain."

"Yeah, pretty cool, but we don't get to see each other often."

Katie nodded, understanding what it was to miss family. "It sounds like you're in a jam. I can come in this afternoon and help."

"Seriously?"

"I've got nothing going, and I need the money."

“Hmm.” Colleen considered the restaurant. “We’re not overly busy on Mondays. Think you can handle the four tables there by the window?”

“I may not be as fast as Lorraine, but I can do it.”

“Mark can handle the rest, and Colin will run the bar. He’ll complain the whole time, but you watch how much fun he has.”

“What time should I be here?”

“Two to seven? Josh and I can come back in then and help close things down.”

It wasn’t easy since Katie hadn’t learned the menu, but she smiled a lot and only messed up one order. She watched the door but was more discreet. She also made $57 in tips, which she didn’t have to share because no one was bussing, or behind the bar. Katie mentally promised herself half of all tips would go into the bank.

Disgusted with his day, the fucking auditors, and life in general, Jack stopped at the liquor store on the way home. He was out of smokes and Jack Daniels. He needed both to get through the evening.

The third drink found him raging aloud, “God damn bitch!” He kicked a kitchen char and headed to the den and the cabinet Katie had refinished. Yanking out all the items she’d carefully collected for her patients, he carted them to the fireplace and set them aflame. He poured another drink and watched the fire.

Chapter 53

On Tuesday, Nick swung by the Crested Iris to visit with his mom. Maggie went into full matchmaker mode, "The new girl waited on your dad and me last night at Tipsy's. She was a little flustered but did a nice job."

Nick nodded noncommittedly. Annie intrigued him. Just that morning, he'd gone to the General Store, in hopes of catching a glimpse. She'd been bargaining with Skinny Tom about using the washer and dryer she'd spied in the storeroom.

"It sure would be nice to do laundry here versus going to the laundromat on the other side of town." She'd turned her green eyes on Skinny Tom.

The old-timers were listening intently, and Nick grinned at Tom's red face.

"You've always got a load of towels sitting there. I'll wash 'em for you, and you'd never have to worry about it again." She negotiated sweetly, and Nick had known Skinny Tom wouldn't say no.

"Sounds like a good deal to me," Jarrod called out.

"Let her use the damn thing," Thad yelled.

As Tom was saying yes, Katie caught sight of Nick. She stiffened and hurried through the rest of the conversation. "So, we've got a deal? You're the best." She pecked Tom on the cheek and ran toward the door. "See ya'll!"

Nick had turned aside, embarrassed. Annie obviously wanted nothing to do with him, and he had no idea why.

Jack looked at the clock and sighed. He'd spent three hours in meetings with the auditors, just as he'd done Monday. The auditors appeared to be buying his story, but there were still twenty-eight contracts to review. At this pace, these meetings were going to take days. It had been a week since Captain Greer had stood in front of the media, discussing Katie's voluntary disappearance. *And here I sit listening to these idiots while Katie gets further away.*

Katie walked into Tipsy's as the Tuesday breakfast crowd was thinning. Lorraine was there, which was perfect. "Colleen mentioned your mom's in a nursing home."

Lorraine looked up, surprised. "Yeah. She's got dementia and had a stroke a year ago. She needs care all day."

"That's got to be hard. Is the nursing home nearby?"

"In Brunswick. So, maybe fifteen minutes or so. Why?"

"Well, it sounds like they're shorthanded. Colin promised me a couple of days here, but I'll barely make my bills."

"You don't want to work there. It smells bad, and the workers are grumpy-ass people."

Katie shrugged. "I think I'd like it."

Katie drove the busier streets of Brunswick. She noted there were more upscale shops: a jewelry store, a spa with an attached boutique, clothing stores. No bookstores, which was good. She found the Silver Linings nursing home on the outskirts of town. She personally thought it was a hokey name but couldn't afford to be choosy.

As Katie entered the building, she was assailed by the smell of urine, antiseptic, and depression. Katie concentrated on breathing through her mouth and walked up to the reception desk. "Do you know if they're hiring here?"

The young woman's surprised expression was comical. "Are you kidding? Let me call the supervisor."

A beautiful woman with ebony skin and long straight hair pulled back in a colorful scarf came out of a back office. "I'm Latrice Copley, the administrator here. How can I help you?" She talked fast and looked at her watch.

"I'm Anne Morrison." Katie held out her right hand. "I'm new to the area and wondered if you're hiring."

Latrice looked at Katie over her glasses. "Really? No one seems to want to work here." She glanced briefly at the receptionist, who quickly found numerous tasks to keep herself busy. "Do you have any experience?"

Katie answered as close to the truth as she dared, "Well, I cared for an elderly uncle who had Alzheimer's and helped a woman who'd had a stroke. My cousin was in traction for six weeks, and I helped him. I'm good with people."

Latrice harrumphed, but she was as desperate for a warm body as Katie was for a job. "Come on back. Let's get more details."

She wrote down Katie's pertinent information. "Anything else we can add? Do you know how to bathe or shower a patient?"

"No, but I'm willing to learn. Oh, and I'm certified in CPR."

It seemed to clinch the deal, but Latrice had one more question. "You're sure you can be here at seven-thirty a.m.?" At Katie's nod, Latrice offered her first smile.

They agreed Katie would work Monday through Wednesday from seven-thirty to four-thirty. "You'll be cleaning rooms, helping patients get dressed, and transporting them to and from lunch and activities. The nurse's aides do the rest. We'll give you more training, when possible."

The pay wasn't great-- $9.00 an hour, but Katie didn't need much.

"If your background check comes back clear, you can train this Thursday, and we'll get you on the schedule."

"Just so you know," Katie rushed to explain the security flag.

Latrice raised her eyebrows and gave Katie a once-over from head to toe. "Huh. We'll let you know."

Katie drove back to Bluff Creek, hopeful.

Latrice called at three. "Well, other than being dead, your report is clean."

There was a pregnant pause that Katie rushed to fill. "I'm fighting with them all the time. I've filled out enough paperwork to kill a few trees. Please, I need a job."

There was a long silence. "Please," Katie whispered once more.

Latrice caved to the request, as much due to Katie's plea as to her own need to fill a position. "We'll need another form of I.D."

"I have a new bank count and lease agreement. Will those work?"

"You bring those on Thursday and submit to a drug test, and you're hired."

"Thank you, thank you, thank you! You won't regret this, I promise."

"You'll need nursing scrubs. Basic white pants, work shoes, and a medical smock."

Katie was fairly certain she'd seen such things at Goodwill. She texted Tanja's to see if she wanted to tag along.

Tanja responded, *Meetcha at 6?*

They found what Katie needed, and Tanja handed over a twenty-percent off coupon. "I was saving this for myself, but I think you need it more."

Katie opened a nearly empty wallet. "You know me well!"

Jack studied maps on the computer. "These are too fucking small." He needed more detail and ordered a four by four map of Savannah, and another one showing Georgia, South Carolina, Louisiana, and Florida. He'd track Katie down. *I can research despite the frickin' auditors. What I do on my own time is none of their business.*

Katie rushed into the General Store on Wednesday morning and pulled out a chair at the old-timer table. "Ask me what's new?" Her youth and enthusiasm were a powerful balm for tired, achy bodies.

Craig beat Jarrod to the punch. "I'll bite. What's new?"

Katie couldn't sit still in her chair. "I have not one, but two jobs! Pretty cool, huh? Now I can save some money and make some real plans." She spent ten minutes answering their questions and noticed Nick had come in for coffee. He was visiting the store each morning, and she suspected it was on purpose.

"Hey, Annie." He waved casually and started a conversation with Skinny Tom.

Katie gave a small wave. *He's not so bad.* The woman in her was flattered, but she kept her distance. *Jack was charming, too, Katie.*

Jack had been chewing on the notion that maybe Katie hadn't left Savannah. By the time his workday was done, he'd half-convinced himself she was still in the city. He drove through a McDonalds and then headed to Mr. Parker's house. *Hell, she could be taking care of him, still getting paid, and no one would know. His niece wouldn't care if Katie stayed there.*

At 6:10 Wednesday evening, Jack parked his car and polished off his French fries as he watched Mr. Parker's house. A car pulled in the driveway, and Jack sat up, peering out the windshield. *Not Katie.* "Shit!" He smacked the steering wheel in frustration.

He watched the woman go into the house. Lights came on, but no one else went in or out. After fifteen minutes, he gave up, cruising slowly past the house and trying to see inside. He inhaled a cigarette and headed home.

Katie sailed through her training day at Silver Linings. "You're a natural with the patients," Latrice commented, mentally congratulating herself on hiring Katie.

Jack spent Thursday night in front of Gertrude Taylor's home. He smoked, ate more fast food, and watched the street. He got home late, disappointed there'd been no sign of Katie. The maps hadn't arrived, either. He mixed a drink and threw his clothes on the floor.

He left work early on Friday and followed Katie's boss, Cheyenne. He stayed a few cars behind her as she picked up her kid from daycare, drove through an ATM, and stopped to get groceries. Jack parked a row over, waiting. Cheyenne finally exited with a full shopping cart. "About time." Jack crumbled his take-out bag and followed her to an older section of town. Jack was disappointed to see a darkened house. He parked and was settling in when he saw a curtain pull back. Jack drove away quickly. "That's all I need is her calling the fucking cops."

Katie worked a busy shift Friday night. She never quit moving and was grateful. It kept her from thinking too much. Instead, she told anyone who would listen about her new job at the nursing home.

As she drove home later, she sang, "Happy birthday to me. Happy Birthday to me." She'd just turned twenty-eight, and no one in town could know.

To make this new life stick, she'd be celebrating Cassie's birthday in February instead.

Chapter 54

Jack spent Saturday morning doing laundry and grocery shopping. "God damn, Katie. These are your chores, not mine." He slammed the door on the dishwasher and jabbed at buttons. "This is bullshit." Grabbing his keys and wallet, he headed for the car.

If she's not in Savannah, then Atlanta makes sense. He spent the drive remembering every place he and Katie had ever visited in the city: restaurants, parks, a mall. *Where would you go, Katie?*

He drove straight to Aunt Susan's, silently seething at all the phone calls between her and Katie. Susan would help Katie. Of that, he had no doubt. Parking nearby, we watched the house and wished for a drink.

Ten minutes passed, and pissed off he was getting nowhere, Jack got out of his car and circled around the house. Sneaking up to the patio door, he peered inside just as Susan entered the kitchen. She puttered around, unaware she was being watched. Jack hurried to the front door and banged on it with his fist. He was positioned immediately in front of the entrance, ready to check for clues---an extra pair of shoes, Katie's purse, anything.

Susan looked out the peephole. Spying Jack, she put the chain on the door before opening it the few inches allowed. "What are you doing here, Jack?"

Jack tried to see around her. Susan moved, blocking his view.

"I need to know where my wife is staying," Jack stated. "I know she's called you."

Susan didn't bother to answer, and Jack tried another tactic.

"It's been too long. What if something happened to Katie?" He whined. "If she wants to leave, fine. I'm just worried at this point."

"My ass, you're worried." Aunt Susan put her hands on her hips. "You want her back like a toy you've lost and need to get back in the box." Susan shut and locked her front door.

Jack sped away. *I didn't expect much from the old bitch anyway.*

Parking in front of Katie's previous apartment complex, Jack scrutinized each person going in and out of the buildings. He sat for over an hour, hating the place as much as he had when he and Katie had been dating.

Giving up on that angle, Jack went to the *City Palette* restaurant. He sat at the bar, not seeing anyone who even closely resembled Katie. Her friend, Renae, was still working there, though. He sent a friendly wave in her direction. *Loser,* Jack thought. *Still working the same dead-end job, in the same run-down, POS restaurant.*

Renae recognized him and hurried over. "Oh, my God! Jack! Have you heard anything about Katie? I've been so worried!"

Jack shook his head sadly and looked at his shoes. He needed information and could play-act if it brought him closer to finding Katie. "No. I haven't. I was sort of hoping you'd heard from her or seen her?"

"Well…" Renae paused.

"What? What do you know?" He popped off the stool and grabbed her arm. His eyes dilated, and his breathing intensified.

No longer believing his con, Renae finished her sentence, "I haven't heard from Katie in five years. Right after she married you, in fact." Renae yanked her arm free and stomped off.

"How about the other girl?" Jack called out, "What was her name? Donette?"

Renae spun back toward Jack. "She quit hearing from Katie, too." She flipped Jack her middle finger and stalked away.

Jack drove back to Savannah in a rage, mentally daring other motorists to get in his way. The need to crush, hit, destroy was high.

Colleen observed Katie on Saturday night, instinctively knowing there was more to Katie's story. *At least she's not watching the door as much.*

Katie still seemed vulnerable, though, which brought out fierce, protective feelings in Colleen—something she'd honed since having her little boy, Josh.

Unaware of Colleen's scrutiny, Katie shared a joke, "In a bar in a remote Alaskan town, a newcomer hears people yell out numbers 23, 56, and so on. And then everyone laughs. He asks the guy next to him what's going on, and the guy says, 'these jokes have been told so many times, people just yell out their numbers instead of retelling them.' So, the newcomer yells out 27! But no one laughs. The guy next to him says, "Some people can tell a joke, and some can't."

Jack's mood improved dramatically when he got home and discovered the maps he'd ordered had arrived. He opened the tubes, unfurling them and nodding appreciatively. "Finally!" He made a drink, sloshing it on the stairs in his haste to examine the maps more closely.

He'd thrown out the mess of Katie's shredded clothes, leaving her half of the closet bare. He taped the maps on the empty wall and circled the medical complex, their house, and the address in Middleburg. "Which way would you go?" Jack scratched at his unshaven chin. *West toward Atlanta and what's familiar makes the most sense.* He remembered Katie talking about her one vacation. Jack circled the Birmingham area.

He nodded once. He'd find Katie and bring her home. *Hell, she'll probably be grateful by this time.* Jack laughed at the idea of Katie trying to make decisions and take care of herself.

He went downstairs and mixed another whiskey and Coke, carrying the bottle upstairs. He gulped his drink as he ran his finger along the possible routes from Savannah to Birmingham.

"You still have to get there, though. You took a bus out of Savannah, and then what? Would you buy a car?" Jack thought about the five-thousand-dollar savings account she'd managed to hide from him, and his fingers clenched the glass in his hand. He retrieved the bottle and poured straight whiskey as he considered options. He needed a starting point—somewhere near used car lots and bus stops.

Jack pulled out his phone, Googling western bus routes out of the city. The Chatham Area Transit Map was a friggin' mess--color-coded lines intersected and traversed the entire city. At least three headed west, but every time he zoomed into an area, the map grew too large, and he kept losing his bearings. "Goddammit!" He threw his phone across the closet. "I need another drink." He filled his tumbler to the rim and retrieved his phone.

He saw an option to order a full-sized copy and filled out information quickly. It would all come together soon.

Jack woke up Sunday morning, with his head pounding and his ears ringing. "This is all your fault, Katie!" He yelled the words and immediately regretted the decision. He dropped an aching head into his hands, willing the blood drubbing through his brain to stop.

Queasy and unsteady on his feet, he crawled back into bed, pulling the covers over his head to block out even a hint of light. He stayed curled and nauseous for hours until a constant knocking had him fighting his way free of the tangled sheets. Wincing at the God-awful taste in his mouth, he swung his feet to the floor and waited to see if the room would stop swimming.

The doorbell had him swearing. He yanked on a shirt and clutched the stair rail for support as he worked his way to the front door. *I'm going to kill whoever is out on that porch.* Jack yanked open the door, his face reflecting his murderous thoughts.

The police officer stepped back instinctively. "Jack? You okay?"

Jack stared at the man, trying to come up with a name.

"Officer Fairchild," Randy supplied. "We met before—weeks ago when Katie was initially missing?" He paused, giving time for Jack to puzzle it through.

Jack grunted.

"We're responding to a call from Susan Garrison."

Jack raked a shaky hand through his already messy hair. "Yeah. That was dumb. I can't help wondering about Katie. I thought maybe she'd gone to her aunt's house."

Fairchild made a note of Jack's appearance and demeanor. "Uh-huh. It seems odd for you to drive four hours to Atlanta. A phone call would have been easier, dontcha think?"

"I had to see for myself."

"I'd advise you to leave Ms. Garrison out of the mix. She's mad as hell." Fairchild turned away and then thought better of it. "Jack, you need to accept the fact Katie's not coming back."

Jack waited until the cruiser backed out of the driveway before slamming the front door. The sound reverberated painfully in his head, but he didn't care. He was damn sick and tired of playing games.

On Sunday night, Colin called Katie into his office. "Ya've done a good job. It's time to make this official." He slid an application across his desk.

She'd been in Bluff Creek thirteen days. With no sign of Jack, Katie accepted the job.

Chapter 55

Nick invented ploys to capture Katie's interest. When she came through the store on Monday morning, he was there having a cup of coffee. "Want one?" he offered

"Already had some, thanks." She rushed out the door.

"She looks so cute in her white uniform," Nick said to himself, but the old men heard him, and news spread. Nick was after Annie.

The next day, Nick brought a flower to the store. "Congratulations on the new job." He held out his gift.

Katie gave a quick, "Thanks," and snatched the yellow daisy as she exited the store.

"Whoo-hoo. She ain't liking you, Nick." The retirees chortled in delight.

"Girl's got good sense if you ask me," Craig added.

Nick shrugged. "She smiled this time, though, right?"

Jack began his second week of meetings with the auditors. They'd reviewed the contracts he'd rejected and were whittling down the seventeen contracts he'd approved, saving the Kane Brothers for last. They studied every minute detail to the point Jack thought he would scream. There was nothing Jack could do but smile until his face hurt and hope they'd finish soon.

Jack drove home, irritated, and pissy. He made a frozen dinner and sat picking at the plastic-tasting food and brooding. Slinging the half-eaten dinner in the trash, he went to the den. *I need pictures of Katie when I start tracking routes.* He pulled up a recent photo and photoshopped it to show darker hair and glasses. Having the police stop by the day before had him thinking up a disguise for himself, too.

Katie had been in town for three weeks, and people were curious about her background. When asked for specifics, she gave vague answers, "Trust me, it wasn't that interesting." Or, "Who cares? I've got Bluff Creek."

Maggie had figured it out, though. Annie's face kept tripping an elusive memory until one day it clicked, and she recognized Anne as the woman the news stations had reported as missing from Savannah. Anne or Kathryn, or whoever she was, didn't seem to have any malicious intent, so Maggie kept the information to herself.

Annie usually dropped by the Crested Iris on her day off. She'd snag a cup of coffee and talk. Maggie inserted cautionary advice and thinly disguised warnings whenever the conversation allowed. If Annie understood the implications, she gave no sign to Maggie.

Maggie knew her Nicky was interested in the woman. *Hell, the whole town knows.* Maggie worried aloud as she made dinner, "They're both gonna get hurt."

"What'd ya say?" Don asked from the kitchen table where he was working a sudoku.

Maggie kissed the top of his head. "Just talking to myself."

Jack received the Savannah Bus street guide and hung it on the closet wall next to his other maps. He traced the three western routes—Blue, Brown, and Orange. He circled bus stops and pulled up Google Maps to make notes on surrounding businesses.

He'd made false business cards, listing himself as Greg Landis, Private Investigator. Looking at himself in the mirror, Jack smiled in satisfaction at the disguise he'd put together: a pair of glasses, fake mustache, longer sideburns, and a hat. *I'm ready.*

Nick visited Tipsy's more often, inviting his parents to dinner, picking up sandwiches for lunch, and having a beer at the bar with his friend, Blake.

Colleen filled Katie in on Blake, "He and Nick used to fight every day in middle school--always shoving and punching. Once, bad enough, Nick broke Blake's nose. Look," she pointed discreetly, "you can still see the little bump. Anyway, they've been best friends ever since. When Nick left for New York, Blake headed to Quantico. Now, he works at the Federal Training Center, near Brunswick."

Blake's profession wasn't welcome news. Katie walked away from the bar, finding other areas to work in the restaurant.

When he struck out at Tipsy's, Nick pretended the General Store needed repairs, but no one was fooled. Katie couldn't help flirting with him occasionally. He seemed a decent guy and certainly wasn't hard to look at with his wavy hair and easy smile. Then Jack's face filled her mind, and she shut down any thoughts of Nick. *You need to deal with Jack.* She then made excuses: *If I file for divorce, Jack will know where I am. Plus, how the hell am I supposed to explain using Cassie's name?*

Tamping down her guilt, Katie kept adding to her new life, and hoping her luck would hold. When a flea market was advertised, she withdrew part of the tips she'd saved and hightailed it to the county fairgrounds. She was delighted to find a cheap, old dresser. The lines were excellent, and she was sick of digging through her belongings on the floor of the closet.

The vendor helped load it into her truck, and she happily headed back to town. She was dragging the dresser frame toward the stairs when Skinny Tom walked into the storeroom.

"What the hell are you doing? You can't get that upstairs by yourself. Hang on a minute." He ran to the front of the store and returned with Nick.

Great. Just great, Katie griped to herself.

Nick helped her carry the dresser to her bedroom and wisely said nothing about the blow-up mattress. His eyebrows went up when he spied the safety ladder under the window, though. "Are you planning on sneaking in, or sneaking out with that thing?"

"Umm, I guess I should have asked. I got nervous about just one exit. Fire or, you know, whatever," she stammered.

It made sense in a paranoid sort of way, and Nick nodded. He walked back to the living room, noticing some of the additions she'd made in the last few weeks. "Things are looking better up here."

"Thanks. A little at a time."

"Want me to cart up the drawers?"

"No. You've done more than enough." Katie scooted him toward the door. She was aggravated to find her palms sweating and wiped them on her jeans.

Nick entered the store and grabbed a chair by the retirees. "You know she doesn't even have a bed?"

The men leaned away from Nick and raised their eyebrows.

"Why do you care if she has a bed?" Jarrod asked.

"What business is that of yours?" Craig leaned back in his chair, waiting for an answer.

"Seems you're kinda forward there, ain't ya?" Thad asked.

"Unbelievable. You've known me all my life, and I'm suddenly an ass for making a simple statement?" Nick stood, and the group had the good grace to look chagrined. "I was trying to say she's sleeping on an air mattress."

"Sorry," Jarrod mumbled, "something about that woman makes a man protective."

Nick pointed at his chest. "I'm a man. I feel protective too." He saluted them and headed out to complete an estimate for a shed a local family wanted Connelly Construction to build.

The old men motioned Skinny Tom over and held a short conference.

The next morning a complete bed, albeit used, mysteriously showed up in the back storage room. A note was attached, "For Annie."

Katie was beside herself. "Who did this, Tom? Was it you?"

"I got no idea, but you can bet your ass I'm gonna be asking who the hell broke into my store." He hurried off before she asked any other questions.

Katie was right behind him. She took in the table full of old men, all gauging her reaction. "Seems I've got a few guardian angels. Anybody going to take credit for the bed?"

They looked around the table and pretended confusion.

"What the hell is she yammering about?" Jarrod asked.

Katie nodded and accepted their generosity. "Well, anyone interested in getting it upstairs?"

The men clamored out of their chairs, anxious to see how she was living up in that apartment anyway.

Chapter 56

Jack sat in his boss's office, listening to a summary of the auditor's final report.

"The auditors have signed off on their review. I do have to add this to your file, though." Barry flourished a single sheet of paper.

"What is it?"

"An official reprimand, listing a high percentage of contracts awarded to Triple C and Kane Brothers Construction. From now on, you need to be more unbiased." Barry handed the form to Jack to read. "You need to sign and date it at the bottom."

Jack glared at Barry and snatched a pen. "This is bullshit."

"It's just a warning, Jack." Barry filed the paper in a drawer.

Jack was still pissed, but he'd survived and without repercussions to the Kane Brothers. Now he could concentrate on finding Katie.

Katie's first paychecks were set to arrive on the first Friday in October. Between the two jobs and her tips, she'd be bringing in almost $2000 a month and could easily make her bills. Moving forward with her dream, she ordered a crate of children's classics on clearance.

"This calls for a celebration." Noting the time, she headed toward Tipsy's and dashed into Colin's office. "Can I steal Colleen and Josh for an hour? I'm so happy I can barely stand it and want to take 'em out to help me celebrate."

Colin acted offended, "Who the hell's gonna watch the bar?"

"There's no one better than you!"

Colin pushed himself out of his chair, grumbling, "Young people got no respect anymore." His twinkling eyes negated the gruff words. "Go on! Get out of here. Colleen needs a friend."

Katie corralled Colleen and Josh into her truck and sped toward McDonald's. Katie and Colleen talked as Josh squealed, with delight, each time he went down the slide.

"This was fun," Colleen stated, "but you didn't have to do anything."

Katie laughed. "Yeah, big spender, huh?"

"I didn't say that." Colleen punched Katie lightly on the arm. "I meant asking Josh and me to come out with you. God, Katie, you're just getting your first paycheck. You should be saving every penny for your store." Colleen cocked her head. "You *are* still going to open a store, right?"

"Yep. That's the eventual plan, but what's the point of having wonderful things going on in your life if you can't share it with the people you love?"

They walked into Tipsy's singing, "This old man, he played three…"

Ten minutes later, Blake and Nick walked into Tipsy's. Blake spied Colleen and Katie and trotted over to the bar area. "Hey, we're going to Rock of Ages tonight. You girls wanna go?"

"Not me," Colleen answered. "I've got a hot date with Josh tonight."

Tanja walked in the door, already calling out her order, "Cabernet for me, Colleen."

Blake made a beeline for her. "Tanja, love of my life, tell me you'll go to Rock of Ages with me tonight." Blake got down on one knee.

"Don't do it, Tanja! He just asked me. He's shameless," Colleen joked.

Tanja studied her nails. "Second choice, huh? Well, I've got better things to do--wash my hair, take out the trash."

Blake clasped her hands in his and pulled them toward his chest. "Please! And tell Annie she should go with Nick."

Tanja winked at Katie. "Well, if *she's* going, it's far more appealing."

"Yes!" Blake yelled, drawing Colin out of his office.

"What do you think, Annie?" Nick asked softly. "You in?"

Katie hesitated. "What's Rock of Ages?"

"Great bar down in Brunswick. Good pizza, pitchers of beer, and," Tanja grinned at Blake, "occasionally good-looking men."

Blake and Nick elbowed one another and added information.

"It's also open-mic night."

"And half-price wings, too."

"You boys don't think you're going to get out of it that cheap, do you?" Tanja brushed past Blake, almost touching him. She batted her lashes, and Blake mimed having a heart attack.

Katie looked at Colleen, silently asking for her opinion. Colleen rolled her eyes but nodded. With the group waiting for her reply, Katie gave in. "Okay. I'll go. As friends," she emphasized.

Nick and Blake cheered.

"Big ruckus, a man can't even think. What the hell is going on?" Colin asked from his office door frame.

"You're just nosy," Colleen yelled out from behind the bar.

"So, okay, I'm nosy. What's all the yelling about?"

Blake grabbed Tanja's hand again. "Tanja has agreed to accompany me on a date night."

"And Annie is going with me!" Nick tried to grab Katie's hand, but she slid out of reach.

Katie pulled Tanja aside. "Fill me in! What should I wear?"

Jack circled businesses along the Blue route and headed towards his car. He patted his jacket pockets, ensuring he had his fake business cards and plenty of pictures of Katie.

Nick and Blake picked up Tanja and Katie and headed toward *Rock of Ages.* As the foursome pulled into the parking lot, the red neon sign blinked on and off, and music pulsed through the air.

Finding a corner booth, they squeezed together, ordering a pizza and a pitcher of beer. They yelled to be heard over the band, and Katie howled with laughter as Tanja, Blake, and Nick took turns telling stories about the others. "You did not steal your teacher's car!" She stared at Tanja, unconvinced her friend had been so rebellious.

They shuffled around the dance floor and tried teaching Katie the 'Cotton Eyed Joe' dance. Tanja and Blake had obviously been dance partners before, but Katie was befuddled by the side-to-side movements, kicking and clapping. She kept going the wrong direction, and the harder she worked, the harder she failed. Nick was relentless. "No, Annie! Left, then right, then you touch your heel."

Katie collapsed on his chest, gasping for air and crying from laughing so hard. "My face hurts," she announced as she slid back into the booth.

"You need some work, girlfriend. Haven't you ever been out dancing?" Tanja asked.

Katie shook her head no. Their shocked expressions had her offering a quick explanation. "Dinner parties, but no dancing." She gulped beer to end the conversation.

The band called "Open-mic," and Blake stood up and preened.

Katie was shocked. "You're not going up there, are you?"

"My public awaits."

Nick thumped his friend on the back. "You go, buddy."

Blake borrowed the lead guitar and spun into a fast riff. He danced and twisted, his jet black hair shining in the lights. Tanja pointed at Blake moving across the stage. "Man's got some moves. I may have to consider this more closely."

Katie snorted.

Five minutes later, Blake called Nick up on stage. "Come on, man. The drummer says he needs a break. Get up here and help me out. Folks, give the man a hand." The crowd, who'd had enough beer to applaud anything, enthusiastically clapped and yelled.

Katie watched in amazement as Nick stood up, took off his long-sleeved shirt, and strode toward the drum set, wearing snug-fitting jeans and a simple white t-shirt.

Tanja then let out a whistle. "Look at that ass!"

Blake raised his eyebrows, and Tanja sent him an air kiss.

Blake played fast and furious on the electric guitar, and Nick smacked every drum and cymbal with a fair degree of talent.

"Who knew?" Katie yelled across the noise to Tanja. *Who knew I'd be on a double date having a great time?*

Afterward, Nick walked her to the back-alley door. "I'll wait here until I see your lights come on upstairs." He wanted to kiss her badly but decided it was too soon.

"Thank you for a nice night." Katie smiled as she locked the supply door and hurried up the stairs. She waved to Nick from her tiny kitchen window. Humming to herself, she practiced the Cotton Eyed-Joe in the living room and didn't think about Jack once.

Chapter 57

The following Thursday, Nick dropped by his mom's shop and picked out a bouquet.

"Don't move too fast, Nicky," Maggie warned.

He sent her a cheeky grin and headed toward the General Store, where the retirees were placing bets on whether Katie would go out with Nick.

"I got five dollars that says no," Craig proclaimed. "If she's smart, she'll choose Blake."

"You're prejudiced because Blake's your son." Jarrod tugged on his overalls. "Nicky's the one showing up all the time."

Thad agreed with Jarrod, enjoying Craig's scowl.

Skinny Tom smacked the table with his towel. "You'll all lose. You know she's only got eyes for me." He sauntered off, leaving them to argue.

Oblivious to the wagers, Nick climbed the stairs to Katie's apartment. When she answered the door, he held out the cluster of flowers. "Wanna take a walk with me by the creek?"

Katie stuck her face down in the bouquet to smell them. "What are these? I've never seen anything like them."

"The big white one is Queen Anne's Lace."

Katie gestured Nick inside. He didn't take the invitation lightly and moved forward.

"And these?" She pointed to the bright red berries and tiny clusters of white flowers.

"Pond Berry and dropwort."

"You brought me Dropwort?" She crinkled her forehead but felt her heart shift a tiny bit, even as her brain sent out a warning, *Don't get involved again.*

Nick rushed to explain, "They're pretty on the inside. The berry has the most amazing arrangement of seeds." He broke one open. "See? It looks like a star. You can't judge a thing by its name, Annie." He brushed his fingers across her cheek.

His words had her wincing at her own lies. *Tell him the truth,* her conscience screamed. Katie squashed the voice of reason. "Let's take that walk."

They ambled along Fancy Bluff Creek, and Nick gave non-stop commentary on every bird, tree, and flower they passed. It was a pleasant hour, and one Katie realized had not required her to look perfect, or offer witty banter, or provide sexual quid pro quo.

On the way back to town, Nick pulled a crumbled flier out of his jacket and handed it to Katie.

"What's this?" She asked.

"Most of us are at a loss once the season dies down. So, we show a matinee on the third Saturday of the month. Wanna go?"

Katie stayed non-committal for a week, wrestling with her lies and dreams. She wanted it all—the town, the new life, even Nick.

She thought through the years after her parents died, the years of living with Jack, and yearned for a true companion—someone she could lean on, confide in, love. *But what if the truth comes out?*

Jack spent his evenings visiting restaurants, motels, and car lots along the western Blue transit route. He passed out dozens of business cards and asked about Katie at each stop. One man found Jack's relentless activity suspicious and called the police.

On Friday, Officer Darrow read the phone message and went to find Hopkins. "Some guy--probably Jack—has been handing out cards listing himself as Greg Landis, P. I, and asking about Kathryn Werner."

"What are you talking about?" Hopkins sipped his coffee and then glared at the contents inside his cup. "God, this is worse than normal." He wiped his lips free of the taste.

Darrow rattled a piece of paper in the air. "Got a call from a Bryce McDermit out near Tremont Park. He manages A.J.'s Auto Mart. He claims this Greg Landis went from business to business two nights in a row. He was showing pictures of a young woman—Bryce said it looked like Kathryn Werner from TV—anyway, he got suspicious because it was in the evening, and this guy made like eight stops in a row. The investigator was not only asking if anyone had seen her but whether she bought a car, got a ride, etc. I think it's Jack."

"There's nothing wrong with Jack looking for his wife."

Darrow rolled his eyes. "Yeah, but Jack's probably not just looking."

Hopkins nodded. "Maybe we oughta check in on ol' Jack."

When Jack pulled in his driveway, after work, a police cruiser slid in behind his car. Jack squinted at the rear-view mirror. *Now what?*

Officers Darrow and Hopkins got out of their car, and Jack groaned. Composing himself, he stepped out of his car and took the offensive, "Officers Darrow, Hopkins. To what do I owe this honor?" He brushed at his dress pants and forced a smile.

"Hey, Jack," Darrow returned the greeting.

Hopkins stayed silent and watched Jack shake a cigarette out of a mostly empty pack. *He looks like shit.*

"Do you have any news about Katie?" Jack asked, blowing out smoke like a professional.

"No, but we heard some rumors about a private investigator asking questions about her. You know anything about that?"

Jack shrugged. "No. Why would someone do that?"

Hopkins jumped on the response, "Good question. You didn't hire anyone?"

"No, I haven't." Jack caught himself shuffling his feet and stopped abruptly.

"Well, we were in the area and thought we'd run it past you," Darrow smoothed. "Gives us a chance to check in on you. It's been what? Five weeks, right?"

"A person can start to get a little desperate," Hopkins added.

"I'm over it. Like you said, it's been five weeks."

"If we hear anything, we'll let you know," Darrow stated

Hopkins gave a veiled warning, "Don't do anything foolish."

Jack watched them drive away and decided to lay low for a week. He didn't want the police interfering with his plans for finding Katie.

Katie took a chance and joined the throng at the high school auditorium for the matinee, *Jaws*. People arrived in groups, juggling bags of popcorn and candy. She watched a family corral their two younger children, and an elderly couple trundle past carrying matching seat cushions. Nick and Maggie spied her and yelled in unison, "Annie!" They motioned her over to their seats. Katie was greeted several times as she made her way across the aisles. Those she didn't know, Maggie introduced her to immediately. "This is Annie, she's going to open a store here!"

Katie fell in love with the entire town that day.

Chapter 58

Nick dropped by Tipsy's on Sunday night. He leaned on the bar, casually talking to Colleen and Mark before turning toward Katie. "Hey, Annie. Wanna go see T*he Conjuring,* with me? It's older, but the Brunswick Theatre is showing it for the Halloween season."

"Hey, Romeo, make a date on your own time," Colleen jibed.

Nick ignored Colleen. "What do ya say, Annie?"

Katie made faces at him but didn't answer.

"It's just a movie," Nick persisted.

Katie bustled around the bar, pushing stools in. "I've got a busy weekend."

"We can go on Thursday. You don't work on Friday morning, right? If I show up a little late on Friday, it'll be okay. I know the boss." Nick grinned and tried to grab Katie's hand.

She pulled away and kept cleaning.

"Plllеееaaaseee," Nick pleaded.

"Damn, man, stop!" Mark teased. "Now, all the girls will expect *me* to beg."

Colleen flung a lemon slice at Mark. "First, ya gotta get a girl to look at ya, Mark."

"Ha-ha. You're funny. I might have two or three girlfriends you don't know about."

"In this town?" Colleen raised her eyebrows and shook her head sadly. "Everybody knows everything. Just like we know Annie's gonna go to the movie, aren't ya, *A Chara*?"

"I will if it will make ya'll shut up!"

A triumphant Nick fist-bumped Mark. "I'll pick you up at 6:00," he yelled over his shoulder and hurried out before Annie changed her mind.

"Looks like you got a date, princess." Colleen winked. "You still have to clean the bathrooms here though," She handed over a spray bottle of Clorox and a clean towel.

Katie snatched them out of Colleen's hands, muttering about "…ungrateful. …supposed to be my friend…why do I always have to clean the damn bathrooms, anyway?"

Nick was on time Thursday night, smiling and joking. Katie was a nervous wreck, alternately talking too fast or falling into silence. *Idiot. Going on a date,* she chastised herself.

Once they were settled and the movie began, Nick realized Annie was the real entertainment. Her pupils dilated, and her mouth hung open. She tossed popcorn into her mouth as fast as humanly possible and gestured wildly. As the movie reached its crescendo, she threw what was left of her popcorn at the screen.

Nick teased her afterward, "You're a big scaredy-cat!"

Katie punched him lightly in the arm and bundled into his car. "I'm never going to go see another scary film again."

"Let's get a pizza," Nick suggested.

Katie's conscience had her asking to go home instead.

Nick walked her to the back door of the General Store. *I will not settle for a handshake and a smile this time,* he told himself.

Under the pale security light, Nick gathered Katie close and kissed her lightly. His hands rubbed up and down her arms, and he leaned in closer, wanting to taste every inch of her soft, full lips. When they opened for him, he felt his heartbeat accelerate. *Ahh. Yes. This is much better.* Nick could feel the heat in his groin. *Easy there, big fella, she's likely to bolt.*

On cue, Nick felt Annie tense and pull away. *Shit. I knew it.* He forced himself to put his hands in his pockets.

"I'll wait here until I see the light go on upstairs."

Katie tilted her head, surprised he was letting her go. *Jack wouldn't.* She leaned in and kissed Nick one more time, then hurried upstairs to her apartment. As was the new habit, she waved from the kitchen window and watched him drive away.

Another car slowed and pulled into the alley. Katie's heart hitched. *Jack.* She ran for the bedroom window and unfurled her ladder, listening for the storage door to open or footsteps on the stairs. With her head partially out the window, she watched the car drive through the alley and make a left. Not Jack, after all.

I need to practice again, to be sure. Keys in her pocket, she backed out of the window and descended as fast as she dared. Her weight made the ladder crash into the building several times. Her breath whooshed out, but she made herself keep going. Once on the ground, she ran for her truck, hitting the key fob as she reached the driver's door. She closed her eyes. *It works. I'll be alright.*

Later, she lay in bed, visualizing each of her new friends. *You've lied to every single one of them, Katie.* Sleep was a long time coming.

Colleen asked for details on Friday. "How'd the movie night go with Nick?"

"It was fine," Katie answered and carried glasses to the kitchen.

When she came back out to the bar, Colleen tried again, "Come on! Have pity. I haven't had sex in over a year, give me something juicy! Tell me about your night."

Katie shrugged. "I told you it was fine."

Colleen texted Tanja to ask if she'd heard anything.

Nope. Got nothing. We should gang up on her.

Nick called and texted Annie over the next few days,
but she ignored his messages, too.

Chapter 59

Colleen rushed to close up Tipsy's. "Hurry, Annie! Tanja's got margaritas!"

"I know!" Katie replied, sloshing the mop bucket in her haste.

They were slated to meet Tanja and Maggie to decorate Tanja's store for the holidays, a.k.a. Girl's Night Out. Unbeknownst to Katie, it was also an intervention. She'd been too quiet the last week, and the girls were determined to figure out what the hell was going on.

Having been without a night out with girls for years, Katie was beside herself, yanking Colleen toward Tanja's store. "I thought you were in a hurry!"

They burst through the door and were met by Tanja holding a pitcher and Maggie extending two glasses. "Finally! We've been waitin' for you two to get here."

Colleen leaned in and wiped the salt from Maggie's top lip. "Liar."

Maggie had the good grace to blush, but Tanja laughed it off. "We had to taste them to make sure they weren't poisonous."

"And?" Katie asked, "What's the verdict?"

"They're fantastic!"

"See, Annie. I told you they'd start without us. Bitches." Colleen tucked her elbow through Katie's. "They got no sympathy for us workin' girls."

Tanja ignored the barb and poured margaritas all around. "Here's to the girls, working and otherwise!"

Glasses clinked, and Katie took in a mouthful. Licking salt off her own lips, she asked for an explanation. "So, what are we doing here tonight?" She held up her glass, "Besides the obvious?"

"We're decorating for the holidays. It's big business."

"Thanksgiving?" Katie asked, and Maggie and Tanja laughed.

"No, Christmas, silly girl."

Katie gaped at them. "Christmas? That's two months away!"

"True, but it's the motherlode." Tanja beckoned Katie over to a corner near the door. "This is what's left of Halloween for the next week." A small table held a few Halloween items and a 50% Off sign. Tanja then pivoted to point toward a carved, cherry sideboard table, where a dozen fall florals were displayed in antique silver and glass vases. "That's it for Thanksgiving. The rest of the store," Tanja twirled once, "is all about Christmas!"

Katie spun toward Maggie. "Is this true? Do you skip past Thanksgiving, too?"

Maggie nodded. "It's all about sales, Annie. You need to understand if you're gonna open a store. We push Halloween—last week in September and three weeks in October."

Tanja nodded and made a face at Colleen, who was pouring herself another drink.

"Then, you do a week or so for Thanksgiving and go right into Christmas." Maggie leaned toward Colleen and offered up her glass to be topped off too. "If someone orders a Thanksgiving display from me, I immediately offer them something for Christmas."

Tanja pulled Katie to the storeroom where a dozen large totes sat, each one marked *Christmas*. 'See?' She switched on the store stereo, and "I Wish You a Merry Christmas" poured from the speakers.

Katie shrugged. "Okay, you're the boss."

For the next hour, they opened boxes, laying out fabulous Victorian swags, delicate ornaments, antique angels with real feathered wings, and yards upon yards of garland. Katie sat in the middle of the treasures, lifting items free of their wrapping and handing them over to the girls, who knew where they should be placed.

As the last tote was opened, Tanja made eye contact with Colleen, who nodded once, picking up the queue. "So, Annie, is Nick a bad date? Bad kisser?"

Katie sloshed her margarita. "What?"

"He's not a bad kisser," Tanja offered, setting aside a two-foot-high reindeer so she could better watch Annie's reaction.

"How do you know?" Katie asked too quickly.

Tanja shrugged and winked.

"She's dated everyone in town, Annie." Colleen shook her head and whispered in a sad, forlorn voice, "I'm afraid our friend Tanja is a tramp."

Tanja twirled—pulling her hair to the top of her head. She posed, jutting out her breasts, and gave Colleen a sultry come-and-get-me look. "You're just jealous."

Colleen marched toward Tanja, pretending to be offended. Nose-to nose, Colleen gave up the pretense and snorted. "Damn straight, I am. The last penis I saw was when I accidentally walked in on Josh going to the bathroom."

Tanja stroked Colleen's hair, "Poor baby."

Maggie pushed past both of them. "Sex. Sex. Sex. That's all you two talk about."

Colleen and Tanja turned wide-eyed expressions on Maggie. "Who? Us?"

Katie sat back on her heels, enjoying the show.

Maggie walked toward Katie. "We're talking about Annie and Nick. Are you saying my Nicky is a bad kisser? No way. It's not in the genes, baby!" Maggie twitched her little butt.

Katie choked on her drink.

Maggie pounded Katies back. "Well? What's going on with you and Nicky?"

Colleen rushed to give Maggie the basics, "She went out with him Thursday night. And she won't say a damn word except, 'It was fine.' No details. No nothing."

Tanja joined in, "We're supposed to be friends. Does she share the details of her date?"

Colleen and Maggie shook their heads no and moved closer to Katie.

"Did she ask for our well-earned advice?"

Colleen and Maggie shook their heads again and stepped forward again.

Katie giggled as she watched their faces.

"Share the dirt," Tanja stated in a deep, ominous voice. She gestured to Colleen and Maggie until it became a chant,

"Share the dirt! Share the dirt!"

Katie put up her hands in mock surrender. "Okay! Okay! I give in! I do, however, require more margarita."

Maggie, Tanja, and Colleen agreed, and glasses were topped off. Colleen looked into the empty pitcher and grinned. "We're gonna need more potion!" Tanja shushed her, "In a minute. Annie's got the floor."

Katie set aside her drink and began, "We had a nice date. But, he's not a good kisser." Katie waited a full two seconds, enjoying the moment when their faces fell, then admitted, "He's a great kisser. Fantastic. Very enthusiastic."

Cheers went out, and Maggie high-fived Colleen. "I knew it!"

"So, what's the problem?" Tanja asked.

Katie fiddled with the bubble wrap in her hand. "It's too soon. I just ended a marriage with a man who was far from easy." She concentrated on unwrapping the ornament. "Nick's a great guy, but he doesn't seem the casual type." Katie's voice rose, "I'm not ready to recommit." Her passion had her pulling too hard at the wrapping, and an impossibly thin glass ornament fell to the floor and shattered.

Katie jumped to her feet."Oh, my God! I'm so sorry." She babbled and knelt, brushing the shards into her hands. In her haste, she cut her palm but didn't notice. She looked around frantic for a trash can. "I'll pay for it. I'm so stupid. I'm sorry."

Colleen, Maggie, and Tanja stood watching her, stunned until Maggie's maternal instincts took over. She caught hold of Katie, pulling her into a fierce hug. "Shhh. Quit. It's all right." She stroked Katie's hair. "It's an ornament, not a crime."

Tanja walked over and wrapped a napkin around Katie's hand. "No big deal. In fact, it's a blessing. I never liked that one anyway." She tipped Katie's chin upward and smiled. "Girlfriend, you just gave me an excuse to go buy something fabulous."

Colleen's face was murderous. "Your husband must have been a real piece of work. Give me the bastard's name, and I'll personally cut off his balls." Seeing Annie's shocked face, Colleen softened her threat, "You did the right thing leaving his ass. Nobody messes with our friend, do they girls?"

They formed a circle around Katie, hugging her until she was overwhelmed and began to cry again. Maggie squeezed Katie fiercely, knowing they'd just seen the tip of the iceberg.

After two weeks of keeping a low profile, Jack had spent the weekend searching the last businesses along the western bus routes. He kept his questions short and wrote them down in a small notebook—precisely what a private investigator would do.

He wasted five minutes following a blond prostitute, fantasizing about taking her hard and fast in a nearby alley.

She pivoted on her high heels and addressed him, "Hey there, handsome. You gonna follow me all night or make something happen."

Seeing her face and how little she resembled Katie, Jack hurried away.

Chapter 60

After the girl's night, it rained for a solid week—making for a soggy Halloween, and an overall depressed feeling in Bluff Creek. Katie was tired of the gray days and lonely evenings. She drove home from Silver Linings, assessing her new life. She'd been in town for more than two months, and there'd been no sign of Jack. The nightmares were occurring less. *Take a chance, Katie.*

She spied Nick's truck parked in front of a nice-sized ranch. Squinting through the rain, Katie could see him working in a half-finished shed he and Don were building. The roof was on, but rain still poured in through the open walls.

She honked once and pulled into the driveway. Climbing out of the truck, she yelled a greeting, "Hey Nick! Mr. Connelly!"

Nick stood grinning like an idiot—the cordless drill still spinning. He released the trigger and blushed. "Whatcha doin' here?" he stammered and turned a deeper shade of red. *Oh, nice one, Nick. No wonder she's not interested in you, can't even put four words together.*

"It's almost five. Let's go do something." She flicked water at him.

"Hey! I'm at work here."

Don smiled into his collar. "Go on, Nick. We can't run the equipment in all this rain anyway."

Nick put away tools and walked back toward his truck. Katie followed close behind. Spying a big puddle, she jumped into it with both feet, covering them both in water and mud.

Nick sputtered and got a dangerous glint in his eyes. "Oh. You wanna play, huh?"

Katie took off running, but Nick caught her from behind and held her arms in place. She momentarily froze, but then saw the mischievous look in his eye.

He kicked water at her until she was soaked, and she shrieked with laughter as they made two full circles around Nick's truck. Don watched from the shed. "Damned fools. Don't you know it's raining?"

Nick grinned at their clothes, "Guess we should clean up, huh?"

"Good idea," Katie agreed, looking at her own splattered clothing. She walked toward her truck.

Nick, finally able to get his brain to work, shouted, "My house is closer." He pointed down the street. "The little blue one is mine."

Katie paused one foot in her truck.

"I'll make you dinner," Nick offered as an enticement.

Come on, Katie. She nodded once. "I'll follow you there."

Nick raced to his truck, praying she'd be behind him. He pulled into the gravel driveway, opened the garage, and ran to the kitchen door. He held it open and gestured Katie inside. "This is one of the Connelly rentals. Nice perk, right?" They stood in a laundry room, and Nick stripped off his shirt and dropped it into the washing machine. He directed Katie toward the bathroom. "Through the kitchen, first door on your left. Towels are under the sink."

Katie hesitated.

"What?" He turned back toward her, rubbing his own wet hair with a dishtowel.

"Nothing." He didn't attempt to follow her toward the bathroom or send sexual innuendos her way. *Not Jack. Definitely not Jack.* She locked the bathroom door anyway and stood under the hot shower for a long time, thinking about Nick.

She had no clothes to change in to and wrapped one towel around her head and one around her body. She opened the door two inches and caught the smell of grilled cheese. "Umm, Nick?"

He came from the kitchen shirtless and had rolled up his muddy jeans. "Nice outfit."

She took in his lean, toned frame. *You too.* "I don't have anything to wear."

"The towel's not working for you?"

Katie shook her head.

Nick asked for her wet clothes and watched her push the door closed. "I'll put 'em in the dryer and find something you can wear." He returned with a T-shirt and baggy sweats and knocked on the door. "Sorry, this is all I could find. I'll leave them outside the door. Come and eat when you're done."

She opened the door and snatched the clothes. Holding the t-shirt up to her chest, she tried to identify what she was feeling. *Safe.* She felt safe.

She made her way to the kitchen, where Nick served up the sandwiches with ravioli. "It's one of the few things I can cook."

They sat at his little table, chatting like old friends.

"I'll handle clean-up," Katie said as she scraped her plate. "Go take a shower."

Nick came out wearing sweatpants and pulled her towards the living room. Katie stopped dead in her tracks staring at the enormous TV mounted between the windows. "Oh, my God." She swiveled her head toward Nick. "I can see why me not having a TV was so shocking!"

Nick shrugged. "I'm a man. We watch TV. What can I say?" He rubbed his arms as he moved toward the couch. The flowered pattern didn't fit Nick's style, and Katie suspected Maggie had donated the furniture. "Come sit with me, Annie."

Katie flinched as Nick reached for her.

"Honest. Just sit." Nick grabbed a throw pillow and placed it beside him, patting it, and making it clear she didn't have to sit directly beside him.

She eased herself down, keeping the pillow between them.

Nick shook his head at her. "Someone did a number on you, didn't they?" It was more a statement than a question. He rested his arm on the pillow, plopped his feet on the coffee table, and closed his eyes.

Minutes ticked by with Nick resting and Katie sitting ramrod straight. Soft evening light filtered in through the windows giving the room a faint amber hue. Nick's breathing evened out, and Katie slowly relaxed her muscles.

"I just realized I don't know how old you are," Katie announced, abruptly breaking the silence.

Nick opened one eye. "I turned twenty-seven in August."

Katie nodded a few times, accepting the number.

"Too old? Too young?" Nick asked.

She started to tell him he was a year younger than she was but caught herself in time. Cassie would be turning twenty-six in February. "Just right," Katie answered and mentally searched for another topic before giving anything away. "Tell me about New York."

"Been checking on me?"

"There are no secrets in this town."

Nick told his story while tracing lazy circles down her arm. "I was your typical college kid, full of grand plans. After graduation, Bluff Creek felt small and old-fashioned."

"What's your degree in, anyway?"

"Finance and property management. I wanted to make my mark but was still working with my dad. He made me crazy--wouldn't upgrade the rentals, never raised the rent, and refused to use spreadsheets."

"Spreadsheets?" Katie giggled. "Don? It's all in his head, right?"

"Exactly." Nick squeezed her hand and kept talking. "Mostly, I was full of myself, and sure I could do better. So, after an argument over drywall…drywall for God's sake," he scoffed, "I packed up my stuff and headed to the city where I'd be appreciated."

Katie snuggled in deeper. "How'd that go?"

"All right at first. I landed a respectable job, got a tiny apartment, and a sexy girlfriend named Erika." Nick paused and pretended to be thinking of Erika.

Katie rolled her eyes. "Erika? Wasn't that the name of a hurricane?"

He tried to look insulted, but he couldn't help but grin. "I don't remember. Maybe."

"Do you know why hurricanes were originally named after women?"

"Why?"

"They arrive wet and wild and leave with your car!" Katie grinned at her joke.

"You're a funny girl." He knuckled her under the chin and settled back into the couch."Where was I? Oh yeah, New York. My bosses were only concerned with the bottom line. Erika only wanted to party. I started to miss Fancy Bluff Creek, lightning bugs, tree frogs, and my parents. Not in that order. So, I came home."

It was Nick's turn to ask a question, "And you? What's your story?"

Katie gave a much shorter answer. "Unlike you, I did grow up in the city and not the right side of it either. I longed for a house with the proverbial white picket fence and married the first man who came along offering such things. He ended up not being nice at all. I left, heading for Florida, and ended up here." Guilt at her less than honest answer had her leaning away.

Nick waited a few seconds to see if she'd say more. When she didn't, he rolled toward her and kissed her gently. Katie accepted it and tried not to respond to the warmth of his mouth. He didn't push for more, leaving Katie unbalanced.

"We should get you home. People will be talking." Nick rose and headed toward the laundry room. "Clothes are done!"

He followed her out to her truck, swinging her hand in his. As she opened the door, Nick tugged her slightly. She turned, and Nick cupped her face gently, feathering his fingers along her jaw.

He looked her in the eye and kissed her slowly, outlining her lips with the edge of his tongue, and drinking in her softness.

Katie melted into the kiss, feeling her skin grow warm. It shook her, and she pulled away. "I thought I was ready, but I can't do this."

Nick smiled and released her. "I'll wait."

She hopped in the truck, fumbling her keys. Nick rapped on the window, and she jumped. He pantomimed rolling down the window, and she opened it four inches.

"Call me when you get home, so I know you're safe."

Katie nodded and peeled out.

She trudged up the stairs, weighed down by guilt. *What are you doing starting a new relationship? Jack needs to be dealt with first.* She let herself in her apartment, texted Nick rather than call, and turned on all the lights to chase away the shadows.

As Katie thought about Jack, he was thinking about her. *Are you with a lover, you bitch?* Jack went into another hacking fit, and his eyes watered while he tried to catch his breath. "Fucking weather," he grumbled. He'd spent a week working the first southern bus route, but it had come with a price. Being in and out of the rain, Jack had caught a bad cold. He was shaking, and running a temperature and knew he'd be calling off again tomorrow, too. He poured Nyquil into his glass of whiskey, hoping he'd finally sleep through the night.

He had to get back to work. Half the office was sick, and reports were due. Barry had already warned him they'd be working Saturday. Jack shook his head, knowing the next few days would be long, and he wouldn't be finding Katie anytime soon.

Chapter 61

Nick called Katie three days in a row, asking her to go out with him again.

Determined to get her life in order, she always refused.

On Friday, Colleen teased her about her time with Nick. "So, I heard you and Nick had a little fun on Monday."

"What? How do you know?"

Colleen smirked. "Tanja told me."

"Tanja? How'd she know? I haven't talked to her all week."

"Mrs. Randolph told her."

Katie plopped her hands on her hips. "Who the hell is Mrs. Randolph?"

"Mrs. Randolph lives next to Nick. She reported the two of you were in his house for hours and then lip-locked in his driveway."

Katie rolled her eyes. "For the love of God. It's not a big deal." She did, however, spend her free time researching local divorce lawyers.

After yet another failed attempt to get Katie to go out on a date, Nick called Blake Sunday night. "You have to go out with me on Thursday night."

"Dude. You're not my type."

"Not me, asshole. With Annie *and* me."

"That seems awkward. I didn't know you were into a ménage a Trois type of thing."

"Shut up! She won't go out with me. Every time I ask, she's got some reason it won't work."

"Losing your touch, bro? I'll make you a deal. If I ask Annie out., and she says yes, we'll know it's you."

"I'll break your fuckin' nose again."

You could try," Blake cautioned with sarcasm dripping.

"Come on, Blake. Help a friend out here and do a double-date."

Blake considered. "Tanja or Colleen? Wouldn't mind Colleen. The girl's always playing hard ass, but man, that red hair, and fiery temper."

"What about Tanja?"

"We're not a thing. I'm simply spreading the wealth."

"You talk like that to Colleen or Tanja, and you're likely to get your nuts kicked in. I don't care who you call, just say you'll get a date and meet Annie and me."

"You'll get a date and meet Annie and me," Blake repeated deadpan.

"I'm on my way over there to break your nose, smartass."

Blake laughed and agreed to a date, but not the broken nose.

On Thursday night, Katie folded herself into Colleen's tiny Ford Fiesta, and they sped off to the maintenance garage. Nick and Blake were already there and waved them into an empty bay. The two women exited the car to music blaring from an old stereo.

Blake wasted no time reaching in and hauling Colleen into a hug. She accepted and then twisted and had Blake's arm bent behind his back. "I'm not so easy, lover boy," she grinned into his face. "If you ask nicely, it might go better."

"Watch this," Nick said, moving closer to Katie. "Those two have been sparring since high school."

Blake suddenly dropped to a squat, spun a half-circle, and came up holding Colleen's arm behind *her* back. He grinned into her face. "Can I please have a hello hug?"

Colleen tilted her head, appreciating the move. "You need to teach me that one."

"Do I get a hug, first?"

As Colleen wrapped herself around Blake, Nick turned to Katie. "How 'bout me? Do I get a hug?"

Katie gave Nick a platonic hug--nothing like the one Blake was receiving. When Nick pouted, Katie was tempted to try again, but the moment had come and gone.

She blew on her hands to keep them warm and busy. "So, what are we doing here? You said you desperately needed help."

"We do. Blake and I have to hang the town's holiday displays," Nick explained. "Each one needs to be checked and ready to go the weekend after Thanksgiving."

Blake grabbed Colleen's hand and headed toward the Skid Steer. He loaded a six-foot crate and showed off twirling circles. Colleen chased beside him and managed to jump aboard. Her bark of laughter eased Kate's nerves, and she settled in to have a good time.

Blake set the crate down near Nick and took off to gather the next one. Nick undid the clasps, and Katie stuck her head in the box, eyeing the four-foot-high, green and wire decorations. Some were shaped like stars, others like candles. Each was wrapped in white lights with big rope at the top of each. Katie fingered one of the loops and looked at Nick questioningly.

"The loops fit over the top of the light poles," he explained, opening yet another crate.

Colleen found a ball of mistletoe and held it over her head. "Wanna kiss me, Blake?"

"Yes. Yes, I do." He jogged over, caught Colleen by the waist, and laid her backward into a dip, capturing her lips in his.

"Wow. That's some mistletoe," Colleen laughed. "You should try it, Annie!"

Nick retrieved the decoration and chased Katie. "Yeah, you should try it, Annie!" She laughed and ran slower, letting him catch her. Nick lowered the mistletoe to shield their faces and leaned in, "Ready?"

Katie licked her lips, "Oh yeah."

Colleen and Blake yelled, "Get a room!" which had Nick and Katie pulling apart.

The evening ended with late-night pizza and beer—an easy camaraderie Katie was getting used to quickly.

After they cleared their mess, Nick offered to drive Katie home.

"That works!" Colleen answered for Katie. "I've got to get home to Josh, anyway.

Nick and Katie headed out, still joking about Blake. "He's in way over his head!"

Chapter 62

As was their habit, Nick walked Katie to the back door and waited while she fished out her keys. "I'll stay here until I see your lights come on."

Tired of worrying and spending solitary evenings at home, Katie pulled Nick toward the stairs. "Why don't you walk me all the way this time?"

As she was about to open the apartment door, Nick angled their bodies, so her back was against the wall. Looking into her eyes, he bent his head and kissed her with such longing, she couldn't breathe. Her hands bunched in his shirt, drawing him closer. Nick pulled away, laboring to get his breathing under control. He smiled and said nothing more.

Katie stared at him. *He'll wait if that's what I want.* She smiled and opened the apartment door fully. "Let's go inside." She pulled two longneck bottles of Bud Light out of the fridge, holding one out to Nick. "Beer?"

He nodded and took off his jacket, hanging it over the back of one of her new stools. He wandered toward the living room and saw her touches here and there: colored bottles on an end table, a curled piece of driftwood on the coffee table, and books displayed here and there. A curious, green tree frog hung from the edge of one of the curtains, but still no TV.

Katie dimmed the living room light and stood with her hands clasped awkwardly together. Nick took them in his and led her toward the couch, gauging her body language, and making sure he wasn't going too fast.

She nodded as though she'd heard his thoughts.

Nick set aside his beer and sat beside her on the couch, kissing and caressing her face. "I'm falling in love with you."

"I feel the same way."

Nick's hands drifted through her hair and down her neck, teasing her shoulders and moving in excruciating circles across her ribs. His right hand stopped over her heart and stayed there. He closed his eyes. "I feel your heart in my hand."

She'd never known a man could light so many fires with just a touch or a few sincere words. Katie snuggled into the cushions, and he followed her, covering her body with his. He stretched to taste her lips again, and she melted under the heat of his tongue. With her mind in a blur, she surrendered to wherever Nick decided to take them.

His talented fingers inched below her shirt, pushing the thin material upward.

Rising slowly from the couch, she allowed Nick to peel it away. She suffered no shame, just a buzzing in her ears and a need to feel him beside her, on her, in her. She reached for his shirt, tugging at buttons, and letting her hands roam across his stomach and up to his chest. The hair there was deep russet, shining brighter red where the light captured and held.

His fingers journeyed over her breasts at the edge of her lacy bra. He followed the material to her shoulder and eased each strap off and undid the clasp. He pulled the bra free, letting it fall to the floor. He stayed half crouched between her legs, gazing at her curves, and the shadows cast by the moonlight filtering in through the curtains.

When Katie blushed and covered herself in embarrassment, Nick lifted her hands away. "Don't hide from me. You're gorgeous."

Feeling her tense as he kissed the top of each breast, Nick leaned back to see her face. "If I forget to tell you later, I've had a great time already tonight."

Katie laughed. It was exactly what she'd needed, and she relaxed.

His mouth came to hers again and brought a quiet sound of pleasure. She moaned when his lips slid down the base of her throat and moved lower to cover a nipple.

Her skin was hot, and Nick ran his tongue from below her breast to just inside her jeans. Her pulse jumped as he found her secret places. The taste of her grew warmer until he wondered how he wasn't consumed by her heat.

Katie reached for him, hungry to taste as well. Her mouth traced along his jawline, running down his chest to follow the line of fine hair from his tight stomach to his waistband.

Their moves were impossibly slow as if they swam through water. Nick's body trembled for hers. Katie felt his muscles tense under her hands.

Nick could hardly bear to wait any longer. "I want you, Annie."

"I want you too."

He undid her jeans and pulled them slowly from her legs. He traced a line from her heel to her hip and cupped her center. Katie cried out, arching helplessly at such a soft caress.

She pulled his belt free. Nick shook with anticipation, and Katie was awed with her power over him. He pulled his jeans off, and Katie watched in fascination, taking in his length and muscles earned from hard work, not weights at the gym. She reached for him, but he shook his head slightly.

Fearing she'd done something incorrectly, Katie sat back. "What's wrong?"

"Umm. Protection. We need protection." Nick turned aside, fumbling in his jeans pocket. Katie heard the crinkling of a package opening and dropped her head to hide a smile.

Nick rolled back toward her and, in one smooth move, had them both lying on the couch once more. He kissed her, building up the heat again. Their senses filled with each other's scent: new wood and musk for him, and mint and flowers for her.

Fingers explored, and he found her center again, damp and ready. She wrapped her hand around his ready erection and squeezed gently. Nick rose over her, waiting for her beautiful green eyes to open.

She smiled up at him, and he slid into her with one powerful stroke. He willed himself to stop so their bodies could adjust to the new texture and feel of one another. He slipped deeper, and she rose with him, fell with him, and recognized her own need building.

She rode a wave of sensation: their labored breathing, a slight sheen of sweat, Nick's soft words, skin sliding against skin. Katie gripped his hips, groaned as she was swept up in a tidal wave of feelings she'd never experienced with Jack. Her body quivered, pulsed, and crested. "Oh, God, Nick. Oh…." She shuddered twice.

Nick's world wavered. He buried his face in Annie's hair and lost himself. Forever.

Minutes ticked by, with their breathing filling the silence. When Katie shifted, Nick flipped their positions so he wouldn't crush her.

Stretching, Katie tangled her legs with Nick's. His arms wrapped around her and he held her, content to stay there for the next two or three centuries. "I could get used to this," Nick mumbled into her shoulder.

Katie sighed, but a tiny niggle of fear ran through her brain. *Oh God. Jack's still out there. What am I going to do?*

Chapter 63

Early on Sunday morning, Jack intentionally messed up his hair and glued on his fake mustache and sideburns. Slipping on a baseball hat and false glasses, he decided he didn't look too out of the ordinary. He was down to the last few stops along the southern bus route, which ended near a highway. Jack had a good feeling about the day. He was nursing a headache, but he'd learned to live with those.

At a stop near Georgetown, Jack noticed a branch of Katie's bank directly across from the bus stop. He scanned the area, noting a run-down motel called *City Manor*. It was too much a coincidence to ignore, and Jack headed toward the motel.

Jack introduced himself to the manager, "Greg Landis, Private Investigator." He handed over one of the false business cards.

"I'm Chad Johnson. Can I help you?"

"I've been working a case for months and wondered if you've seen this woman?" Jack showed a picture of Katie.

Chad leaned in to see it better. "Hey, that's the woman who disappeared, right?"

"How about this woman?" Jack showed the photoshopped picture of Katie, with darker hair and glasses.

Chad widened his eyes. "That's Anne. Why do you have her picture?"

Jack went on high alert, and he made up a quick lie to keep Chad talking. "Well, it turns out she's missing, too. I think this may have been the last place she was seen. What can you tell me? Time is critical."

Chad didn't ask why a private investigator was involved. He'd never heard from Anne, and his bruised ego was soothed by the notion it hadn't been purposeful. "That's Anne. Anne Morrison. She stayed here a couple of nights."

Jack jerked his head toward Chad. "Morrison?" *Same as Cassie. I'll be God damned.* Jack shook his head in appreciation. *Smart move, sweetheart.*

Jack settled in to chat, buying Chad and himself lousy coffee out of the motel vending machine. Jack read the situation and offered a few compliments. "She's a good looking girl. I bet she liked you."

Chad disclosed her job at the bank and her gray Nissan.

"Well, Chad no one at the bank location has ever heard of her. She's missing, and we need to understand the situation. You understand?"

Not willing to be disloyal to Anne, Chad offered excuses instead. "Well, I'm sure there's an explanation. She even rented an apartment."

"Do you remember where?"

"Sure. Ashley Commons. It's not far from here."

Jack scribbled the name down.

"She's never there, though. I've gone by a few times."

Jack worked to stay congenial. "Well, I'll check it out myself. You've been a big help, Chad." Jack thumped him on the back, and resisted the urge to punch Chad in the face for even daring to look at Katie, let alone pursue her. As he drove away, he spoke the name "Ashley Commons" into Google Maps and followed the directions.

The apartment manager remembered Katie too.

"She put down a deposit and never came back. Non-refundable."

He dug for the file. "Here it is. Cassandra Anne Morrison."

For a hundred bucks, the sleazy manager gladly gave up a copy of the lease agreement. As expected, it contained all the pertinent information.

Jack rubbed his hands together in glee. "Gotcha." He peeled off the stupid mustache and headed for home.

Armed with Cassie's full name, birth date, and social security number, Jack logged on to AnnualCreditReport.com. He completed the online form, using the address from Ashley Commons. The program asked if 'he'd' lived there for two years. When Jack clicked 'no,' it asked for a previous address. Yanking out his phone, he typed in the Morrison's address.

As the credit report page processed the information, Jack laughed aloud and guzzled his second drink. A message appeared on the screen, "Your report will be finalized and sent to the email address indicated in 3-5 business days. Use passcode XWbJ39DcC to open."

"Shit!" If he was lucky, he'd have information by Wednesday. Jack didn't believe much in luck and figured it would be Thursday or Friday. Looking at his calendar, he flung his glass. "Goddammit. Thursday is Thanksgiving." He doubted the report would show up on a holiday, either.

He poured another drink, talking to himself, "What am I supposed to do 'til then?"

Unwilling to wait, he headed toward the Morrisons. Anger and humiliation had him banging on their front door, rather than using the doorbell.

Bob yanked open the door with a scowl.

Jack started in immediately, "Katie stole Cassie's identity. Has she contacted you?"

Bob bristled at Jack's tone. "You came here two months ago, asking questions. What the hell is going on?"

Julie came to the door. "Who is it, Bob?" Seeing Jack, she frowned.

Bob and Julie stood side by side, barring the entrance.

"I know you helped her!" Jack screamed.

Bob leaned forward. "You're not going to come to *my* house and dishonor *my* daughter's memory or accuse us of anything. Do you understand me?"

Julie interrupted. "We haven't seen Katie in months. She's a lovely woman, and I hope she's all right, but we have nothing to say."

"What about Katie using Cassie's name? How could you not know?" Jack glared at them.

Julie clapped her hands on her hips and shot back, "We have no idea what you're talking about."

"I trust the police have this information?" Bob asked. When Jack said nothing, Bob added, "Well, they will. We'll be calling them immediately."

Julie tugged at Bob's arm. Long married, he understood the signal and closed the door.

Jack drove away with no new information and a foreboding he'd hear from the police. He wasn't wrong. Hopkins and Darrow were working on another case but sent Randy Fairchild out to Jack's house, again.

Fairchild didn't waste time on niceties, "Got a call from the Morrisons."

Jack nodded. "I was upset."

"According to them, you were angry and making accusations. Why are you still trying to find Katie?" He waited, eyebrows at attention, ready to write down whatever Jack had to say.

Jack ran his finger through his hair, grabbing at handfuls. "I want my life back. If she wants to be gone, fine. But make it official, get a divorce, move on. I'm sick of this shit."

Randy wrote it down and headed back to the precinct. Jack had been warned.

Chapter 64

Katie woke on Thanksgiving morning feeling blessed. Carrying her coffee to the second bedroom, Katie admired the second crate full of books that had arrived the day before. She sat cross-legged on the floor, pulling the books out one by one. Despite Giovanni nagging her into getting insurance on the truck, her little account was growing. There was no reason to believe she couldn't keep adding to her savings.

Life was good. *I have friends and, more importantly, Nick.* The two were getting more serious and spending all their free time together.

Yet, Katie still debated telling him her real story. *He needs to know.* She was afraid--afraid she'd waited too long, afraid of his reaction. *Soon* she told herself.

She called Aunt Susan, needing to hear her voice.

"Oh, Katie-girl, I'm so glad you called. Things still okay?"

"Better than okay," Katie filled her in on her two jobs, her apartment, her friends.

"Any men down there?" Aunt Susan asked.

When Katie hesitated, her aunt pounced, "Oh-ho. Tell me everything!"

They talked so long Katie worried she'd run out of minutes on her phone.

'You need to tell the truth, Katie. This is a bad way to start what seems like a good relationship. Jack came here weeks ago looking for you. He's still out there."

Katie's head dropped to her chest. "I know."

Jack received Cassie's credit report on Friday. The county office was closed for the holiday weekend, so he settled in to read. The report showed a credit check by Don Connelly in some town called Bluff Creek. There was a vehicle registered too. "A God damned pickup?"

Jack drove an hour and a half, cruising through the old section of town. It was a sorry-ass collection of businesses with only a few restaurants and stores, most of which were already closed, including Connelly rentals. Jack shook his head in disgust.

He coasted along slowly, hoping to get lucky and see Katie on the sidewalk. His right hand caressed the handle of the hunting knife, holding down a place of honor in the passenger seat. One look at it in his hands, and Katie would be convinced to get in the car.

Jack looked for the truck, too, but never saw it since it was safely tucked behind the General Store.

She's here somewhere. She thinks she's safe, which buys me time. Jack drove away, contemplating ways to lure her into the open.

Unbeknownst to Jack, he'd driven past Katie. She'd talked Nick into showing her the retail space next to Tanja's Antiques. "Please? I want to get a feel for the overall area and whether it'll work." It would be a thousand dollars a month, which she couldn't afford yet. Still, she wandered the large open room, trailing her fingers along the walls, and visualizing bookshelves and comfortable chairs. Her mouth was slightly ajar, and her eyes were far away and dreamy. She inhaled once. "I can practically smell the coffee brewing." She turned toward him, her face aglow with sunshine and dreams, and Nick fell the rest of the way in love.

On Saturday, the whole town gathered in the square. The decorations were hung, and everyone had come out to see the lighting of the tree. Standing beside the Connellys, Katie was happy. Here among old buildings and narrow streets were genuine people, making a decent living and content with their slower pace and smaller lives. Here she, too, could make a beautiful life.

As Nick reached over to hold Annie's hand, Maggie looked at the two young lovers and sighed. She and Don shared a secret--Nick was planning to propose after the lighting ceremony. One part of her was happy, the other scared by Annie's past. Don, oblivious to the back story, rubbed Nick's shoulder and grinned from ear to ear.

The Christmas tree came to life with a thunderous round of applause. Candles were distributed, and the townsfolk began to sing "Silent Night." Nick squeezed her hand, and Katie understood he was a man she could love forever. With the realization came an awful truth, *I can't live this life as Casandra.*

As the town's voices swelled to sing the chorus, Katie's heart broke. All she'd hoped for and dreamed of shattered because she'd been a coward. She caught her breath on a sob. Bewildered, Nick gathered her in his arms.

Watching Katie's face change from happy to horrified, Maggie felt her gut clench. *Uh-oh. Here we go.* She leaned across Nick and patted Annie's hand. Crying harder, Katie pulled away and ran toward her apartment. Many of her new friends, stopped singing as they watched her leave—their faces a mix of concern and confusion.

Fumbling with her keys outside the General Store, the wind whipped Katie's hair and dried her tears but couldn't whisk away the sense of despair.

Nick had followed her and called out, "Annie, what is it?"

"I love you, Nick."

"I love you too, Annie. What's wrong?"

"For starters, my name isn't Annie. I'm not who you think I am." She left him standing in the alley and locked herself in her apartment.

Nick called multiple times and banged on her door. Maggie and Tanja called. Katie never answered. Curled on her couch, she sat in the dark for the rest of the night. "I have to tell the truth." She had no idea what the consequences meant where Jack and Nick were concerned. She crawled into bed and cried herself to sleep.

With her mind in a whirl, she plodded through the next day, working her shift and avoiding her friends and any conversation.

Nick tried to catch Katie at Tipsy's, but she focused on other customers. "Annie, we've got to talk. What's going on?"

Colleen caught Nick's eye and shrugged her shoulders. "I haven't been able to get anything out of her either. Hang in there, big guy."

On Monday night, a frustrated Nick banged on her door once more. "Annie, please let me in."

She opened the door, and Nick noticed the circles under her eyes. "What's going on?"

Katie paced as she told him the truth in bits and pieces. "I married a selfish, awful man. I've got documents showing he may have been taking bribes. I think he'll harm me or worse. Cassie wanted me to do it, and it made sense at the time."

"Whoa. Slow down. Who's Cassie?"

In jerking sobs and a voice sometimes reduced to a whisper, she poured out the entire story, "…and then I met you. I couldn't keep pretending to be someone else. I love you, Nick, but I'm still married to Jack."

Nick was incredulous. "You're married?" He stood and glared at Katie. "You lied to me." Nick strode to the door. "You were right the other night, you're not who I thought you were at all." He slammed out of the apartment with Katie's pleas following him down the stairs.

Nick headed straight to his mother's kitchen. "God, Mom, what am I going to do? Anne isn't even her name. It's Kathryn Werner, and she's married. I'm a damned fool."

Maggie sat across from him and let him rant. When he'd exhausted all words, she laid her hand on his. "You're no fool. Look how hard she's worked to build this new life. You don't know all the details. She's still the same person. Her story's just bigger than we imagined."

Nick pulled his hand free. "Why didn't she tell me?" He chewed on the situation for almost a full day. With no clear ideas, he called Blake, hoping he'd have advice.

As friends do, Blake agreed with Nick. "What a fucking mess. It's not your fault, man. You were upfront and honest. But here's the thing Nick, she could be in real trouble--with the law and her husband. Want me to talk to her?"

"No."

"Come on, let me help."

Nick finally agreed, and Blake went to Annie's apartment on Wednesday evening, catching her as she came home from work. "Hey, girl. Can I come in?"

She held the door open but remained guarded and quiet.

"I can't help you until you tell me the story."

As with Nick, she shared her story. Blake encouraged her to show him the paperwork, the letter from Cassie, the pictures of her bruises and the broken ribs. When Katie was done, she hung her head. "What am I going to do?"

Blake let out a long sigh. "Stealing an identity is a crime, but, as far as I can tell, there's no new money involved, right? You didn't take over Cassie's accounts or use her name to open a credit card. I think the best thing for you to do is to turn yourself in and make a deal of some kind. You need a lawyer."

"Am I going to jail?"

Blake looked away and mumbled, "Probably."

Katie nodded. She'd come to the same conclusion. Hearing it, though, made it sound frightfully final. "Can you give me a day? I need to explain myself to a lot of people. I'd rather they hear it from me."

Blake agreed. "I'd like to do some background work, and maybe drive to Savannah to meet with the officers in charge of the investigation. Maybe we can come up with a plan."

As Blake headed out, Katie called Aunt Susan.

Susan consoled as much as she was able. "You're doing the right thing—the hard thing--but it's the right choice if you want this new life."

"I do--but jail?" Katie burst into tears.

"We'll do what we have to do. You've already proven you can start over. It'll be okay. Maybe not today, but it'll be all right."

Katie agreed to keep her in the loop and hung up, resigned to her task. She spent the rest of the evening practicing her speech, pacing, and crying in frustration and rage, "Why can't I just have a normal life?"

Blake used his federal credentials to download and read Katie's missing person reports and the police findings. Afterward, he called and set up a meeting with the Savannah police detectives Hopkins and Darrow, for the next morning.

Chapter 65

Early Thursday morning, as Blake was headed to Savannah, Katie searched out Maggie and Don, relieved to find them at home. Katie started and stopped her explanation a dozen times until she'd shared all the details.

Maggie folded Katie into a hug. "Nick told us part of it, but I already knew. I figured it out months ago."

"You knew? You're not mad?"

"No. How could I be angry? No one knows what's in your head, or your heart but you. You were obviously desperate."

Don sat at the table, rubbing his forehead. "What a mess. You're gonna need a lawyer, Annie." He smiled. "Sorry, I can't get used to Katie yet."

Katie sniffed. "It's okay. How about Katie-Anne?"

Don patted both women and headed toward their den. "I'm callin' Montgomery."

"Who's Montgomery?"

"Montgomery is Don's cousin and just happens to be a semi-retired lawyer." Maggie mopped at Katie's face. "Are you going to be okay?"

"I think so. The faster I tell everyone, the better. God knows when Blake will come back to arrest me." She tried to laugh, but it broke apart on a sob instead.

Maggie rubbed Katie's shoulders, "You're doing the right thing, and I'm proud of you. What are you going to do first?"

Tell everyone, Katie answered as she ticked off names, "Tanja, Skinny Tom, the retirees, Colleen and Colin in that order."

Darrow and Hopkins were waiting when Blake arrived. They all grabbed a coffee and headed to the conference room.

"The whole disappearance was a frickin' mess from day one," Darrow announced.

"We'd already concluded she faked the disappearance and skipped town. You're telling us she wants to turn herself in? Why?" Hopkins asked.

"She's tired of looking over her shoulder and worrying about Jack. The lies don't sit well with her, either. She's made a place for herself in Bluff Creek, and I don't mind telling you, the town loves her. I do, too."

Hopkins and Darrow frowned at Blake.

"No, not like that. Katie's special. You'll see."

"The husband was the principal suspect. We've kept an eye on him but could never put the pieces together." Darrow kept his comments respectful.

Hopkins had no such reservations. "My opinion? Husband is a real piece of shit. All the signs of an abusive marriage were there. Isolated her. Scrutinized her every move. We've got reasons to suspect there was some violent behavior."

"Katie shared some stories with me. She has pictures of bruises and busted ribs to back up her claim. She also has some possibly incriminating evidence which may show Jack's been taking bribes, too, but it'll be hard to prove."

Darrow let out a long sigh. "Jack Werner's not going to handle any of this well. Not Katie coming back into town, and, sure as hell, not any information that makes him look bad."

"He could be a real problem," Hopkins picked up the conversation. "He's been trying to find Katie all along. He showed up at the Morrisons a week ago, screaming about Katie using their daughter's name for a fake I.D."

"She's not safe," Darrow said, voicing what they were all thinking.

Blake waited for them to come to the same conclusion he had. It didn't take long.

"Well, identity theft is a crime." Hopkins looked at Darrow, who nodded once.

"If she's in jail for the weekend, Jack can't cause any problems," Darrow added, and Blake tilted his head, acknowledging the statement.

"If you bring her in later tomorrow, she can't be arraigned until Monday," Hopkins concluded. The three officers agreed.

As they were shaking hands, Darrow made one last observation. "The press followed this story pretty heavily." He let the statement hang in the air, and Hopkins nodded, impressed.

"You're right. They did." Blake said and didn't commit further.

Tanja took one look at Katie's ravaged face and turned the store sign to "closed." She pulled Katie toward the back room and sat her on a colonial revival couch. "Talk." By the time Katie was done, Tanja was crying too. "Why didn't you say anything? Don't you trust me?"

"It's not about trusting you. It's not knowing what to do about the truth. What was I supposed to do? Walk-in here and announce, 'Oh, hey, by the way, my name is Katie, not Annie. I'm running in fear for my life, my husband is trying to find me and may or may not kill me. Let's have lunch.'" Katie's voice hitched. "I swear I just didn't know how to fix it. And, I thought you'd hate me."

"Hate you? You're one of the bravest women I know. Whoever you are!" Tanja swept her hair away from her face and held out her hand. "Hi, I'm Tanja."

Katie gripped her hand and laughed. "Hi. I'm Katie. Glad to meet you."

Tanja shoved chocolate into Katie's hand. "You're going to need this for fortification. Now, keep going until you've told everyone."

Katie headed toward the General Store and told her story. When she got to the end, Jarrod shook his head, "Hell of a secret to keep, Annie." The rest of the retirees nodded.

"I'm sorry. I was so scared. Scared word would get back to my husband. Scared this new life would fall apart."

Skinny Tom flipped his towel back and forth. "Hell, I already knew."

Katie couldn't believe it. "You did?" Two people had known her story from the start? *First Maggie and now Tom.*

"I got years of watching faces come in and out of this store," Skinny Tom explained. "I pay attention, and you seemed familiar. You were so skittish, I got to wondering why, and then it clicked. The woman from Savannah."

The retirees grumbled at Tom, "Why didn't you tell us?"

Skinny Tom scoffed, "It wasn't any of your business. Besides, none of ya'll can keep a secret."

Katie looked at the old men who'd been watching out for her. "I love this town. I love you guys." Tears trickled down Katie's face.

Craig stood up and took her hands. "You know you've committed a crime?"

Katie nodded.

"You may have to go to jail."

Katie nodded again, and Jarrod nearly fell out of his chair.

"You know we'll help you in any way we can?"

Katie laid her head on Craig's wide shoulder and sobbed.

The others gathered around, patting her on the back.

Katie hiccupped and asked, "Can I come back here when this is over?"

"Well, you'd better." Skinny Tom was the first to answer. "You can keep all your stuff in my storage area."

Katie kissed him on the cheek, and he blushed as he'd been doing for the last three and a half months.

Thaddeus tapped her on the shoulder. "News travels fast in small towns. If there's anybody else you're fixin' to tell, you'd best hurry."

That Thad had uttered two full sentences was noteworthy. Katie ran towards Tipsy's.

Colleen was pissed. "I knew something was wrong, the way you were always watching the door…." It turned into a royal ass-kicking speech about honesty and loyalty, and 'we're friends for God's sake!'

Katie hung her head. "I know."

Katie's back story was spreading like wildfire. After three phone calls from townspeople wanting to know more information, Don called Nick. "Son, things are ramping up fast. Katie needs you."

"She should have told me," Nick repeated for the hundredth time.

"Well, it seems to me she did. You've got to see it from her side, too. When things got serious between you two, she didn't run. She told the truth as hard as it was. Why do you think she did that?"

Sometimes his dad was a lot smarter than Nick gave him credit for being.

Blake called Nick on the way back to Bluff Creek. "I met with the Savannah police force. Katie's husband does have a violent streak, and he knows she's using Cassie's name. I know you're hurting, but we need to get her safe. Fast. I need your help. You've got to be at Katie's apartment with me tomorrow."

Nick wasn't sure what Blake meant, but he agreed.

"Call her," Blake barked into the phone. "You're being an ass."

Nick started to defend himself, but Blake had already hung up the phone.

Nick was sitting on the bottom step to Katie's apartment when she opened the storeroom door. Her heavy heart lifted, but she paused, waiting for him to make the first move.

He stood and opened his arms to her, and relief flooded her.

On Friday, December 6th, Nick and Blake showed up at Katie's apartment early. Blake wore a suit and laid out the plan, "I'm gonna take you back to Savannah, and you'll be in jail. I'm sorry, but it turns out Jack's been looking for you all along."

All color drained from Katie's face.

"The best place for you is in jail. Jack can't get to you, and we can sort out the legal end of things." Blake regarded Nick, then Katie, and released a long breath through puffed out lips. Pushing himself up out of the chair as if he'd aged twenty years, he withdrew handcuffs from his belt. "I'm sorry, Katie, but it's time to go."

Katie stared at the cuffs.

"Handcuffs? You're not serious?" Nick's hands curled into fists, ready to take on a fight. "She hasn't done anything wrong."

Katie turned sad eyes to Nick. "That's not true. I used my friend's identity."

"But it's wasn't a vicious crime. Cassie told you to use her name."

"Look, Nick, if it were up to me, I'd just drive her to Savannah. We've got to make this look good. If Jack's watching, he needs to see Katie in cuffs and in jail."

Katie blinked two slow blinks and offered her hands.

Blake fiddled with his phone. "We need video showing Katie's been taken into custody."

"Why?" Katie and Nick asked in unison.

"We need the media. They're gonna be crazy for this story since they covered it back in September. They'll keep Katie safer than anybody. The entire state of Georgia will be watching her *and* Jack."

Nick looked at Katie. "You're gonna divorce his sorry ass, right?"

Katie leaned over and gave Nick a kiss. "I am."

Blake handed Nick the cell phone. Nick was incredulous. "Me? You want me to film it?"

"No one else is here. Giovanni was supposed to help, but he's working a big accident out by the highway."

"Jesus Christ." Nick held the phone up and lowered it again. "I'm sorry, Katie."

"Me too. Let's get this over with."

Nick filmed as Blake read her Miranda rights being and placed her in the backseat of the car. Blake unlocked the handcuffs and put his siren on top. When Katie smiled bravely from the back, Nick wanted to throw-up.

"Now what?" Nick handed the phone back to Blake.

"We send it to WSVA, the Savannah station, anonymously."

"Can I go with you?"

"Give us a couple hours, and then you can head up. I need to get her processed." Blake didn't use the siren and planned to sneak out of town, but Katie's friends were out on the street, waving and calling out encouragement. "Hang in there! It'll be all right!"

Colleen even jogged along with the car for a half block, keeping her eyes locked on Katie, lending quiet strength.

Katie slid low in the back seat more humiliated than she'd ever been in her life.

Three hours later, Katie lay curled in a ball on her cot. She hadn't expected a jail uniform and scratched at the thick, yellow material. She prayed as she'd never done before and hoped Cassie would put in a good word for her.

Chapter 66

Katie's arrest hit the news at five p.m. "Kathryn Werner, believed to have disappeared from Savannah three months ago, has been arrested for Identity Theft." Jack caught the tail end of it on his way home from work.

Jack's fist slammed the steering wheel. "Fucking bitch! Serves you right! I've got you now!" He pulled into a small sports bar, found a stool, and watched the broadcast. He smiled when he saw her in cuffs.

He laughed aloud when the crazy woman news anchor, Lindsey Shepard, tore into Katie's reputation. "We believed her. We felt sorry for her and wondered what could have gone wrong. And what do we find? She's been hiding out along the Florida border all this time. This woman took on the name of her deceased client." A picture of a smiling Cassie filled the screen. "What kind of sick person does that?" People were encouraged to call in and tweet. Most responses were ugly.

Jack giggled, and the people sitting nearest to him scooted away.

The guard rapped on Katie's cell. "You've got visitors."

Nick, Blake, and Tanja had driven up to see her. She couldn't touch them through the visitation glass, but their faces and voices gave her courage.

"There are news vans parked outside already." Tanja preened. "I'm sure Hollywood will be calling soon."

A roar went up on Saturday morning when Jack showed up in the jailhouse parking lot. "Mr. Werner! Can you tell us what you're thinking? Mr. Werner! Why are you here?"

"I want to see my wife."

Unfortunately for him, Katie had listed him on the "No Visitation" list, and he was refused entry. Jack fumed and killed ten minutes in the restroom, before walking back out to his car. The media didn't know he hadn't seen Katie. "No comment," he stated to the reporters who were yelling out questions.

The three Kane brothers had a quick meeting. "This is getting out of hand," Scott said. The other two agreed. "Jack's a loose cannon." The three brothers made eye contact.

"We'll keep an eye on things. If it starts to unravel, we fix the problem."

Business was booming in Bluff Creek as reporters scurried there to get the back story and the dirt on Katie. The townsfolk didn't say much, but what they did was positive.

"Girl worked her arse off. Never sick, never late. I got nothin' else to say." Colin glared.

Colleen and Mark refused to give an interview.

Skinny Tom scowled at the camera. "Girl made everybody feel special. We like her. I don't care what you say." His towel flipped back and forth, and the retirees could be heard voicing their agreement in the background.

They found Silver Linings and Latrice Copley. "She was fantastic with our patients. I personally hope she comes back soon."

It was extremely disappointing to reporters who would have enjoyed dragging Katie through the mud and exposing her as a cheat, a fraud, and an all-around despicable person.

Saturday afternoon Don, Maggie, and Skinny Tom drove up to visit. "Hang in there, Katie. The whole town's on your side.

"Nick's back in Bluff Creek running interference with the media, but he'll be back tomorrow." Maggie smiled, and Skinny Tom nodded and told her the retirees were waiting for her return. "They're bored without you."

"Montgomery will be here in about an hour," Don said.

"I can't afford a lawyer."

"We've got it covered. You need good legal counsel. I'll have his butt if he gives any less."

Katie hung her head and whispered, "Thank you. I'll find a way to repay you."

"We know you will."

Montgomery Causely had seen the media coverage and was ready for the press, "Kathryn Werner is my client, and we're preparing for court." His air of professionalism and three-piece suit were notably distinguished.

Katie was taken to a stark white room and placed on one side of the table. Montgomery entered, sitting on the other side. "Ms. Werner, I'm Montgomery Causley." He held out his hand.

Katie took in his stark white hair, handlebar mustache, and deep southern drawl, and accepted his handshake. "I can't tell if you come across as a Southern gentleman or a grandpa, but I'm glad you're here."

He'd heard plenty about Katie. As he took in her demeanor, Montgomery decided she lived up to the glowing testimonies. "Well, I've got seven grandchildren and a soft place in my heart for ladies on the wrong side of the law. Just don't tell the state prosecutor."

Montgomery opened his briefcase and pulled out papers. "First, you need to get familiar with the law. Your arraignment's on Monday. You don't have to go." His eyebrows lifted.

"What do you think?"

"The media is crazy. Yesterday you were a monster, but the tide is changing. No one can point to any harm you've done. I think it's in your best interest to go to court." He glared at her prison jumpsuit. "We don't want you filmed in a corrections uniform. Can anybody bring you some nicer clothes?"

Katie nodded. "If you get word to Maggie or Tanja."

"Fine. The prosecutor's going to start by using all kinds of legal jargon. Don't let it rattle you. You sit up tall and look straight ahead. Understand?"

"Yes."

Montgomery plucked a paper out of his bag and began reading the charges word for word. "You are charged with Aggravated Identity Theft under Federal Statute 1028a, Title 18.

"Georgia laws concerning identity theft vary depending on how the information was used." "It is overall punishable by imprisonment for not less than one year and no more than ten years. The prison term can be reduced or paid as a $10,000.00 fine if the violation does not involve the intent to commit theft or appropriation of any property. We'll argue some of those items later."

Katie grew deathly pale.

"You okay?"

"No. It sounds awful."

"As I said, it's just jargon. But you need to hear it all." He cleared his throat and continued to read verbatim, "It is considered Aggravated Identity Theft if the person uses any data for the purpose of obtaining employment. They have you on that one."

"You're right. They do."

"All we're going to do is enter a plea of 'Not Guilty.' This is not where we argue, show your value, or try to strike a deal. All we do on Monday is say…." He waited.

"Not guilty."

"The judge will set a date to hear motions, and possibly a trial date. Bail will be set. Then we get busy proving how wonderful you are and how you didn't intend to be malicious, etc."

"Mr. Causely?"

"Call me Montgomery."

"Montgomery, I don't want anyone to pay the bail."

"Your husband, right? I got an earful from Blake and Nick, so I'm aware of the situation. Are you sure you want to stay in jail?"

"Yes."

"We should put your request in writing. Could come in handy later."

Katie nodded.

"Once the arraignment is done, we'll work through what to do about your husband. What's his name? Jack?"

"Yes, and let's not beat around the bush. I want a divorce."

Montgomery pulled at his mustache. "I think a restraining order first. We'll leak the information to the press, ensure your safety. Once that's firmly in place, bail can be paid, and you're out of here until trial. Sound good?"

Lindsey Shepard, who'd started the media rant and the Twitter firestorm, was the first reporter to change her tone. By Sunday morning, she was asking different questions.

"Why would such an obviously sweet young woman feel the need to do these things?" Clips of positive interviews with Katie's previous clients and people from Bluff Creek were peppered throughout the segment. "Why would she feel she had to take on her patient's name? Run? Try to start over?" The questions had all eyes on Jack again.

Colleen and Josh arrived at the jail simultaneously with Aunt Susan and a woman Katie had never met. Using multiple visitation phones, the four talked at once. "I needed a ride. So, me and Ethel here broke out of the assisted living complex," Aunt Susan explained.

"Mom took me to McDonald's."

"They almost didn't let Josh in. I guess you're limited to three visitors." Colleen ran a hand through Josh's jet-black hair as she talked.

"Know how people stop being crooks?" Aunt Susan talked over the group, "They straighten themselves out!" Susan cackled, and everyone groaned.

Jack slumped in his chair, having finished off most of a bottle of Jack Daniels and a whole pack of Marlboro. He'd pulled the shades against the reporters camped outside the house. He'd unplugged the phone too, which was unfortunate as the Kane brothers needed to talk.

Tim Kane went to Jack's house after dark, circling the property to make sure reporters were gone, and there was no outside security. He met an inebriated Jack at the door. "Just checking on ya, Jack." Tim spied a camera mounted by the stairs and stepped back out of sight. "We don't need any trouble, Jack."

Jack swayed on the porch. "Miserable bitch. Katie doesn't know about you guys."

Tim leaned away from Jack's whiskey breath, but now had an idea of how to make Jack disappear, in an accident, if necessary.

That evening, the guard came to Katie's cell again. "Girl, you got more visitors." He led her to the overly bright visitor's station. Another sheriff rested against the wall, arms locked watching and listening.

Lindsay Shepard held the visitor phone, ready to talk.

Katie recoiled. "What do you want?"

Lindsey tapped the receiver gently on the glass, begging Katie to pick up her end.

Katie reluctantly picked up the phone and waited.

"I want to interview you and hear your side of the story. It might help others, Katie."

Katie sighed. "Maybe you're right. I need to talk to my lawyer first. And the Morrisons. I owe them an explanation."

"I'll see what I can do," Lindsey agreed. "I want to do this as soon as possible."

Nick came later in the evening, and the media thronged around him.

"Mr. Connelly! Did you know Kathryn before she left Savannah?"

"Nick! Over Here! What are your intentions?"

He waved but said nothing. Nick handed the guard an outfit Tanja had picked out for Katie's court appearance.

Katie told him about not paying bail, the restraining order, and Lindsey Shepard's request. "What do you think?" Katie asked.

"The interview might help. Montgomery's right about the restraining order, too. You should have done that a year ago." Nick immediately apologized, "Sorry. That wasn't fair."

"You're not wrong. I thought about it several times. But I knew a restraining order wouldn't have stopped Jack. Besides, the road I chose took me to you."

They each placed a hand on the glass, touching as much as they were able.

As he was leaving, Katie asked if he would contact the Morrisons. "I have a feeling they're going to hear from Lindsey Shepard, but I'd rather they hear from someone I care about. Please ask them if we can meet." Katie rattled off their phone number.

No one slept well that night.

Chapter 67

On Monday, the guards led Katie to a changing area and stood directly outside while she dressed. She donned modest black pants, a white dress shirt, a black sweater, and no makeup. The guards patted her down and transported her to court.

Katie studied the sea of faces. Many, like her, had been arrested over the weekend, and the courtroom reeked of desperation.

The bailiff entered and announced, "Chatham County District Court is in now in session. All rise for the Honorable Joseph Knowles." His voice reverberated in Katie's head, and her knees shook.

The judge acknowledged the courtroom over his glasses. "Be seated, and we'll begin."

Katie willed herself to sit quietly, awaiting her name. It took an hour. "The State of Georgia vs. Kathryn Anne Werner."

She and Montgomery stood facing the bench.

"Does the defendant have counsel?"

"She does, your Honor," Montgomery answered in a loud, clear voice.

The judge nodded, and the State Prosecutor stood to read the charges. "Kathryn Werner, you are charged with Aggravated Identity Theft…." He read the exact words Montgomery had shared on Saturday.

The Judge looked at Katie. "Do you understand the charges placed against you?"

"I do your Honor." Her hands trembled.

"How does the defendant plead?"

Montgomery answered, "The defendant pleads not guilty your Honor."

Judge Knowles reviewed his calendar. "Date for motions is set for January seventeenth. A trial date with a jury of your peers will be established at that time. Due to flight risk, bail is set at two-thousand dollars."

The gavel banged once, and Katie jumped at the sound.

She was back in jail, wearing the hated yellow uniform, and worrying about her future.

"You got more visitors." The guard unlocked the cell and led her to the communication area again.

Katie was tired and shuffled behind him. Her face flushed with shame when she saw Bob and Julie Morrison sitting in identical chairs on the other side of the wall. Lindsey Shepard was there, too, but wasn't allowed to film. She sat behind the Morrisons, taking notes.

Bob and Julie Morrison hesitated and then picked up the phone on their side of the glass. Katie did the same. She squeezed her lips tight and waited.

"Why'd you do it, Katie? How could you drag Cassie's name through this?" Julie asked.

Bob glared at Katie, unmoving.

"It wasn't supposed to be like this. I loved Cassie as a friend, as a sister. Cassie wanted me to do it, take her name, start over. Neither of us considered the consequences."

"What do you mean, Cassie wanted you to?" Bob allowed his anger to spew out.

The Morrisons repeated Katie's answers due to their incredulity at the situation. It allowed Lindsey to get a feel for both sides of the conversation.

"Cassie figured out I was in trouble at home. She'd seen the bruises, multiple times. Remember when you two took me to the Emergency Room?"

"The ER?" Julie stopped and rubbed her temple. "When you fell in Cassie's room?"

"I didn't fall there. Cassie made up that story. Jack, my husband, had broken those ribs."

"Your husband broke your ribs?" Bob's ears turned red.

Oh, this is good, Lindsey scribbled notes.

"Why didn't you tell us? Why lie?" Julie asked.

"If I'd told you or the ER doctor, it would have ended up in a police report, and then what? Jack would have found a hundred different ways to make me pay. Anyway, Cassie had enough of me hiding. The ER visit was the last straw for her, and she began to plan and made copies of her documents."

"Cassie made copies of her papers? Not you? Why would she do that?"

Katie shrugged. "I didn't know she was doing it. I swear. She gave me the money from her savings account and even wrote a letter explaining she'd knowingly given the documents to me. I still have her note begging me to use her name."

"Cassie did it? You didn't steal her ID?" Bob asked again.

"I'd never disrespect you, or steal. You can read Cassie's letter."

Bob shook his head, even as a slow smile grew. "My girl always did have spunk."

"Yes, sir, she did. More than me. I'd have never done it on my own. She insisted she could keep living through me."

The statement reduced Julie to tears, and, on cue, Bob patted her shoulder.

"Ahhh, Katie." Julie wiped a hand down her face. "How are we going to get you out of this mess?"

"I'll find out more in the next week. It's not horrible. I didn't rack up debt. I have two jobs and was saving money. All opposite of what an actual identity thief would do. There's hope the state prosecutor may be willing to deal." Head tilted, Katie looked at them through the glass. "Some of that may depend on you two."

"Well, we sure as hell aren't pressing charges." Bob glanced over his shoulder to make sure Lindsey heard him and wrote down what he'd said. "If you've got the letters from Cassie, then we believe you. It wasn't the smartest thing, but I can see how the ball got rolling. We'll do our best to help any way we can."

Aside from the funeral, it was the longest speech Katie had ever heard Bob give. It was Julie's turn to pat his shoulder. They left consoling one another.

On Tuesday, Katie put more pieces in play. She asked Nick and Tanja if they could drive her truck to the Morrison's. "It's in Cassie's name anyway. Oh, and there's two-hundred dollars under the passenger floor mat. I'm gonna need every dime I have."

Julie and Bob initially refused the truck. Eventually, a deal was worked out where they would keep the vehicle until Katie's release. They would then sell it to her for $900.00, effectively recovering Cassie's savings but leaving Katie with a car. Montgomery put it in writing along with another paper giving him permission to handle Katie's bills.

Montgomery was finally able to meet with Steve from the fraud unit of the District Attorney's office late Wednesday afternoon.

Steve was adamant. "Look, I get it. Kathryn intended no harm, even had permission from the deceased. What she should have done is legally changed her name, gotten a divorce, and followed the law. We can't let this go. Lots of people out there trying to start over."

"There were extenuating circumstances."

"Kathryn Werner isn't the only one in such a boat." Steve consulted his notes and sighed heavily. "I'll throw out malicious intent."

Montgomery pulled his mustache, a sign he was thinking. "She purchased a truck, rented an apartment, and held down two jobs. She didn't enter into any loan agreements or open a credit card. She even took out car insurance for God's sake." Montgomery was on a roll. "Hell, Steve, she turned herself in to the authorities."

Steve wasn't giving in so easily. "She did all of those things using a deceased person's name and social security number. Misappropriation of property."

Montgomery leaned back in his seat and stayed silent.

Steve waited too but eventually acquiesced. "She turned herself in, you're right. That makes this unusual," he paused, "but the law is the law."

"I think we can work this out. The girl's been in jail for six days, with another week to go before we're back in court. She made arrangements to give the truck back to the Morrisons." Montgomery fished a paper out of his folder and pushed it toward Steve as proof of the truck deal. Montgomery tapped the paper. "Your office can take credit for the truck deal. Make it a condition." He kept talking before Steve could interrupt, "She's still gainfully employed. Neither employer is willing to let her go. She has some money saved. She could pay a small fine."

Steve read his notes. "She didn't break *all* the statutes. I can reduce it from aggravated felony theft to a Class B offense. It would reduce the sentence to one year and a fifteen-hundred dollar fine."

"How about time served, return the truck to the Morrisons, and a two-thousand dollar fine?"

"You want to pay more?"

"I want her out of jail."

"Time served, repay the nine-hundred *and* give the truck to Morrisons for emotional distress. Add in community service and a twenty-five-hundred dollar fine. Final offer."

The two men shook hands. The bargain was notarized and in Montgomery's hand in less than an hour. He headed out to get Katie's signature.

A restraining order was served to Jack at work on Thursday, December 12th. He lost his mind and stormed out of the office, ranting and cussing. He sped toward Bluff Creek, intent on finding Nick Connelly and beating him senseless. The need to destroy overrode any potential consequences.

Nick, however, was on his way to visit Katie, and the two men passed each other on the highway.

Finding the Connelly office closed again, Jack realized he had no idea where to find Nick. Entering Tipsy's, Jack hurriedly scanned faces. Colleen identified him immediately. "Something I can do for you?" She rapped the bar twice with a beer mug, the signal which always brought Colin out of his office.

Colin stuck his head out of the door frame, and seeing Jack, joined Colleen at the bar. "What's going on here?"

Colleen pointed her chin at Jack. "Nothing. Jack was just leaving."

Jack narrowed his eyes and exited the restaurant. He went to the General Store next, remembering Katie rented an apartment overhead. Skinny Tom recognized him and came out from behind the counter.

Craig joined him, watching Jack's every move. "Something we can help you with, Mr. Werner?"

Thaddeus and Jarrod walked over, arms crossed and scowling.

Jack wisely walked away.

Giovanni received a call from Skinny Tom and drove the main street looking for Jack. When he noticed a strange car parked crookedly in front of Connelly Rentals, he put the lights on the cruiser and pulled behind Jack's vehicle.

Jack lowered his driver's side window with his left hand and used his right to tuck the knife down between the seats. *That's all I need right now, some fucking cop seeing a knife.*

Giovanni approached. "License and Registration."

Jack shook his head. "What the hell? I was parked. I didn't do anything wrong."

"You were parked illegally. License and Registration, please." Giovanni stood ramrod straight, watching as Jack dug in the glove box and pulled his wallet free from his back pocket. Giovanni took his time walking back to the police car and running the plates through the system.

Giovanni sauntered back. "Mr. Werner, this is a small town. Strangers are noticed. Sorry to stop you like this." Giovanni tore off the warning ticket and handed it through the window.

Jack got the message and headed home.

Chapter 68

Lindsey Shepard set up the interview with Katie for Friday afternoon. Despite the fact live dialogue was risky, the reporter wanted the piece to run over the weekend. She and the sound crew built in a three-second delay in case someone dropped an F-bomb or said something inappropriate. She'd asked the Morrisons to be present, and they agreed. Guards stood outside the jailhouse conference room.

The segment opened with Bob and Julie hugging Katie and her hanging onto them so fiercely, her knuckles lost color. They sat on either side of Katie, while Lindsey sat on the opposite side of the table. It wasn't ideal. She'd love to have had a living room scene, but time was of the essence if she wanted this exclusive.

Lindsey opened the discussion, "Katie, it seems everyone in Georgia is aware of your story— How you and Cassie collaborated to use her name. We now know you left Savannah in September, changing your hair, appearance, and moving around. Why didn't you just file for divorce?"

"I didn't believe Jack would grant a divorce, and I needed to start over on my own."

"Why did you stay in the marriage so long? Five years is a long time, and it appears to have gotten…well, messy."

Montgomery had coached Lindsey and Katie not to accuse Jack directly or use words such as abuse. Conscious of his warning, both women let the sentence hang for a few seconds knowing the audience would fill in the blanks.

"I didn't grow up with much. Your network gave the backstory, filmed my old neighborhood, and reported on my parents' deaths. When Jack came along, he was answered prayer.

He was smart, handsome, and he made me feel special. I would have done anything for him." Katie lowered her head. "And did." She took a deep breath and continued, "When a person never has love, they'll accept a sorry substitute, because they don't know better. A compliment or display of affection is perceived as love. You don't stop to ask if it's real."

"When did you realize things weren't going well?"

"Things were less than perfect from the time I moved to Savannah, but I thought it was me. I wasn't working, and there was a lot of stress over money. I thought if I got a job, worked harder at the relationship, things would smooth out. Looking back, I can see red flags, but at the time, I considered them normal problems in a new marriage. By the time I understood our arguments and fights weren't typical, it was too late."

Lindsey cocked her head, "What do you mean?"

"I made a lot of adjustments over the first year--things I couldn't take back: Moving away from the only family I had left, agreeing not to carry cash because we were budgeting. I didn't fight his tracking my phone initially because I was in an unfamiliar town and lost most of the time. It seemed a good idea for him to be able to find me." Katie shrugged. "To keep the peace, I'd let my friendships dwindle because Jack wanted my time. Which, if I'm honest, was flattering. Later, when I fully understood the situation, I was alone with few resources."

"Things changed when you met Cassie, didn't they?" Lindsey spent a few minutes filling in details of Katie and Cassie's friendship and showing a photo of the two women together. Drawing the Morrisons into the interview, Lindsey asked, "Did you ever have reason to suspect what Cassie and Katie were planning?"

"Never." Julie shook her head. "Katie added so much to Cassie's last months. We were glad they found each other."

"If we'd known, we would have shut the idea down and encouraged Katie to take other avenues." Bob glanced at Katie apologetically. She nodded, understanding.

"Are you angry she used Cassie's name?"

"I was. Very. But now, knowing the whole story, it makes us sad." Bob patted Katie's shoulder."

Lindsey turned back to Katie. "We can only guess as to how this will end. Do you have plans? Plans for afterward?"

Katie smiled. "I'm going home."

"To Savannah?"

"No. Home is Bluff Creek. I want to go back to work, spend time with my new friends, maybe open a store someday."

"How about Nick Connelly?"

Katie tilted her head, considering what she should and should not say. "I hope so."

"That seems optimistic, given all you've been through. Is there anything else you want to say?"

"I don't understand the question."

Even Lindsey, usually so razor-sharp, had fallen in love with Katie. Lindsey paused and softened the question, leaning toward Katie. "A price has to be paid. You're incarcerated. What would you say to others who are in similarly bad circumstances?"

Katie looked momentarily at the ceiling. Gathering herself, she faced the camera. "I would tell any woman, or man, to stand up for themselves. Fight for what's important. Don't settle for less because you think it's all you deserve."

"Even in jail?"

"Even in jail. People often toss clichés at a situation—'there's no time like the present, or there may not be a second chance.' Cassie and my new friends in Bluff Creek taught me otherwise. As long as we have breath, we can choose to move forward, to change, to create new opportunities. You just have to do it within legal parameters." Katie had the gall to laugh.

Julie squeezed Katie's hand. "Cassie would be so proud of you."

"She knew how to live each day to the fullest." Bob choked on his sentence.

Lindsey allowed the moment to sink in, recognizing good television when it happened. After a few seconds had passed, Lindsey continued, "Katie, there's one more thing you should know. A friend of yours, Colleen McQue, opened a Go Fund Me Account for your legal fees. The goal was ten-thousand dollars." Lindsey paused. "The fund currently holds fourteen-thousand-two-hundred and thirty-three dollars."

Katie's hands flew to her face, and she wiped away the instant tears. "See? There are second chances. For the most part, people are good, and I'm so grateful."

The segment aired on Saturday and Sunday morning, and Jack admitted his life was over. There was no fixing this, and no second chances regardless of what Katie said. He'd divorce her and move on, literally. New place. New city. Her optimism was his ultimate demise. He could never return to his job or live on Forsyth Park without being a constant conversation piece.

To avoid questions, Jack called work Sunday afternoon, leaving a message that he would not be in the next day

The Kane Brothers watched the interview, too and met together on Sunday. "All eyes are gonna be on Jack," Scott, the oldest, concluded. He turned toward Tim. "You've been watching Jack. What do you think?"

"He's losing it. Been driving all over the city, drinking a lot. There's a lot of pressure on him right now."

"What's he going to do if they ask other questions?" Scott asked.

Tim shrugged. "It's probably time for Jack to disappear. I think a drunk driving accident would work."

Ronnie joined the conversation, "Nah. Too messy with no guaranteed outcome We need to cut our losses. Clear our tracks. Leave it a mystery. His life's falling apart, his job is questionable, and his wife is leaving him. It could just be too much for the man."

Scott leaned forward. "What are you thinking?"

"We take him out and dispose of him far away from the city," Ronnie answered, "Make it look like he ran."

The three brothers sat thinking through the possible scenarios. Tim cocked an eyebrow, "It works for me."

Scott stood, indicating the meeting was over. Pointing at his brothers, he said, "You two, make it happen. No clues, no fingerprints, keep it clean."

Tim agreed, already wondering how to get into Jack's house and bypass the alarm.

Nick drove to Atlanta and hand-delivered an envelope to Lindsey Shepard's intern. It was marked 'Kathryn Werner. Urgent.' Nick walked away quickly before anyone asked questions.

"What happens next?" Katie asked Montgomery on Sunday evening. "We file the plea bargain and motions on Tuesday. If the judge accepts the deal, you walk out a free woman. You'll pay the fee and the payment to the Morrisons, and it will be over and done. Then you figure out how to start over again." He smiled. "What is it now? The third time?" "I guess we get as many as necessary," Katie answered. "See you on Tuesday."

The Sunday evening news had a new tidbit. "An anonymous source has sent information indicating Mr. Jack Werner was involved in a county audit earlier this year. There are purportedly papers showing evidence money laundering may have taken place." Lindsey Shepard wiggled her eyebrows. "Who could have access to this information? A co-worker? Kathryn? The papers show receipts of money paid to Jack Werner."

Scott called Tim. "You see the latest news?"

"Yeah. God knows what that asshole has on us."

"When you get to Jack's house, you need to take the computer, files, thumb-drives, and any kind of records, too."

Tim grunted and hung up.

Jack watched the latest broadcast, hearing the latest nail being pounded into his coffin. He swirled his drink. Who'd found his receipts?

It had to be Katie. *How the fuck did that Bitch get ahold of those?* He sat drinking and hating her with a passion. Two more drinks had Jack passed out in the living room chair.

Chapter 69

Jack woke up Monday morning stiff and momentarily unsure of his surroundings. Taking in the living room, his clothes still on from the day before, he figured it out. In the small recesses of his brain, he admitted he was losing control.

Groaning, he worked his way out of the easy chair and stumbled toward the kitchen needing Tylenol and coffee. The microwave showed it was ten a.m., and Jack was stunned he'd slept so late.

Jack listened to his voicemail while playing with his knife. It was always nearby anymore and had become symbolic of Katie and all that she'd done to him.

His boss Barry had left a message. "Jack, I got your call about not coming in today. But we're going to need you in the office tomorrow. There's a meeting scheduled at 9 a.m." It was a cryptic statement, but Jack knew what was coming.

Three reporters had called asking if he had comments about the allegations of money laundering, or Katie's upcoming court appearance.

His dad had left the longest message, "We just saw the news…" he blathered on a few minutes, "Your mom and I are concerned by what's being implied. Do you need anything? A lawyer, maybe?"

Jack slammed his phone on the counter, regretting the noise and hanging onto his throbbing head.

Tim and Ronnie Kane had risen much earlier than Jack and were discussing options while sitting in a construction garage—far away from reporters or investigators. Scott was laying low, staying in an alternative place in the city, and steadily removing evidence and creating alibis.

Tim and Ronnie worked out a strategy—Tim would go in the back and Ronnie through the front. Having been to Jack's house before, once to give a bid for the kitchen remodel and once to issue a warning, Tim knew the basic layout—mostly secluded backyard, kitchen and den in the back, all the bedrooms upstairs.

The security cameras were the first priority. "We gotta knock those out," Ronnie stated, and Tim nodded. "Yeah, I have a plan for that."

"Once that's done, we grab Jack, and the files and get the hell out."

Jack spent the afternoon preparing to leave. His phone never stopped ringing, and he turned the damn thing off. He poured a hair-of-the-dog drink at two.

The rest of the day was spent shredding documents and cleaning out files. He turned the cameras off, not wanting his last moves recorded. He made a quick trip to an ATM and came back home to pack. He'd leave town in the morning. There was no way his life was going to return to normal. He'd be fired tomorrow, and potentially arrested for fraud. The irony of his situation compared to Katie's wasn't lost on him, and he poured another whiskey and Coke.

Late that night, Tim and Ronnie moved into place, circling the block where Jack lived. Tim pointed at the house where one faint light glimmered from an upstairs room. "Perfect."

Ronnie nodded as he slid on gloves

They left the car on the street and made their way toward the house—Tim towards the back and Ronnie positioning himself near the porch. 'Let me know when you're ready," Ronnie whispered.

Tim slid past the garage, staying low and looking for the line bringing wi-fi into the house. Seeing it attached low and entering a basement window, he removed wire snippers from his bag and snipped the ethernet cord. With that problem fixed, he hurried toward the kitchen door.

It had been a miserable day. Jack couldn't get his head wrapped around his situation and had no idea where he was going to go or how he would survive. The alcohol kept him numb, and he headed toward the kitchen for more whiskey.

Halfway across the darkened room, Jack caught movement outside the window and stopped. Squinting, he could barely make out a form by the backdoor.

Jack reached over, grabbed the knife off the counter, and pushed himself against the wall by the door. He could hear tools working the lock and raised the knife, ready to strike.

The door clicked open, and a man walked through.

Jack's knife arced and found its mark. The intruder dropped to the floor with a loud thud. His breath gurgled out as he clawed at the blade, plunged deep within his chest.

Jack barely had time to register what had happened when he heard the front door open. Ronnie Kane's unmistakable voice called out, "Tim? Did you get him?"

Jack's survival instincts kicked in, and he raced for the stairs, catching sight of Ronnie. The streetlights showed a hint of silver in the right hand.

Gun! Jack's brain screamed and took the stairs two at a time. Jack slid into his bedroom and heard Ronnie pounding up the stairs. *Shit! I'm trapped.* Jack looked around frantically for a weapon and spied Katie's candlestick on the corner table. *The only thing of hers I ever liked.* Grabbing it, Jack stayed just inside the door, waiting for the right moment.

As Ronnie reached the top landing, Jack sprang forward and swung his weapon, connecting with a sickening thwack. Ronnie fell backward, thumping down the stairs, the gun clattering alongside him. Jack rushed after him, reaching the bottom at almost the same time. He struck two more times until Ronnie laid unmoving.

Jack flipped on the foyer light and stood, looking at Ronnie's bludgeoned face and the pool of blood around his head. Jack sank to the floor and turned off the light. He didn't want to see, and sure as hell couldn't have neighbors looking in either.

Jack crawled to the kitchen, identifying Tim Kane, bloodied and dead just inside the door. "Fuck." *Now what?* The action had sobered Jack up, and his mind whirled with scenarios.

Do I get rid of the bodies? Call the police and report a break-in? No, these are the Kane brothers, and I'm associated. I'm screwed. Charges against Jack flittered across his brain: Fraud. Bribery, Double murder.

"This is all because of you, Katie!" he screamed and staggered back toward the foyer. "What am I going to do?" His toe kicked the gun, and Jack picked it up and put it in his pocket without thinking.

"I've got to get out of here." He ran up the stairs, changed his clothes, and grabbed the suitcase he'd filled earlier. Snatching the bottle of Jack Daniels on his way out, Jack pulled Tim's body into the kitchen and exited.

He spent hours driving aimlessly, brooding, and pounding drinks. His fist slammed the steering wheel, and he lit another cigarette. He remembered Katie's hearing started at ten and made his way towards the courthouse. Finding a parking space nearby, he slouched low in the driver's seat, waiting for her to arrive.

On Tuesday morning, Katie was on her way to the courthouse for what she hoped the last time.

A horde of reporters thronged the steps and walkways in front of the building, cameras, and microphones ready. A hum of excitement carried across the crowd as journalists spied the police car approaching.

The cruiser parked, and a guard exited, helping Katie out of the backseat. Montgomery hurried over to walk beside her, while extra police officer, pushed journalists back, clearing the way for Katie.

Questions came from all directions.

"Kathryn, will you plead guilty to reduce your sentence?"

"Has there been a plea bargain?"

"Mrs. Werner, tell us what you feel."

"Katie? Katie-girl!" a sing-song voice called from the crowd. Katie turned to find her Aunt Susan waving frantically.

Katie released her first smile of the day. A whole entourage from Bluff Creek was with Susan. Don, Maggie, and Nick were clumped together. Colleen and Tanja stood nearby, their arms linked. Katie's spirits lifted. *It's going to be all right.*

Nick began walking through the crowd, keeping pace with Katie. Don followed him for a bit, then realized he couldn't keep up with Nick's long stride.

A disheveled man pushed through the crowd, a cap pulled low over his forehead, and his right hand firmly in his jacket pocket. The hurried pace caught Don's attention. *Is that Jack?* Don moved closer, following him on instinct.

The man shoved his way to the front of the crowd, getting in front of Katie and the guard.

Katie saw the man and recognized him as Jack. She took in the five-day beard, and the red-rimmed eyes and began to shake.

Seeing Katie's shocked face, Jack reacted, yanking Ronnie Kane's pistol out of his pocket.

Don, close behind, caught the glint, and reacted without thinking, propelling himself toward Jack.

Jack pulled the trigger, and the sound reverberated in the confined space between the courthouse and other buildings. The impact had Katie screaming and falling sideways.

As he was ready to fire again, Jack was tackled from behind and fell to the ground. A second shot went off, and all hell broke loose. Reporters screamed and stampeded over one another to get out of the way.

Jack landed on the concrete near Katie, and her brain struggled to make sense of Don Connelly, lying on top of Jack, motionless. Blood seeped out from underneath the two men.

Nick ran into the mix, leaping over and around anyone who was in his way. Taking in the scene as fast as he could, Nick saw Katie move and beelined for his dad. Maggie was right behind Nick, screaming, "Don! Oh My God! Don"

Nick reached his dad, pulling him off Jack. Don blinked twice,
then wrapped his arms around Nick. "I'm okay. Go to Katie!"

Police had already dropped to defensive positions, and their own guns were drawn.

"Shooter!" One Cop yelled.

"Everybody down!"

"Lockdown the courthouse!"

With just two feet between them, Jack and Katie's eyes met and held one last time. As the life-light began to fade from Jack's eyes, Katie looked at him unblinkingly and whispered, "There was a crooked man…"

It was the last thing Jack heard.

Legs and arms and people and voices were suddenly all around Katie, and she could no longer see Jack. The scene was mayhem and unfolded in slow motion. She was a spectator watching a movie, distanced and not wanting to accept it as reality.

"Katie! Are you all right?" Montgomery shouted in her ear.

Katie's guard crouched down, putting pressure on Katie's wound. "Are you hit anywhere else?" He asked, examining her as fast as possible.

Katie shook her head. "What happened to Jack?"

"He's down. Hang on. We've got an ambulance on the way."

The siren's wail grew louder until it became the only focus in her world.

Nick and Colleen tried to get to Katie, but police, unsure who was who and whether there were other shooters, shoved them backward, "Stay down!"

Paramedics ran into the melee, whisking Katie into an ambulance. Two more emergency personnel lifted a bloodied Jack onto another stretcher and covered him with a blanket. Seeing his lifeless body, Katie sobbed. "Oh, Jack. What have you done?"

Hours later, a panic-stricken group filled a tiny waiting room at the hospital, anxious for news concerning Katie. A police officer sat outside, keeping the hallway clear of journalists and curiosity seekers.

The doctor came out and shared the results. "She's doing fine. She took a bullet to the shoulder, but the surgery went well. She's resting now and should be able to see visitors soon." Looking at the size of the group, the doctor amended his statement, "Three at a time."

When they were allowed, Nick, Aunt Susan and Maggie rushed down the hall and into Katie's room. Nick was the first one through the door, grabbing Katie in a fierce hug.

"Easy there." She grimaced and put her hand on her left shoulder.

Nick released her. "God. I'm sorry. I just need to touch you. Jesus, Katie!" He ran frantic hands through his hair.

Aunt Susan pushed forward and kissed Katie's cheek. "Oh, baby girl. Are you all right?"

Katie squeezed Aunt Susan's hand with all her might. "I am now."

Maggie hung back, giving Susan time. When she couldn't wait any longer, Maggie stepped forward, running her hands down Katie's hair. "Oh, my God. Katie. I'm so glad you're all right. You know Jack is gone?"

Katie nodded, and fresh tears rolled down her cheek. "He got two shots off—one at me, and the other struck him high in the abdomen when Don tackled him." Her voice shook, "How could it have come to this?"

Nick and Susan refused to leave Katie's side, and the rest of the group came in two at a time, defying the doctor's rule.

Colleen and Tanja came in, talking fast, "They had us on lockdown for thirty minutes, and we had no idea if you were okay."

"No one would tell us anything and even took our cell phones."

"God! We were so scared!" Tanja admitted.

Don and Montgomery entered the room next, and Katie smiled at Don, "My hero."

"No kidding," Nick shook his head, "I couldn't believe it. I see this guy jumping on Jack, and then I realized it's Dad."

Don grinned. "Old man's still got some moves, huh?"

"You'll be telling this story for years, won't you?" Katie asked

"And it will get bigger and more dangerous with each telling, too," Nick laughed but kept his arm slung around Don's shoulder, ensuring himself all was well.

Don approached Katie, "Don't even think about blaming yourself. This was Jack's doing, not yours. Katie."

Montgomery jumped into the conversation, "Damn straight. There isn't a judge in the world that won't grant you a reduced sentence and set you free. Anyone can see the Bastard was deranged, and you did whatever was necessary to escape."

The house in Forsyth Park was searched, The Kane brothers' bodies removed, the computer hauled away, and the surveillance tapes confiscated. It would take longer to complete the corruption and murder investigation than to dispose of Jack Werner. No autopsy was necessary, and his body was released on Thursday.

A private graveside funeral was conducted on Saturday morning. Three people attended: Jack's boss Barry, and Fred and Sylvia Werner. Jack's mom cried. His dad did not.

It took another week to unravel the paperwork, get statements, release Katie from the hospital and set up the new court date.

Katie arrived with Montgomery and Nick. She'd asked everyone else to wait at home. She was tired of seeing the faces of the people she loved on television.

Judge Knowles nodded as District Attorney Steven DeWitt read the reduced charges. "If all parties agree, I do too, except for the part requiring community service. In this court's opinion, Kathryn Werner has been through enough. Case closed."

The gavel banged once, but this time, Katie didn't jump. Instead, she turned to find Nick.

Acknowledgments:
Thank you to my friends and family, who listened to me as I tried to put all these pieces and parts together into a believable story. Thank you to my mom Deanne Heitkamp, my life-long friend Karen Pemberton, and writing partner Larry Scott who read pages and pages then offered clarity and advice. Thank you to my five special readers who slogged through the manuscript and gave feedback. Thank you to my husband, John, who not only helped me write the details of the vehicle breaking down in this story, but put up with my thousand-mile stares, and less than focused evenings as I thought through changes and edits. Thank you to my children, who are always my champions. I hope the end result makes you as proud of me, as I am of you.

Katrina lives in Westfield Center, Ohio, with her husband, John. They are blessed that their three children, Michael, Spencer, and Deanna (and her family!) live, work and go to school nearby. The author keeps herself busy working within the community, writing two additional books, delivering motivational speeches, and teaching interactive writing classes.

Other books by Katrina Morgan: *These Animals Are Killing Me* and *Echoes in the Walls.* Follow on: Tumblr, Twitter, Facebook, LinkedIn, GoodReads. Or, visit the website www.Katrinabooks.com

Made in the USA
Monee, IL
27 April 2020

27989943R00229